PENGUIN BOOKS

The Inside Job

After studying Mental Philosophy at Edinburgh University, Felix began his career as a writer for radio and television. A change in career took him into the City where he worked for the major US brokerage Cantor Fitzgerald. Soon after, Felix launched his own company which he later sold to MF Global in 2008, just moments before the financial system imploded.

Felix Riley lives with his wife and two daughters in Surrey, England.

The Inside Job

FELIX RILEY

PENGUIN BOOKS

PENGUIN

Published by the Penguin Group
Penguin Books Ltd, 80 Strand, London WC2R ORL, England
Penguin Group (USA) Inc., 375 Hudson Street, New York, New York 10014, USA
Penguin Group (Canada), 90 Eglinton Avenue East, Suite 700, Toronto, Ontario, Canada M4P 2Y3
(a division of Pearson Penguin Canada Inc.)
Penguin Ireland, 25 St Stephen's Green, Dublin 2, Ireland
(a division of Penguin Books Ltd)
Penguin Group (Australia), 250 Camberwell Road,
Camberwell, Victoria 3124, Australia (a division of Pearson Australia Group Pty Ltd)
Penguin Books India Pvt Ltd, 11 Community Centre,
Panchsheel Park, New Delhi – 110 017, India
Penguin Group (NZ), 67 Apollo Drive, Rosedale, Auckland 0632, New Zealand
(a division of Pearson New Zealand Ltd)
Penguin Books (South Africa) (Pty) Ltd, Block D, Rosebank Office Park, 181 Jan Smuts Avenue,
Parktown North, Gauteng 2193, South Africa

Penguin Books Ltd, Registered Offices: 80 Strand, London WC2R ORL, England

www.penguin.com

First published 2012

001

Copyright © Felix Riley, 2012

The moral right of the author has been asserted

Typeset by Palimpsest Book Production Limited, Falkirk, Stirlingshire
Printed in Great Britain by Clays Ltd, St Ives plc

A CIP catalogue record for this book is available from the British Library

ISBN: 978-0-241-95169-9

www.greenpenguin.co.uk

MIX
Paper from
responsible sources
FSC™ C018179

Penguin Books is committed to a sustainable
future for our business, our readers and our planet.
This book is made from Forest Stewardship
Council™ certified paper.

ALWAYS LEARNING   **PEARSON**

To the 99%

Peterborough City Council	
60000 0000 73411	
Askews & Holts	Sep-2012
THR	£6.99

'I rob banks because that's where the money is.'

Willie Sutton, United States bank robber
1920s–1950s

I

Tokyo, 6.33 a.m.

Yukio Sato squinted at his face in the mirror with its too-bright-for-this-time-of-morning lights. His face stared back at him, twenty-five going on fifty. That last bottle of shochu was a big mistake. He was actually getting nostalgic for sake. Half the strength and twice the taste. Even the bourbon those Ame-koh bankers from Chicago had plied him with after he made them a cool million dollars, American, with his options strategy hadn't felt this bad. Or had it? Come to think of it, hadn't he sworn off drinking for ever after that night? Did anybody on any part of the planet ever stick to that promise? Unable to hold on to his train of thought, he held on to the small sink in his tiny shower room instead. His stomach was posing the hungover dilemma: to vomit or not to vomit. A wave of nausea tilted the argument one way before subsiding. He gave it a moment. It was getting better.

Five years. Five more years and I'll have earned enough to get out of this rat race. Go be a teacher, go live on one of the other islands, just get the hell away from Tokyo. Anything that doesn't involve waking up feeling like this.

Frankfurt, 10.38 p.m.

The group of young, suited Germans were pleading with their boss.

'Just come in for one drink.'

'We're buying.'

'It's not as if any of us can tell our wives.'

The middle-aged banker examined the neon sign above the nightclub's doorway in the heart of the city's red-light district. *Das Liebe Haus.* He smirked and looked at the greedy grins of his team before him as the burlesque sounds within rose and fell with the opening of the entrance door by a well-dressed doorman. Inside the club could be glimpsed the red velvet wallpaper with its promise of decadence beyond.

The banker spoke, his manner not unlike a Bavarian doctor, thoughtful, careful. 'Boys, there is a key around my wife's neck. It is gold-plated to disguise it as jewellery, but it is, in fact, a real key.'

The gaggle of young men paused to listen. Part smiles, all attention.

'Once a year, on my birthday, my dear wife opens the safe in our bedroom. The safe to which only she knows the combination. Inside the safe are her more expensive necklaces and earrings and other such stuff. But if you look closely, you will detect another door at the back of the safe. Into this she places the key from around her neck, turns it, and the door pops free to reveal a plain metal box. Very carefully she brings this box to the matrimonial bed, where I will be waiting with the cup of tea that she has made me. Remember, it is my birthday. Then, very carefully, she opens two latches in a very particular way. And, might I add, were I to grab this box and open the latches the wrong way, the contents of the box would be destroyed for ever.'

The door to the venue opening for new clients momentarily invaded the story with its nightclub noise before closing again.

The men had unconsciously gone quiet, their drunkenness abating as they listened rapt to their boss. He was the head of the most profitable division of Weltbank, one of the country's leading investment institutions. He was shockingly intelligent, understated and kind to his hard working team. He did not say much, so when he did his team of acolytes paid attention. He was – almost – everything they wanted to be.

'Then, and only then, does my good wife lift the lid to give me a brief glimpse of what she keeps inside. And do you know what it is she keeps in such a box?'

As one the group shook their heads.

'Inside the box she keeps . . .' The bank executive looked at each of his team in turn before continuing. 'My testicles – and I would like to see them again someday.'

A roar of surprised laughter met his punch-line, and the protesting started again. He gave a small wave to a black S-Class Mercedes waiting at a discreet distance.

'Go be young and enjoy yourselves, we've had a good year, you deserve it. *But* . . . be at your desks nice and early.'

They half groaned, half laughed in response.

He replied with a smile and slipped into the limousine, which smoothly took him away.

The group had forgotten him within five seconds, as their attention turned to who had the twenty euros per person entrance fee in cash. It was not a transaction they wanted showing up on their platinum American Express statements.

London, 9.48 p.m.

'If you gentlemen would care to come this way.'

The Maître d' was as crisp as the white linen surroundings. He was impeccably dressed and struck a tone as refined as the after-dinner port yet as light as the salmon mousse. Everything the head waiter of a three-star Michelin restaurant should be. When the four bankers had tried to book earlier in the day they had been told the truth: that every table was taken. However, the manager had overheard the name of the disappointed customer, listening in as he was because the customer was at least important enough to have the number of the restaurant's private line. With rising panic the manager had almost snatched the phone from the elegant reservations girl and, adopting his smoothest possible tones, had given his assurance – seasoned with just a hint of grovelling – that a table would be made available to the customer in question for that very night at the time of his choosing. Restaurants will do that for certain people. Celebrities, heads of state and for their very favourite diners: those who left four-figure tips last time they had dined with them.

Rich or very rich, it was surprising how intimidated people could become in an internationally renowned restaurant. They walked self-consciously, spoke more quietly, all the things they thought were required to fit in. The gentlemen, however, were bankers from the private arm of one of the country's biggest finance houses. They put in long hours, were smart and – to a man – felt that they deserved to be there. Their bank did not disagree. Tonight's meal was on the company. The quartet just had to pick up the tip.

The bankers took their places and smiled with satisfaction at their genteel surroundings. The Wyatt was not only at the top of the Michelin tree, it had not been out of any respected food guide's top three restaurants for one year short of a decade. Even a food-poisoning scare five years earlier had not threatened its three-star crown. The restaurant itself often surprised diners on their first visit. It was the size of a very large living room and no more (in fact, the result of knocking through two terraced houses in the Chelsea district of West London). The clientele were a mix of City, media and the wealthy. But no bad-boy behaviour was ever on display here. It was The Wyatt. It was, by any measure, genuine class.

'Now, sirs,' the Maître d' continued, 'what is it tonight? A special occasion?'

Every banker tried to fight a smile and every banker failed. Terry Stephenson, team leader and captain of his troops, spoke for all of them.

'Not bloody half. Now, champagne all round, François, and no scrimping like last time.'

'Of course, Mr Stephenson.'

The Maître d' turned smoothly on his heel and glided away, even at this early hour mentally spending his portion of the tip. It was going to be a good night.

Tokyo, 6.55 a.m.

Yukio Sato shuffled into the elevator on the eleventh floor of his residential apartment block, Motoazabu Hills, in the Minato-ku area of the city. For the first two years at the bank his modest income had made living with his parents in the suburbs an easy decision. His family thought it was his rocketing salary – with the exception of one bad trading year – that had led him to move to one of the swankiest new condos in the Japanese capital. It was never that. It was the hours he was working. A star trader he might have been, but his 24/7 approach to trading the options market quickly took its toll. So he moved to the financial district and started grabbing priceless extra shut-eye every day. The sky-high rent was worth every yen.

Yukio considered his appearance in the elevator's mirrored wall. Slightly more twentysomething post-shower, helped by the spiky styling of his jet-black hair and his long, smooth sideburns. Nothing garnered more looks from his seniors at the bank than his hair, but with each successful quarter their displeasure appeared to subside. Doubtless it would all come down on him if he had another bad trading year. But he had learned from the past. His sideburns were here to stay, of that he was determined.

The elevator delivered him smoothly to the ground

floor. He hoped his boss had been true to his word and sent a car.

Frankfurt, 10.59 p.m.

The gaggle of young German bankers, ties adrift, top shirt buttons swiftly undone since their boss's disappearance, had positioned themselves in front of a small cabaret stage with three poles spaced along it. The five young men were bang in the centre, on a red velvet crescent-shaped bench seat with enough room for them and any hostesses who might wish to top up their earnings that night. They were sat round a half-moon table, a long-legged step from the stage, where hard-working girls could grind out some extra euros from the clientele. And, in the right frame of mind, nobody spent more than the banking brigade.

A round of Wasmas cocktails – beer, coke and cognac – had appeared in front of the men, and they didn't care that it was probably a ruse by the management to fiddle the evening's bill. They were out to celebrate their bonuses for a bumper year and the cost of tonight – whatever happened – would be negligible.

As the stage's spotlights whirred and twisted into life a stocky, red-headed trader at one end of their bench leaned into his neighbour.

'Hey, Axel, are you going upstairs later?'

'Of course, I want a return on that entrance fee . . . Hey, where you going? The show's about to start.'

But his bulky, trader colleague was already standing.

'I won't be able to concentrate on the show until I've got my end away. I'll be back in fifteen minutes.'

'You're a bitch on heat, you know that, Jurg.'

Somewhere in his drunk mind Axel knew he had mangled that metaphor, but his friend had already staggered off to the staircase. Crimson-red carpet, naturally. Red like every inch of the decor, red like the lips of the scantily clad girls gliding about the room, serving drinks, accepting drinks, accepting invitations to join the wolfish men around them. Then whistles and cheers filled the air as the curtains began to draw apart at the rear of the small stage to signal the beginning of the act.

Jurg turned with the stairs as they took him up to the nightclub's first floor. Below him Beyoncé's 'Naughty Girl' began to pound out in the cabaret lounge. He reached the top landing and saw a petite blonde girl in purple corset and high heels. Instinctively he smiled at her. His eyes flicked down to her unabashedly on-display and ample cleavage before returning to her face, where even in his semi-drunken state he could not miss the look of abject fear he discovered there.

London, 10.00 p.m.

The bankers lifted their cut-glass champagne flutes in salute to each other. They were in no rush to drink. Not because the bottle cost more than the average person took home each month, but because they had earned it and they wanted to savour it, savour the *why* they were drinking it.

They had invested their clients' money and – whisper it quietly, since the bank was still part-owned by the British taxpayer – some of their bank's money and bought gold all the way up to its recent high, doubling up as everybody else was taking their profits off the table. They had been fearless while everybody else had been fearful. The fury of their bank's executives that their desk had been caught massively overexposed during the Credit Crunch had been replaced by back-slapping smiles and hearty laughs. Everybody was friends again – and everybody had grown richer.

Terry cleared his throat and grew mock-serious. His accent was upper-middle-class English. Posh. Yet a keener ear, that of a linguist – that possessed by *My Fair Lady*'s Henry Higgins perhaps – would have detected an East End undercurrent. What they call a 'boy done good' in some quarters. A boy who had battled to move from one social stratum and one wealth bracket to another. Posh house, posh car and – just as importantly – posh wife. And boy, had the boy done good. And he had taken his team with him. He was a 'grumpy old bastard' according to those on his desk. Petulant, boozy and foul-mouthed. And everybody loved him.

'Boys,' Terry began, 'boys, when I met you, you were nothing. Less than nothing. It would be an insult to nothing to bring nothing into the conversation to describe just how nothing you were. Right?'

With a mock-seriousness to match Terry's own they all nodded and agreed.

'But I took pity on you. I saw in each of you a germ, a germ I could nurture into something ever-so-slightly better than shit.'

The youngest and liveliest of the four broke into a grin. 'What, even Sammy?' Referencing an absent colleague.

Terry didn't break from his scholarly pose. 'No, you're right there. Sammy will always be shit.' The other three guffawed with pleasure. 'But my point is this, boys. I found you in the gutter and I raised you kicking and screaming to be the wealthy men you are today. But never forget this: I could put you back again in the blink of an eye. Right?'

Again, they all nodded, this time with mock-humbleness and concern.

'And that's because, without me, you are nothing. What are you?'

'Nothing, boss.'

It was the one joke speech he knew and Terry repeated it at every opportunity. It never failed to raise a smile or a laugh. Why should it? He'd paid each of them millions during their time at the bank.

At the front of the restaurant were two bay windows looking out on to the street, each with floor-to-ceiling silk curtains. Between the curtains, hidden from customer view, was a large chemical fire extinguisher. In the case of a fire it would be used to suppress the flames. In the case of a fire it would not have worked.

Tokyo, 7.00 a.m.

If Yukio Sato could have smiled he would have, but in his fragile state a sense of relief was all he could muster. The car was waiting. Or rather, a car was waiting. A large, black, executive Lexus LS. Typically the driver would be standing obediently to open and close the rear passenger door for him. But on this occasion he wasn't. Perhaps it wasn't his ride after all?

The exit to his condominium was past a hotel-style reception to a car drop-off point outside, covered by the residential tower above. The young trader crossed to where the car sat idling before the main doors. He looked around. There was no one else about, it had to be his. Tentatively he opened the rear door and leaned his head in.

'Yukio Sato?'

The driver didn't look round but assented and gave a small nod. This was a level of disrespect Yukio was not used to, but his delicate state made it a side issue. He gratefully slid into the back, closed his door and sagged in his scat.

The car pulled away with a screech that forced the young trader back, bouncing his head off the head-rest.

'Hey, could you drive a bit more gently, please.'

The fast turn the Lexus took back around the loop of the condo's driveway told Yukio that the driver couldn't.

Frankfurt, 11.09 p.m.

What met the crowd on the small stage of the club both puzzled them and delighted them. Four girls in army fatigues. Head to toe. Balaclavas covering their faces. Breasts exposed. AK-47 semi-automatic rifles slung over their shoulders.

As the stage lights began to swirl their blue and red lights about the women, Beyoncé's pounding song teasing the audience, uncertain laughter flickered about the room, excited noises rose and fell. And then subsided altogether.

Because something was wrong. Very wrong. The breasts . . . They were fake.

London, *10.12 p.m.*

The four bankers *chinked* their flutes together, swathed in the serenity of one of the world's most refined restaurants.

'Cheers, lads. You've earned it.'

Terry's three colleagues looked at the head of their desk with genuine affection.

'Cheers, Terry.'

Outside, a motorcyclist in a blacked-out helmet sat on a Kawasaki trial bike and watched them toast each other. He turned to face the street ahead, pulled on the accelerator and sped off into the London night.

Tokyo, *7.11 a.m.*

'Stop! Stop! What the hell do you think you're doing? Damn it . . . !'

Yukio was being thrown into the rear left corner of the Lexus as the driver continued to drive at perilous speed around the condo's large looped driveway, round and round to the right, smoke pouring from the rear wheels as the car slid round each corner in ever faster circles.

The confused and terrified trader, his hangover

tormented by the driving, made a lunge for the rear of the front passenger seat and succeeded in gripping it enough to pull himself forward.

'What the hell do you think . . . ?'

But the words caught in his mouth as he saw the pistol lying in the driver's lap.

'Oh my –'

Yukio turned and grabbed his door handle.

Frankfurt 11.12 p.m.

Axel gestured at the girls in frustration. 'What is this? Show us your titties – your *real* titties!' His colleagues nodded and jeered in agreement.

The four girls responded by pointing their AK-47s at the young bankers. The phallic nature of their weapons was too much for some, who reacted with more whoops and cries, egging the eccentric show on with mimed weapons of their own.

Then the slaughter began.

As one, all four of the balaclavaed performers began to empty their weapons into the bankers, sending their cocktail glasses and drinks into them as they were sprayed with gunfire. If the sight of the young men pinned to the back of their seat as bullets pumped into them was not enough, the noise alone induced complete and utter panic amongst the customers present. Tables and chairs were upturned as people raced for the exit, charging into each other, punching and kicking to get through, anything to escape the massacre behind them, the grotesque lap-dancers murdering four young men on a night out, riddling them with bullets, slicing them to death at almost point-blank range.

Upstairs Jurg had turned from the gun inches from his face to the sound down below. He returned to his captor open-mouthed with horror. The perfect target for the bullet that cannoned out of the gun, splashing the falling man's brains across the wall opposite. Crimson blood on crimson velvet.

London, *10.12 p.m.*

Every one of the fourteen tables at The Wyatt was occupied as they were virtually every night. Despite the downturn, business had been good.

As the champagne flutes touched the City bankers' lips they were met by the force of the blast. A fireball of an explosion that blew the windows and entire façade of the Chelsea restaurant across the street into the front gardens of the houses opposite, an explosion that killed – instantly – every diner and member of staff present, the floor above collapsing down into the main restaurant, crushing the remains of the people whose terrible luck it was to be there when the four bankers had chosen to visit.

Tokyo, *7.12 a.m.*

Gravity alone would have tossed the young trader out of the circling Lexus, but the bullet fired into the back of his head made the event a certainty. He was dead before he hit the sidewalk, where he tumbled and rolled towards the feet of two reception staff members who had run out to investigate the commotion. This, coupled with the change of direction of the car – out of the driveway towards the freeway outside – was too much for the young female concierge who screamed hysterically as much in fright as confusion. The wide-eyed manager beside her covered his mouth with his hands as he looked from the man on the ground to the manically departing car.

Yukio lay as only a dead man can lie. Limbs twisted impossibly under his body, feet almost back to front, the large exit wound in his forehead answering any questions about his mortality. His wide-open eyes somehow holding the look of alarm he felt in his dying moment.

The car screeched off into the main thoroughfare, along the front of the complex and away.

Frankfurt, 11.14 p.m.

Nobody moved in the nightclub. Either because they had gone, because they were surveying the destruction they had wrought or because they were dead. The four women stood in the cloud of smoke coming from their guns, the blue and red lights twisting and turning around them, Beyoncé bringing to a close her song of sin and seduction. Then, slowly, as if the prospect of capture was an irrelevance, they tore off their Velcro-attached fake breasts, dropped them to the stage floor and turned wordlessly away.

London, *10.16 p.m.*

A black taxi cab lay on its side as flames licked their way out of the now-exposed restaurant's interior. The air was filled with distant but approaching sirens, as every emergency service reacted to the barrage of 999 calls that had lit up the switchboards almost immediately. A car's security alarm whined along with the warning flashing of its rear and front headlights.

An elderly man lay slumped against a glass and debris-covered Bentley Continental GT. He held a T-shirt donated from somebody's gym bag to his bloody head. Half a dozen others leaned against cars or front-garden walls, outnumbering the few passers-by attending to them as best they could. A middle-aged man gently placed his raincoat around the shoulders of a young girl, her face streaming blood that she was oblivious to.

'What happened?'

'I don't know.' The girl, twenty years old and laden with gold jewellery and make-up, was in shock. 'I was walking down the road. I just wanted to walk down the road. I was going for the bus. Who would do this? Who? I only wanted to get the bus.' Unable to stop the tears now.

The middle-aged man put his hand on her arm and gave her a comforting squeeze. He saw an ambulance approaching from the far end of the road and steered the girl towards it, away from the confusion and the flames. Away from the carnage.

2

Anenecuilco, forty miles outside Tijuana, north-west Mexico. Fifty miles from the United States border

The Sikorsky Black Hawk helicopter landed in the two-hundred-yard stretch between the adobe mud walls of the villa's garden and the cliff-top four hundred feet above the sea. The Mexican police chief stood by his jeep, his head turned from the dust cloud being tossed about by the incoming aircraft. The large helicopter settled in a stately fashion upon its three fat wheels and the blades began to wind down.

The chief looked at the three young police officers in attendance and shouted over the noise of the bird. 'Yankees. Always kicking up a storm wherever they go.'

A large door slid open on the side of the helicopter and a small series of steps were tipped over the side to the ground. A fifty-year-old African-American woman put a hand on her hair and stepped carefully down in black suit trousers and polo neck, the lack of jacket on this occasion a concession to the midday heat of the setting.

The woman kept her hand on her head until she had cleared at a stoop the spinning blades above, then made her way directly to the police chief, hand extended at the earliest opportunity.

'Special Agent Diane Mason of the United States Secret Service, a pleasure.'

The Mexican gave the hand a perfunctory shake, his disdain for her person and title writ across his face. 'Pedro Carranza, likewise.'

The younger officers smiled at their dusty shoes.

Special Agent Mason ignored the slight and looked towards the ranch. It was around ten acres in all, she had got a good view of it coming in from the sea. The outer perimeter was marked out by a crude but effective barrier of razor-wire along three sides, the cliff-top being left clear perhaps due to its natural defences, or perhaps because its owners liked to enjoy the view. At the heart of the ranch was a villa surrounded by a twelve-foot-high wall around a two-acre garden. It might have looked like a classic red-mud adobe affair, but the wall's thickness suggested it could withstand a mortar attack. The near wall, facing the cliffs, had tall black wrought-iron gates. They had been opened and revealed the back of the property itself, a large if modestly finished villa. She noted that it was low-key even by Mexican drug lord standards, even if it wasn't meant to be his main residence. No two- or three-storey boxy building with terracotta tiles to cap it off. It was a breeze-block bungalow, painted white, with a flat roof jutting out of what was evidently the back. *Maybe for a quick helicopter getaway.* She noted a few small trees in pot plants which had been stationed about a plain courtyard, a lacklustre attempt to give a feeling of homeliness, prompted by his wife, perhaps. But she couldn't imagine Señorita Lazcano spent more time at her husband's hideout than she had to.

Shutters – doubtless bullet proof – on the rear of the villa suggested the presence of windows and maybe large double doors. It looked like a roadside store closed for the holidays.

Special Agent Mason and Chief Carranza walked towards the building.

'Thank you for making the journey, Agent Mason.'

'It was nothing, really, I was already in Mexico City for a conference.' It was a lie, but she didn't want him to know she had taken such a personal interest in the matter, that she had her own reasons for the trip from New York.

As they reached the wide-open gates the wind from the aircraft's blades had abated, and they got their first proper look at each other. The African-American Secret Service agent inexplicably looked a decade younger than her years; her figure was more fulsome Monroe than stick-insect super-model, but she was comfortable with it. She was, by any standards, attractive. He was, by any standards, grizzled. A weathered face with a thick, bushy black moustache and full facial beard to distract attention from the relentless pockmarks of teenage acne decades earlier. His attire was a world away from her chic casualness. His khaki outfit with its militaristic overtones was dishevelled and older than most people's gardening clothes. But the Department of Homeland Security file had singled out his most important quality. Behind the misanthropy and pessimism was honesty. And that Mason could do business with.

'Secret Service? Protecting the President?' Spoken loudly against the slowing engine and blades of the Sikorsky. The police chief's question betraying his confusion.

'Financial investigations. Fraud, terrorism, drug money, that kind of thing.'

'Ah.' The peso dropping.

'Care to tell me what happened here?'

He gave her a somewhat ironic look. 'Don't you mean, what *didn't* happen here?'

The night was deadly still, deadly quiet.

I was falling, falling spreadeagled through the sky in near silence except for the unavoidable fluttering of my clothes. Above me a glider banked away into the darkness, back towards the United States.

For a moment I was in freefall as I approached terminal velocity. My preference had been for a HALO jump, high altitude, low opening. Hit them hard. But it wasn't going to work. The noise of the parachute opening at the last moment, the brief violent flapping of the canopy, was too risky. I had to come in silently. I had to come out of nowhere, because if anybody happened upon me with their night goggles I was quite literally going to be hanging out there.

The night was devoid of light due to full cloud cover. I was dressed head-to-toe in a lightweight black combat outfit topped with a black tactical vest, every inch of my face covered in black camouflage paint, with black night-vision goggles to round it off. Even the Heckler and Koch 416 assault rifle hanging round me was black. I was all but invisible. I needed to be.

As soon as I was clear of my ride I pulled my rip cord and experienced the yank of the black chute billowing open above me. I kept the sea on my right as I guided the parachute along the coastline, seeking out the landing point, seeking out the building down below. But for now nothing, just darkness. Jumping into the pitch-black was a fairly desperate measure on my part, but if there was another way it had escaped me. There was a whole world of trouble waiting for me when I got where I was going, but my main concern was not slamming into the deck – which was a distinct possibility if no lights turned up.

I kept the pace as slow as I could, having started my descent as far from the landing zone as possible. I had to strike a balance between accuracy and the need to hit the ground running. Most of all I had to land inside the compound's walls, but where the hell was it . . . ?

There below me. Muted lights by normal standards but distinct hotspots in my night-vision goggles. About a thousand feet below and the same distance ahead, the cliff-top ranch. The ghostly green images on the goggles confirmed what intelligence had suggested: two armed guards along the cliff's edge, a further two patrolling each side of the outer perimeter, the villa itself with a guard at each corner of the high inner wall. The major drug cartels were no longer protected by thugs and gangsters. The guards here would be ex-police, ex-military – even ex-counter-narcotics special forces. Trained at the Mexican people's expense and now dedicating themselves to sticking it to their fellow countrymen and women as ruthlessly as any junta. They would be armed and they would be dangerous. Landing outside the villa would be suicide, landing inside was hardly better. But hardly would have to do. My information was that the coastline protection was increased to include shore-patrols when the Lazcanos were in residence but that they weren't present tonight. This suited me just fine. I wasn't here to see the head of the Lazcano cartel. I was here to see somebody else.

With the rising sound of waves crashing down below me, I tugged my left hand slightly, the parachute drifting me in that direction for a hundred yards before I corrected myself, coming in on a line at the rear of the property. I had been descending as slowly as possible but I couldn't risk this pace as I got closer to the rear of the outer wall and so allowed the parachute to gather speed. My goggles showed the electronic green spectre of a guard standing sentry on the corner itself, looking west towards the sea. So he was not ready for the two boots that came from the north, that I smacked into his head, delivered with an extra kick. We landed inside the compound at the same time, me trotting to a halt ahead of my parachute, him crippled by the fall.

Hit them hard.

I found myself halfway along the inside of the rear wall by a tall metal gate, nearer to the south-west corner than I would have liked. I didn't wait to assess my situation but pulled my HK416 assault rifle into my shoulder. As I trained the sight on the guard in the far corner of the wall I saw momentarily that he was reacting to the pained grunt he had heard from his colleague on the opposite corner and was sweeping his gun's night-sight from the now-empty command post down towards me. Not waiting for any understanding of the abandoned post, he drew breath to yell the alarm. I pumped three bullets into him, the suppressor of my gun limiting the sound to a deadly *phutt-phutt-phutt*. The guard hovered for a moment before falling forward into the compound. If he wasn't dead before, the twelve-foot drop directly on to his head would have sealed the deal.

The police chief pointed to two corners of the courtyard. 'We think the men entered at the back of the property.'

'What men?'

'The men who attacked the Lazcanos.'

Special Agent Mason looked at him almost askance. 'Just a moment. Are you saying the Lazcanos asked you to look into this? I thought they worked these things out between themselves?'

'That is how they typically resolve matters, yes. But this wasn't an attack by another cartel. It was way too sophisticated for that. A place like this? The cartels would fight each other through the front door. The men who did this, they were more like, what would you say, special forces.'

'Mexican?'

He paused before speaking. 'United States.' He eyed her, wanting to gauge her reaction. He seemed uninterested in her incredulity and walked off, suppressing the anger that he felt at the perceived disrespect. From her and her country.

I crept back towards the first guard, my 'chute trailing behind me. I found him at the foot of a ladder leading up to his sentry post. He was dazed, moaning in a heap, trying to right himself. I knelt down behind him, took his head in my hands and snapped it to the right. I held on for a moment, wanting to be certain he had gone still. A sigh-like breath escaped him. And no more.

I released the harness of my parachute and reeled it swiftly in. I wouldn't be needing it again and figured I would rather any cameras caught sight of a large cloth than a dead guard so laid it over him. I leaned my back against the wall of the inner perimeter and listened intently to the large courtyard before me. Everything seemed as still as the warm evening air. There was nothing that I could detect.

The easy part was over.

'That's a hell of a claim. Chief Carranza, I can assure you that the US government did *not* authorize this – I'm telling you that on *and* off the record.'

The police chief did not react but instead proffered her a small, narrow, metal can. It looked like a cross between a tiny vacuum flask and a used firework. 'You can't buy this on the open market, Special Agent Mason. Are you telling me the US government permitted somebody else the use of its equipment? Or perhaps it was stolen to order?' His sarcasm coming through loud and clear.

I scanned the garden. The villa at the centre was as plain as they got. It was a building whose main purpose was clearly functional. Which exact function I was aiming to find out. Down the right-hand side I saw an unshuttered door. If I had the luxury of a choice, that would be my preferred point of entry, but guarding my route were four closed-circuit cameras along the top of the rear of the building. I had to assume that I wasn't going to get any-where near the premises without coming up on their monitors – if I hadn't already. I had no idea what the lack of security personnel inside the villa walls themselves meant. Was it attributable to it being night? Was it because the boss of their cartel was out of town? Was it for a more sinister reason?

I withdrew a small canister from my tactical vest. I pulled a wire ring out of the top, which produced a tiny hiss, before rolling it to the centre of the courtyard. I winced at the clattering sound the smoke grenade made as it skittered across the paving stones and instinctively tensed. Before it had come to a standstill a non-toxic smoke began to pour out, gently pushed this way and that by the minimal breeze. As the mist occasionally rose, thin red laser beams revealed themselves about two feet off the ground, marking the distance between myself and the main residence like the yard lines on a football pitch, the villa at the halfway point. What did the laser beams trigger? I didn't want to find out. I looked up at the cameras then scanned the characterless garden once again. So far so undetected, it appeared. I deliberated over whether to approach by stealth or speed. If the cameras were watching for heat I was going to stand out like the Rockefeller Plaza Christmas tree. Crap.

The villa was about one hundred yards away, and my rifle was good for four or five times that. Once the cameras were out there would be calls to the now-dead guards, and then it would be lockdown time. I gave myself a minute from the first bullet. I had to kill the surveillance, get to the villa and avoid the lasers. And not get shot. All in sixty seconds.

I pulled another smoke grenade out of my vest and

with one hand pulled off its cap before setting it at my feet, where smoke began to seep out.

I took aim at the camera on the far left of the building. Here went everything and nothing.

Special Agent Mason considered the incriminating gas canister in her hand. The incriminating gas canister in her hand. She looked up with a deadpan face. 'This doesn't mean it was authorized.'

The police chief snorted derisively and led the way across the courtyard towards the villa. He waved a hand around the garden as they passed through it. Dotted about were scores of small chalk circles. 'Note the bullets, Agent Mason. We believe they were actually fired by Mexicans.'

Sixty seconds from the first shot. Sixty seconds to mayhem. I delivered a three-bullet burst into the first camera. The sound of the bullets landing in the camera's guts was louder than the *phutt* of the suppressed gunfire, like lightbulbs being stepped on. I needed to squint to stop the impact flaring up into my night goggles and blinding me. I tilted right and took out the next camera, then the third and the fourth, squinting each time against the light. Ten seconds.

I picked up the smoke canister at my feet and – as fast as I dared – moved through the courtyard, smoke ahead of me. The hazy red of a laser beam appeared in its mist, and I hopped over the virtual wire. Twenty.

I moved further forward. Behind me, one of the dead guard's comms units sprang into life. Another red laser beam. The comms device blaring out, the voice more urgent this time, becoming alarmed. The beam stepped over. Thirty seconds.

Further forward. From the other corner behind me the other dead guard's comms unit, straight to the urgent tone. A red line, stepped over, me by the farthest smoke canister now. Forty seconds.

I moved faster, more sure of the distances, but as I approached where the line should have been revealed a gust caused all the smoke to swirl about before blowing towards me. I couldn't find my line without the smoke. I had no choice but to wait for the wind to settle. Just then a siren whirred into life, its warning wail reminiscent of air-raid sirens. I could hear a shutter grinding into life, moving rapidly, my entrance to the building being closed off. The wind changed direction. My canister of smoke discovered the lost laser beam, inches from my leg, and I wheeled over it. Fifty-five seconds.

There was no more time for stealth, and I made a dash for the right-hand side of the building. I ran through the next beam, which the turning wind had pointlessly rendered visible. On breaking the beam I learned its purpose immediately: the entire courtyard erupted with illumination as floodlights sunken into the walls came into life. I was unprepared for this, and as the courtyard became swathed in a super-bright white my night goggles flared over completely, the image blinding me mid-run.

I staggered and rolled to the bottom of the building, my outstretched arm breaking my fall, my eyes filled with all the stars in the galaxy, a jagged pain tearing through my head. I dragged the glasses down around my neck, almost gasping at the agony of the sudden assault on my senses, my brain raging. The side door was a distant goal now: regaining control was everything. Mexican voices began to call vigilantly to one another. Lockdown was in full motion. I looked around but couldn't see a thing, my vision bright patches of amorphous white. As the shutters came to a close I knew that I was helpless and that they were closing in.

The world-weary Mexican police chief was pointing at the roofline of the villa above them, where a thin rope dangled from one of four security cameras. Closed-circuit cameras which had clearly been shot to pieces. 'The invaders disabled these.' He gave his American counterpart a deadpan look. 'Ballistics tell me the invading cartel members used US special forces bullets.' He *tutted* sarcastically. 'That will never do.'

Diane Mason saw enough deniability to stick with it. 'Chief, I give you my word I will investigate this, but I did some preliminary checks, and nobody ordered this on our side. With all due respect, this is circumstantial, it could just be a diversionary tactic.'

He played along. 'What, like a smokescreen?'

'Yes, exact . . .' She stopped mid-sentence, seeing the chief rolling another gas canister between his fingers. It was a hell of a long way to travel just to be mocked.

She went to speak, but he broke in. 'And is the body a smoke screen as well?'

A thousand thoughts ran through Mason's mind. Byrne had been off the radar for almost a week. Since two days before this attack. Mason wanted to tear a strip off him.

She also wanted him back alive. 'Who . . . I mean, which body?'

'The American body.'

He scrutinized her face once again as she tried not to react. He hoped for her sake she wasn't a poker player.

It was the worst possible predicament. I needed to keep my eyes closed to regain my sight, I needed to keep my eyes open to see the approaching guards. The courtyard was about to become a shooting gallery and I was the only attraction. Then I heard her voice running round my head. I squeezed my eyes as tight as they would go to get rid of the blindness, to get rid of the voices. Final conversations. With her.

'Where you going?'

'It's a secret.'

'As in Secret Service?'

'As in, you don't want to know.'

'Don't do it, Mike, don't go after this guy.'

'I can't . . . leave him.'

'Can't leave him or can't leave *it*?'

She had me there. I couldn't leave it. And this was what I got for my pains.

The scraping of feet on gravel above me. I looked up with my naked eyes, large white spots obscuring my vision. I was bathed in light – but the roof was not completely lost to me. I partially saw something, somebody. On instinct alone I fired at the figure above and was rewarded with a pained yell as somebody fell backwards and away.

Where would they be coming from? They wouldn't abandon the perimeter, they would be looking for attacks from all sides now and hold their positions, and the twelve-foot-high inner wall would keep them out as much as anybody else. No, they'd stick to their patrol positions until they understood the security breach. It was inside the villa itself that would be the warzone. It was inside I needed to get to.

I held my breath as I heard more movement alongside one side of the villa. I pulled a grenade off an ammo belt and withdrew the pin. I counted to eight and tossed it just past the corner of the building. There was a yelp of alarm as somebody retreated – but not before the explosion caught up with them.

I cast my mind about for a way round until the obvious hit me. The roof.

I reached into a thigh pocket and pulled out a slim length of rope. The scuffling of feet was closing in now, and it was down to this. I looped the rope up over the remains of one of the security cameras and pulled on the fixture. It seemed safe enough. Safer than down here at least. I retrieved a grenade from my tactical vest and pulled the pin out with my teeth. Ten. A diversion. Nine. Anybody moves. Eight. They get a treat. Seven. Foot-steps along the wall. Six. I needed to clear the side of the villa. Five. I needed to clear the roof more. Four – I tossed it up on to the single-storey extension. Three. The silence. Two. A yell of dread. One. A man turning on the gravel of the roof. Zero. A blast followed by the clump of a falling body off the side of the roof to the courtyard below.

I pulled the rope taut and walked up the wall, feeding the rope into my hands, seeing people emerging down below, grabbed the roofline, swung my feet up, breeze-blocks shattering about in a hail of gunfire behind me. I knew my silhouette would be the perfect target and threw myself to the dark floor just as another hail of metal flew over me, me rolling to the right as bullets traced a line I was believed to be in, a line that was dead centre a second earlier.

I crawled on my belly past a dead guard, towards a square of light in the roof ahead of me. A cautious head popped up, a flashlight on his gun barrel searching the rooftop, turning left then right.

Grenade. Pin pulled. Shots to make him duck down. Me rolling the grenade ten yards into the trapdoor ahead of me. Me crawling as fast as I could towards the cries of confusion and panic. A Mexican screaming at his colleagues to get the hell out. Too late. A thunderclap inside the room below. Bullets strafing the rooftop now. Me launching myself into the trapdoor, bullets chasing me along the roof, a steep wooden staircase, me upside down, running my hands ahead on the steps, trying to break the fall but falling all the same, tumbling, landing on my back, landing on a dead Mexican. I pulled my gun up where I lay and saw the furious guard charging through the doorway just in time, a burst from my gun, his feet skidding from under him as his head took three bullets.

I righted myself, and flattened my back against the wall by the door. Switched my HK416 to safety mode and placed it on the floor. I didn't want my assault rifle at these close quarters. Maybe I'd get it on the way out. Maybe.

A metal extendable ladder had been found and leaned against the single-storey rear extension. The chief of police started to climb it before stopping halfway up and looking back down at Agent Mason.

'Are you coming, Special Agent Mason?'

She hadn't come round yet, hadn't buried the emotions her worst fears had realized, that this guy's idea of humour would be to stand over Michael Byrne's dead body with a cigarette in his mouth. She had to control herself, had to control the situation.

'Certainly. I'd like to see all the evidence.'

The chief was climbing up the small distance to the flat roof before she'd finished speaking, the ladder clanging metallically under his military boots.

The room I was in was like a large closet but served as the emergency exit to the roof. I was on the ground floor. At least one floor too high up.

I was kneeling by the doorway, my Sig Sauer service pistol in my hand. I quietly stood, listening for any movement outside. People were shouting to each other in the grounds, but inside I could have been alone. I slipped out my gun's suppressor and screwed it to the end of the barrel. The element of surprise was in short supply but I'd use what was left.

I took a step into the doorway and swung my gun left to right. Nobody. A short corridor with a right turn. A clattering noise coming towards me. I stepped back and to the side of the doorway as somebody's grenade reached the passageway's elbow. A flash burst into the large closet beside me. I immediately stepped out and slid my back along the wall, facing the corridor where the grenade had come from. Two guards ran into view, the second one's line of sight to me blocked by the first, the first slower on the trigger than me. Two bullets, two down.

I stepped across them and rounded the corner to see movement from a doorway at the far end of the corridor. An exclamation of almost surprise from the man standing there. I squeezed off a bullet and moved swiftly towards him, passing two opposing doorways along the way. Servants' quarters, I had been told. I reached the Mexican I had just downed, the door half closed beside him. I crouched and pushed it slowly open with one hand. A large kitchen with a long table, maybe a dozen chairs around it, the windows, like all the windows here, shuttered closed. In the corner a tall gas canister serviced the stove and oven, with their dozen pots and pans hanging above them. No utilities would service a house this far out, which meant even the electricity was generator produced. I was banking on it.

I moved cautiously through the room, assuming the entrance opposite could burst open at any moment. A bullet whizzed past the left side of my head from behind: the servants' quarters.

I dropped to the right, down behind the kitchen door. I pushed it closed with my foot then immediately stood up behind it. It was a rustic-looking door and would hardly slow my bullets. I placed four in the rough centre. An almost-whimper went up. I ejected the empty magazine on to the floor and slammed in another. I yanked the door open and then immediately stepped out of sight. A couple of bullets flew into the kitchen. From the position they landed in the wall opposite they seemed like fairly wildly placed shots. The sort of shots a badly wounded man might make. Still, just to be sure I stepped out and took aim at him twenty feet along the corridor. The bullet in his forehead put us both out of his misery.

Special Agent Mason stepped down off the steep wooden stairs into the closet-like room. She looked beyond Chief Carranza in the corridor ahead and saw the signs of grenade damage. She turned into the corridor proper, where two bloody body outlines were traced on the ground. To go with the one at the bottom of the stepladder.

The chief of police nodded at the white outlines on the floor and the brutal holes in the walls. 'As you can see, there was an exchange of gunfire at this point.' He turned, not interested in Mason examining the minutiae of the evidence – a mere sideshow, a distraction – and made his way towards the kitchen, stepping round another two body outlines en route. 'Also here.'

Mason followed without speaking, the growing body count adding to the pit in her stomach.

I opened the far kitchen door. A long, gloomy corridor reached back into the villa with various doors coming off it. But it was the two opposing doors nearby I was interested in. Both were in darkness, except that some kind of light was playing under the left-hand one. The kind of light a television might make. Or maybe a number of televisions. I stood outside, raised my foot, aimed for a spot left of the handle and gave it a hard kick. The door flew open to reveal a small, raggedy-looking Mexican nervously holding a gun. I was slower off the mark than usual, needing to aim carefully. He got off the first bullet. But fear or inexperience saved me — it didn't even get outside the room he was standing in. Small mercies.

I shot his gun-hand. The gun jumped out of his grasp as he recoiled in surprise. A surprise that was replaced by a scorching pain in his now-three-fingered hand. He looked aghast at what I had done, held the hand aloft in disbelieving fright as the blood ran down it.

I spoke in Spanish. 'Open the basement door and I won't shoot you in the head.'

He clasped his wounded hand to his chest, taking a moment, taking a moment to register the situation. He looked at me with a mixture of fear and desperation. This clearly wasn't what he had signed up for when he took the job with the Lazcano drug cartel. Being a cog in the machine that spread misery across northern Mexico, the southern United States and beyond, yes. Having a gun pointed at him for his pains, no. He weighed up the situation, the outcome for him.

'You promise?'

'I promise.'

He looked at the desk of buttons and switches beside him then back at me. I extended the gun towards his forehead.

'OK, OK. But you promise.'

He waited for my nod then reached down and flicked three switches in succession. On a screen in the middle of the bank of monitors I saw the flickering black-and-white image of a heavy metal door swinging open on a hinge, matched by a sound across the hallway.

He dipped his head appeasingly. 'Remember – you promise.'

I fired two bullets into his heart.

I'd remembered my promise.

Special Agent Mason looked around herself, at the kitchen, at the corridor beyond. Black from flames. Half a dozen forensic personnel from the Tijuana police force in white paper boiler-suits were travelling between the different rooms, requiring her to step out of their way. The police chief was standing between two doors ahead of her, both open. He indicated one.

'The invaders broke into the control room and killed the security guard. In the heart, execution style.' Looking at her with a look that just might have suggested that that was what he would expect of drug gangs, not the US military. 'They then made their way down here.'

He indicated a basement stairwell opposite. It too was burned black and, to Mason's eyes, significantly damaged by explosives. He held an arm towards the lower floor, inviting her to lead the way. He answered the question running through her mind.

'The American's body is still down there.'

She could feel his eyes probing her face. What the hell was Spanish for *screw you*?

I stood at the top of a cold stone staircase. A large diesel engine could be heard at work somewhere in the bowels of this place. Presumably supplying the electricity. The walls were the thickest of any so far, unnecessarily thick for any normal purpose. As sure as anything soundproof.

What went on down here was not for the ears of the people upstairs. What went on down here was the production of the cartel's most powerful weapon. Down here was the fear factory.

For now, I took a grim appreciation of the soundproof nature of the facility. Had they heard the commotion up above them? Were they on alert? Were they waiting for me? These walls plus the noise of the generator gave me hope they weren't.

I walked down the steps in a low crouch. In any other setting the bare concrete stairs and breeze-block walls would magnify every sound I made, but the sound of the generator was getting louder. The walls were unpainted, the air cool. Purely functional. The function of the building.

At the bottom of the stairs was a single, short passageway with two doors on each side, all open, and one at the end. Closed.

I moved closer to the first doors, my gun at the ready. The door to my right was an armoury of some kind. It figured that it would be in the most secure part of the house. I stepped into it, swept around the room. Nothing but enough hardware to kick-start a small military coup. Gun rack after gun rack of Glocks, Smith and Wessons, Thomsons, SLPs, accompanied by metal crate after metal crate of what were clearly grenade and rocket launchers, plus all the ammo that went with these things. All doubtless bought in America. All paid for with drugs money. What a whirlwind waiting to be sown.

I checked the corridor. Nothing and nobody. A scream escaped from the locked room at the far end.

'Please! Please, I don't know anything!'

The voice young, American, weak, descending into weeping and unabashed sobbing. As terrified and desperate as a person could get.

I stepped into the doorway opposite. The generator room. As loud and as foul-smelling as I'd expected. Two large diesel engines in cages. The prominent industrial-sized on/off switch in the far wall under lock and key with them. Pipes leading the fumes out and away some place.

Back into the corridor. I moved quietly, but the rumble of the diesel engine made any incidental sounds I made irrelevant. The second door to the right was some kind of cell. A bare room but for an iron bunk with a single blanket. There was a lot of blood – dried and fresh – on the floor and bedposts.

'Please! Oh please, I've told you everything I know.'

And more weeping that morphed horribly into an inhuman howl, suddenly cut off.

I switched sides in the corridor, my back to the right wall looking into the last room before the closed door. As I thought, a bathroom. A stainless steel metal bathtub with a stainless steel toilet, every surface white tiles. Even the ceiling. Every last tile wearing the blood of the infernal function of this place. Hand marks dragged through the crimson on the wall by the bath. Scuff marks covered the floor.

A primordial moan escaped from behind the closed door. Was I too late?

I unscrewed the suppressor from my gun and slipped it into a thigh pocket. Gunshots would be the least of my problems. Mobility would be the priority, reactions would be everything. I put my left hand on the door handle, readied the Sig Sauer in my right. Took a moment to prepare myself.

Behind the door, a clipped, academic-sounding Mexican speaking English. 'Just tell us how to get it back.'

'I don't . . .'

I wrenched the handle round, swung the door open and moved my gun across the three men present.

No.

Jesus wept.

I thought I was ready for anything but I wasn't.

Three men, side on.

I was ready for the interrogator on the left, an older man in a white shirt, sleeves rolled up. I was ready for the torturer on the right, a younger man, shirt off, sweat pouring off his bald head. But I wasn't ready for the American, the man tied to the chair between them.

He looked at me. What was left of him. He faced me, but I couldn't face him. A picture of hell. Jesus *wept*.

The white-shirted guy threw his hands up and confused me even more by pleading instantly, 'Please, I'm just a lawyer.'

In my shock I was completely unprepared for the bald man launching himself at me with a roar. I was slammed into the concrete wall on my left, where we both bounced to the ground at the lawyer's feet, the torturer on top of me. I tried to bring my gun hand round, but he had an impossibly strong grasp of it. I saw the lawyer creeping out. Son of a bitch.

I leaned myself and the bald man to one side so that my gun was aiming low out of the room. I got off a round.

Directly into the lawyer's leg. He fell to the ground yelping with pain.

I was grappling with a man who was pure muscle, a man I could outrun over any distance, but a man who could squeeze the life out of a boa constrictor before it squeezed the life out of him. And now he had a hand round my neck and he was tightening his grip.

I rolled towards the wall, he shifted his balance to keep me pinned down on my back, I heaved back the other way with all my might and managed to reverse our positions but what the hell did he care. I was the one on top but he was still choking me and still had the wrist of my gun hand in his iron grip.

I tried to punch him in the face with my left hand but couldn't get round his arm. The colossus just seemed to absorb it. My knife was in my right thigh pocket. Unreachable. And I needed oxygen. Desperately.

With difficulty I patted my tactical vest looking for what I could reach, what I could use. I found something and hoped he hadn't noticed me slipping it out. I was running out of air and time. He was gritting his teeth, using all of his strength. I needed him to open his mouth. I ran the fingers of my left hand down his right arm to the inside of his elbow. Ninety times out of a hundred you could disable a person by putting pressure on the right nerves. A man this big had muscles blocking the very nerves I was trying to reach. I dug my thumb into where the brachial artery inside his elbow should have been. Pure muscle. I rocked us to one side, he shifted his weight, thinking I was trying to wriggle free, I dug the thumb inside his elbow again, not a lot of space but enough, dug in hard with all my might. Any other person would have recoiled in agony, would have had to escape the pain. The torturer kept functioning with nothing more than a cry of distress. That was enough. I brought my left hand round and rammed a smoke grenade into his mouth and immediately covered it with the same hand.

He heaved in a convulsion of choking, his massive chest rising under me as it was my turn to hold our position. I bore down with all my force, my hand on his face, keeping the gas in there, the man's eyes wide open now, barely comprehending the turn of events. We were locked together in a battle of wills, him trying to crush my neck, me wanting that smoke to overcome him. He wouldn't let go, he wouldn't let –

He buckled. He swiped my arms away and reached a hand into his mouth to retrieve the canister.

As he tried to unblock his throat I brought my pistol round into the side of his head and put a bullet in his temple. Still astride him – gasping for air myself – I turned to face the corridor. Limping out of the armoury was the lawyer with an Uzi submachine gun. Before he could aim at me I emptied all but one of my bullets into him, the Uzi spraying wildly about the walls and ceiling fleetingly before he fell backwards to the base of the staircase.

I rose, coughing and sucking in much-needed air at the same time. I looked down at the torturer at my feet. The smoke pouring out of his motionless mouth told me I wouldn't be needing to use that last bullet on him.

Mason paused at the bottom of the stairs. Venturing into the room at the end of the short, near-destroyed corridor was the last thing she wanted to do. The acrid smell of the burned-out basement, the smell of weapons, of cauterized bodies, was almost more than she could bear. But if she ran it would be left to somebody else. Somebody else who wouldn't be as keen to cover it up.

She looked at the room at the end, the room that mattered. More people in their white paper outfits were testing everything and anything. The room the quiet hive of activity that attends a murder scene.

The police chief was holding a handkerchief to his mouth and nose, quietly revelling in Agent Mason's discomfort. He wanted her – somebody from the American government – to see the butchery wrought by the Mexican drugs and the American guns. To taste for one hour the bitterness of the war that his country lived with every minute of every day. Then he realized his anger was getting the better of him and tried to put it to one side.

'Forensics is still trying to piece together what happened, but preliminary reports suggest that the invading force killed everybody down here before the explosion occurred.'

Special Agent Mason had to wrench her eyes away from the room at the end to take in the basement area he was indicating.

'I see.' She knew she was in danger of giving in to her worst fears and mentally reprimanded herself. She walked past the police chief determinedly, setting the pace. 'Well, let's see what you brought me here to see.'

The police chief watched her face as she passed him. Maybe she could play poker, after all.

Mason navigated the debris of twisted metal and small

pieces of rubble to reach the doorway of the room at the end. Obediently, as if they had agreed beforehand, the trio of forensic experts stood back to let her take in the scene.

She couldn't bring herself to look at the body straight away but instead made a show of being the detached observer, even though the effort was tearing her nerves apart. She looked down to her left and saw a clean patch amongst the wreckage, knowing immediately it had been made by a body that had since been taken away, a body that must have been lying there when the explosion occurred. She stared at it, making a pretence of somehow absorbing this important information. Putting off the task she knew she dreaded so much. Putting off the inevitable.

She slowly turned her head to the body in the middle of the room. It took every ounce of her self-control to not let out an involuntary cry.

I took a moment to get my breath then realized I almost wanted to put off the very task that had brought me all this way. Get a grip, Byrne. I turned towards the American, who had watched on as hopefully as a man in his condition could. He made an effort to look up at me in his enfeebled state. He spoke in a mumbled whisper.

'Are you here to take me home?'

I had to fight to form the words, my heart in my mouth. 'Yes. Stay calm and it will all be all right.'

'I've got no feeling in my hands or feet.'

'You've been tied up, that's all, the circulation, you know. It's going to be OK.' Me choking on the words.

'I'm an American citizen. My name's Simon Turlington.'

'I know.'

'Who . . .' He weakly spat some blood out that trailed from his bottom teeth down on to his chest. '. . . are you?'

'I'm Mike Byrne. I'm with the American Secret Service. Look, Simon, we haven't got much time. I need to know who set up the meeting.'

'Mr Byrne?' Barely audible above the generator down the hall.

I took a breath. 'Yeah.' I wanted to weep for him. I wanted to weep for his parents. 'What is it, Simon?'

'I think they cut my face . . .' The words trailing off. He didn't have much time. We didn't have much time. Only a high dose of morphine could explain his physical and mental togetherness right now.

I had to fight the emotion. 'Who set up the meeting, Simon? I need a name.'

It took a moment then it came out like a sigh. 'Sec . . .' But once again Turlington trailed off with the words.

'Sec? Your secretary? No, Simon, who arranged it?'

He seemed to shake his head. He turned his eyes slowly in their sockets and stared at me for the first time. I had to give him the dignity of returning the look, knowing it would haunt me for ever.

He tried to speak, but his tongue seemed to grow thick in his mouth, and he lowered his head on to his chest.

'Simon, can your secretary tell me who arranged it? Is that it?' I looked across to a silver trolley, where various medical-cum-torture utensils were laid out along with a BlackBerry phone.

His mouth moved a minuscule amount, but no words came out, no sound at all.

'Simon? Simon, can you hear me?'

Now just a stare at the ground. And yet there seemed to be so much pain inside. An infinite torment.

I stood up and steadied myself, steadied my emotions. I walked round the back of the dying young man. One bullet left in the chamber. I held the gun pointing towards the ground, my fingers twitching as I did. I needed to get the hell out but I stood frozen with inaction.

Then, suddenly, the American threw his head back and – with a strength I couldn't have imagined he possessed – cried at the top of his hoarse voice, 'My hands and feet, they –'

I put my last bullet in the back of his head.

Mason walked out of the basement room, out past the accusing look of the chief, anger replacing the pity she felt on seeing the young man's charred body, not giving two hoots what the people about her thought of her display. She was good at her job. Hell, she was damn good. But she never wanted to be that good that she felt nothing when confronted with a scene like that.

'Vete a la mierda,' she told him. She'd remembered the Spanish for it, after all.

I stood at the top of the basement stairs.

'Throw out your weapon.' A Mexican ordering me to surrender.

I tossed out a pistol and stepped after it, away from the basement doorway.

On both sides, in front and behind, were two very nervous Mexican guards. Four in all. They had their guns trained on me. They had me with my hands in the air.

My edge?

I knew what was coming.

A blast from the basement – the result of weapons and explosions and diesel generators – rocked the corridor, sending the villa into total darkness. I dropped to the floor in time for each pair to fire wildly at each other. A new gun from the back of my pants in hand I put a bullet into the two between me and the exit and sprang over them as I started my sprint back towards the rooftop. As I got past the kitchen I turned back and fired a bullet into the gas canisters for good measure, already on my way as the gas bottles erupted in a fireball.

As I neared the turn in the corridor a dark figure emerged ahead of me. I side-stepped into the doorway of a servant's room as gunfire filled the corridor. As soon as I heard six bullets emptied from the gun I stepped back out, but the figure was gone. I raced round the corner to see a lone Mexican standing at the bottom of the step-ladder to the roof exit. The clouds must have broken because a beam of moonlight through the trapdoor lit him up. He was holding my HK416 assault rifle, he was holding it three feet from my stomach.

'Drop your weapon or I shoot.'

I looked at the rifle then at him. I shook my head, angry at myself. He squinted warily in bemusement. I raised my gun. He pulled his trigger.

Realizing the assault rifle's safety catch had been left on was the last thought he ever had.

I peered over the lip of the trapdoor to see the far end

of the villa in flames. There were men attending to it, but had they pulled all the patrols off? All I knew was that I had to get the hell out before every helicopter in the Lazcano cartel arrived with paramilitary backup.

I ran at a crouch along the rooftop in relative darkness, the villa's floodlights killed by my manoeuvre with the generator. But the moon was doing its best to pick up where they had left off.

A Mexican voice. 'Over there!'

Some wayward shots cracked my way, and I could hear the remaining men snapping into action. I leaped off the roof on to the courtyard below, rolling to kill the impact. Voices were building around me, the group coordinated now. I righted myself and sprinted at full pelt away from the villa, towards the far left corner. They saw my moonlit outline and fired after me, but the darkness, the panic, the limitations of them or their weapons all rendered the shots ineffectual. I reached the far wall at the end of the garden and bounded up the stepladder to the sentry point, pausing only to scout for the cliff-top patrol. Nobody.

The cloud-cover was returning, covering the moon, and darkness was my friend again. I vaulted over the wall and landed heavily on my feet. Badly. Damn it. I fought through the pain as best I could towards the edge of the cliff, aware of guards leaping over the wall behind me and a Humvee approaching down each side of the outer perimeter wall. The Humvees would be packed with heavily armed guards. The Humvees took away all my options.

As I half limped, half ran towards the cliff edge the bouncing headlights were picking me out against the skyline. Guns burst into life as the Humvees bore down on me. I didn't even stop to look back, to learn more about the automatic gunfire aimed my way. The cliffs, four hundred feet above the rocky coastline, were the only exit plan I had left. As an extra wave of guns burst into life I pitched myself over the edge, bullets filling the air above me.

Into the darkness for the second time that night. One hundred feet.

The gunfire fading as the air rushed past me. Two hundred.

The sea crashing noisily on to the rocks below. Three hundred.

Pull.

My reserve parachute billowing into position for the briefest of glides before splashdown.

Mason was leaning against the rear wall of the villa, staring out past the motionless helicopter, past the cliffs, to the Pacific Ocean. It would take a bottle of wine to unpack all the emotions she was feeling. Jesus. What a day.

The Tijuanan chief of police walked up behind her and came to a halt by her side.

'Sorry, Agent Mason. I should have given you some breathing apparatus, those places can play hell with your sinuses.'

Mason smiled joylessly to herself and kept staring at the sea. 'I can promise you that wasn't a United-States-sponsored mission, chief.'

Carranza was in no mood for more stonewalling. 'Let's cut the bull, shall we, Agent Mason? This was not the work of the cartels, it was way too professional for that.

You know it and I know it. And please don't insult my intelligence by suggesting they used American equipment as some kind of elaborate ruse. You saw what happened to the Lazcanos: we're talking about a small goddamn army here.'

'No we're not, Chief Carranza.' Mason turned slowly to look at him, at his defiantly questioning expression, the steel of her senior position in the United States Secret Service fully present in her bulletproof stare. 'We're talking about one man.'

3

'Michael!'

I sensed she was mad on the phone on my way into the New York field office on Adams Street, Brooklyn. I suspected she was angry as I approached her actual office, Special Agent Mason moving about too precisely, working herself up. She left me in no doubt that she was pissed when I sat down at her desk. She was standing behind it, a picture of the President behind her. Diane claimed it was a patriotic gesture. I knew it was because she'd voted for him. Then she confused me by twisting her rear round for me to see.

'You see this butt, Michael?' She pulled a *Well, do you?* face. 'It's prosthetic. I got the real one chewed off at the Department of Homeland Security this morning. They think we've got a rogue agent going postal down Mexico way.' Looking at me accusingly. 'Well, have we?'

I hated these conversations. Or maybe I hated causing these conversations.

'I . . .' I was going to give some bullshit answer then couldn't be bothered. I didn't need it and she didn't need it from me. 'They had my star witness.'

She slapped the large cardboard file she was holding down on the table, creating an unexpectedly loud thump. She really was pissed. 'Star? Don't you mean *only*? *Only* witness in a case who had *only* talked to you . . . Technically known as . . . ? *Hearsay* evidence.'

'He was prepared to testify in front of a Grand Jury. I told him not to go to Tijuana, but he was worried about his bonus. They threw him to the lions, Diane, they killed my star witness.'

'And your case, Michael, don't forget your case.'

I waited in the hope that some of the steam would go out of her. She looked away to calm herself then looked back again. 'What were you . . . ?' She shook her head, too angry to talk. Her anger rising. 'I mean, what were you planning to do, Michael, shoot your way into a heavily armed drug lord's hideout then walk a kidnap victim out the front door?'

'Well, that was more like plan B.' As a rule we were on the same side. Diane's zeal for her job made my contribution look like indifference. It was rare that she was *really* mad at me. But it did happen. Especially when I handed it to her on a plate. Like today. 'What did you tell the Director?'

'What do you think I told him, Michael? I said it looked like inter-cartel violence dressed up to seem like we did it. They'd have both our behinds in a sling if I said otherwise.'

I pulled a conciliatory face. 'Sounds plausible to me.'

Wrong move. Now she was really angry. 'Does it? Does it, Michael? Because it sounds like baloney to me. Because the ballistics report only showed bullets from two guns, two guns that we both know I could track to one person in *this* department.' She dropped heavily into her chair for emphasis and glared at the file rather than me. 'What were you thinking, Michael?' Angry and disappointed.

As my mother used to counsel me, when all else fails tell the truth. 'I was thinking of the young banker, Turlington.'

We stared at each other, her angry and worried, me sympathetic to the shit storm I'd clearly kicked up in DC for her. Then a dark cloud crossed her face, and the anger was put to one side. 'So, what happened? How did Turlington find himself tied to a chair in a basement outside of Tijuana?' Keeping it at arm's length, factual.

'Sovereign Bank are telling us that Turlington flew down to Mexico to meet an unnamed businessman, a prospective new client, but that he never made it to the meeting.'

She tapped a long, ivory-coloured fingernail on the tatty brown file in front of her. 'And the truth?'

'I think the unnamed businessman is Lazcano, and that Turlington was met at Tijuana airport by his people. I think that *was* the meeting.'

She took her time about the next thing she wanted to talk about. I could see her coming at it from different angles, her look softening, turning to something approaching compassion. She spoke quietly.

'I saw what they did to him, Michael.'

I didn't react. I didn't know how to.

We both sat in silence for a full ten seconds, the occasional phone ringing in the large open-plan offices outside Diane's own glass-walled office. I didn't want to talk about Tijuana, and she didn't know how to proceed.

'I . . . I saw what you did to him.'

One bullet left in the chamber. I held the gun pointing towards the ground, my fingers twitching as I did. I needed to get the hell out but I stood frozen with inaction.

I was getting hot, and it wasn't the temperature of the room. I couldn't look her in the eyes, but she saw the passion rising in my face as I went to protest, went to explain. But she held up a hand.

'It's OK. God knows I'm not judging you, I know the how and the why of it. But nobody can live with that kind of thing, Michael. Nobody. And I know you, Michael, you're blaming yourself for what happened to Turlington.'

I wanted to look away, wanted to shove that moment deep down inside, away from the light. Then I remembered how that must appear and did my best to return her a steady gaze.

'No I'm not.'

'You ever lie to me again, Michael Byrne, and I'll have your badge before you draw another breath. You blame yourself because you always forget that people like Turlington are chasing the next dollar, just like his bosses, which is how these crimes happen.'

I didn't say anything, mainly because she'd told me not to lie, and all I had was bullshit denials.

'Michael, you should see a counsellor.'

'I'm fine.'

'I don't want you walking round with that kind of baggage.'

I did my best take on nonchalance. 'It's hand luggage at worst. I'm fine, really.'

She leaned forward in her chair. 'You're no good to me like this, Michael.'

'Like what?'

'Like somebody who's treating it personally.'

'I'm not treat—'

'We win some, we lose some. That's all there is to it. *We don't take the work home.*' Enunciated clearly for my edification.

'I'm fine, really.' I thought I meant it.

'See a counsellor. It's not a request, Agent Byrne.'

She took a card off her PC screen and placed it in front of me. I looked at the address, somewhere in Grace Court, towards the Brooklyn docks.

When she saw that I wasn't picking it up she looked heavenward for help. 'You know, all the . . . garbage we deal with, Michael, it's like landfill. You can only bury so much of it.'

I had to concede her something, if only to move the conversation on. 'I'll take some R&R.'

'Mexico was *meant* to be R&R.'

'I know, but I got a lead on the Sovereign Bank case.'

'Michael, I told you that case was closed.'

My turn to lean forward. 'Diane, they're doing exactly what Barclays and Credit Suisse did with Iran and Libya, only Sovereign are doing it with a Mexican drug cartel, right under our noses: trading with the goddamn enemy.'

'Michael, we're not pursuing it.'

'But I've got new evidence. Before Turlington . . . died, he said "Sec". I think he was trying to tell me something.'

'You went all that way for half a word?'

'And this.' I put the young banker's Blackberry phone on the desk. 'It's not going to send anyone to jail but –

used the right way – the emails on this will turn up the pressure on their legal team . . .'

Diane looked at me, pained by either my refusal to give up on this or something that was eluding me. 'Michael, even if it were admissible – which I seriously doubt – we're not pursuing it.'

'But Sovereign Bank are washing Lazcano's money . . .'

'I know, Michael.'

'Great, then let's subpoena their asses and take it to trial.'

'We're not pursuing it.'

I half threw my hands up in frustration. 'Diane you keep saying that . . .'

'It's not me saying it, Michael – it's Washington.'

'What do you mean, it's Washington?' Me confused now, not sure if I was annoyed at her obtuseness or at the dawning realization that I was about to hit the biggest brick wall of all.

'It serves a purpose, that's all you need to know.'

I was lost. 'What? What serves a purpose?'

'Sovereign Bank, Lazcano, you know the rest.'

I was momentarily lost for words. 'Allowing Lazcano to launder hundreds of millions of dollars and deposit it in a New York bank account serves a *purpose*? What sort of bullshit is that?'

'CIA bull. They've got some kind of strategy in play.'

'With Sovereign Bank?'

'No, not them, nothing to do with them at all. But if we blow the lid on Sovereign it'll shine a light on certain activities of the Lazcano cartel that everybody would prefer kept in the dark. For now. Let's just say you're in a queue on this one.'

'Jesus H.' I shook my head at the floor. *What was the point? I mean, what the hell was the point?* I was remembering why I'd left the service once before.

'I'm sorry, Michael. Wheels within wheels. Tell you the truth, they were kind of embarrassed you spotted it. You've landed more than one person in hot water over at Langley. So, let it go.'

'Let it *go*?'

'Michael, we're not the DEA or ATF. All of this is now outside our remit, stop taking it personally.'

'It's not that I'm taking it –'

'Case closed, let it go. That's. An. Order.' Almost barked, surprising me and perhaps her.

It wasn't like her to speak to me like that. She was my boss, and we'd known each other over fifteen years. But I had a very long leash. For a moment I wondered if the shit coming down the pipe from HQ was getting to her worse than I had imagined, before remembering my un-authorized foray at the weekend.

And she was right. I hadn't let it go yet. 'What about Turlington, do we let that go as well?'

'For now, yes.'

'Diane, "for now" has a habit of becoming for ever around here.'

When she eventually spoke it was with a certain lack of conviction. 'Apparently Lazcano has been told not to repeat that kind of behaviour. Not with Americans, any-how.'

'Ah, the word of a drug lord. Well, if you can't take that

to a bank, what can you take. Oh yeah, laundered money.'
I shook my head in disgust.

'Is this you not taking it personally, Michael?'

'Diane, when the proverbial hit the fan in 2007 we both
know that a hell of a lot of banks used drug money as
their liquid investment capital of choice. That's not my
personal opinion, that's the UN's findings. Are you telling
me we're not going after those banks?'

'For the record, I'm telling you we're going to balance
the national interests and the interests of our fellow law
enforcement agencies.'

'And not for the record?'

'Oh, Michael, it's a pile of BS, and you and I both know
it.' She levelled a stare full of conflict at me. 'Let's fight the
battles we can win, shall we?'

I tightened up inside, thought about it and knew I could
have reacted fifty ways but found myself smiling in defeat.
Well, it was that or punch a hole in the wall. I suppressed
a sigh before speaking.

'So, if I'm not investigating the money-laundering case
what do you want me to look at?'

She opened a drawer in her desk and pulled out a document labelled 'Confidential: Department of Homeland
Security'. She slid it towards me.

She spoke while I read. 'The bank murders in Tokyo,
Frankfurt and London two nights ago.'

I looked up, interested. If we were talking remits this
was a world away. 'The bank murders? Interesting case,
but what do you want from me?'

'What's your take on them?'

I continued through the few pages of the report. There

wasn't much to read, pretty much summarizing what was being repeated across the media, except without the thrill of reporters interviewing each other to fill air time. I placed it back on the desk.

'I think whoever did it are very good at what they do. Has Interpol confirmed who they think was responsible?'

'It's not definite, but an outfit calling itself Nemesis were the first to come forward – very quickly by all accounts. However, there's no confirmation that they are the ones, and there are no trusted lines of communication yet.'

'I thought we didn't talk to terrorists?'

We smiled ironically at each other at that line of bullshit.

'What about targeting bankers, Michael? Do you think it's going to prove political or good old-fashioned extortion?'

I shook my head as I thought about it. 'They attacked three different banks – and very publicly. Extortion? Possibly, but a banker somewhere should have broken cover by now and run to the authorities. But the name, Nemesis . . . it's interesting.'

She cocked her head at me. 'Nemesis? Means archenemy, doesn't it?'

'Yeah, but Nemesis is derived from the Greek for "dispenser of dues". She was the embodiment of resentment against others, a kind of angel of vengeance who punished those who acquired undeserved fortunes, like thieves or gangsters . . .'

'Or bankers?'

I smiled as if the thought had never crossed my mind, which was rewarded with a mock scowl from my boss.

'Michael, how in the hell would you know all about Greek mythology?'

'*Clash of the Titans*. Big fan.'

She gave me a look that told me she wasn't going to lower her dignity by replying to that remark. 'So, do you buy that Nemesis might be out to punish "undeserved fortunes"?'

I mulled it over for a moment. 'Yeah, I'd work with that for now. I think if it is Nemesis then they're going to be your classic Baader-Meinhof world-changing types. Let's face it, we should have expected something like this after the banks busted the global economy then used the bail-out money to pay themselves bonuses. The moral outrage getting physical? That's not too surprising. But this, this seems a little excessive.'

A twinkle of mischief appeared in Diane's eye. 'Getting sentimental on bankers now?'

'What can I say, Diane, I play both sides of the Street.'

She smiled before getting back to business. 'What else?'

'Well, it feels like an unusual network – global, world-wide. That's a very hard thing to keep secret. Cells in London, Frankfurt, Tokyo – something ought to come up on the radar. What's the intel on chatter?'

Diane shook her head. 'Nothing so far. The NSA are rechecking thousands of internet groups, but they're not connecting anybody with this yet.' Then she cut to the part that was bothering her. 'Do you think they're planning anything here?'

It was a guess and my face said as much. 'I can only surmise, but, yeah. I'd say New York was on their To Do list. I mean, if it is a political movement then they'll see Wall Street as the biggest offender.'

She nodded like she was slotting that piece of information into the jigsaw in her head. 'And the biggest target.'

'Pretty much.'

'Michael, I want the Market Abuse Task Force to look into it for me. Tell me who you need and I'll have them seconded.'

'Isn't it one for another agency?'

'Normally, yes, but it's pretty much the *only* thing anybody's looking into right now. I want the financial angle on all of this.'

'You really think this might have anything to do with market abuse?'

'Michael, when did you ever look anywhere and *not* find somebody abusing the markets? And besides . . .' She creased her brow, uneasy about her main concern. 'I don't want anybody to die in New York.'

And that was why I worked for her.

'OK. Any thoughts so far on where to start?'

She made a slightly helpless gesture. 'Well, one thing's for certain, we're looking for people who hate bankers.'

I raised an eyebrow.

'No, *really* hate bankers.'

I raised both eyebrows.

'OK, OK, we're looking for a bunch of nut-jobs who are actually doing to bankers what a lot of people would like to metaphorically do to bankers. Speak to the SEC, make sure we're not duplicating any workload here. Now, get on with it.'

Meeting over, only my interest had been piqued by the

inches-thick file she had been kicking around her desk, and she saw that I was looking at it too.

She nodded at the years-old beige document holder. 'Your personnel file.'

'Oh.'

'The results of your medical came through.' She pulled it towards herself and tilted it away from me as she opened it. 'I mean, this was before your recent suicide mission.' She hovered a pen over the page. 'Do I need to update this at all?'

'A slight sporting injury. I'll walk it off.'

She perused the page at her leisure, enjoying reminding me of the world order around here. She stopped her reading and took me in where I sat across from her. She studied me long enough to make me slightly self-conscious of my large hands resting on my jeans, nicked and scarred in the line of duty. Then her eyes travelled up my chest so slowly I was wondering if I had left one of the buttons of my white shirt undone. I was regretting wearing my leather jacket to the meeting, the temperature was rising all over again.

'You seem to be getting down the gym all right.'

I smiled awkwardly. 'Well, between filling in paperwork.'

Then she flicked a glance down at the medical file and then looked back at me quizzically.

'You haven't got any fillings.'

I waited for the significance of that.

She looked over her glasses at me. 'At your age?' Half compliment, half suspicion.

'Well, I am the right side of forty.'

She took her glasses off with mock indignation.

'Are you saying there's a *wrong* side of forty?'

I looked at her age-defying ebony skin, her figure-hugging black polo neck, her curvy figure, and had to admit she made me look at older women in a different light. 'Diane, they say fifty *is* the new forty.' I hoped it sounded better than any sense it might have made. Hell, I'd given her enough compliments in my time. She knew where I stood.

She put her glasses back on, replying with nothing more than a crooked smile.

'That'll be all.'

I was glad we'd managed to end it on a better note. I stood from the chair but then realized I was reading the mood music all wrong, or perhaps I was too eager to move things on. Something was troubling her, troubling her to the point that she didn't know where to start. The brief moment of levity was exactly that – brief. She had something on her mind, maybe it had been there the whole time. She kept her hand on my personnel file as she spoke.

'Michael, the Mexican adventure.'

'Yeah?'

'I can't put any of it in your record because (a) I've already covered for you and (b) upstairs would be on you like NRA lobbyists on a new gun-control bill. But Michael, there's something you should know.' She watched me, trying to get a read on my mood before continuing. 'You do anything like this again and you're out of the agency. Understood?'

I squeezed my lips together and nodded slowly. 'Understood.'

'That's all.'

I made straight for the door. I had it open when she spoke next.

'And Michael?'

I turned, holding the door behind my back.

'Who the hell doesn't have any fillings?'

I gave her a lopsided smile. 'Oh, I had fillings, Diane. I just got them knocked out doing your dirty work.'

4

The large, open-plan precinct room was as busy as it was crowded. Nests of desks formed lines, and around each were detectives, NYPD officers and a ragbag of New York's not-so finest in a variety of handcuffed poses. Most in custody slouched as they sulkily went through the motions of being arrested yet again. Some – the optimists – sat earnestly forward in the vain hope that they could convince the arresting officers otherwise, some sat stone-faced, and some sat stoned out of their faces.

Every officer was busy and every officer was tired. And every officer was thinking the same thing. *It's only ten o'clock in the morning.*

But no matter how tired and jaded and ground-down some of them felt everyone could sense the change in atmosphere when Detective Jenni Martinez entered the office. Not because of anything about the five foot and a half Latina herself – though more than one detective had tried and failed in the past to move the relationship beyond the purely professional. It was the lumbering and furious African-American figure she was shoving ahead of her. A young, gangly man in his faux-prison style of knee-sagging jeans and tight orange bandana across his head, his wrists cuffed behind his back. A man all but spitting as he jutted his head in every direction – a head with a very noticeable abrasion above the eyes.

'I'm gonna sue you, I'm gonna sue the NYPD – I'm gonna sue the City of New York. I'm gonna make you bitches pay.'

Detective Martinez guided him firmly through the room by his upper arm, wearing a look that was as tired as it was sceptical. 'I'd be disappointed if you didn't.'

Behind them was Martinez's partner. The broad-chested, chisel-faced African-American, Detective Ashby. Her senior in years and experience and, right now, in mirth. An overweight colleague spotted this and had to ask.

'Hey, Ash, where d'you find that sewer rat?'

But Ashby just shook his head, too amused to speak. The gangly youth, however, was having none of it.

'Hey, who you calling a sewer rat? I want your name, officer, I'm putting your name on the law suit.'

A female Korean detective on the other side of the aisle spoke across the room. 'Better put me on that – I've got library books going back years.'

'Fuck you. I been assaulted. Look at my face. Anybody can see I been assaulted.'

Martinez had reached her and Ashby's desks at the far end of the room where she half guided, half shoved the suspect into a chair.

'If I'd assaulted you, Wayne, we would have needed to drive you to ER, not the precinct.'

This earned a short, sharp kick from Wayne into the desk drawer in front of him.

Martinez barely acknowledged it as she booted up her computer to start the paperwork. 'Good luck with that, Wayne. I haven't been able to open that drawer since I inherited this piece of junk.'

'The NYPD will regret the day it assaulted me.'

Ashby was by the Korean officer, who flicked a glance over at the fuming youth. 'Martinez getting heavy out there, Ash?'

Detective Ashby had trouble talking through his smile. 'Dumb idiot tripped on his baggy pants as he tried to run away. Slammed his face into a dumpster. Martinez actually cried with laughter.'

The Korean looked sagely at the angry youth. 'Ah, pride coming after the fall, eh? How d'you find him? We've been looking for Big Wayne for months.'

Ashby gave another little laugh, only this time mixed with slight disbelief. 'Marty, man. We're grabbing a coffee when she sees Little Pepe.'

'The dealer?'

'And known associate of our new house guest. Martinez is out of that deli before her cup's down. Chased him up five flights of stairs before knocking him to the floor. Gave him the choice between giving up himself or Big Wayne.'

The Korean looked across the room ruefully. 'Whatever happened to loyalty?'

Detective Jenni Martinez hovered a finger over her coffee-stained beige keyboard.

'Name?'

'I want a lawyer.' All lower lip and resentment.

Martinez typed one letter then paused. 'Is that a capital "W"?'

Big Wayne gave her a confused look as Ashby joined them.

'You wanna coffee, Marty?'

The desk phone rang, and she nodded as she picked it up. 'Detective Martinez.' She held a finger up to indicate that things had changed and she wanted Ashby for something. 'OK, I'll be right down.'

She replaced the phone and was immediately on her feet. 'Change of plans. I'll get the coffee. You beat the confession out of Big Wayne.'

The suspect's confusion deepened as well as admitting of a little alarm. 'Say what?'

A suddenly tired Ashby took the chair behind the PC and began to type one-fingered.

'Where's my lawyer?'

'Shut up, Wayne.'

'What do you want?'

'A warm welcome just like that one.'

Martinez looked at me like the last time I'd seen her I'd left her standing at the altar, which was pretty much how she treated any transgression on my part. She looked away, exhaled a long patience-tried breath, then gave me a look that suggested my answers had better get better.

'I'm serious, why are you here?'

'Because I promised I'd come and see you as soon as I got back.'

Suddenly – in her own never-understated way – she was speechless. 'Because you *promised*?' Now she was looking about us, looking about the entrance to the station house. 'Not because you wanted to, not because you missed me, but because you were *obliged* to?'

My body and mind needed rest, and I really couldn't tell

if she was still sore from our car-crash of a parting or if I really was putting both feet in my mouth.

'What did I say?'

But she was already shaking her head. 'It wasn't *what* you said, Byrne.'

She turned, still shaking her head, and walked back up the stairs, leaving me with nothing but a confused head and, admittedly, a great view of her rear.

'"Because I promised."' It was Judy, the duty officer on the front desk. She was staring down at me through her grey-ginger hair and outsized glasses with a look of pure disappointment. I'd bumped into her enough over the past year to be on first-name terms, and she didn't need any encouraging.

'Was it that bad?'

'"Was it that *bad*?"' Quoting me again, believing intonation alone would damn me.

'Is that a yes?'

'"Is that a *yes*?"' Shaking her head at me now.

I was being out-argued by a person parroting my words. It seemed like the time to leave.

5

The skin of the war-bird darting across the mountain range was pure polished aluminium. Clear blue light shone off its upper half, pure white reflected off its lower, the snow-capped range and clear blue sky ensuring that. Its nose was noticeably long, like an E-type Jag's, its propellers a blur of technology from a bygone era. The engine's sound had an uplifting burr as it roared through the air. At fifty years of age the fighter aircraft was (slightly) older than its pilot. The Cavalier F-51D was a modified Mustang P-51, surplus to requirements after the Korean War. A Rolls-Royce plant powered the four blades at the nose, giving the aircraft and its pilot the confidence to hug the slopes, to come in fast and low, as one might for an attack run. Not that the pilot needed the reassurance of such a reliable engine. The pilot didn't want for anything.

A Bell 407 charter helicopter hovered six feet off the crest of a snow-covered ridge that ran along the top of the Catskill mountain range. The first hints of the coming dusk were tinting the sky a darker shade of blue. A small number of long, thin clouds hung lazily above the white-peaked mountains in every direction. It was cold and still and beautiful. A door had been slid open and sitting on the edge of the exposed side of the aircraft was a young man in full skiing gear, a snowboard under his right arm.

Up front the pilot waited patiently for the last of his passengers to exit. He was a patient man by nature, but the top-end fee he was charging the group of skiers today would have inspired him to give the Dalai Llama a run for his money.

Below the helicopter, standing in a flurry of snow whisked up by the chopper blades above, stood four other young men. They were all standing with their snowboards in their hands looking up at the last of their group.

'Come on, DB!'

'Yeah, come on.'

The remaining snowboarder swung his feet out and nervously dropped down beside his colleagues. An ironic cheer went up and they all looked to the pilot, all five of them giving him a hearty thumbs-up, which the pilot returned before leaning the helicopter to one side and heading away down along the descending ridge.

All of the young men watched on, impressed by the sight of the lone craft leaving them atop one of the highest peaks in upstate New York. The tallest of them, Ace, filmed their departing ride and his colleagues' reaction to it on his HD camera. Another, the gym-fit Duke, leaned close into the lens.

'Fucking A, man. We are on top of the fucking world, my man, you hear?'

Ace panned the camera round to the others. Even in their all-encompassing ski gear, the excitement was palpable.

FiDi held his hands aloft like a headline act taking to the stage. He was the only African-American guy amongst them, lean without being skinny. He was also the coolest and made sure they knew he was the coolest at every opportunity.

'Bro', I am so amped about this. So fucking *amped*!'

The last word shouted out across the breathtaking view they were witness to, its echo disappearing along with the helicopter across the snowscape. The white mountains, the silence, the sense of being the only people in the world right now, the majesty of the reddening sun as it almost touched the tip of a mountain across the valley from them, was too much to not generate a sense of awe in every last one of them. They took their time to take it all in, knowing it was special, knowing they were special.

The stocky DB nervously looked at his watch. 'Maybe he's not coming.' His Polish accent – which he made no attempt to hide – making everything sound exotic and gentle.

The others did not jump to agree, Duke speaking for them. 'Man, he's coming. Anyway, this is going to be fucking amazing.'

DB tested his snowboard with one foot, sliding it backwards and forwards on the spot, wondering about the twenty-foot drop at the beginning of their off-off-*off*-piste run. 'Yeah, but how can he be so sure he'll find us? There's so many slopes out here.'

The others laughed at his fretfulness. FiDi used the tip of his snowboard to toss some snow over him to the amusement of the others. 'You nose wipe. Those things have got, like, super satnav and shit, even the old ones. Didn't you see what we did over in Iraq? If we can find Saddam Hussein in a fox hole in the middle of the Arabian deserts we can sure as hell find a mountain top.'

Cartman, so-named because of his mild likeness to the overweight and less-than-angelic South Park character of the same name, wasn't going to let FiDi get away with that. 'You douche, it was the Marines that found Saddam, not the Air Force.'

'Oh yeah, and how'd the Marines get there? Flap their freaking arms?'

Cartman and FiDi started to square off with an antagonism that would have seemed real to anybody who didn't know the horseplay in the group.

'They got there by road, Mr FiDi Cent.'

Chest to chest now, the others switching their attention between their faux alpha-male stand-off and the breathtaking world of snow and mountains and trees about them.

FiDi stabbed the overweight Cartman's large, jacket-padded chest with a finger. 'What, all the way from Texas? We building roads across the Atlantic now? Whassa matter, you don't know jack about geography 'cos your mamma covered the globe in chocolate, deep-fried it and fed it to you as a child? Is that what you got under there, an entire fucking planet? Is that it, Mr Blimp?'

'Maybe she did, and maybe I had diarrhoea for a week after I ate too much Africa . . .'

Nodding at each other like territorial birds fighting over a prospective mate.

The aircraft dipped and rose with every contour of the land, the pilot swapping a comfortable flight that cruising altitude would have afforded with the demanding task of keeping the plane a constant height above the rising land at over three hundred miles per hour, an unnecessary diversion but one that demanded every last ounce of his concentration, total dedication to the task at hand, the blocking out of every other thought in the world. In short, a break from everything.

The target would not know what had hit it. The target would have nowhere to run. They would have to take whatever he threw at them. He who knew every slope of these mountains, they who knew only that he would be joining them at a pre-agreed time. The pilot looked through the almost invisible spiralling blades and saw the mountain top ahead. His goal. His target.

Cartman and FiDi were now bumping chests off each other, gripping each other's lapels in their hands.

FiDi had slipped into his accent from the 'hood that he'd spent his young life working to escape. 'Yeah, well, I heard that when your mamma couldn't get to the store one week 'cos she'd growed so *fat*' – almost spat into Cartman's face – 'that she couldn't get out the house, that Wal-Mart's stock fell ninety per cent on the news.'

Cartman in FiDi's face. 'Really? I heard their stock fell 'cos you and all your brothers were stealing early for Christmas . . .'

DB checked his watch again.

'Shhh!'

Everybody stopped to look at DB.

'Do you hear that?'

And they could. The whine of a plane engine straining at what sounded like maximum revs. But no sight matched the sound.

Everybody stopped and stared out at the peaks about

them, FiDi and Cartman remaining as they were, holding each other's lapels, the rest standing with their snowboards, Ace ready with his camera. A mixture of readiness, nerves and electric anticipation. The sound was getting louder at an incredible speed and yet no plane could be—

Then all at once it was upon them.

Tearing up from the blind side of the mountain, ripping the fabric of the sky apart as it burst up and over them at no more than fifty foot in distance, impossibly appearing like a winged beast rocketing up out from the Underworld.

Every last one of them met the sight with an unsuppressible cry of elation. 'Fuck me . . .' 'Oh my god . . .' 'What the . . .' 'I don't believe . . .' 'Yeah . . . !'

All of them, all at once, twisted, the breath and reality stripped out of them, watching the ancient fighter plane trace a wide loop in the sky before barrelling on to its back then its front then aiming itself at them once again. But this time they could see it coming, this time they were prepared – or so they thought. Because now came the attack noise, the air rushing so fast through the former gun-ports and air ducts that the metal bird added a whistle to the roar of its engine that could only be the harbinger of an attack, this World War Two bird of prey tilting left then right as it gunned towards them, every schoolboy fantasy of what such a vision would truly entail realized before their very eyes. Their eyes glued to it, mesmerized by it, believing themselves to be immune to any further shocks until – at what seemed the moment *after* the last moment – the pilot once again barrelled the plane on to its back and buzzed the group of men no more than forty, thirty – they would swear that if they hadn't ducked the blades would have sliced through them – feet away.

They all resumed their upright positions as the Mustang shot over them and corrected itself, hugging the slopes of the valley as it disappeared down the mountain and out of sight. Even DB's ass-backwards capitulation to the event was not remarked upon – for now. They were all there when it happened and they had all had their young, high-earning, swaggering cynicism blown away.

Nobody spoke for the longest time. To have done so, so soon after the spectacle, would have been indecent. Then, after a while, as one, they also sensed it *was* time to do something. Somehow, being part of something *that* cool made them *feel* cool.

The tallest of them, Ace, an Ohioan, slipped his camera into his pocket, zipped it up, then let his snowboard fall flat before him. This last act breaking the spell itself.

'Last one down buys the drinks.'

They all shared a smile and followed his example. FiDi punched Cartman in the arm.

'Hey, fat boy, mine's a Bud.'

And as one they pushed off, as one falling the first twenty feet off the summit on to the deep-piled snow of the treacherously steep mountainside, before beginning to expertly weave their way down the virgin slope, the setting sun burning red to perfect the moment.

6

Mexico City. A city synonymous with narcotics-related violence and a government struggling to impose order as well as reversing the rising body count from the drugs trade. An unofficial truce between the drug cartels still held here, and even the most bloodthirsty and punishing of the cartel heads could feel relatively safe. But safe was not the same as stupid.

The residential street in the Lomas de Chapultepec district was more Beverly Hills than Miami. More tasteful than one might have guessed from one of the wealthiest areas in the whole of the Mexican capital. More tasteful than one might have guessed given that the street was host to at least five heads of the country's leading cartels. But the truce held good. And living in bling houses was completely at odds with their aim here – to lie low. If anything, it was almost a competition to see who could live in the most humble abode. Walled mansions, yes, that was a no-brainer given the security situation. But expensive and expansive, no.

The long alley running along the back was almost down at heel. It was a long-since concreted road broken apart by weeds a decade earlier. No house boasted a garden to speak of, and the rears were mostly garaging and parking within the safety of the residences, all high walls and large, thick metal gates.

As the sun dipped behind the houses one of the gates was opened by two vigilant security guards. Guards who looked more like members of an unsavoury SWAT team than domestic protection. Bullet-proof vests, black military garb, dark glasses, ear-pieces. And guns. A pistol and submachine each. Travelling in Mexico City was relatively safe. But safe was not the same as stupid.

Three cars roared out of the rear parking area, all with heavily tinted windows. A Chevy Suburban turned right, a Ford Lobo pickup turned left, then a Jeep Grand Cherokee also turned right. All kicked up dust as they got the hell away from the sitting duck that was the rear entrance to their employer's house. The security guards scanned the immediate neighbourhood menacingly, as if their tight jaws alone might deter attacks. Then they closed the gate, disappearing back inside behind it.

The Ford Lobo bounced along until it turned out of the alley on to a better and more typical road surface, and a smooth ride commenced. Up front sat two bodyguards kitted out like their gate-minding associates. One driving, the other with an Uzi submachine gun held across his chest. All this so that the two passengers in the back could ride in relative safety.

The two passengers were the Lazcano brothers. Eduardo Lazcano, the eldest and most senior, was a large man. Not in an obese way. He was large in an expansive way. Large in a patriarch-of-a-huge-extended-family kind of way. Capable of a room-filling gregariousness. And capable of murder. Beside Eduardo sat the fortysomething Gabriel. Younger, leaner, sharper, with the looks of a Mexican daytime *telenovela* star. He was smart, diplomatic and, that rarest of things, truly loyal. The rear bench was lacking in space, and both resented the discomfort, Gabriel as ever giving up the most space to placate his elder brother's temperament.

Eduardo gestured with a newspaper about the interior. 'Why always the small car, Gabi?'

Gabriel was watching the roads and surroundings. Hating travelling between two locations. Not much happier when he reached his destination. 'We don't always take the small car, Eduardo. That would be a pattern. You know we don't do that.'

The elder brother returned testily to his newspaper. 'Well, it always feels like the small car.'

The younger one considered his brother's rotund stomach, considered whether to make a quip. He thought better of it. Days, weeks, *months* passed with his brother in good humour until the most random event caused the most violent of reactions. Violence that never failed to shock the younger one. Gabriel returned his gaze out of the pickup truck as they slowed by an intersection. Having to come to a stop. The worst part of any journey.

Eduardo tapped his newspaper with a pleased finger. 'Ah, look, the new series of *NCIS* is on. I love that show.'

His younger brother was too intent on the events outside to feel the need to respond. He only relaxed – a touch – when the car pulled away from the lights. A cell phone began to ring inside his jacket. He retrieved it and opened it up.

'Yes?'

Gabriel listened attentively for a full twenty seconds without uttering a single word in reply, then snapped the phone shut. He turned to his brother and spoke matter-of-factly.

'We know who raided our Tijuana compound.'

Eduardo did not look up from the TV listings page he was marking up with a pen. 'Who were they?'

'It was a he.'

The head of the Lazcano cartel jerked his head up to look at his brother, who completed the answer before tempers frayed.

'Michael Byrne of the United States Secret Service.'

Eduardo swilled the name around in his head, making sure it reached every part of his memory so that it would stay with him, the way a wine-taster might consider this year's Beaujolais.

'Byrne? Hmm.' Returning to his newspaper. 'I think we should talk to this Señor Byrne.'

The car headed west, out of the city and the traffic. Into the fiery crimson ball that was the setting sun. Back towards Lazcano territory.

7

The hotel's large wooden bar had four sides, a big wrap-around affair that stood in the centre of a lounge that had expected more customers than it was clearly getting. There was a muted television on each side to add a bit of life to the mostly empty tables. All facts of which the gang of young bankers were blissfully unaware. They were flushed with the adrenaline-charged journey down the slopes and the first two drinks of a long Saturday night ahead.

When their boss arrived he was greeted with a well-earned cheer that his body-language suggested he didn't need but which his heart lapped up. Then the young men burst into a well-practised Kinks song for special occasions such as these.

'Louie Louie-ay, Oh baby, I gotta go. Yeah yeah yeah yeah.'

Doug McCarthy raised his hands to receive the high-fives that capped off his greeting. McCarthy was forty-four and still in the trim shape he had been in when he left the United States Air Force over a decade earlier, the 'Louie' being a reference to his then rank of first lieutenant. He was from the south side of Chicago, second-generation Irish, and if he were any more proud of his roots he'd have had to dye his hair green. He had entered Wall Street late, in career terms, via an introduction from one of his airmen whose father was a senior equities trader at Sovereign Bank. It was a favour the father found easy to perform given that he had every reason to believe that McCarthy had saved his son's life in Kosovo, which he had, earning an Air Force Cross into the bargain. And if the father had worried that the ex-Air Force pilot would struggle to adapt to life on the Street then he had worried in vain. McCarthy was a star trader from the off, and, much to the delight of many in senior management, a trader from the old school. He traded from the gut, living and breathing his favourite stocks and knowing just how they would feel about every bit of news macro and micro, every commercial development big and small. He just seemed to *get* banking stocks. 'The right man at the right hour' was how he had been described when he burst on to the scene. (2008 had been a bad year – OK, a terrible year – but then it had been bad for everybody at the bank. And, anyhow, the bank bailouts had smoothed over everybody's trading records at that time.) His favourite way to trade, however, was second-guessing everybody else's reactions to news. He followed his sector closely but very quickly took the view that it wasn't what news *should* mean to a stock that mattered, but how *everybody else* viewed the news. It was the *reaction* of banks and hedge funds and pension funds that he was trading, believing them to be a herd of bovine patsies. And it served him well.

But McCarthy brought something else to Sovereign Bank that quickly impressed his peers and helped his rapid ascent up the ranks. He brought *esprit de corps*. Nobody – *nobody* – had worked harder to bond his team together than McCarthy. Birthdays, engagements, pay days – *bonus time* – were all celebrated to the max. In addition, he took his entire team, at his own personal expense, away each quarter for a weekend of activities. Stock car racing, Vegas, golfing, yachting, this weekend in the Catskills, all on McCarthy's tab. Even when somebody wasn't passing muster and he 'had to let them go' he never once in seven years of running his desk threw anybody out until he had helped them secure a job in a different department or company. He always said he owed them, which made them feel like they owed him all the more. His team didn't just like him, they *loved* him. And they didn't just love him, they would take a bullet for him. (Or so it was joked around the office by snarkier, envious, less successful colleagues.) On this particular weekend, one of their number, Excel, had had to stay back in the office. It was devastating to him, but he had, by his own admission, caused an almighty snafu – deleting a week's worth of data inputting – which *had* to be ready for Monday. His mistake, his problem. 'Any other weekend and we could have left it, Excel, but the board need this for Monday,' McCarthy had explained. Excel was almost sick with disappointment but sucked it up and stayed behind.

'So, losers . . .' The team grinning at the expectation of the wild night out McCarthy had doubtless arranged. 'Who came last – who's buying the drinks?'

There was sniggering all round as DB held his hands up in gracious defeat. 'I fell over right at the end.'

Ace almost spat his vodka and tonic back into his glass. 'Yeah, he was checking his watch.'

The group burst into laughter, and DB nodded gently, taking it all in good part.

McCarthy patted him good-naturedly on the shoulder. 'Tell you what, DB. Get me a JD on the rocks and I'll put the drinks on my bill.'

'Oh, Mr McCarthy, you are too kind.' The Pole's face had lit up at the near financial miss and he revelled in the groans of disapproval that his good fortune elicited from the others.

The bartender, who had no other active customers at present, had the drink ready before DB could turn to order it. DB thanked him and passed the drink to his boss. Ace then raised his glass in a manner that requested that they all follow, except for his boss.

'To First Lieutenant Douglas McCarthy, flight commander of Sovereign Bank First Airborne. May the only near misses we experience be the audacious stunt you pulled off this afternoon on Hunter mountain.'

The group roared their approval, irritating the few other customers present. McCarthy allowed it to subside then said what everybody had studiously avoided saying all day.

'To Turlington.'

As their faces fell he raised his glass. Slowly they all followed suit. Then, as one: 'Turlington.'

They supped at their drinks, and there was a risk of the mood tipping into the maudlin or even depressive. Their boss, ever alive to the pack mentality didn't want this – nor Turlington - discussed at length. Despite their desire to discuss that subject it had acquired the status of off-limits immediately after it had happened. McCarthy wanted all the facts in before he discussed it, wasn't interested in fevered speculation. But there it was again, threatening the light mood.

'So, who was the most scared during the fly-by?'

Grins leapt to their faces, and Duke pointed a gleeful finger at DB.

'DB fell over on his ass!'

Laughter broke out, and the conversation turned to where it had been straining to turn since the ex-pilot had walked in to the bar. For the next half hour they told and retold him how mind-blowing they had found the amazing events of the afternoon. From the helicopter ride to the extreme snowboarding to, of course, the greatest fly-by they were ever likely to experience. They pestered McCarthy for every detail of his flight and he delighted in telling every moment of it, right up to *swearing* he could see the looks on their faces as he flew by.

McCarthy's trading desk. Excel, Duke, DB, Ace, Cartman and FiDi. No person on the team was actually called by their real name because McCarthy ran his team like a military outfit, breaking down his men before rebuilding them again the way he wanted them. And step number one was the name. Excel was easy because he was landed with their data-inputting at the end of each day and was a whizz at the eponymous software. Duke was Duke because he went to Duke University and – his boss insisted – because he walked with John Wayne's swagger. DB was from a moment of comedy where every member had failed to say his full name, Dobieslaw Beisiadeck, correctly late one night and so McCarthy reduced it to his initials – 'for the sake of sanity'. Ace was from Ohio and played cards sharper than anybody, but he got his name from a shooting weekend McCarthy had organized where Ace had not only got the lowest score but, in the words of the old coot who ran the ranch, 'shot worse than a blind Sunday School teacher with a racoon running up her skirt'. The old coot had been calling him Ace all weekend, and it stuck. Cartman was volunteered by the others in recognition of his constant craving for food, as well as his size, and when McCarthy saw that he didn't take offence – in fact, revelled in the acceptance of his belt-threatening diet – he co-opted the name, and Cartman it was. But McCarthy's crowning achievement – at least, he felt – was FiDi Cent. The young African-American man had arrived with his degree from Columbia University as polite as you like and as presentable as any prospective employee could hope to be. But McCarthy was 'from the south side of Chicago' and could spot a fellow traveller from the projects at a hundred yards and called him on it in the interview. FiDi had wriggled and turned and insisted he was just your average middle-class kid from your average middle-class family, terrified that it was a trap, that anything else would get him shown the door. This was the fabled Sovereign Bank, after all. Then McCarthy had misquoted the rap artist Fifty Cent at a later point in the interview, and when FiDi corrected him the die was cast. FiDi let down his guard and admitted he was from Washington Heights and that McCarthy had called his background correctly. Then he picked up his coat with a face like his mother had just slapped it and made for the door. Only he hadn't taken two steps before McCarthy had offered him the job of trader on his desk, before adding to the speechless young man, 'You'd have had it half an hour ago if you'd just admitted what made you tick.' Then, this being FiDi, the Financial District, McCarthy dubbed him FiDi Cent from there on in. And, truth be told, he always wondered himself if part of his reason for giving the young man from the Heights the job was because he was so tickled by the nickname he had invented on the spot. Well, so what, FiDi was good at his job. They all were. He made sure of that. Lastly, there had been Ninja, now dead. Simon Turlington, named after the Mutant Ninja Turtles, a cartoon that was a bit old for his group. But somehow, by some unspoken agreement, his nickname had not been repeated since his ill-fated trip to Mexico. He had become simply Turlington again.

Talk of the day's events had moved on, and Ace held up his hands by way of requesting the floor.

'Louie,' – McCarthy's self-inspired nickname – 'Can you settle an argument for us?'

McCarthy sipped on his new JD. 'Shoot.'

'Duke here . . .' A cheer as everyone knew what was coming. 'Duke was saying before you came in that Duke University is the "Princeton of the South".'

Laughter met this statement and, even though he was laughing too, Duke was in earnest when he spoke. 'It *is*, I'm telling you. That's what everybody calls it. Duke is an Ivy League university, *the Princeton of the South*.'

Ace was amused but exasperated. 'Then why doesn't Princeton call itself the *Duke of the North*? Huh?'

Duke was stumped. 'It just doesn't.'

FiDi jumped in. 'I know the Duke of the North: Ferman Penitentiary.'

Laughter erupted once more as everybody raced to agree, drowning out Duke's attempts to redeem himself. It wasn't until McCarthy spoke that they stopped talking over one another.

'Guys . . .' Pausing while they shushed. 'Let me tell you how I know Duke University ain't no Ivy League outfit. I'm from the south side of Chicago, and the last thing I need is to have some Harvard dickwad staring at the markets like he was *entitled* to have them go the way he wanted.' Nods of approval all round. 'If Duke was an Ivy League university I wouldn't have you on my team.'

But the laughter and cheers that followed suddenly trailed off as they saw the serious look on McCarthy's face.

'Those sons of bitches.'

He pointed with his glass of bourbon at what had caught his attention, at what had changed his mood. The television screen behind the bar. It instantly changed theirs.

On Fox News they were showing a live report from Hong Kong where a torn-apart Lamborghini lay smouldering outside a bank in an early-morning street, vehicles from every emergency service present. The headline read, '*Bank Killing, Nemesis Strike Again?*'

DB shook his head in disbelief. 'Another one.'

So close after Turlington's death, so close to the other bank murders, the mood plummeted.

Duke clenched a fist and felt the blood pumping through his jock veins. 'Fucking scumbags, I'd like to see them try that over here.'

FiDi looked like he was about to throw his bottle of Bud at the screen – he'd done worse before. 'Those motherfuckers should come to the Street and go a few rounds with our traders. That would be one short motherfucking fight, I tell you.'

Ace, taller and more thoughtful, shook his head.

'Terrorists, that's what they are. I mean why bankers? It's the regulators they should be going after.'

Hollow laughter met the crack. McCarthy studied the faces of his team as they took in the muted news report, the pictures telling it all. McCarthy watched the bartender wiping and emptying his way around his work space. And McCarthy knew that look. Knew exactly what the hotel employee was thinking: *Those bankers deserve everything they've got coming to them.* Mr Minimum Wage delighting in the Masters of the Universe being brought down to earth, brought to book. He could see it, see the furtive glance and the head-down-in-case-I'm-caught-doing-it behaviour. A younger McCarthy would have called him on it, would have wanted to turn it into a full-blown argument, nothing less than a fight. But that was the younger McCarthy. He returned to his team.

'London, Frankfurt, Tokyo and now Hong Kong. You know where this is headed, don't you boys?'

DB looked on wide-eyed. 'Do you really think so, Mr McCarthy?'

'Think so? I know so. They'll be on our streets in weeks if not days.'

Ace felt a shiver run down his spine and hoped nobody had noticed it. 'You for real, Boss?'

McCarthy answered that with a look, then replaced it with a curious one. 'What would you really do to this Nemesis outfit?'

The young men looked at him, not expecting that particular question.

DB spoke first. 'What? If they came to America?'

'Yeah, what would you do?'

Duke slammed a fist into his other hand. 'Take those mothers out.'

FiDi mimicked a hand-gun with his fingers. 'Only one thing to do. Like, what? We're gonna wait for *them*? To shoot *us*? You kidding me? We do an Afghanistan – take it to the enemy.'

Ace pulled a sceptical face. 'Yeah, 'cos that really worked out. You think it's really gonna happen here, Louie?'

McCarthy knew they looked up to him not only as a boss but as somebody who had *been there and done it*. He got nothing but respect from his team for his time in the Air Force. Shit, he'd *killed* people. And when he spoke they listened.

'Why not? If it's a war against bankers there's no bigger theatre than the United States. It's where I'd choose to take the fight.'

DB contemplated the conversation anxiously. 'You really think it's a war?'

McCarthy nodded very slowly. 'Yeah. Yeah I do. And you gotta ask yourself what you're prepared to do about it.'

'Fucking kill them.' 'They'd be dead meat.' 'I'd pay money to get a shot at them.'

McCarthy gave careful consideration to their youthful answers. ''Cos, you know, if that's the way the wind's blowing, if those psychos are declaring open season on us, you gotta think about what you'd be prepared to do. *Really* be prepared to do. You really have.'

The former Air Force pilot looked from one member of his team to another. They met his look with serious stares of their own. The group silent as they tried to convey their commitment to the idea and each other. Then, when he judged the moment was right, McCarthy broke the ice with a smile, turning the mood upside down on the spot.

'Fuck it, let's not worry about the things we can't do anything about right now.'

DB nodded sagely. 'Yes, like Excel's finger over the delete button.'

Everybody laughed again, as much in relief that the subject had changed as anything else. Then McCarthy lifted his near-empty glass in the air. 'Gentlemen . . .' They raised their glasses as one. 'To absent friends.'

Then as one. 'To absent friends.' Thoughtful, since Turlington was in their thoughts.

After a pause DB spoke. 'Let's not forget Excel.'

Then everybody laughed, not sure if he was just joking or really hadn't included Excel in the toast. So they raised their glasses again.

Ace had his camera out and took a group picture from his long, outstretched arm, squeezing himself on to the end of the photo. He checked the result and thought it was priceless.

8

'Bankers are dying, Kieran.'

'We're all dying, Mike, what's your point?'

I didn't respond immediately in that way that was meant to signal that such comments weren't going to help the conversation. Kieran O'Meara was the deputy head of the Office of Investigations for the Securities and Exchange Commission. His was the office that investigated the investigators, policed the police. His was the office that I felt might provide the path of least resistance towards my trek up the Amazonian rainforest that was the regulatory system. Kieran O'Meara was in his fifties and out of shape in a well-to-do kind of way. That is, fat with a tan. And tonight he was dressed in that most flattering of outfits, a tuxedo for the black-tie event he was attending: the annual Bank of the Year awards at the Waldorf-Astoria on Park Avenue. I'd dragged him out between courses and his demeanour told me he was less than happy about it. Given enough time and energy I could have given a damn about his feelings, unfortunately he was in a hurry.

'I think we have a duty to investigate all avenues.'

O'Meara shifted his heavy frame from one foot to the other, his dress shoes hurting him. Or maybe he was afraid the free wine would run out.

'This couldn't have waited until the morning?'

I looked around the foyer of the hotel, rich couples in tuxedos and ball-gowns, moving carelessly about. The whole thing made me uneasy. The whole lots-of-bankers-in-one-place didn't feel good. Diane had tasked me with setting my mind to the banker killings, and I didn't like the obvious conclusions that I was reaching.

'No, Kieran, I want to get to work on this right away, tonight.'

He let out a sigh for my benefit, to let me know the clock was ticking.

'And what exactly do you want from me?'

'I want you, the SEC, whoever, to reach out to the regulators in the United Kingdom, Germany, Japan and the rest and get me the trading records of every one of the victims of these attacks to date.'

He pulled a face that said he could probably swing that. 'That it?'

'Then I want the trading records of every desk of every bank on the Street.'

The laughter began almost before I'd finished speaking. Heads turned at his walrus-like noise, the regulator properly amused by my suggestion.

'Oh, you've got some nerve, Byrne.'

'What's that supposed to mean?'

'Come off it, Byrne, shall we cut to the chase, shall I just send over Sovereign Bank's first?'

I almost felt naive that I hadn't foreseen his cynicism. 'I don't care what order you send them in, just as long as I get them all. I want to see if there are any clues as to who is being targeted by these people. I want to know if any Americans are in their sights.'

But it was too late. He'd taken his position. One of profound disbelief. 'You yank me out of a networking session for this? Well, nicely done, Byrne. Dressing up your obsession with Sovereign by going through the motions of investigating these other crimes? Catching me off guard and exploiting these crimes to do it? Nicely done.'

I didn't mind personal, but reckless was making me grit my teeth.

'Kieran . . .'

'Put it in an email, and I might treat it as a matter under inquiry.'

We were momentarily stopped by a passing crowd of bankers and partners laughing loudly at jokes of their own.

'Everybody's meant to be working together on this, Kieran.'

'Fine, then we'll work on it and take the necessary action. But you can forget any Wall Street trading records. We'll carry out our own investigation.'

Suddenly my anger at the system was rising, rising and I either didn't care or couldn't stop it. 'That's all very well, Kieran, but the SEC has gotten into the habit of smacking banks on the wrist and sending them on their way, and while that might suit you and your friends right now we will all come to regret not establishing the facts in this particular instance. In this particular instance the banks will wish they had told the truth, and your fig-leaf protection will hurt them in a way that even they can't buy off. The downside isn't a smaller bonus this time, Kieran. The downside is death.'

The regulator smiled at me and tugged at his cuffs. 'Well, so glad we've dispensed with any hidden agendas, Byrne. Now, if you don't mind, I have to get back to my dinner.'

'It's not dinner, Kieran. It's networking. Remember?'

I turned on my heel and left without waiting for an answer.

9

The BlackBerry on the bar vibrated and trilled at the same
time. The young, sandy-haired Californian, who was
blessed with West Coast good looks when he wasn't jaded
and tired, put down his Bud and picked up his cell phone.
The subject read, 'Soz u not here. Not same w/o u.' There
was an attachment, which he opened to see a photograph
of the rest of the trading team in a bar up in the Catskills,
clearly getting by without him. Any envy he had felt, any
disappointment he was feeling just doubled. He smiled
ruefully, shook his head, then put his phone face down on
the bar. His night was over. *Another boring day in the boring
life of Excel.* A thought he might not have had if he had
observed the attractive girl with the unnaturally red hair
eyeing him from the far end of the bar.

The Excess on Broadway did everything it needed to in
order to be hip – soft furnishings, coloured up-lighting,
illuminated bar top, dance music, extensive cocktail selec-
tion – yet it somehow lacked the magic ingredient. It was
one of those bars that people visited on their way to the
real party. Maybe it just came down to location. This was
Lower Manhattan. Most of the clientele were in finance,
and finance didn't happen at the weekend. That it was
even half busy on a Saturday night was deemed a success
these days. But, despite this, the stressed-out manager felt

the kooky-looking girl at the end of the bar was taking up valuable real estate, being as it was that she'd been nursing the same beer for almost an hour. *Still, chicks bring the guys in, so I won't start dropping the hints just yet.* And he had to admit if you were going to look at a face you could do worse than look at hers. It was a strong face, quite masculine in a way, but the lips and the eyes and the slender hands, well, they all seemed to fit together quite well. A fact noticed by more than just the manager as he moved away from her.

A group of young men positioned themselves next to the redhead. One sitting with his back to the bar beside her, two others standing. Smart casual clothes, a slightly preppie look. Like hedge fund managers' idea of how to look cool. Which is exactly what they were and what they thought. The two standing urged on their associate with looks and heads jabbed in the girl's direction. The seated guy leaned towards her.

'You come here often?'

It was lame, he knew it was lame, but he wasn't going to use a line from one of the how-to-pick-up-girls websites in front of his friends. She eyed him up and down, eyed them all. From their Ralph Lauren sweaters hanging over their backs to their Brooks Brothers shoes. And an idea formed in her head.

'One of me, three of you. What are you hoping for, like, a gang bang?'

Her unapologetic Kansas accent, sharp tone – and words – took them by surprise. The men were out of their depth with no game-plan for dealing with such an unexpectedly confident and hostile reaction. But they needn't have worried. Before any of them could form a meaning-ful sentence she had picked up her bottle and very large canvas bag and moved round them to the other end of the bar. Excel had an empty seat next to him, and it was here that the redhead stopped.

'Do you mind?'

Excel proffered a disinterested hand at it. 'No, it's not taken.'

She dropped her bag down and seated herself with a slight show of annoyance, giving no regard to the non-plussed looks she was getting from the trio she had left behind.

'I'm sorry. Those jerks were giving me a really hard time.'

Excel was so down in the dumps that he had barely registered that a very pretty young lady with long, curly, shockingly crimson hair had chosen him as her compan-ion at the bar. He tipped his bottle to his mouth. 'Yeah, well, it's a Saturday.' He put it down and made no effort to suppress a long sigh. Or engage in conversation.

She was watching him out of the corner of her eye, looking for a line of her own. 'Long day?'

He glanced at her, seeming almost to notice her for the first time – crazy hairstyle, a bit racy for him – then chuck-led mirthlessly to himself. 'Long week.' He saw her watching him expectantly and decided to answer her questioning stare. 'All my work pals are having this, like, major weekend, and I'm stuck here. Got a really urgent job from my boss and I was the only person who could do it. You know.' He twisted his bottle in his hands under the bar-top light.

'Well, their loss is my gain.'

It took a moment but then he looked at her with mild surprise and no less pleased for it. Single men, as well as some married, hit bars with long elaborate flow charts in their heads. Scope out the action. Home in on the action. Try an opening line. If yes, go to offer of drink. If no, go to ask-about-her. If no, turn to the less attractive friend. If, if if, and so on. There are an infinite number of variations of these mental flow charts and they are a source of infinite frustration to the male species. But however different they all might be, they all have one thing in common: the final box of the flow chart is 'Have sex'. For a woman to begin the talking skips a few stages. For a woman to begin the talking *and* hint that she's *interested* in you – *you* – is like you're one step away from the end of the chart. For the first time since Friday afternoon Excel stopped feeling sorry for himself.

He noticed that she was empty. 'Another one?'

She looked awkward. 'Oh, well, if you're expecting someone . . .' She placed her hand on his arm as she spoke but didn't move it when she'd finished. She didn't have to move her hand up to his heart to know that it was beating faster.

'No, no, I'm . . . Well, I was expecting you.'

Excel grinned at his own smoothness then held two fingers up to the barman who nodded his understanding, pleased to see she was finally paying her way in his joint.

She withdrew her hand and smiled in acknowledgement of the humour of the line then, seemingly despite herself, added, 'Well, you've got me.'

Excel had difficulty swallowing and was hoping that the

low-lighting was hiding his blushes. He couldn't look at her out of a sudden shyness and looked down, noticing what was at her feet.

'Travelling?' Indicating the large canvas bag, tied together at a hole at the top with thin rope.

Her face fell. 'Oh, don't. Missed my flight back to Kansas, next one's tomorrow morning. So, I was gonna get a hotel room for the night.' Saying the last bit just right. Saying it so that the guy sat next to her knew that, if he played his cards even *half* right, that the room she would be staying in would be his.

Excel received the two bottles from the barman with only one thing on his mind. She needs a room and she has to be out of my hair first thing. Wait till I tell the guys about *my* weekend.

'The name's Stephen. But everybody calls me Excel.'

'Alice. But everybody calls me Alecto.'

'*Alecto?*'

'Four brothers. Don't ask. *Please.*'

Alecto laughed with embarrassment at the memory, then smiled a sweet, pained, lovely, intimate smile, hinting at a girl trapped in a boyish childhood, a girl who just wanted to play at being a girl. Excel thought it was a nice smile – a *great* smile. The sort of smile you played over in your mind on the ride home. Then, to cap it all, she ended the smile with a self-conscious downward glance, like she'd given too much away, maybe realized she was wearing her attraction for him on her sleeve. Not that he had a problem with that, no problem at all.

In as much as anybody could read anybody's mind she read his, knew that he felt he'd hit the jackpot and was going to invite her back to his place. She was pleased with that. It meant that everything was going to plan.

The apartment door swung open but nobody entered. Excel and Alecto were kissing in the hallway like long-separated lovers. She started to untuck his shirt, at which point he stopped her hands. She pulled away surprised, apologetic.

'Too fast?'

He seemed torn between staying and running. 'Oh, God no. I just need a piss real bad.'

He dropped her bag inside the front door and dived into a room off his living room which, being Manhattan, even the East Village, doubled as his entrance hall. She stepped into the apartment and looked around herself. A small place, compact, kitchenette off the living room, one bedroom off that. Predictably untidy, dirty even. She didn't like that part of it. She did, however, like the computer sitting on the small dining table shoved up against the wall.

The young woman crossed to it and pulled a lipstick out of her cut-off jeans. She took off the lid to reveal a usb-connector. She stuck it into the front of the machine. A dot on the lipstick/usb-stick glowed intermittently and a jiggle of the PC's mouse woke up the sleeping machine. She selected the icon for her device and a series of folders popped up. She chose *WS1*. It contained a number of pictures.

'You OK, Alecto?'

Excel saw her using his PC as he left the toilet. His tone betrayed his slight irritation at her presumption, hoping his intonation might stop her using his stuff too casually. She returned a relaxed gaze.

'Yeah. Bit hot. Mind if we open a window?'

'I mean, what are you doing?'

'I was just checking you had everything.'

He smiled at her as he crossed the room, unsure of the sense of her words, unsure of her new businesslike tone. 'Had everything? I don't understand?'

She waved a hand around the apartment. 'You know, somewhere to live, good location, PC – though I'm more of a Mac person – internet connection. You know.'

He twitched a hesitant smile at her then looked at the pictures on the large computer screen. That she should have pulled up her own pictures was enough to . . . But then something even odder. He recognized the pictures. Of a building. The headquarters of Philadelphia National. People coming out of the office. One face recurring. One man closed in on. Grainier as they trained in on his close-up, unsuspecting face coming out of the building.

He pointed dumbly at the pictures. 'They're like private detective pictures. What's going on?'

Excel so uneasy now that thoughts of sex were secondary to understanding what *was* going on. He watched dumbly as his date – this different person now – undid the cord of her bag and pulled out a compact 3.5-inch-barrel Jericho 941 Desert Eagle semi-automatic pistol.

'Jesus Christ.' Excel half-raised his hands. 'What is this, I mean, what's happening?'

'What's happening?' The woman almost annoyed by the question, her soft Kansas accent hardening, becoming less city, more country. 'The fucking world's, like, going to shit and you're pulling down seven-figure salaries, that's what's *happening.*'

Excel was at a complete loss. 'I'm not . . . Alecto, I barely made one hundred thousand dollars last year.'

She rolled her eyes. 'Barely? *Barely?*' Shaking her head now. 'Anyways, I don't mean you. Not *you*. I mean, your type.'

Excel felt sick. All he wanted to do was to look at the weapon pointed casually at him but he was worried that if he thought about her gun she would think about her gun and then she might actually use it. He was a slight man and something about her physique, her way of holding herself, something told him she would win in a fight. With most men.

'Look, what do you want? Anything.'

'Gosh,' playing with him right now, stepping towards him. 'Anything? Well, I want you to pay.'

'Pay? I'll pay anything. Really. Take my wallet.'

This actually made her laugh before her face took on a vile look. 'Fucking . . .' Not finishing it. Too furious.

'I'm sorry, I didn't mean to . . .'

'Mean to what? *What?*'

She slammed the butt of the gun into the top of his head. He recoiled at the pain, throwing his hands up to his head.

'I'm sorry.'

Another hammer blow with the gun, Excel buckling at the legs, reaching out a hand for the kitchenette counter, missing, crashing to the floor, the redhead leaping on to him, sitting astride him, pounding the gun into his head again, his weak arms covering his face, doing nothing to halt her, the gun smashing down again, the man crying in pain and misery, another hammer blow, whimpering, another, nothing, another, nothing, another, blood, *another*, blood trickling on to the linoleum floor.

Straddled across him, Alecto assessed his condition. Excel lay motionless on his back, blood draining out of his head. He was, at the very least, disabled, out. She sat back on his crotch exhausted. She took a couple of breaths to collect herself before needing to address her temperature. With her non-gun hand she reached up and pulled off her red wig and tossed it on to the two-seater IKEA couch, revealing close-cropped brown hair. Cropped like an army recruit's. But it wasn't enough so she popped all the buttons on her checked shirt. That was better. Not as good as it should have been, but it was better. She took her top off and added it to the couch.

The young man mumbled something, a plea that never quite translated into understandable words. He opened his eyes for the last time to see a strange woman astride him. Hot and sweaty, short hair, with a different top on. Some kind of . . . No, not a top. Something wrong. Something he didn't like. *Oh God* . . .

She watched with malicious satisfaction as his eyes closed and the life faded out of him. She looked around the room, still somewhat out of breath. The place really did have everything she could want. Good location, a PC, internet connection, a dead banker . . .

She reached for her phone on the dining table and pressed #1 and held it for a fast dial. After a moment it was picked up.

'It's me. Hey, you know how I always said I'd kill to live

in Manhattan? Well, *I just did.*' Saying it like she'd just come top in her math class. 'Now, why don't you come over and see what I've done with the place. Plus, I need a fuck.' She rutted her body playfully where she sat astride the dead banker. 'You too.' She closed the phone, pleased with her situation and the prospects for the night ahead. Pleased that she had found a moment of sexual boldness, of abandon on the phone. Her old sexual boldness, pretty much gone these days.

Her eyes alighted on the computer screen, which was running a slideshow of her usb pictures. *Fucking rube.* 'They're like private detective pictures.' She scoffed at his ignorance as the picture of the bank entrance was replaced with a closer, grainier shot of a particular man exiting the building. Wished fleetingly she could bring Excel back and tell him. *They're reconnaissance pictures, you idiot.*

10

William Webster was not an overly tall man but he was a man of presence. He was built like a bootcamp instructor, intimidating, hard-faced, yet for all that attractive in a twinkle-eyed charismatic way when occasion required. A small scar on his left cheek did little to soften the effect of a man who you did not doubt had walked paths most of us would run from. And he *had* walked these paths, in the service of his country, for as long as he could. But there had come a time when he had had to slow down. Not the physical pace. At fifty he was as fit as most men would hope to be at thirty. But his spirit was eroding. He had sensed it beginning a decade earlier, had fought it, but when his life became as pointless as the missions he was being asked to carry out his self — his inner self — told him he had had enough.

When he was very young he had seen his father work the mines in West Virginia, and to him his father was nothing less than Superman. The biggest man who ever roamed the earth. A barrel-chested colossus able to pick William and his three brothers up on his outstretched arms at the end of a working day. William wanted to grow up to be *that* strong. And then the mine shut down, and his father had been laid off. And there had been work for a while, but then the town pretty much shut down too. And then there had been no work. And houses where he had visited his friends now stood empty because they had moved away. 'Abandoned the town the way the mine abandoned us,' spoke his father. It was bewildering to a child that the world was so uncertain. Boredom set in, and soon the sport was to play inside these desolate homes on the few pieces of furniture that had been left behind. And then the sport had been to smash the windows, smash the furniture. They even burned one of the houses to the ground. Why not, nobody was using it.

Then his father began to drink. And he stopped being William's father and instead became a barfly. Not a violent one or self-pitying one, just a broken one, a silent one. So that William came to think that he didn't have a father, not one that he knew. And with all certainty about the universe gone he decided he did not now wish to be his father when he grew up. Because his father was adrift and had cast his family away with him. And William craved a new god that he could pledge himself to, aspire to and be at one with. And finally a god presented itself to William Webster. Bigger, better and more powerful than he had ever imagined a god could be.

That god was the United States Air Force.

When William first enlisted he triumphed over his peers physically and mentally. Not through being larger or stronger – he wasn't. Not through being smarter or sharper – he wasn't. He beat them through sheer force of will. He *wanted* it more. And if his fellow airmen were slow to pick up on this, his superiors were not. He was rewarded with responsibility and promotion and, above all, trust.

But only when William Webster flew for the first time did he realize what he was put on this earth to do. *Fly.* And only his spirits ever soared higher than the jets he raced across the Texas sky. Flying was *it*. The certainty of his life was back. His career was mapped out. He would carry out sorties over the Middle East during the first Iraq War, embark on a career as a test pilot – the more to be around the metal birds that he loved so much – gain promotion into the lower ranks of Air Force command then enjoy a well-earned retirement. It was written in the stars, a fact about the universe. It was what would be.

Only nobody had told Delta Force about this. And nobody had told the CIA about this. And, clearly, nobody had told fate, because in his late twenties his boundless energy was drawn towards the escapades of Delta, the USAF's elite fighting force, which offered a new challenge and new adventures. And when his body could take no more of that the CIA had their uses for him. And once there he lied and cheated and killed for The Company. Did it as well as anyone. Put his life on the line time and again so that a tiny piece of the ever-shifting billion-piece mosaic Uncle Sam wanted to build could near completion. Befriended devils in human form, assassinated these same people, befriended the people who replaced them. It got so he could barely tell right from wrong, the good from the bad. All that was left was the ugly.

When his mind could take no more of that, when his life both professional and private had paid every price imaginable, he woke one morning and asked himself what the hell he was doing – and what the hell he was doing it for. He had executed his duties and people for his country such that he didn't know what his country stood for, didn't know what *he* stood for.

He needed a change, but he also needed money and he needed it bad. And there was only one place on earth that he knew of that overflowed with money – legally recognized money, at any rate – and that was Wall Street. He approached a recruitment agency and told them (some of) what he had done and could they parlay that into life on the Street. He had barely left their office before the offers began to flood in. And all from names he'd never heard of. European banks, Arab banks and Wall Street banks, all virtually anonymous and all liking it that way.

He went for a slate of interviews with a bunch of people who outlined their security concerns and he felt like they were having him on. The internet and data issue were IT's security concern. The banks were worried about disgruntled employees taking client details out of the office, adulterous employees giving the company a bad name and lowering morale, insider trading . . . They thought these things were *problems*? It's not like they even had branches somebody could hold up. And they thought he was the right man for the job. Because he was. Because they didn't want these problems dealt with – they wanted them *eliminated*. They wanted *total* security. And they were prepared to pay.

And life had gone from hard to soft, poor to well-off (by his standards, not his employer's). He knew where he would be at night and didn't have to regard every stranger as a potential threat. He did, but he didn't *have* to.

He considered this new life. He could get used to it. He *did* get used to it. Got used to it and wanted more of it. The limousines, the fancy restaurants, the world-class resorts, the private jets – all in the name of business?

People on Main Street didn't *relax* this well, let alone do it at work. He liked it, liked it lots. But he rode his employer's coat-tails on these occasions, enjoyed these perks as perks of the job, not perks that would be there for ever. The bankers would enjoy them for ever, but not him. Like Scott Fitzgerald said, the rich were different.

And then the music stopped.

During the Credit Crunch every bank had been scrabbling about for money. Before the government opened up its wallet there had been bona fide panic in Lower Manhattan. Credit had dried up. Money had dried up. Every institution closed its doors and everybody closed their wallets to everybody else.

Almost everybody. Clients that had been turned away before, clients on the fringe, clients with money, grey money – black money – were reached out to. By certain banks. By Webster's bank. 'Just till it blows over.' Webster watched his bosses use these words and considered them the worst kind of lies. The lies we tell ourselves.

But William Webster knew that it never blows over – it blows up.

Like life at the bank and his dreams of a very comfortable retirement. Most banks were rudderless during the Credit Crunch. They begged and screamed and threatened the Treasury until the money flowed like a tsunami, dollars flooding into Lower Manhattan. Webster had smiled at the way the banks outplayed the government, admired their smarts. But his real admiration was reserved for the few players – the very few players – who made money during the market crash. He knew from experience that for every loser there had to be a winner. It was why the Chinese had the same word for 'crisis' as 'opportunity'. Hell, he'd instigated enough crises in South America to know that sometimes they were the *only* opportunities.

But, as far as William Webster was concerned, these banks were not so different from the cartels and despots he had had to deal with all his espionage life. You do the deals you have to do and then you do other deals to add a little sugar on top. It had made him smile. But because he had walked the wicked pathways of those worlds he also knew something his bosses did not . . .

The past may be dead, but the dead sometimes come back to haunt you.

The office was large. The only light was a desk lamp, a computer monitor and the moon-bright sky coming through the slatted blinds behind the desk itself. As a result, most of the room lay in darkness. Hidden.

The two men behind the desk had watched the film with very different reactions. Anthony Cochran, CEO of Sovereign Bank, was small, slightly shrewish, with short-cut hair around a bald head. Fifty-six years old, he sported a permanent tan, but even in the dim light of the room his look of loathing and terror had drained all the colour from his face. Behind him, wanting to put a consoling hand on the man's shoulder but feeling constrained by hierarchy, was William Webster, the bank's Head of Security. He had watched more in sorrow than disgust.

Webster looked at the desk, at the padded envelope torn open. The writing scrawled casually. 'Have I got your attention?'

They sat without speaking. Cochran unable to, Webster wanting his boss to process the moment first, get his head round it.

Cochran broke the silence. 'What do you think we should do?'

Webster didn't rush to answer. He could only offer advice and while he found the conclusion easy to reach he didn't want to ram it down his boss's throat. When he spoke he spoke softly.

'Do as he says.'

Cochran turned from the screen filled with disbelief. 'Do as he says?'

'Yep.'

Cochran tried to look back at the screen, blank now, but so filled with potency from the horror it had just displayed that he couldn't bring himself to do so. His mind fogged over. 'What . . . what exactly did he say?'

Webster felt like he was walking on eggshells, like a courtier breaking terrible news to a king. 'If I heard correctly, he said that you should pay Lazcano $250 million.'

Cochran wanted to throw up. He wanted to scream *and* throw up. He was confused and scared and horrified. 'Are you . . . Bill, are you, are you sure?'

Webster frowned uncomfortably. 'Well, I do think we should listen again.'

Cochran looked up at the blank screen. He struggled to reconcile himself to what Webster had suggested, then looked guiltily at his office door in the dark beyond, as if a horde of police officers might burst in at any moment.

'Do we have to?'

'Sir, let me just check. You don't have to watch.'

Cochran made no attempt to get out of the security chief's way as Webster used the mouse to jump the film back thirty seconds from the end, turning the volume up as he did. Webster flicked a glance at Cochran, wondering if he should get permission, before getting on with it anyway.

The face of the young banker Simon Turlington took up the screen. A dark hand – a Mexican hand – was holding his head up by gripping a fistful of his hair at the back of his head. A fraction of a second told the viewer Turlington was beyond doing anything much for himself. A fraction of a second was all Webster would allow himself to look at the poor, wretched creature. Any more would have sent him into a downward spiral of revulsion that would have made him unable to carry out the job at hand. The young Wall Street banker in a room somewhere in Mexico being tortured. The young man's voice on the monitor, with the weakness that only the dying possess, suddenly boomed out of the too-loud speakers, which Webster hurried to correct. Neither of the men looked at the screen. Both were ashamed to be looking away. Cochran because of what he had allowed to happen. Webster because he was meant to be stronger than this.

'. . . Please, Mr Cochran . . . Please . . .' Turlington begging, half wheezing, half whimpering. '. . . Pay back the two . . .' The effort more than he could bear, the breathing heavy for a moment. '. . . the two hundred and fifty million doll . . .' The last mumbled. The last words before unconsciousness took him. Both men shocked to the core by what they had seen. The beaten face. The unrecognizable face. Cochran waved a wild hand at the monitor, signalling for Webster to *stop it*. Webster, momentarily nervous, unsure whether his boss meant for him to pause it or to make it all go away, turned off the monitor instead.

The two men both struggled to wrestle their minds from what they had just seen.

Webster stood and looked out of the window, speaking as much to break his boss's torpor as to resolve the issue. 'Sir, you have to pay.'

Cochran pointed threateningly at the now blank computer monitor. 'What makes him think we won't take this to the police? Huh? We could.'

Webster gave him a level stare, a *think about what you just said* stare. 'Could we, sir?'

Cochran rocked back and forth slightly, considering the floor beneath his desk bitterly. 'But . . .' Finding some strength in the basis of business. '*He* lost the money.'

Webster picked his words with the care of somebody sifting through broken glass. 'Sir, technically, we lost it.'

'No, no, no, *no*, Webster. He put his money into a fund that he knew would be traded. We told him this, we told him the risks, we told him everything.'

'Sir. You don't lose money for people like Lazcano.'

'Webster, this is Wall Street. We don't pay back people's losses, if we did that we wouldn't last a week.'

'If I may, I think the subtleties of our business model may be alien to our client.'

'Our former client.'

'I think that he thinks his account is still open until he gets his money.'

Webster looked away from his boss, giving him time to think it over, himself watching the midnight traffic way down below on Barclay Street. Not a lot of it. The odd limo, the odd taxi cab.

'Connie almost opened it.'

The security chief turned back and took a moment to register the dazed statement before his boss's dread-filled gaze at the envelope answered his question.

'The post-girl left it on her desk, and ninety-nine times out of a hundred Connie would have opened it but she was late for her personal shopper. My PA almost *opened it.*' Suddenly a sob escaping the CEO as he dropped his head into his hands and let the trauma flow out.

Webster stood uncomfortably to one side. A film like this was meant to have an effect, so, this was it having an effect. The crying continued for a moment before Cochran got a hold on himself and fished out his handkerchief, blowing his nose and his tears away with it.

'And where the hell has the figure come from? I mean, he didn't lose a quarter of a billion, he lost a hundred and fifty million. Where did the other hundred come from?' Cochran throwing his hands about as he demanded an explanation from people invisible.

'Erm, I believe that's what they call the *vig.*'

Cochran looked at Webster like he had just spoken Arabic. 'The what?'

'The – the *vig*, sir. The interest. On monies owed.'

Even in the near dark Cochran's eyes clearly widened. 'One hundred million dollars? Interest? Who the fu . . . ? How dare he expect a bank to pay such fees.'

Webster felt his boss was reading from the wrong part of the operation manual and felt it was time to lay it out for him. 'Sir, you have to understand how these people operate. If you steal from them —'

'We did *not* steal from them.'

Webster hunched apologetically. 'If you lose their money and refuse to pay it back? Well, you've disrespected them. They won't let a thing like that pass. You're telling everybody they're weak. You've made them lose . . .'

Neither of them needed or wanted to hear the end of that sentence.

'You'll have to tell him no, Bill.'

'Sir, I think that's a mistake.'

'Tell him no. We have no choice.'

Webster thought this was completely the wrong reaction. Thought this was about to get a whole lot worse. For everybody.

11

'Dinner tonight?'

'Dinner tonight!'

'LB@9?'

'LB@9! ;-x'

I didn't need to reply to her last text. If dinner at that restaurant didn't get me fully back into Martinez's good books it would be time to join a monastery. I slipped my cell phone back inside my leather blazer pocket and looked around me.

I was standing on the corner of Broadway and Wall Street. Seven o'clock on a Sunday morning. Too early for me, and everybody else it seemed. It was quiet, a light spray falling from the sky. Tomorrow there would be a constant flow of people funnelling into the heart of the city's financial machine. Bankers, traders, back office, admin, secretaries, security guards, office cleaners, thousands of them. Today there wasn't even a trickle. The chilly, grey February morning weather was reflected in the faces of the few people who passed by.

I'd been standing there so long I'd had to flash two different sets of cops my Secret Service badge to justify my behaviour. But what I was interested in was the behaviour of everybody else. They were doing exactly what they ought to be doing – getting on with their lives. But today I could only see the threats.

Today I could see the coffee vendor fifty yards away along Broadway being all fingers and thumbs as he opened up for the day. First day on the job or maybe it wasn't his job? I'd seen the same cab circle the block three times. Looking for a fare or looking for something else? Opposite Wall Street itself, the guy tending the Trinity Church cemetery, on a Sunday? Why hadn't he looked up – because he was the real deal or because he was damned careful not to be caught looking up?

The price of freedom, the homeland security headache, the balancing act we had to strike every day in our country. Only, I had a feeling it was about to become unbalanced, about to be pushed off kilter by events. Upward of three-quarters of a million people work in Lower Manhattan. In my estimation, the overwhelming majority did not feel like the targets of this new group that had been hitting bankers, but tens of thousands were. They would be . . .

Then I saw something high up in the bell tower of Trinity Church. I didn't trust what I'd seen. Was it somebody at a window? The shadow of a passing bird? The Neo-Gothic church front faced directly down Wall Street. A tempting, if obvious, vantage point for any would-be attackers. I guessed they'd be ringing the bells for Sunday service just before eight. But that was almost an hour away. It was not something I could resist investigating.

New York didn't fall quiet behind me when I entered the building but it certainly started to speak in a whisper. The mute sounds and cold smell of stone was a million miles away from the incessant noises and odours of the metropolis outside the church's heavy, bronze-laden doors. In days gone by churches were a sanctuary from your enemies, now they felt like a sanctuary from the twenty-first century.

I looked about the expansive space, the nave separated from the aisles by soaring terracotta columns, up to the high, arched oak ceiling above. A magnificent stained-glass window took up most of the far wall behind the altar. The pews taking up the centre were almost empty except for two people. On the left, an elderly lady fished through her handbag, on the right, sat a solitary male figure. From his suit and grooming I guessed he was a well-remunerated banker. From his painfully stooped position I'd guess he was currently on the wrong side of a trade.

I made my way quietly up the narrow bell-tower stairs. They were a stone spiral twisting up to the left around a tight central column. If somebody was waiting they were above me and with a better view. From outside the church the bell platform looked about one hundred and fifty feet from the ground. After about ninety steps I slowed down. Slowed right down. My gut said nobody was up there, but my brain said there was no upside to being careless.

I pulled out my Sig Sauer P229 service pistol and held it low behind my leg. To hand, but out of sight if I bumped into a chaplain on bell-cleaning duty. As quietly as I could I made my way up, one step at a time, listening for the slightest noise, cursing myself for not wearing pumps instead of my black shoes. Thankfully their leather soles were near-silent on the stairs, it was my breathing I felt was the loudest, the illusion of amplification.

I ascended a few more steps then saw an unwelcome sight.

A ladder. Or something between a steep set of metal stairs and a ladder, a wall hard on both sides.

The final part of the journey was up that ladder to the bell platform itself. If I was exposed on the stairs this was trouble squared. A blindfolded person could hit me on this thing. Stealth somehow felt like a pretence at this point, but I persevered. I put one foot and my left hand on the ladder, the right hand with the gun pointed up above me. I strained to hear any noises above. I thought I could hear something but at the same time didn't trust myself. I hauled myself up, silence taking priority over speed. The stone channel around me insulated me from every last piece of noise so that I now knew that anything I heard was either from the room above or my heart beating. And there was something. For a moment there was a tap. Something briefly rapping something up above, then a scuffing noise, quiet but there. Then it stopped. I stopped and waited. I waited a full minute, but nothing followed. I continued up.

Up above I could see that when I got to the top of this stepladder there was another ladder bolted to the wall waiting to take me up to yet another floor. I didn't know if the noise I could hear was in this room or the room above. There was only one way to find out.

I completed the last half-dozen rungs to bring my head to just below room height. And there it was again. A tapping on wood. The briefest of sounds but a sound nonetheless. But definitely one floor up.

With infinitesimal care and caution against noise I chambered a bullet into my gun, every click and slide of the mechanism sounding like a bag of spanners rolling down a ship's staircase in my ears. I gave it another full minute after I'd completed the action before making another move. There was no repeat of the tapping, which I didn't know whether to take as good or bad news.

I dared a peek over the rim of the first floor.

Nobody.

I was entering from the corner of the room, railings around the gap in the floor I was emerging from. On three sides the room had large, round recesses, ten foot or so in diameter. Within each of these was a ring of Gothic rose-shaped windows allowing the room a dim visibility. There was a bench set into each window, a dozen or so bell-ropes hanging through slits in the floor above, and that was pretty much it.

The noise had come from above. And it was coming again. A tapping followed by a fierce scuffing like some-body was snapping a plastic shopping bag into shape by whipping it through the air.

I knew that sound. And I knew why it had stopped.

I looked around the bare room I was in. Nothing.

I mounted the ladder opposite, two rungs at a time, still in near silence. When I got – quickly – to the next floor I saw it.

A pigeon. Battering itself against a slatted shutter that allowed in limited streams of light, the rows of bells impeding its attempts to take flight even in this generous portion of the tower. I remembered these shutters. Trinity Church had had to install them when local residents complained about the peel of the bells during the church's practice sessions. God and mammon. But seeing me was too much even for this overweight bird, and it half flew, half hopped out of sight.

I was glad of its presence. It explained the noise but more than that it covered any sound I might have made on my way up. Nevertheless, I scanned the room. Nothing and nobody presented itself. Just streams of dust shown up by the thick bars of light coming in through the shutters.

For good measure I carefully paced round the edge of the dark room, around the bells, all twenty-three of them.

Just me and the pigeon.

I was going bats in the belfry. That's how antsy I was about the bank killings. But that's how antsy everybody was about to get, if they weren't already.

I went over to the east window, a tall lancet affair, narrow with a pointed arch at the top. I hit a switch on the wall, and the shutters began to open. As the light began to flood in my new-found friend waddled over in his half-curious, half-fussy manner, a bundle of ticks and shoulder twitches. With a speed that probably said more about hunger than bravado the pigeon launched itself ungracefully through one of the stone window frames and wobbled out of sight.

I watched after it as it made its anxious way along Wall Street. Tomorrow people would be pouring in like a river down below. Oblivious to the enemy setting its sights on them. Oblivious to the vantage points on offer. Oblivious to what was coming.

12

Captain Novak was a man from the wrong era, at least he looked that way. It bothered everybody who ever met him. Not just that he *was* so goddamn handsome but that, what was it, what *was* it . . . ? That's right, he looked like a matinee idol, from the thirties or forties. And when it fell into place for people they could never look at him the same way again. After that he was Cary Grant or Clark Gable or whatever knockout black-and-white movie star they could recall. He was dapper and, to top it all, his habit of always thinking before he spoke was ever-so-slightly-arch, like he'd learned his lines before he said them. And yet, while it screamed out to everybody around him, he seemed thoroughly oblivious to all of it. And, to his credit, never played up to it. He was handsome – so what? If he had ambition it was not on the silver screen but within the NYPD. Lived it, breathed it. A third-generation cop. Wore his careerism a little too obviously, kissed the carousel of butts up at City Hall whenever he could, but, in his late forties, was doing all the right things. Like not getting precious about the law enforcement hierarchy.

The squad room was packed with detectives and uniformed officers, some on chairs, most leaning against the walls or sat on desks. Coffee was in abundance, waking people up, combating hangovers. They talked the usual shit to each other while their boss collated his papers at the front until his trademark cough had them going quiet.

'OK, what I'm about to say is not to leave this room, understood?' Captain Novak looked around the people present. 'In the light of the terrorist attacks on bankers in Europe and Asia we're stepping up security around Lower Manhattan.'

Everyone took in the news as Detective Jenni Martinez, at the back, raised her hand before asking her question anyway. 'Captain, is there any material reason for this?'

He was straight with them. 'Nothing firm, no. But this is an exercise in pre-emption and deterrence. We will be reassigning almost the entire Counter Terrorism Division and all available personnel to the Financial District for the time being. But we're trying to keep it low-key.'

There was a ripple of groans until an older detective spoke for them. 'You're putting us on patrol, Cap'n?'

'Yes.'

As disaffected groans began to rise from the detectives, Johansson, a tall Scandinavian male, spoke for the uniformed officers. 'With all due respect, sir, is babysitting detectives a good use of our time?'

He got something approaching a cheer from his class of policeman before the captain raised his hands *very funny* style. 'Keep it for the canteen afterwards. Think of this as a visit from the President with the same vigilance and attention to detail that I would expect of each of you during such a time. We don't want the death of a banker on our watch.'

A slightly mutinous whisper rippled round the room.

A crumpled-looking male detective sitting on a desk

said, 'Sir, can't the bankers hire their own security? They're the reason we've had our budget slashed.'

The remark was greeted with mumbled and louder-than-mumbled support.

Novak stared about the room until all dissent had quietened. 'Judson, when you want to run for mayor you've got your platform. Until then you do your duty. If anybody doesn't understand their duty I'm happy to send them back to police academy for some retraining.' Nothing from anybody. 'Good. Now, we don't want to alarm the good citizens of this fair city with this course of action so it is *imperative* that we do not broadcast our new procedure to the wider population. By which I mean the media.'

He stared at them, the look telling them that he knew someone or other in the room was in the habit of doing just that.

'Remember, this is an opportunity for us to show people the effectiveness of our counter-terrorist capabilities. We will, of course, be working with all the other lead agencies, and very likely the FBI will use this precinct as a temporary base.' Groans poured around the room, nobody making any attempt to hide them. 'It should also indicate the seriousness with which this situation is being viewed by the Department of Homeland Security.'

Martinez's partner, Detective Ashby, shook his head in disgust. 'Just what we need, a bunch of Fibbi hard-ons running the show.'

Muttered support met his remark.

Novak, wanting to wrap things up, had no small measure of sympathy but needed to run a tight ship all the same. 'Well, Ashby, you could always join them and run the show yourself.'

'You kidding? Then *I'd* be a hard-on.'

Martinez was leaning against the opposite wall to her partner. 'Oh, don't worry, Ashby, you'll always be a hard-on to me.'

An amused jeer met her taunt of her partner.

Ashby shook his head again, like he was most unimpressed by his partner's effort. 'Eat me.'

'When I go on a diet I'll call you.'

More cheering.

Judson talked into the Starbucks cup he was pulling to his mouth. 'Better call him soon.'

A collective 'Oooh' went up at the near-the-knuckle remark. Martinez whizzed her half-full bottle of water at Judson's head, smacking him square in the forehead, eliciting an 'Ohhhh' from the room, impressed by her accuracy and the raising of stakes.

Martinez was quick with the follow up. 'And that was my *bad* arm.'

Judson didn't know if it was his head or his pride, but something was hurting. However, it was too much too late for the captain.

'All right, all right, that's enough games for one day. Let's remind everybody why we're called New York's finest. Now, go protect the city.'

13

'What have you got?'

'So many STDs I ought to be in an incubation tent.'

I waited patiently on the edge of Park's desk, where I had perched myself. For reasons going way back to my first stint in the Secret Service, Park didn't like me. It wasn't professional, it was personal. It wasn't profound, it was petty. But that was the way Park was and how he liked it. The Korean continued working at his computer in the vain hope that it would infuriate me. When he realized it didn't, he looked up in his best Judy Garland manner.

'Can't it wait?'

'No.'

Park huffed like his soufflé had failed to rise in the oven for the third time in a row. He tracked his wheelchair backwards, grabbed a report off a nearby desk and – rather petulantly – handed it to me. I looked at it. *Interpol, Initial Findings Into London Restaurant Attack*. I skimmed through it, past the factual description of the crime scene to what I believed was the most salient fact. '*The bomb retains many characteristics of improvised explosive devices actively employed in Iraq.*' I leaned back to consider it.

Park waved a hand at the document. 'Yeah, apparently we're looking for a network of Iraqi insurgents. Go figure.'

'Or somebody with experience of their work.' There

was a clue in here, maybe even a starting point on the trail. 'What have we got on the restaurant's security cameras?' Asked, even though I could guess the answer.

'Destroyed in the attack. They were using an old VHS format, which Scotland Yard are trying to salvage as we speak.' Park rolled his eyes. 'They'd have more luck salvaging Mel Gibson's career.'

I rescanned the report. No, this was the thing, at least, the only thing to go on.

'Park, get me every bit of footage for the approach to the restaurant –'

'Michael.'

I turned to see Diane Mason standing in her doorway.

'Could you join us?'

I nodded then stood by the AV expert's desk. 'Park, I want a name to every face on the restaurant films. Start with the twenty-four hours before, then keep going back every twenty-four hours until we find a face that fits this.'

'But it's a Sunday.'

'This is top priority.'

Park knew what that meant and did nothing to hide his displeasure. 'I've got plans tonight.'

I tossed the Interpol report on to his keyboard. 'Cancel them.'

When I entered the conference room I understood the meeting immediately. To his credit, the Treasury Secretary had the courtesy to stand as I entered and offer his hand, his high, bald head blocking the low morning sun like a mini-eclipse.

'Mr Secretary.'

'Agent Byrne.'

We all sat around the top of a conference table and got down to it.

'Michael, Secretary Peterson was asking about progress on the Nemesis killings.'

I adopted a look of mild surprise. 'Are we officially going with "Nemesis" in this, Mr Secretary?'

The sixty-plus head of the Treasury caught the mood. 'Well, they called immediately before the most recent attack in Hong Kong. It feels fairly solid.'

I looked from one to the other. 'Who did they call?'

Diane now. '*The New York Times*.'

I didn't like that one bit. 'Bit close to home. Did they make any demands?'

Diane and I looking at the Treasury Secretary. He shrugged, disheartened.

'Said another banker "had" to die and that we should "get used to it".'

We all three paused to consider the implications of such a threat.

Diane creased her nose in thought. 'Maybe you were right about those Baader-Meinhoff types, Michael.'

'What's that?'

I took the question. 'Well, Mr Secretary, if it's global, and if it's bankers, the terrorists' goal seems to be the eradication of the banking class.'

Peterson looked from Diane to me to the room almost despairing. 'Jesus wept. They're sociopaths. They have no regard for any of our values. How do we stop them?'

'The bankers or the terrorists?'

They both rocked back at my seeming flippancy.

'Michael, that's in poor taste.'

'But that's how these terrorists see the bankers. As money-grabbing sociopaths with no regard for any of our values. And as the Occupy movement has shown, that plays to a fairly wide audience, Mr Secretary. London, Frankfurt, Tokyo, now Hong Kong – everybody's still paying off the debts of their bankers. That's a lot of angry people, sir.'

He nodded to show he took my point, however unsavoury.

'But what do we think are the terrorists' demands, Byrne?'

'So far they have been very targeted in their killings, specifically killing pre-identified victims. They're not using the usual terror tactics, they're not trying to vaguely attack bankers and if innocent bystanders die so-be-it. They want to zero in on certain individuals.'

Peterson unconsciously sat forward in his chair as he addressed us. 'Do you think there's a link between the deaths above and beyond just being bankers?'

'That's what Michael is working on, Mr Secretary.'

He nodded, then frustration got the better of him. 'But they must *want* something – they must have demands? Are they anti-capitalist? Are they communist? Do they want to replace our current economic system? What?'

I exhaled partially out of fatigue, partially to signal my lack of ideas. 'Maybe they haven't got any demands, sir. Maybe they just want to kill bankers.'

The Treasury Secretary's face showed his bewilderment at such a prospect and yet he didn't move to deny it.

After a brief silence from all of us Mr Peterson drummed a finger on the conference table. 'So, what have we got?'

The question aimed at me, Diane happy for me to take the spotlight.

'Well, we have to assume that another agency will get there first. I mean, you have to understand that crime-scene investigations, surveillance and good old-fashioned tip-offs are our most likely route to success here.'

He nodded in a way that acknowledged that this was nothing more than preamble. 'And you understand that the President wants everybody on this? What's your angle, your personal take on this, Agent Byrne?'

I opened my hands helplessly. 'I haven't got one until the banks start cooperating.'

Peterson looked from me to Diane, confused.

'What Agent Byrne means, Mr Secretary, is that we, that is, *he* has requested the trading records of all employees from all the banks in Manhattan.'

The Treasury Secretary's eyes narrowed. 'Why?'

'Because everybody killed so far has been a trader. And not just a trader but a bank trader. Without exception. The coincidence is too great.'

Peterson to Diane again. 'And getting these records is a problem, why, Agent Mason?'

Diane wore a look that confessed to the tricky nature of our position. 'Because they are worried that once we have these records that we will do more than just investigate Nemesis, that we will use them to pursue other lines of inquiry we have had frustrated in recent years.'

Peterson again. 'And would we?'

Diane. 'Hell yeah.'

The Treasury Secretary shook his head, frustrated.

'Well, you'll just have to assure them that you won't – and then be true to your word.'

I didn't like this development. 'But, Mr Secretary, do you realize the number of cases we could bust open with this sort of information? I mean, proper, non-filtered trading records, not the BS they give the regulators, but really what they're up to?'

He gave me a level, inquiring stare. 'Like Sovereign Bank's activities in Mexico?'

I was slightly taken aback that this was on his radar but didn't feel I had to apologize. 'Yeah. After this is all out of the way, yeah, why not?'

Peterson made what he thought was a discreet glance at Diane. 'Didn't Agent Mason tell you that case was closed?'

I was torn between pressing my case and dropping Diane in it. I had to figure that she had told me about the CIA's operations in Mexico without Peterson's blessing. Which tied my hands, to say the least. 'In no uncertain terms, Mr Secretary. It was just an example, there's plenty more we could break with this kind of information.'

Peterson took a moment to order his words and the look between himself and Diane gave me an insight into the nature of their conversation before I had joined them. 'Byrne, I've taken a hell of a gamble in sponsoring your Markets Abuse Task Force. They're convinced over at the Department of Homeland Security that it's a power play by Treasury to get the Secret Service back under our remit. And you want to know what? They're right. Between you, me and these four walls, they can keep Protection, but what the hell is Financial Investigations doing under another state department? I want it back where it belongs, in Treasury. If they see my little experiment running off with its own agenda I can kiss goodbye to getting every financial investigative and regulatory body under one roof – ours. We have to be seen to play ball. Are we playing ball, Agent Byrne?'

'Of course, sir.'

He interrogated my eyes for a moment, looking for me to flinch. When I didn't, the mood relaxed. 'I'll get you your trading records.'

I couldn't believe it.

'They'll have to be put into an escrow account. An IT team will be watching activity on this account and any abuse of the information – any attempt to copy it, print it off, *anything* – will be deemed you breaking your end of the bargain. Are we agreed?'

It was better than where we were. 'Yes, sir.'

'Then that's everything.'

He stood, and we both followed suit. He shook hands with Diane and then with me. Only he kept my hand in his.

'Byrne, I've got to see the President today. He's going to ask me my assessment of the likelihood of an attempt to kill a banker on American soil. What should I tell him?'

'An attempt?' I paused to order the words in the most palatable fashion possible. But there was only one answer. 'Sir, tell him one hundred per cent.'

14

Detectives Ashby and Martinez sat in his 1973 Ford Mustang Mach 1. Apart from being a classic American muscle car it was also, on occasion, his unmarked police car of choice, on this occasion parked on Broadway and Liberty Street. They were, along with seemingly every uniformed officer in New York, watching the street outside. Boredom had quickly set in, both convinced this was a fairly desperate and unimaginative measure by the powers-that-be. People were milling past, but it was just weekend traffic. Nobody stood out from the crowd, partly because this was one of the biggest melting pots in the world, and diversity was what was to be expected, and partly because this was New York, and you had to be just a little bit crazy to live here.

Nothing unusual happened for a bit longer until Ashby tapped his partner's arm. 'Hey, check out this threat to national security.'

Walking along was an old African-American man with the sunken mouth of a toothless tramp. He had a sandwich board hung over him. It read: 'The end is nigh . . .' Ashby and Martinez followed him with their gazes as he walked past their car, looking at them and mumbling some profanity to himself. They watched him cross Broadway, reading the back of his sign as he did: '. . . For bankers'.

They both chuckled grimly and swapped a sorry *Whatever next?* expression.

'How's it going with Byrne?'

Martinez didn't know whether to smile or scowl and settled on a frown. 'OK.'

'You do that whole "Maybe I'm not interested any more" thing when he got back from his trip?'

Now she did smile, amused. 'Of course. Gotta make them work for it.'

He eyed her narrowly through his chiselled, grave-looking face. 'Don't make him work too hard.'

She gave him an unimpressed look. 'You seem to be forgetting what awaits the fruits of his labours.' She waved her fingers down herself for emphasis.

'Low-hanging fruit, more like.' Before anything could escape from her amused and outraged mouth he pressed on. 'You seen him properly since he got back?'

This new thought batted away any lingering mock-hurt. 'Actually, he's taking me to Le Bernardin tonight.' She waited for some kind of reaction from her partner to the mention of one of the city's best restaurants but sensed she was going to get nothing. 'It's French.'

He raised an unimpressed eyebrow. 'No merde.'

She took a moment to realize he was teasing her and guffawed at his behaviour. They both resumed looking out of the car windows at the street, at the constant flow of people passing by, at the seemingly futile nature of their exercise. Martinez, only half her mind on the job, and none on her partner, missed that his mood had darkened since they had stopped talking. Since he had resumed scrutinizing the crowds of people that made up the financial district.

'You know, Marty, I always thought this would happen sooner.'

She took her eyes off the street and turned them on Ashby. 'What would?'

'People feeling this way about bankers, you know, the whole Occupy Wall Street thing.' Ashby talking with his hands, the way he always did.

'Really?'

Shrugging. 'Well, yeah.'

She gave him a pointed sideways look. "Cos of the money they earn? Come on, Ash, this is America – the Land of Opportunity.'

'For who?'

She held his stare for a moment, only now realizing how the issue was eating at him, and now he had to get it out.

'I mean, look at the way they paid the bailout money to themselves. Wall Street paid itself $150 billion the year after the bailouts – as *bonuses*. That's money that should have been paid back. Can you imagine if the NYPD said it had a budget crisis and then when City Hall gave us an extra billion we just put it in our pockets? Shit, Marti, my kids' school just laid off two teachers because of budget cuts. People *should* be mad.'

'You condoning the violence, Ash?'

'I'm understanding it. I mean, busting the economy, getting trillions of dollars in bailouts, paying themselves bonuses I couldn't even count to . . . Wouldn't you expect a little anger? Ain't you angry?'

'Come back to me if I'm still sitting here in a week.' She grimaced as she took in the street scene about her. 'I guess it was kind of creepy the way they stopped driving their bling cars and living their bling lifestyles for a while after the crash. Like they knew they ought to be ashamed.'

Ashby could not stop a snort from escaping. 'Yeah, like gangsters after a major haul. Lie low for a while before starting to spend the cash again.' He shook his head, fighting down some cuss words. 'They ain't so different from wiseguys, not when you think about it. Scams, skimming off the top, politicians in their pockets, not giving a damn about the lives they wreck. Shit.' Shaking his head.

They both sat quietly with their glum thoughts about the people they were protecting and about the ugliness of the situation that was now facing them.

'Ash, do you really think cramming the streets with New York's finest is going to stop these crazies?'

'Come on, Martinez, this ain't about stopping them. This is about showing people we're doing something.'

'You got that right. Hey, I thought of something we could do.'

'What's that?'

She tapped her watch. 'Our shift's over. Let's go get a coffee.'

Ashby reached for the ignition. 'Finally, some real detective work.'

The car eased away from the sidewalk, and Ashby and Martinez turned left up Pine Street, unaware that they were being watched. Watched in the circular setting of a telescopic lens. The view through the lens swept back to where they had been parked then further south along Broadway to the entrance of a bank's offices. Philadelphia National. The view slowly scanned up, one, two, then more floors, till the tenth was reached. Still below the level of the viewer. The viewer scanned across to the right, three offices along. The blinds were pulled up on a plain room, empty but for a desk and chairs. The viewer zoomed in on the desk. On to a picture, framed, in pride of place. A man on a yacht.

Alecto lowered the telescopic lens. The detached lens from a long-range rifle. She looked the street up and down with her naked eye. Looked at the route she would have to take into the area and the route she would have to take out. Disciplined. Planning it, like a military operation. Planning it so she would live to kill another day.

She returned to looking through the telescopic lens, looked at the angle of the shot one more time. The desk. The man absent. Just the picture of the man. The man on the yacht. Possibly his yacht.

What did it matter whose yacht it was? He'd be dead tomorrow.

15

Be careful what you wish for, Byrne.

My Sunday evening. I'd sat in the living room of my Brooklyn apartment just as I had sat since mid afternoon, just as I expected to sit for a long time to come. The Treasury Secretary had been true to his word and gotten me access to all the trading records from all the banks, and it was a *lot*. Like Mount Everest was tall. He'd told me the data was being watched and if I attempted to copy it my career was over. God knows I was tempted to, and God knows I could do it without being spotted by an IT security 'expert' who had a quarter of an eye on me and one and three-quarters on his Facebook page, World of Warcraft online account or whatever it was he was doing. I could do it with him watching me. But I wouldn't. I'd given my word and I'd been raised to not break my word. What was it my mother had said? Oh yeah. It was 'wrong'.

I'd stopped counting at ten thousand traders currently or recently working in Lower Manhattan. I could throw the net wider in terms of time or geography, but getting some kind of handle on the ocean of data was my first task. Thankfully, long gone were the days when I would wade through such information manually, sending algorithms crawling over the data was my preferred approach. Set my parameters and let the wonders of number-crunching software do the work for me. Not that framing the right inquiries didn't provoke a lot of head-scratching on my part. I hadn't asked a question of the database that hadn't spewed a river of answers at me. Too much information, too much data – needles and haystacks. What was I missing?

My duplex windows were half covered by a series of shades. I'd done that to make viewing my home projector possible. On my lap was the computer tablet I was working on, its display mirroring the information on the large home-cinema screen opposite. I had the tablet's display resolution as detailed as possible, making everything on its screen as small as was practical. It meant I could get a hell of a lot up on to the high-definition cinema-screen. The way I had come to work. On the cinema screen was a spreadsheet with countless tabs at the bottom, countless sheets still left to examine.

I looked about my room, needing to rest my eyes off the wall-projected screen. My gaze fell on the dark outline of my guitar. Poor thing actually had the beginnings of a layer of dust on it. Either I was neglecting it or I had a problem with my air-conditioning. I remembered the arguments I'd had about that exact guitar, what I'd gone through with a guitar of all things, how much of my undeniably troubled youth I'd spent with it. How it was my escape, my constant friend, my refuge from the screaming and the shouting, how my guitar could echo and shout down any and all noises, how it could raise the devil or sweet-talk angels out of heaven. How I would obsess about emulating an exact riff by a particular guitar hero, for the briefest of moments matching an ounce of their skill. Thinking how that guitar was my escape. Thinking how I hadn't made much time for it recently, how I hadn't made much time for me. Thinking how I felt tired. Because if it wasn't one thing it was another, the world full of people looking to get one over on people by not playing by the rules and me always against that and finding myself sitting alone on my couch giving a minimal shake of my head as I wondered if that was some innate sense of morality or my way of imposing a structure on my world. And not really knowing the answer. I never had.

I'd pick that guitar up soon. When order had been imposed.

I smiled ruefully at it.

I dragged my eyes back to the screen and the galaxy of data.

The Le Bernadin barman was hovering by Martinez. He'd opened with breezy, respectful banter, moved on to small talk but was now feeling nothing but awkward for her. Just over an hour before she had arrived early, wearing her best dress and a smile the size of their waiting list. She had perched atop one of the midtown restaurant's bar stools, her near-backless electric-blue dress facing the hungry eyes of the room behind her. She had ordered a martini like she had something to celebrate, the catwalk barman suggesting as much. She'd suppressed a grin of excitement and assured him she had heard a lot about the restaurant.

Three Michelin star tables don't wait for ever. Tables in midtown New York don't wait for ever. Three Michelin star tables *in* midtown are left empty for the amount of time it takes a snow flake to melt in Death Valley. When Byrne was already twenty minutes late Martinez had asked for the menu, so they could order as soon as they sat. The menu made her mouth water, though what ingredients like wasabi, wagyu beef or Hawaiian escolar had to do with French cuisine she had no idea. Not that she cared – she wanted to eat it all. More than all of it as the minutes rolled by.

Martinez had felt a wave of embarrassment after half an hour, knowing that everybody waiting had arrived after her and would know she'd been left hanging. At three-quarters of an hour she could barely look the staff in the face, the bar staff tag-teaming to try and lift her mood. Now the young barman who looked like his every spare minute must have been spent in a hair salon with a set of weights nodded at her empty glass, wondering how he could politely ask whether the table would be being used or not. Because the next person to ask would be the Maitre d'.

'Ma'am?'

But Martinez was watching the clock on her phone reach 10.26 p.m. She held up a finger, indicating he wait for whatever it was that was about to happen.

'Hang on, he's about to beat his personal best.'

She spoke to him without any rancour, a strange calmness about her which he found unusual in stood-up ladies. She lifted up her cell phone from the counter and hit the *call* button.

I was in the middle of writing down the code to my umpteenth algorithm when I heard the vibration from my cell. I'd muted it earlier and was annoyed that it must have slid on to a harder surface than the cushion I'd tossed it on to. I didn't want distractions. I didn't want . . . *Oh hell.*

I snatched the cell phone up, my tablet falling off my lap. 'Jenni.'

I heard nothing but a sigh from the other end. My mind had already done the calculations – I could never get there in time to secure the table. But I was about to be worse than that.

'You're working, aren't you?'

'Oh Jenni . . . I'm so sorry. Are you mad?' Not asked to force her into letting me off the hook, asked because a long time before we'd both learned to get it out in the open quick.

At Le Bernardin Martinez looked at the wall of distorted glass that artfully separated the bar area from the dining area. A wall she would not be walking round tonight. She swilled the last drop of drink in her glass, studying the lipstick marks she'd made around the edge.

'No, I'm not mad, Byrne. I *was* mad. At about quarter to ten, but that was only after I'd been bored, anxious, depressed, amused, followed by a prolonged period of questioning my own sanity.'

'Jenni, I'm sorry.'

'At one stage the waiter thought I was crying but I was actually choking on the olive from my martini. My second martini.'

'Jenni . . .'

But she could sense I wasn't offering to repair the situation.

'It's work, isn't it?'

I forced myself to look away from the projector screen, give her my attention, but I couldn't force myself to lie.

'Sorry. It's the bank murders, I'm doing my bit on it,

you know, looking for any kind of pattern in the numbers. Look . . . Do you mind if we do this another night?'

I waited, waited for the explosion . . . that never came.

'It's OK, Mike, I . . . you know.'

I couldn't believe how she was holding it together, how she was holding back the dam.

'You seem very calm.'

'Feel like you're off the hook?'

I managed a small smile, her humour was staying alive. 'Actually, yeah.' Laughing as I spoke, wondering if I'd made a mistake.

'Look . . . I know the deal. But ring, you son of a bitch.' Spoken in a way that told me all was well with the world. 'Two things, Mr Byrne.'

'Anything.' Me more relieved that she wasn't torn to shreds than at my narrow escape.

'You're going to make this up to me.'

'Like you wouldn't believe.'

'And you're going to pay my bar bill while I see if there's any men available here.'

'How much have you drunk?'

'I'll tell you in the morning. Now pay my bill.'

In the restaurant, Martinez handed her cell phone to the bemused barman who put it tentatively to his ear like a jet of fire was about to burst out of it.

'Hello?'

Then she rattled her empty cocktail glass at another barman. One for the lonely ride home.

16

Doug McCarthy put the phone down. He checked his watch. 9.20 a.m. Late. It bothered him. Everything bothered him since Turlington had gone down to Mexico. The part he played, the things he could have done differently – should have done differently. *Not now* . . . He lifted up his head to look at his team.

'Hey, anybody heard from Excel?'

His team, exhausted from the weekend, hungover from a party in the Meatpacking District the night before, answered in the negative.

They were sat around one long desk, one of dozens in the huge open-plan trading floor of Sovereign Bank. Each trader had a nest of six screens – three above, three below – each displaying the information of their choice, but invariably they all chose the same. Their company's proprietary trading platform, a market news source, a Bloomberg or Reuters market price feed, a live S&P chart, then all the information they could possibly need – and more – about the exact stocks they were following.

The polite young Pole, DB, the keenest to please, answered first, 'Maybe he pulled an all-nighter.'

Ace was unable to help himself. 'Maybe he pulled his cock.' A crack appreciated by all the juniors.

McCarthy was wearing a concerned look that they immediately understood to mean this was no time for locker-room banter. 'Has he emailed anybody the work he did at the weekend?'

The group collectively shook their heads.

'Check your emails and phones. I want to know if he's contacted anybody. And *don't* cover for him. This is too important. I need that report.'

His team swapped uneasy looks before conscientiously looking through their email accounts, each wearing a face they hoped their boss would recognize as proof that they were looking *really* hard. After a minute or so Duke fell back in his chair.

'Oh man, that sucks.' When nobody asked he continued anyway. 'Compliance have said we have to give twenty-four hours' notice to *them* before we take off a trade on our PA accounts.'

All but McCarthy groaned. Cartman, as pissed as Duke, spoke with his mouth full of his second BLT ciabatta roll of the morning. 'We gotta wait a whole *day* before we can take a personal trade off? That's a joke. How the hell can you trade like that?'

FiDi cussed to himself. 'Shi-i-i-t. How's a guy to top up his salary without a bit of side action? Personal trading's the reason I dress so well.' Shooting the cuffs on his Armani suit for emphasis.

McCarthy reared his head towards them. 'Hey, all of you, what have I told you? What have I said?'

There was a silence eventually broken by a sheepish DB. 'Don't get high on your own supply.'

McCarthy stared them all down. '*Don't* get high on your own supply. I don't need any of you worrying about your personal trades when you've got a desk to watch. If you're personally long Cisco and we're short Cisco as a desk how the hell are you going to trade *that* position? You think I want you missing crucial trades for the bank because you're on the phone to *your* broker? Million-dollar trades going AWOL because of your pissy little five hundred dollar PA position? Are you *serious*?' He looked from each to the next to make sure the message had been driven home. 'If you've got such a hot tip share it with the desk, otherwise trade for the bank. Now, why don't we all get our heads down and start buying up some Bank of America.'

Ace was confused. 'We covered our position last week, Louie. I thought we wanted to be flat in that?'

McCarthy checked his screens. 'Not now that they're about to post some unexpectedly strong quarterly numbers.'

The juniors looked at each other slightly bewildered.

'But they haven't made any announcements about that.' As much a question from Ace as a statement.

On a television screen Bloomberg was showing the Opening Bell of the New York Stock Exchange. Almost every screen began to flicker as market numbers began to change at the start of trading – Bank of America's share price ticking up with every passing second.

McCarthy pointed at them then at their keyboards, indicating that they get busy. 'Welcome to Wall Street.'

17

McCarthy was the last to enter. 'Sorry everybody.'

Around the epically long mahogany table – and present on an expansive video-conference screen – were the board of directors of Sovereign Bank as well as the heads of the Bond Division, Global Equities, Treasuries and Currencies. In addition were the head of Compliance, head of Legal, selected heads of desks, a senior PA, the COO, the CEO Anthony Cochran and, next to him, a man people had glimpsed about the building for the past few years and yet who had never wanted to introduce himself or be introduced to anybody. William Webster, the shadowy figure who reported directly to Cochran. His anonymity merely added to a mystique that both he and his boss were happy to cultivate. The rumour was that he was a former government agency man, the agency changing with each conversation. For a while he was ex-FBI before graduating to ex-CIA until the continuing silence led people to conclude he wasn't watching threats outside of the bank but threats within it. At which point gossip moved him to ex-NSA. His gruff manner and seeming disdain for what passed for rank in the organization fed the suspicion and, truth be told, nervousness he generated.

The fifty-year-old Webster was the subject of everyone's discreet attention. It was their first ever really good look at him, and they saw a little something of what he was. Strong muscles, strong features, strong eyes, a small but noticeable scar under the left one. Some looked closer still and saw that the hands also revealed scars big and small. What they couldn't see was that more than one digit on each hand had been broken, to go with the other previously broken bones that the smart dark suit covered up. He was a man whose travels were measured not just in miles but also in experiences. Experiences the least of which would have made every last person in the room shudder with fright. His previous career a world away from their comfort and privilege. Comfort and privilege he had been tasked with the job of protecting.

McCarthy was last in, which meant he could prop himself up against a low-running cupboard if he wanted a seat, which he did. He received that one-second-longer-than-usual look from his colleagues that he'd been getting since the news of Turlington's disappearance in Mexico, the unconfirmed rumours of his death generally believed. Cochran gave him a little hand signal that meant *Don't worry* and continued on.

'. . . So that the meeting we were meant to have today will have to happen next week, after the conference, instead.' Cochran turned to the PA on his right. 'Is there anything else before we move on to the main business, Connie?'

His attractive, ambitious, Chinese-American PA flicked through her pad.

'That's everything.'

'OK.' Cochran looked around the table with the air of a man about to make something of an announcement. 'Ladies, gentlemen, I'd like to introduce you to a man to whom, if he will forgive me, I hoped never to introduce you.'

The CEO indicated the man on his left. Webster did not react, the revelation of his identity a moment of fascination for the assembled staff.

'This is William Webster, our Global Head of Security.'

The tension heightened, and were a person to drop a pin on the table now it would have been heard up and down the room.

It was apparent that the CEO was in a humourless mood, and his brooding manner gave the vast majority a growing sense of paranoia, that the finger of accusation was about to point at them or that a devastating piece of news was about to be revealed. Almost to a person they realized that they hadn't felt this fear since the dark days of the Credit Crunch, when they felt the very building about them could have collapsed, so close was the bank itself to the brink. At that time the staff felt they could be ruined, personally wiped out, if the bank had dropped into the abyss. It wasn't until the storm clouds had dispersed – blown away by the government bailout – that perspective was restored and the staff remembered that the worst that could have happened was that they could face unemployment. The imagined Damoclean sword being just that – imagined. The world did not end, neither did their existences, and, in reality, pay had climbed steadily since the bailouts. So steadily that a nostalgia for those turbulent days was already forming in some breasts as they identified it – correctly – as the upturn in their fortunes. But the fear of the terrible unknown was in the room again today.

Anthony Cochran continued. 'As we are all well aware, a lunatic fringe called Nemesis are carrying out atrocities against bankers around the globe. Whilst we have to hope against hope that it doesn't come to this, it is perfectly natural for us to assume that they might wish to commit their acts of terrorism here in the United States.'

The room was full of very busy people from the highest echelons of the bank – and therefore the banking community – but he had every last cent of their attention.

'But I will allow Mr Webster to explain further. Mr Webster.'

Webster moved slowly, knowing they were rapt with intrigue. But unbeknownst to the assembled crowd he was a little nervous. He'd waited a long time to get in front of them in a situation like this. He'd been patient. He'd been around these money men and women long enough to know that they made their money by being around wealthy people. He was thinking of his retirement and how it all hinged on his performance during this new-found threat. He mustn't put a foot wrong. He had to provide the protection these bankers deserved.

'Gentlemen, ladies, thank you for taking time out of your busy schedules to attend this meeting.' They liked the fact that he was seemingly well educated, well spoken and polite. It played well that his manner was not showy in any way. It was factual in a way that the listener felt that everything had been fact-checked to the nth degree and beyond. Factual like he knew what he was talking about. Which he did. More than anybody in the room would ever know.

'Mr Cochran has asked that I present to you my assessment of the threat level posed by the group known as

Nemesis. I know time is money to you good people so I will keep it brief and I will try to keep it non-technical. The bottom line, to borrow a phrase, is that the threat to Sovereign Bank, whilst remote, is, I regret to say, also very real.'

Something approximating a gasp came to everybody's lips, with the exception of McCarthy and the pre-warned CEO. Webster noted the evenness of McCarthy's manner and was privately intrigued by it. Then he held his hands up in a placatory fashion.

'Now, please remember that no member of the law enforcement community – let alone myself – could ever sit here and say otherwise. On a very simple analysis, bankers are being murdered, you are bankers . . . We can all fill in the blanks.' He paused to allow the undeniable logic to permeate the room and for pulses to slow down slightly. 'So, I *would* say that there is a threat, regardless. But, please remember, getting out of bed doubles your chances of dying every day, so let's put this threat into context. The more important question is, is there any *particular* threat to Sovereign Bank and its employees? To that, I would say that presently there is no reason to think so.'

Again a room-wide reaction. Relief all round.

A sharply dressed African-American banker raised his hand but didn't wait to be invited to speak.

'What about Turlington? How can we ignore that?'

There were as many reactions as there were people in the room. Many curious, many considering the question inappropriate, with Cochran the CEO and McCarthy staring venomously at the banker. Webster's demeanour was calm but no-nonsense.

'I will only comment on this once. What happened to Simon Turlington was an isolated incident totally unrelated to events unfolding around us in New York. As you will know all meetings on Mexican soil have been suspended until further notice until we can assure your safety in doing business there.'

Cochran coughed slightly. 'No more need be said on that matter.'

The African-American banker tugged his suit jacket into place, despite it already sitting perfectly. He understood the rebuke but didn't like it.

The Human Resources Director, a nervous-looking middle-aged woman, could not keep a lid on it any longer. 'Excuse me, sir?'

The CEO's brow furrowed in displeasure, but Webster invited her to continue with a wave of his hand. 'Sure.'

'Is there anything we can do, you know, to keep ourselves safe?'

There was a collective nod of interest since she had spoken for almost everyone. Webster caught McCarthy's continuing implacability out the corner of his eye. The Head of Global Security considered his reply. Personal safety? What was the point in telling the truth? What was the point in reminding them that the bank murders were almost all committed at a distance, professional hits that they would have about as much chance of surviving as a mouse thrown into the snake enclosure at Brooklyn zoo. If Nemesis wanted these people dead then dead they would be. Even Mr Cool, Calm and Collected leaning against the furniture by the door. Even him. But what was the point in saying that?

'Just go about your normal business and, at this juncture, trust the various law enforcement agencies to do their best by you. I have instructed security around this and all other Sovereign buildings to be raised as a precautionary measure.'

People accepted the report stoically, along with the very human desire for a more emphatic reassurance from their newly introduced security chief. Then McCarthy raised a finger, to which Webster nodded his assent.

'Mr Webster, Doug McCarthy.'

'Mr McCarthy.'

'It seems a bit, erm, strange with all our resources to just play patsy whilst we wait for these Nemesis – or whatever the hell they call themselves – to come after us. Isn't there anything proactive the banking community can do?'

Webster took the question in his stride. 'Sure there is.'

A mood of interest, optimism almost, swept the room as people's antennae switched to a new hope, a new way through this situation.

Webster looked around at the assembled crowd and spoke very steadily. 'We hire some mercenaries to hunt down every last one of these sons of bitches and put a bullet in the back of their heads.'

A silence hit the room with the immediacy of a light being switched off, almost sweeping the very air out with it. People's stares went from Webster to each other with a slowly rising alarm at how this situation could turn out.

Then Webster's mouth broke into a smile and he laughed lightly. 'Just joshing. The report I've written for Mr Cochran includes a number of recommendations which I believe are to be circulated to all bank employees.

The truth is that, statistically, we're all at more danger from domestic hand guns or road deaths than we are from Al Qaida, let alone these upstart Nemesis folk. Putting this in perspective is as important as preparing against it. If you want my honest advice, lobbying the Mayor and your local congress representative to increase spending on law enforcement is probably the most proactive thing you can do about this and any lunatic outfit.'

The CEO felt the moment was right to wrap it up. 'Well, there we have it. A copy of Mr Webster's report will be sent to you today. Now unless there is anything else to add . . . ?'

McCarthy spoke. 'There is one precaution I've already taken.'

The room paused for his contribution, nobody's interest piqued more than Webster's.

Cochran looked at him, worried that this ex-Air Force officer may have gotten all alpha-male and gung-ho on them. 'And what is that, Doug?'

'I'm short all the banks. Any of their share prices plummet we stand to make a tidy profit. If there's going to be a killing we might as well make one.'

The room's response to his ruthless profiteering was divided. Half of them impressed, amused, the other half finding his candidness distasteful. Their no-nonsense star equities trader choosing his moment as ever.

'And on that note . . .' The CEO stood, not reacting to McCarthy's contribution, but secretly pleased at his unabashed treatment of the opportunity. The meeting started to break up.

Even though McCarthy was nearest the door he moved

against those filing out towards Webster, still standing by his chair. McCarthy put his hand out and they shook.

'Thank you for that, Mr Webster.' Two men with military backgrounds instinctively treating each other as so.

The security chief nodded at him, and his face tightened. 'I meant to get together with you. I wanted to apologize about Simon Turlington.'

McCarthy felt the room close in about him. 'Ah, it's not you who needs to apologize, I should never have let him . . .' But not knowing what to say or how.

Webster shook his head dismissively. 'Look, don't blame yourself one bit. Nobody could have known that it was going to happen. It was meant to be a routine meeting with a prospective client. He wasn't even in a dangerous part of Mexico. He was kidnapped. It's me who should be apologizing to you.'

'Then you have nothing to apologize for, either.' McCarthy not wanting to admit the partial relief the pardon made him feel.

The ex-CIA man shook his head again, only this time ruefully. 'No. My job is to pre-empt the unexpected and above all protect you all. I failed on both accounts.' Then he locked on to McCarthy's eyes with an earnest gaze. 'But trust me, I'll find the people who did this.'

The banker would normally have dismissed such a remark as so much bravado but Webster's face seemed to quell such scepticism.

McCarthy began to feel slightly awkward. 'I was wondering if you had a card?'

Webster reached inside his jacket and retrieved his wallet. 'Sure.'

The security chief handed him a modest card with his name, number and email details. McCarthy flicked the card between his fingers.

'Gotta get back to the desk but maybe I'll give you a call.'

'Sure, anytime, Mr McCarthy.'

A polite smile and McCarthy was the last bank employee to leave.

Webster watched him go, watched him walk along the corridor and out of sight. Knowing he'd call. Knowing he'd call before he'd even walked into the room today. And knew one thing for absolutely certain: McCarthy was walking towards a whole mess of trouble.

18

He looked at me. What was left of him. He faced me but I couldn't face him. A picture of hell. Jesus wept.

I woke with a start – my phone was ringing.

My cell phone. In the semi-dark.

Night time? No.

Oh I hated that. My living room. I'd fallen asleep. When? My mind catching up with me. Sometime after six in the morning. What time was it? I pulled the ringing cell up to my face and looked through bleary eyes. 10.23.

I put it to my ear. 'Yup?'

An unimpressed sigh came down the phone. 'You didn't go to bed did you?'

'I went to sleep.'

Martinez not buying it. 'On the couch?'

'The bed's not the same without you in it.' Said rather flatly, I had to admit.

She laughed disbelievingly. 'Oh, you're good, Byrne, you're *good*. I can't believe you would try to sell me that line of bullshit.'

I looked around myself: the tall windows virtually blacked out by blinds, my computer tablet on the couch beside me, its display still projected on to the white wall opposite, too bright to look at right now.

'You there?'

I needed a coffee. I got up off the couch and crossed

the room to the kitchen area to the island, talking to her as I organized a drink. 'Yep, I'm here. Sorry, waking up.'

A faux-sulky tone intruded into her voice. 'Oh, I told you to let me come round and make you breakfast. I could have made you bacon and eggs. You know, once I'd beaten you senseless for standing me up last night.' I could hear the smile in her voice.

'Yeah, I'm . . .'

'Hey, I'm the one who should feel bad – it wasn't you who went home with a waiter.'

'So the night wasn't a complete washout.' Relieved that she really wasn't holding it against me.

'Oh, that reminds me, I should wash those sheets after what we did. Oh, and the throw on the couch, and the kitchen counter, and –'

'*Jenni Damita Tierra Rosa Martinez.*'

We only used each other's first names in times of intimacy. We only used each other's full names when the other one had crossed the line from good taste into . . . I was rewarded down the line with one of Martinez's trademark laughs – the filthiest of any twentysomething in the whole of New York.

'Jesus, Martinez, shouldn't you be catching bad guys someplace?'

'Talking of which, did *you* catch the bad guys?'

I took advantage of the pause to turn on the coffee grinder which complained loudly as it decimated the beans I'd poured into it. I stopped it and continued with the all-important task of making a hot caffeine-based drink.

'No. Treasury sent over tens of thousands of trading

records – including the recent bank victims in London, Frankfurt, Tokyo and Hong Kong – but nothing.'

'I don't understand how you can read those things. It must be like sifting through grains of sand on a beach.'

I put the coffee pot on to the stove and lit the gas under it. 'I don't read them, I just send algorithms over them. You know, ask it to look for certain patterns. Like, were all the dead bankers trading the same thing, the same time, the same way? You know.'

'I see. So the result's only as good as the question?'

I paused my search for a coffee cup underneath the island to give her my full attention. 'You know, if your brain was as smart as your ass you could do well in the NYPD.'

We sat on the phone silently for a moment. Both knowing we had to get on with our days.

'I . . .'

'Look . . .'

Talking over each other. I pushed ahead.

'Look, I gotta get on.'

'OK. Speak to you later.'

'Speak to you –'

'Oh, Byrne.'

'What?'

'Don't forget your appointment with the counsellor.'

'What –? How did you . . . ?'

But she'd ended the call. I ran over how the hell she would know about the counselling session Diane had booked for me, how the . . . Then I realized. I turned round and saw the business card on the kitchen island where I'd left it two nights before. She had a key to my place, she must have been round since I'd gotten back from Mexico. She'd seen it and not said anything. She'd been *round* and not said anything. Somehow I was irked at myself for leaving the details of the appointment lying around. Revealing too much about myself? One insight too many? I smiled at my pettiness. One for the therapist. I picked the card up. An appointment for 11.30 this morning. Good. I'd hate to have slept through it and missed it accidentally instead of this way – on purpose. The coffee kettle started boiling behind me. I turned and pulled a thin white mug up next to it in anticipation. The coffee brewing. My mind percolating. *What the hell was the connection between the dead bankers?* Wondering how long I had left before it happened again.

Because it was going to happen.

Somebody else was going to get killed by Nemesis. Here in New York.

Excel's apartment was immaculate. Any untidiness had been banished and cleaned along with every surface by Alecto over the weekend. She surveyed her work with quiet satisfaction, the space much more acceptable to her now. Even the bloodstains had come out of the linoleum with some hard scrubbing. Everything was orderly. Much better, much better this way.

Alecto crossed over to the computer and opened the web browser. She chose Options then History. Only one website was listed. *The Xia Chronicles*. She deleted the browsing history then went into Settings and selected for the history to be deleted whenever the browser was exited.

This done, she logged off the machine.

It was time.

I stepped out of my wet-room and wrapped a large white towel around myself. Coffee and a shower had done the trick. I was running over the different angles I could approach the trading data from as I stepped into my walk-in closet to look for some fresh clothes – jeans, white shirt, smart leather jacket. Like somebody doing a cross-word it was my early wrong answers that kept coming back to me. The dead ends and false starts repeating themselves, blocking any attempt at fresh thinking. *Nemesis* . . . Would they give themselves away with their choice of victims? Was there even a pattern to look for or was I trying to link up random events arbitrarily? Maybe there was nothing to find. But looking was better than nothing. And nothing was all I had right now.

Alecto pulled on a black skiing jacket she had found in the dead banker's bedroom closet. Slightly large but not overly so. As she stood by the apartment door looking at herself in the nearby full-length mirror she thought it was perfect for a cold February day. Perfect for hiding the long, thin, heavy sack around her neck. She checked herself in the full-length mirror by the entrance. Perfect. Right up to the fake auburn hair.

She slipped her iPod on and pressed PLAY. Radiohead's 'Everything In The Right Place' hummed into life, its hypnotic synthesizer rhythm transporting her thousands of miles away to a foreign desert to when she was happy.

*

I refilled my coffee mug and took it back to the couch where I placed it on the circular redwood coffee table. I sat forward on my seat and looked up at the screen. Spreadsheets. Thousands of them. *Where to begin?* I had to clear my mind. *Think visual.* I tapped the computer tablet a few times and the picture on the screen switched to a map of the world with a photograph of each of the victims by their geographical locations. London, Frankfurt, Tokyo, Hong Kong . . . Looking for the connection. Why were they Nemesis's nemesis? London, Frankfurt, Tokyo, Hong Kong . . . A taxi, a nightclub, a restaurant, a street . . . And all of the cities big markets, leading markets, but the traders killed: bond traders, currency, derivatives, rarely trading the same thing, no historical or corporate connection, no nothing. Maybe the answer wasn't here, maybe it was in their spending habits, their affiliations, their personal histories, their *something else.* Maybe it was completely random. In fact, why the hell not? Society wasn't trying to discriminate between being angry at the bankers who'd gamed the system and those that hadn't, why should the killers? Maybe the reason I was barking up the wrong tree was because there was no tree. Maybe, maybe.

I took another gulp of my coffee, almost managing a smile at the thought that the reason behind Nemesis's choice of victims was all Greek to me. Ancient Greek . . . Oh Jesus. I was rambling to myself. They talk about snow blindness, what about investigation blindness? Me going round in circles. Me wasting time – mine and everybody else's – when there were killers on the loose. Wasting time. Precious, precious time.

*

Alecto was eating a McDonald's breakfast as she walked along, the brown paper bag screwed up in her left hand. She stopped at the north end of Columbus Park and consulted a map. She ran her finger along the route again, looking up to double-check the landmarks. Worth Street, Centre Street, Park Row, Broadway. Almost there. She hadn't needed to consult the map. She could have walked this route in the dark, blindfolded for good measure. She wanted to be able to look around herself with an air of innocence. Wanted to see if anybody was watching her. They weren't.

She put the map back inside her pocket and looked for a trash can for her food bag. There was a can at the intersection of some pathways. She crossed over and dropped the ball of paper into it. Everything in its right place.

I drained the cup of coffee, the flavour I craved somehow tasting bitter with my mental block. Nemesis, bringer of dues, punishing undeserved fortunes. Punishing bankers . . .

I rose from the couch, exasperated at my lack of progress. I would go into the office and tell Diane I had nothing, the other agencies would have to solve this, it wasn't one for the Market Abuse Task Force. I put my coffee mug in the island sink and ran some water into it. I pulled open a cupboard under the sink where the trash was kept and tossed the counsellor's appointment card into it. I checked my watch. 11.31. Couldn't make the session now if I tried. I smiled bleakly as I closed the cupboard. Somehow realizing that it wasn't until this moment that I knew for certain I wasn't going.

*

Alecto mounted the stairs silently. The stairwell was for emergency use only, and she had it to herself. She had pulled off the iPod and was wrapping the headphones around it as she climbed the building. She undid the padded jacket as the exercise heated her up, slipped the iPod into the inside pocket, zipped the pocket closed. Making sure of everything.

The American. 'Are you here to take me home?'
　　The memory haunting me day and night.
　　Punishing me for my undeserved fortune.
　　The fortune to be alive.
　　I shook my head.
　　I cupped a hand under the running water and rubbed it over my face. I felt better. Then I felt worse. What was I washing away? The young banker I'd let down? My obsessions? My sins? Jesus, maybe I did need to see a counsellor. See what she thought of my being alive, my undeserved fortune.
　　Undeserved.
　　Un-deserved.
　　Not deserved. Not earned. *Un*deserved.
　　Something, some synapses pulling two ideas together –
　　Undeserved.
　　Just a moment.
　　Undeserved.
　　It was there in front of me.
　　Undeserved. Undeserv*ing*.
　　I stared into the sink as the water drained over the edge of the cup, worried that my train of thought would drain away with it. Wall Street . . . Bankers . . . Traders . . . That's

what Nemesis was thinking. That was it . . . That was it: some bankers *were* more undeserving than others.

I looked up at the projection on my far wall. A map of the world, the victims' faces by the cities they died in. Wealthy men. Wealthy men who had come by great fortunes. Great fortunes that were seen by Nemesis as excessive, extravagant, but most of all *undeserved*. Fortunes that had seen retribution visited upon them because, because, *because* . . .

That was it.

I could stop it. I could stop the killings. I could predict the bankers in danger –

The simple algorithm I was going to use sprang fully formed into my mind as I dashed towards the computer tablet . . .

Alecto crouched behind the low wall running around the roof of the building. A grey sky keeping the air wet and chilled. A thin, long sack sat between her knees. She held a half-finished rifle in her hand as she screwed the barrel on to the muzzle of the gun.

Everything in its right place.

The dead traders, each and every one of them, had had a terrible losing year. At some time or another in their careers they had lost *millions*. All of them had lost more than they had ever earned for their banks. If it was their own money they were using they would have been personally ruined, wiped out. But the bonus system of banks was such that they had all taken millions off the table all the same. They had made themselves millionaires

— *multimillionaires* — but had lost their banks *way more* than that. Only in banking could that happen. By any normal standard it was outrageous, fine, OK. But somebody, some people — *Nemesis* — were so outraged that they were killing. But why? Killing out of anger? Killing to make a point? Killing to punish? Killing for killing's sake? Damn it.

I grabbed my cell phone.

Alecto tucked the butt of the rifle into her shoulder. She looked through the lens and hummed to herself. Hummed the Radiohead tune as she scanned the bank down below. Hummed as she thought about the bullet. Hummed as she thought about the bullet being in the right place. Not in her rifle but in a banker's skull. Everything . . .

Special Agent Diane Mason was in conference with two of her juniors when her desk phone began. She glanced at the incoming number, not inclined to pick it up — but changing that inclination when she saw who it was. She held a hand up to her staff and plucked up the phone.

'Diane, it's Mike. I know why they're killing them.'

'Michael . . .'

'Diane, it's their trading records. These traders are net trading losers but net earnings winners. It's revenge, it's a punishment for their undeserved fortunes.'

'Michael.'

'What, Diane?'

Diane's head sank forward as she spoke. 'It's too late.'

The subway train doors slid closed on the auburn woman in the black ski jacket. She had heard the police cars screaming into action. Had heard the uniformed officers in the street alerting each other, events moving too fast to stop her progress up Broadway to Fulton Street subway station, where she had disappeared underground. Away from the panic. Away from the man lying dead on his desk, blood forming a pool around the silver frame containing the picture of his happiest memory from his time on earth. Away from everything.

19

'There's been a shooting! I just got a call from my friend over at Phili National, somebody's been shot!'

Even before the words had left Duke's mouth the mood had changed violently on the trading floor. Suddenly voices were raised to shouting level, shock and worry battling with the need to attack the markets; phones began ringing off the hooks; people were pointing at television screens; employees were entering the room and asking, apprehensively, 'Have you heard the news?' or being pointed in the direction of the live news broadcasts, every network clearing the schedules for the story they had wanted to break for the last week, to breathlessly cover the moment it reached the United States.

Duke and the other junior traders on the desk looked up at the television, trying to gauge how close the threat was, but somehow more excited than nervous. Ace changed over to Fox News. A blonde reporter, with plastic good looks, was at the bottom of the steps leading up to Philadelphia National's Broadway offices, her urgent body language somewhere between Oscars night and a war-zone.

Fear was stalking Wall Street. Fear . . . and Greed.

Ace looked to McCarthy to see if he would mind if they turned the sound up, but his boss was in another world. McCarthy was staring around his screens like a jet pilot in a dog fight, a phone hanging from the crook of each shoulder, furiously typing into his keyboard as he pulled up new data to inform his decisions. His eyes shifting from one set of incoming data to another across his six monitors. He lifted one of the phones to his mouth.

'John, I'll buy twenty at forty-two and a half. OK, done.' He switched to the other phone. 'Susan, am I filled on that order yet? I'll have another million at five cents lower . . . Trust me, Susan, it's going lower.'

He punched a button on the trading board that connected his phone directly to everybody he gave a damn about in the markets.

'Gustav, work an order to buy back the whole position at this price . . . No, Gustav, I don't want cute, I want to get filled. The whole position, OK? Good.'

McCarthy's team watched on, unsure how to act. Their boss's feverish activity told them they should not be standing around shooting the breeze but somehow emulating his example. Only he was working at an altitude none of them could touch. At this point in their careers they wouldn't know where to start. McCarthy continued inputting data, trading on the screens, impervious to life in the office around him, travelling at a speed his colleagues could only dream about, a supersonic trader watching the markets with an eagle eye, spotting the changes across the banking sector as he jumped from one stock to another. His phone rang again, McCarthy slamming it up off the cradle with the heel of his hand.

'Gustav? . . . Completely? Well done. *Very* well done.'

He scanned the various market numbers appearing on screens with satisfaction. 'I saw you get in ahead of everyone there – drinks are on me next time I'm in Chicago . . . No, there are no good bars on the north side.' Grinning at his own joke, at the money he had just made.

He put the phone back and sat back, his work affording him a respite. He saw his team watching him. Rather blankly he thought.

'What have you been doing since the news broke?'

His juniors stammered incomplete responses. He answered for them.

'Talking shit. And what have I been doing?'

FiDi the first to say it. 'Trading.'

McCarthy rose slowly and stood at his desk, considering them all. 'Terrorist attacks are goddamn golden opportunities to make money. How much money – to the dollar – have you made since the news broke?' Staring at each of them, nobody saying the obvious.

'What are you going to do next time somebody gets attacked?'

DB now. 'Be ready to trade.'

McCarthy pointed a rigid finger across the desk at the young Pole, in a *listen to that* manner. 'Be ready to trade. This is like picking dollar bills up off the street. If you can't make money off news like this you can't make money full stop. Have I made myself clear?'

All of them. 'Crystal.' His preferred response from them.

They all stood at their desks, waiting for McCarthy's lead, maybe a hint about the trading he'd just done. A mousy-looking young girl approached them, slightly uneasy with her task. She saw they had the news on and misread their current poses as ones of shock.

'I guess you all heard the news about Phili National?'

McCarthy turned his head slowly in her direction, stretching it unnaturally. 'What is it you want, Katie?'

She was back office, and traders hated back office. They only ever approached you to take up your time and, in traders' minds, time was money. Back office were admin, data-monkeys, the lowest of the low, lower than the caterers down in the cafeteria, lower than the Mexicans who cleaned their offices in the morning, lower than the people on *Main Street* for God's sake. At least you had to credit the people from Main Street as having the dignity to *not* work in back office.

'D-d-d-d-did you have that trading r-r-r-report for the board, Doug?' A stammer brought on at times of stress.

'No, Katie.' McCarthy unabashed about his mocking. 'So why don't you f-f-f-f-f . . .' Her eyes widening at his expected aggression. '. . . Forget about it and I'll send it over when it's ready.'

She went to speak but then, quite correctly, thought better of it. With a very closed mouth she turned on her heel and left.

McCarthy's brow creased and an anxiety crept over him. 'Hey, has Excel called in yet?'

DB's face brightened a little. 'No, but he emailed to say he had food poisoning and expects to be in tomorrow.'

McCarthy's face screwed up like a bad smell had filled his nose. 'Emailed? Doesn't he know to call in?' There was a muted wince from his team, but he softened a little, on them at least, remembering there had been a shooting, after all. 'DB, keep ringing him until he picks up, will you. I want him to tell *me* that he's not coming in – and I don't want any goddamn emails.'

'Yes, Louie.'

McCarthy looked up at the news. 'Turn it up.'

Ace did so, and they heard the agitated reporter describing to viewers what they could see with their own eyes.

'. . . Police coming and going, as well as paramedics attending to his shocked colleagues. As you can see, the police have stopped us going beyond this point, but the bank has promised to make a statement in the next hour. Judy, I have to tell you that the mood here in Lower Manhattan is one of panic with everybody I've spoken to asking themselves, "Could I be next?"'

McCarthy shook his head at Ace, who muted the coverage. He looked at his team. 'Any of you feeling panicky?'

His nonplussed juniors shook their heads.

'No.'

'Not at all.'

'Why?'

McCarthy could see they weren't. Edgy maybe, excited, but panic was the media's word, not theirs. He nodded slowly to himself as he thought about something. Then looked at them until they were all looking at him.

'Remember what I asked you? Whether you'd be prepared to step up if this all kicked off?'

They all remembered back to the bar in the Catskills, all grunted in the affirmative.

'Well, would you?'

They were very still. The other desks around them were moving, trading, talking about the news. But not

McCarthy's. They stood stock still, considering each other. Considering what he had just asked. Because he was deadly serious. Then, one by one, earnestly:

'Sure.'

'Definitely.'

'Bring it on.'

'Boo-yah.'

'Yep.'

McCarthy said nothing but nodded again, like this was all he had wanted to know.

He looked at his keyboard. Sticking out behind the top row of function keys was William Webster's card. McCarthy picked up the security chief's details then the phone. He went to dial. Went to dial then stopped. Stopped, thought about it and thought better of it. His head said yes, there could be a way to use this guy. But his gut said no. His head said yes, his gut said no. Instead he dropped the business card into his shirt pocket. As always, McCarthy went with his gut.

20

Ashby and Martinez both exited the Ford Mustang together then took in the scene on Broadway. It was like somebody had ordered everyone in uniform out on to the streets of Lower Manhattan. Police officers, dog units, SWAT teams, the FBI, everybody was here, patrolling the street, setting up police barriers, organizing around large, imposing armoured vehicles. More police than regular citizens. The only presence giving law enforcement a run for its money was the media. The area was swarming with film crews and journalists from around the world trying to interview cops, witnesses – anyone. Those not giving forth panting reports into cameras were busy trying to wriggle through the impromptu police barriers going up.

'Mother Mary, Martinez. It's the whole nine yards down here.'

Her head was almost spinning from the police presence. 'The only people missing are the Home Guard and I hear the Mayor asked for them.'

Ashby looked from the street and up along the skyline. 'No snipers yet. There will be.'

They looked about themselves, acclimatizing themselves almost. Both of them shaking their heads at the sight, Ashby more annoyed than impressed. 'Shit, the FBI will want to run this show now, just you see.'

'Life's a bitch, Ashby, suck it up.'

Ashby caught the tough tone but wasn't fooled. They'd been partners for over seven years and he knew what she did to get through the day. And today she was fortifying herself against the coldest icy chill of all. Love.

'You seen Byrne yet?'

She shrugged then looked away at the army of different agencies and media people. 'Nah, he's been busy.'

Ashby wasn't about to argue with that. 'Man's got his hands full chasing after these bad guys. It's not like the terrorists take days off, is it?'

Martinez gestured phlegmatically with her hands. 'Hey, I've only got myself to blame. I always said I wouldn't date a cop, right.'

'He's not a cop.'

'OK, a super-cop or whatever the hell he is.' Strapping on a smile that fooled nobody including herself while she said it.

Ashby reached into the back of his car and pulled out his brown leather jacket to wear in the February cold. 'Uh-huh. Well, just be careful, that's all I'm saying.'

Martinez pulled her long dark hair off her shoulders and round the back of her head. 'Careful? Why?'

'Your mood. It seems to be tied to how much you get to see Byrne these days.'

'That's –'

'Bullshit? Marti, you're like a puppy in a dog pound whenever he's away.'

'That's not –'

'Fair? That's what you were like when he was away for a few *days*. Think about it, Marti, what he does, it's not a regular job.'

'I know.'

'It's dangerous.'

Martinez, eyes down, hating being chided. 'I know.'

'What's your mood gonna be like if it doesn't work out?'

She stood her ground now. 'You know me, I'll deal with it. I'll be pissed off for a while and move on – like always.'

Ashby reached behind his car seat and brought out his police pistol. He checked his mood, wanting to make sure he didn't come across as mean spirited with the next thing. He slid his gun into his shoulder holster then flicked a look around what was going on about them.

'I meant, what if it doesn't work out for him?'

21

His handshake was firm, too firm. The handshake of a man who'd practised it, worried about it and measured it for its impact on the other person. A handshake that tried to say something before anything had been said. He needn't have worried. The Guggenheimesque entrance to the bank's headquarters, the original artworks hung along every white space I had passed, the hushed tones of his team of staff, the PA (to his PA) bringing me upstairs to meet the *actual* PA, who then personally took me along the corridor bedecked with photographs of the CEO meeting anybody who was anybody – in the world of money. The CEO needing not just a glory wall but a glory *avenue* to make his point. That the head of the bank barely topped five feet in his shoes hardly surprised me – nor that he probably wore lifts. I left it to him to worry about the twelve plus inches difference between us.

The Sovereign Bank CEO invited me to sit on the couch opposite his own in his opulent office atop the bank's skyscraper on Vesey Street, one block from the New York Stock Exchange. I took in the room. Capacious was one word for it. One polite word for it. Anthony Cochran must have caught my thinking.

'Nice isn't it? I'm the second to occupy this office and, before you ask, I haven't spent one dollar of the bank's money redecorating it.' Probably a reference to the former

Merrill Lynch boss, Jon Thain, who spent $1.22 million on his office during the dark days of the Credit Crunch. Over $87,000 on a new rug, over $18,000 on a George IV chair, over $1,400 on a wastepaper basket – the irony of the word 'waste' clearly lost on him – as well as over $35,000 on a toilet, exactly when his bank was going down it. I smiled a noncommittal smile and glanced around at the original Picassos and original Art Deco furniture and silk rugs from who knew where. It felt like a slightly chintzy Beverly Hills hotel. This guy may not have spent the bank's money on it but somebody sure had.

'So, what can I do for you Mr . . . ?' He paused as if he had to retrieve my name from his memory. Possibly he'd forgotten it. Possibly he was trying the old sales trick of taking you down a peg or two by suggesting you weren't exactly memorable. 'Mr Byrne, sorry. Special Agent Diane Mason was most insistent that I take this meeting myself when she called.'

'We just wanted to give you the chance to handle a situation that has arisen in your own way, Mr Cochran.'

'Fine. But, may I insert a clause into this meeting?'

I nodded by way of assent.

'If this discussion strays on to the matter of any particular clients then the meeting is over.'

'Is that a reference to Mr Lazcano?'

The Sovereign Bank CEO's face became slightly taut before he reasserted himself. 'It's a reference to any client.'

'What about the young banker I found in Mexico, Simon Turlington? Can we talk about him? Can we talk about the condition I found him in?'

His face seemed to freeze, Cochran offended, almost.

He wasn't prepared to take this off me, or maybe anybody. He took a moment to collect himself.

'If you insist on talking about this matter I will ask you to leave.'

'Can I speak to his secretary?'

'He didn't have one, but the matter is closed.'

He stared at me with the sole intention of letting me know it was strike two. One more and I was out. But I'd had a lot of requests for meetings knocked back by this man and I was intent on using it to the max. That he didn't have a secretary . . . that was interesting to me.

'OK, Mr Cochran. But you know there can only be two outcomes to this Mexican affair, don't you.'

'And what would they be?'

'Either I will have your bank – and its executives – indicted before a grand jury for money laundering. Or you'll be killed by your customer.'

He bridled at my last remark. 'Any business we trans-acted with Lazcano was with his legitimate business interests. We would never go near so-called drug money, and it is mischief-making of the lowest order to suggest otherwise. We have nothing to hide.' Blurting it out despite his self-imposed embargo on the subject.

'Everybody's got something to hide, Mr Cochran. By my reckoning this bank has transferred almost $400 billion into dollar accounts from Mexican *casas de cambio*. You think because it comes through their currency houses that it's clean?'

'It is public knowledge that Sovereign Bank has since tightened its anti-laundering procedures in light of some unfortunate lapses.'

His tone less sure now, given that the US district court in Miami was about to slap a multi-million dollar fine on his bank for that one. A fraction of the profits made. Nothing more than the price of doing business. It was like asking a burglar to give back half the goods and promise to not do it again. Where was the deterrent?

'In the absence of any proof, Mr Byrne, I think it unfair and unwise to label all monies of Mexican origin as drug-related. It's rather an insult to our Hispanic community, don't you think?'

'It's rather an insult to the people who suffer at the hands of the Mexican drug cartels that you facilitate their activities. It'll be indictment or death. Take my word.'

He went to speak but was in two minds as to whether or what to say. Good. I wanted to shake him up, but you didn't become the CEO of a Wall Street bank without a little backbone.

'I'd have to be a careless man to let either of those things happen, Mr Byrne.'

'In my experience, you only have to be careless once.'

He sat staring at me, indignant that I would say all this but knowing I was right. He took his time collecting his mood, losing control not something he was prepared to do in front of me, it would appear.

'I'm a careful man, Mr Byrne.'

I glanced up at one of the Picassos hanging on the wall. A woman in harsh, unnatural colours made out of geometrical shapes, biting her fingers, tears popping out of her eyes. Brilliant. I could have stared at it all day and still not understood it. Maybe there was lots to it, maybe what you saw was what you got. Which one was this CEO?

'Does that explain the beefed-up security that met me downstairs?'

He smiled like he'd been expecting that. 'That's in response to the raised threat to all staff in the banking community, Mr Byrne.'

But that smile, a flicker of nervousness behind it? Or was I just looking for evidence to reinforce my own theories? Either way, I answered with a questioning look. His impatience with me and at the use of his time was rising. As I'd intended.

'From these psychopaths running around the world shooting people.'

Like I was slow to get it. 'Oh, Nemesis.'

He dismissed the name – and them – with a wave of his hand. 'Well, whatever they're called, how are the law enforcement agencies getting on with their job of protecting us from them?'

He flashed a sardonic smile at me.

'Well, whatever they're called, Mr Cochran, they're the real reason for my visit here today.'

'So we come to it. And what is that reason?'

'You're on their list. You're one of their next targets.'

He stopped. Stopped what he was about to say. Stopped in his tracks. Stopped and tried to make sense of what I had just said. Most people would have wanted to know more immediately, get me to explain myself, tell them everything. But not Cochran. He was juggling my statement with other thoughts, other information.

'You seem, very certain, Mr Byrne.'

'You seem very relaxed, Mr Cochran.'

'I'm trying to establish the facts. You said Nemesis

would target us. That's quite a statement, Mr Byrne. Would you care to . . .'

There was a knock at the door. Cochran's Chinese-American PA stepped in. 'Douglas McCarthy to see you, sir.'

Cochran hadn't been expecting this. 'Connie, we're busy at the moment.'

I rose to meet him. 'Actually, Mr Cochran, it concerns Mr McCarthy. I invited him.'

Cochran was now more confused than ever. 'Well, then, send him in, Connie.' Less than pleased that I would set the agenda.

She smiled a hesitant smile, unsure if she had done the right thing or not as Douglas McCarthy stepped into the room, and left us to it. McCarthy was slightly shorter than me and well built. Gym fit, not basic training fit, not US Air Force fit. He was jacketless, his shirt sleeves rolled up. A man in the habit of getting things done. I shook hands with him.

'Mike Byrne, United States Secret Service, Markets Abuse Task Force division.'

'Doug McCarthy.' He looked at both of us, waiting for the bombshell. 'Am I under investigation here?'

Cochran gave a small, bitter laugh and spoke like that would have been an upturn in their fortunes. 'Christ, no, Doug. Take a seat.'

McCarthy, confused, joined his boss on his couch as I sat down on the one opposite.

'Mr Byrne here was just telling me that he believes Sovereign Bank will be targeted by Nemesis.'

McCarthy looked from me to Cochran and back

again, staggered by the news, amazed at Cochran's casualness. 'How do you know? Has there been an arrest? A tip-off?'

I shook my head. 'There's been a pattern.'

'What pattern would that be, Mr Byrne?' Cochran was treating it like a business problem. Understand it, then understand what you could do about it.

'It is my belief . . .'

'Belief, Mr Byrne?'

I smiled at his need for intellectual posturing. 'It is my analysis which suggests that Nemesis have been targeting individuals who, whilst personally enriched from their banking careers, have been net losers for the banks they have worked for.'

Cochran was incredulous. 'But that's insane. Finance is *filled* with people like that.'

However, the slightly sickened look on McCarthy's face told me that his conscience was fully alive to the situation. I decided to turn the screw.

'Have you had any big losses, Mr McCarthy?'

He reddened as he spoke, a mixture of shame and anger. 'You tell me, you're the one doing the analysing.'

I laid it out for both of them. 'Lehman Brothers, 2008. You had one of the biggest positions in the market when the Treasury let it go pop. You were holding a whole bunch of swaps that said it wouldn't.'

Cochran almost leaped off the couch, clearly still smarting from the incident. 'That was bad economics, Byrne. That was done to spite Dick Fuld, it was a dumb play all round. No Treasury Secretary in his right mind should have let it happen.'

I continued to look at McCarthy. 'Or so Mr McCarthy gambled, anyway.'

The former fighter pilot wasn't going to take that lying down either. 'Mr Byrne, the collapse of Lehman Brothers was totally unprecedented, nobody could have predicted it.'

The angrier he got, the calmer I wanted him to think I was. 'Really? Nobody could have predicted it? *Nobody* took the other side of your trade?'

He went to speak, but words failed him. If he was using derivatives to bet Lehman Brothers was going up somebody had to be using them to bet it was going down. Somebody was as right about it as he had been wrong about it. It's the bit market commentators and hedge fund managers and bankers forget to add when they say, 'Nobody could have seen it coming.' Somebody always does and somebody always makes a packet out of other people's mistakes. Popes and bankers, infallible both. McCarthy glared at me like throwing a punch was the only comeback he was interested in.

Cochran was back to business. 'Are you saying, Mr Byrne, that Doug is in real, *actual*, danger?'

I looked at the trader. 'Mr McCarthy, I understand you commute from Florida in your own private plane every week, is that correct?'

'Yeah.' McCarthy cooling his heels slightly.

'An old Mustang, am I right?'

McCarthy was secretly pleased that I knew about it. Secretly very pleased. 'Yeah, that's right. The Cavalier, it's a modified version. They're quite affordable, I mean, by Lear Jet standards. I saw one advertised on eBay recently.'

I smiled, indulging his small talk. 'Well, my advice to

you, Mr McCarthy, would be to get in that plane and fly as far away from Wall Street as possible.'

'*What?*' McCarthy disbelieving.

'Lie low for a while.'

'*Hide?*'

'Yep.'

McCarthy's ego was cut to the quick. 'I am not *hiding* from those goddamn terrorists. I am not hiding from *anybody*.'

Cochran had thoughts of his own on this. 'Doug, we may have to consider the bank's position here as well . . .'

His trader turned on him. 'What you gonna do, Anthony, put out a press release telling Nemesis that I'm not here so please don't hurt us?'

He had a point, and Cochran's face admitted as much. They clearly had a security headache here. McCarthy turned to me.

'What else do we know? I mean, what the hell are the terrorists' demands?'

I pulled a helpless face for show. 'They haven't made any. They're just killing traders who have benefited from the unique pay structure of banking. I think they think you're overpaid.'

Cochran was instantly stung by this perennial complaint. 'What would they have us do, stop being so profitable? That's like asking the Mets to win but not by too much.'

I was all sympathy. 'Yeah, well, I believe what's sticking in their craw is that the Mets don't trash the economy then pay their players eight-figure bonuses using bailouts from the government.'

I stood before they could articulate their outrage. I wanted them angry, rattled. 'I gotta go. But, Mr McCarthy, please remember, there's nothing cowardly about running and hiding. I mean that, really.' Me, Mr Sincerity.

McCarthy wanted to be off the couch, but his boss put a restraining hand on his arm.

'*Cowardly . . . ?*' The ex-Air Force pilot gagging on the word.

And, watched by two incensed people, I left them to it.

I walked past Cochran's PA, who was looking at me and her boss's office to try and understand all the excitement. I'd left behind me two grown men in hot dispute. For my part, I was perfectly happy with the meeting. Diane was worried about the strategy but I'd won her over to my logic. Nobody had any leads on Nemesis, but the evidence suggested they would be coming after McCarthy soon, possibly even next. He fitted the profile perfectly. And after my taunting he wasn't going anywhere voluntarily. Which meant Nemesis would know where to find him. Which meant we would know where to find them. It was a fairly desperate roll of the dice, but that's where I'd found myself.

'Anthony, I am *not* going to run from these people.'

The CEO was walking back around behind his desk at the far end of the room. 'My first duty of care is to my employees, Doug.'

'This is America, Anthony. We don't give in to terrorists.' McCarthy bringing his hand down on the desk between them.

'That doesn't mean we have to paint targets on our

chests, Doug. Let's be sensible here. A leave of absence, that's all I'm saying.'

'Leave of . . . Don't ask me to hide in a foxhole, Anthony.'

'Doug, go sick, go flying, go anywhere.'

'I want to go about my business.'

The CEO slumped into his chair and shook his head regretfully, his stomach tying itself in knots at the thought of Turlington's face. The violence dished out by Lazcano, now this new threat against his employees, his bank, him. It was almost more than he could bear. 'That goddamn Lehman position.'

McCarthy threw his hands up in despair, exhausted by the subject. 'How many times – the government bailout covered every cent of that. And it was never my idea to bury that loss, so don't use that, Anthony, don't. It was a tradable fund, I didn't break any laws, I just broke my winning streak.'

Goddamn tradable funds . . . The CEO took a deep breath as he remembered the almighty cock-up and desperate times that were 2008, the desperate search for money as everybody withdrew their credit lines, the meeting in Paris with the Lazcanos. 'Doug, we have to be realistic here . . .' Then he saw a glimmer of compromise – a way to buy time. 'The Sovereign Bank conference in Aspen.'

'What about it?'

'You do it. Take the team. Treat it like a vacation. Come to a couple of meetings then go skiing, whatever. We'll pick up the entire tab.'

'The conference? It's an executive snooze-fest. Are you kidding me?'

'Doug, it's that or I'll have security take away your pass.'

'You can't do that, Anthony.'

But a moment's thought told them both that it was not McCarthy's best ever bluff. They eyed each other, the CEO the victor. He spoke, conciliatory now.

'The conference isn't till Friday, Doug, that's a few days. Wind down your positions . . .'

Now McCarthy really was outraged. 'Wind them *down*? These terrorist attacks are a goldmine – what about my bonus?'

'Jesus, Doug, these people want to kill bankers – they want to kill *you*.'

'And I want to make money out of it.'

Christ, Cochran thought to himself. The greed of some of his people. But then his added fear. *It was Lazcano's money I'd given McCarthy to trade on Lehman Brothers. The money in that tradable fund came straight from Mexico. What if Lazcano finds this out? Do I get a film of McCarthy tied to a chair, tortured beyond reason?* Cochran thinking, *this is all too much.* He ran a hand over his face and sighed. 'OK, OK. I'll see you're looked after at the end of the quarter.'

McCarthy stared at him, feeling slightly better now that his remuneration was safe, but not saying as much. He reached up to his shirt pocket, touched Webster's business card to make sure it was still there. Thinking that his gut had changed its mind.

I reached the elevator turning the plan over in my head. In the complete absence of any intel, a dragnet around these offices was our best hope. I'd step down security for a

188

block until it was invisible to Nemesis, then, when they went to make their move – bam. Well, that was the plan.

There was a Latin American guy about my size and age waiting by the elevator already, looking slightly lost at which of the two elevators – one on each side of the lobby – to take. He was facing the wrong way, the elevator on the other side coming up first.

'This way,' I informed him as an elevator opened behind us, letting him go first. 'After you.'

He smiled at my gesture then slid a gun out from under a raincoat draped across his arm. 'No, after you Mr Byrne.' A thick Mexican accent.

I looked at him. I looked at the empty elevator. I looked at the gun.

You only have to be careless once.

22

I stepped into the large gold-coloured elevator with my hands up, as instructed. Each wall was a full-length gilt-tinted mirror, a hand rail running round the middle. This being the top floor, we were the only passengers. I reached the far wall and turned around. The Mexican – or so I guessed – held his gun calmly in his left hand, waiting for me to complete his instructions. Leftie was a problem.

Feeling confident of the distance between us, the Mexican stepped in after me, coming no closer than he had to. Not moving his eyes off me, he reached out with his right arm and felt along the buttons. He must have memorized them because he hit the button for the basement level first time, not taking his eyes off me, not even blinking. If the rest of his plan was anything like as slick as he was I knew I could expect a welcoming committee downstairs. At which point I'd have a problem squared.

The doors slid closed behind him as he stood implacably facing me. Nothing about him unnerved, nothing about him excited. Moving carefully, deliberately, calmly. Watching me the way a factory worker might watch a production line, because it's a job and nothing more. Lazcano had sent his best. The elevator began to ride down the forty floors.

'Stand in the corner, Mr Byrne and put your hands down.'

Spoken without emotion or fuss.

For the briefest of moments I wondered whether to stand still and see what he did about it. Except I had a feeling I knew what he'd do about it, without batting an eyelid into the bargain. I stepped to my right and put my arms by my sides. For his part, he carefully moved to the other rear corner, faced the front and, crossing his left arm across his chest, wriggled the gun back under the raincoat across his arm. His eyes on me. Constantly. No attempt to pose otherwise. Let people be suspicious. When did anyone ever challenge anyone else about odd behaviour? He'd be an oddball and they'd get out of the elevator and get on with their lives. And he'd get me down to the basement, where my options would run out.

But it was worse than that. This Mexican would have less than no regard for human life and if somebody got into the elevator and he suddenly had any second thoughts then he'd have no qualms about slaying everybody present. I might be the first to go but I wouldn't be the last. I couldn't risk that.

Floor thirty-two. The elevator slowed. People were about to get in. People he wouldn't give two pesos about killing.

He spoke in his unwavering, unruffled manner. 'Just act natural, Mr Byrne.'

The doors opened to reveal a thirtysomething African-American woman with a short skirt and jacket that revealed more than some might have of what was a very nice body.

I could do natural.

She took a step into the elevator.

Strangers wouldn't necessarily notice anything unto-ward, friends though . . . I lit up my face.

'Mary!'

An unplanned-for variable. A witness. Somebody who might do something about any odd behaviour. The Mexican's eyes flicked momentarily to my new best friend. I whipped my arm up to his elbow and vaulted him against the left-hand wall, the Mexican getting off a shot before I could barely move him, the bullet mercifully hitting the control panel. The woman was backing out and screaming as I landed a punch into the side of the Mexican's rib-cage. She was turning and running when I wrapped my arms around him from behind, pinning his arms to his body, keeping that gun penned in while she got away.

The doors were closing when he began to lift one leg up. I was grappling with my left hand, trying to locate his hand under the raincoat, trying to get to the gun. He had his leg half up as I got my hand over his, began to dig my fingers into his wrist, looking for a nerve to pinch, his leg up in front of him, a scream building inside him as the pressure in his wrist started to shoot a pain up his arm, a pain that would make him feel sick to the stomach, a pain that would make him retch in less than five sec– he kicked us both off the wall, shoving us back with all his might, me still wrapped around him, slamming my back into the opposite side of the elevator, the hand rail mercilessly cracking into my lower back as we landed.

I couldn't contain a roar of pain, and he began to thrust his arms out against mine, trying to break the hold I had on him. Once. Twice. I couldn't hold him. Three. I released him a fraction of a second before his last attempt, bringing my cupped hands up and smacking them as hard as I could around both of his ears at the same time. The impact concussed him for one second. One second I used to reach round, grab the gun inside the raincoat and wrench it out of the Mexican's hand, spinning him away from me in the effort, but him still holding one end of his raincoat.

Both of us holding the coat, inside it the gun. Both of us glancing down at it and back at the other, calculating the odds of getting to it, the factors involved, using the time to take a breath. The raincoat tensing between us as both of us pulled harder and harder. Him releasing it, my tension throwing me back to my right as he swept a leg under both of mine, dropping me to the floor on my back. Immediately he dropped a knee down on to my throat, except I'd rolled away as he came down with all his force, landing his knee agonizingly on the floor, distracting him with the pain as I righted myself.

The gun was in the corner beyond him and he was reaching for it as I jumped and stamped my foot down on it, crushing his fingers into the bargain. As he cried out I grabbed the back of his head and slammed it into the handrail, his right hand under my foot. I remembered he was left handed only when he brought his fist into the inside of my left knee. I buckled, he stood and pushed himself up and backwards at the same time, once up slamming his left elbow round behind him into my head, forcing me to block it, and again, and again – screams – the doors had opened – a group of bank employees waiting to get on – their faces horrified as the doors closed – the Mexican spinning round to his left, bringing a punch round with it. I blocked with my left forearm and chopped down on his neck with my right hand at the same time. My assailant staggered back, I stepped forward, punched his jaw with my right hand, followed through with my right elbow, dropped my right side down to deliver my elbow into his stomach, turned, rose up, bringing the same elbow up under his chin before kicking him in the stomach behind me, thrusting his body into the elevator wall.

But he'd held on to my foot, was twisting it, forcing me to see it broken or twist with it. I spun round in mid air landing heavily on the floor. Before I had righted myself he had reached down and grabbed the pistol with his left hand. He brought the gun up, I grabbed it in my right hand, twisting it away from me, delivering a punch to his face with my left followed by another and another, using the time bought to grab the gun with both hands and turn it viciously over the top, the gun reaching an angle he couldn't hold and snapping the trigger finger, a cry of pain, the Mexican having no choice but to release it, leaning into me, shoving me towards the wall, slamming his head into mine, square in the face, almost a knock-out blow, me falling backwards, down, against the far side, away from him, my eyes whiting out at the pain, the last thing I saw – flat – from his sleeve – a blade – swinging it in an arc towards me – everything blurred – my one shot with the gun, fired into him.

The doors opened.

'Nobody move! This is the police!'

Us in profile to them. The group outside. Guns, half a dozen, pointed into the elevator. The Mexican standing over me, me lying back, gun pointed up at him. If I shot him again they'd finish me off. Had I done enough?

The Mexican did not obey them but instead clutched at the hole in his Adam's Apple, blood pouring over his hand, gasping, choking as he tried to suck air into his lungs, sucking down blood instead. The knife dropping from his hand. Maybe trying to say something. Maybe trying to breathe. He fell to his left, into the corner of the elevator.

'Do not move!' Again from outside in the lobby.

'Mike Byrne, United States Secret Service.' Me trying to keep everybody calm.

'Put the gun down, now!'

Me lowering the gun to the floor. 'There's a car, probably a truck, in the basement car park – we have to stop it.'

'Put the gun *down*.' Caution and control everything.

I lay it where the lead officer could see it, and looked outside. An entire SWAT team pointing their weapons at me. I lay my head back, exhausted, and sighed. I could almost see the dead Mexican's associates calmly driving away down Broadway.

23

Diane Mason looked around the table. Almost four billion dollars. That was her very rough and very conservative estimate of the wealth represented by the twenty men – all men – in the room. And that was before she factored in the Treasury Secretary's quarter of a billion that he earned during his time at Goldman's. These men had taken that money off the table running their banks. Almost four billion dollars between twenty men. Not entrepreneurial wealth – salary. Their living wage. What their remuneration committees felt was their collective worth. Never mind that these same people necessitated eight trillion dollars to be injected into the economy to pay for their mistakes. Never mind. She had her own particular coping mechanism for this peculiar fact: she didn't think about it. Because if she did she wouldn't be able to do her job. Smile and take down the bad guys, that's how she'd soldiered on all these years. Except nowadays, she asked herself, who were the bad guys? Her department was either in the process of prosecuting, investigating or suing every bank around the table for one thing or another. And every single time the ultimate fine would be a fraction of the profits from their ill-gotten gains.

She'd noticed a creeping change in her sensibilities of late. She noticed it the night before when she'd dropped off some food at one of the soup kitchens near her mother's house. She'd never seen the queues so long or so early. She noticed that her compartmentalizing of banks and their recent effects on the economy were not the Chinese Walls they used to be. The way the banks had chased profits so recklessly that the government had had to step in and step in and step in since 2007, how the government had had to hock the country's future to save the banks . . . And the way the bankers had literally deposited a big chunk of the bailout money into their own personal bank accounts . . . Some days she struggled.

'It's impossible to get in and out of the Financial District. You can't move for press people.'

'Our COO had his application for an apartment building turned down when the other members of the co-op learned that he was a banker.'

'We've had to cover up every window in our offices. We've had to cover up everything.'

Diane Mason thought that at least that last complaint deserved some kind of quip, but her mood was failing her. She was sat at the top of the long walnut table in a conference room on the executive floor of the Federal Reserve Bank of New York. In the middle of the table, lest the attendees forget, was inlaid the seal of the august institution itself. At the far end from Diane Mason sat Treasury Secretary Peterson. Filling up both sides of the table between them were twenty of the most powerful bankers in New York. Bankers who were demanding *something be done*.

A wire-brush-haired young CEO spoke across everybody to the Secret Service agent. 'Our people are scared, Agent Mason. We've got everybody we can working from home. That's not how we should have to live our lives.'

There were vigorous nods of agreement around the table.

Anthony Cochran stabbed the table with his finger. 'There was a shoot-out, a *shoot-out*, in our headquarters earlier today.'

The other bankers voiced their concern, alarm, despair at such a development, each with their own worry about the anarchy they perceived to be running riot through the city. Mason had made a bet with herself that she could stay composed all day. A couple of glasses of that 2006 bottle of Napa Valley Cabernet Sauvignon if she won. Somehow she felt she'd be going to bed stone-cold sober tonight.

'Gentlemen, the incident at the Sovereign Bank head-quarters today was, to the best of our knowledge, unrelated to the current terrorist threat to New York. In fact, it was a targeted attack on a member of law enforcement in the course of his duties. I can, however, today shed some light on the nature of the threat posed by the group call-ing themselves Nemesis. We believe we have identified the rationale as to the victims they have been selecting.'

The bankers were all quiet for the first time in the meet-ing.

'Having studied the available data, there is compelling evidence that Nemesis are targeting traders and bankers who, though well remunerated over the course of their careers, have actually lost more than they ever earned. This analysis is borne out by the attacks in Tokyo, Frank-furt, London, Hong Kong and, most recently, at the headquarters of Philadelphia National here in New York. Each of the victims was a very big net-loser as a trader.'

There was nothing less than shock throughout the room until a perma-tanned CEO spoke. 'But we've all got people like that in our employ.'

There was a ripple of agreement from his peers.

A Greek-American who could have stepped out of *GQ* magazine shook his head. 'Don't they realize that that's just how it is? You win some, you lose some, but you win enough to show a profit as a bank.'

Nods and mutters of approval.

From another, 'That remuneration model has served us well for over a century.'

Increased nods, increased mutterings.

Mason spoke next in the spirit of education rather than antagonism, though the latter would surely win out. 'Gentlemen, you also paid yourselves generous bonuses with government bailout funds.'

The Greek-American smarted at this. 'You sound as if you sympathize with these people?'

A chill ran through the score of bankers as they looked suspiciously at the Secret Service agent.

Mason despaired at the mood in the room, so divorced from the reality on the ground. 'Gentlemen, it is my job to understand not only the actions and planned actions of such people but also to understand their motivations.' She fixed the Greek-American with a stern unwavering eye. 'Please be so kind as to not label me in such a manner again, as my agency and all the other agencies do their best to protect you from any harm. And please do not forget that we are protecting you with budgets rcduccd because of the need for that same government bailout.'

The egos in the room were about as big as they get, but they also got where Agent Mason was coming from and all pulled in their necks slightly.

'Do we know their demands?' The speaker a white-haired Southern gentleman, professorial, elderly, though still a force to be reckoned with.

Mason had no reason or desire to be less than frank with the leading lights of the New York banking community. 'They haven't made any demands. We're surmising.'

'Guessing?' The professorial CEO reproaching in his tone.

'Sir, it's the best information we have, and I'm sharing it with you at the earliest opportunity. The welfare of your staff and the people of New York are our paramount concern.'

A moment of contrite silence followed before a sixty-something, incredibly chic Indian-American stepped in from the far end of the table. 'What practical advice are you giving us here today, Agent Mason?'

'Well, as should be obvious to you all, the Mayor has raised the profile of law enforcement in the Lower Manhattan area. Every available police officer has been assigned to counter-terrorist duties, and we have contingency plans to draft in officers from neighbouring boroughs if the need arises. I can assure you that this is the President's number one security concern right now and that he is providing every resource available. In addition, the New York Police Department will be carrying out a full review of your protective measures to advise on how best to mitigate the possibility of a breach of your own security.'

Cochran snorted a derisive laugh. 'Why don't you go the whole hog and suggest we set up a banking neighbourhood watch initiative? This is *not* what we pay our taxes for, Agent Mason.' The strain of the last few days bleeding into Cochran's manner.

The disaffected CEOs murmured in support. Mason allowed their discontent to quieten before responding.

'Mr Cochran, I agree.'

That confused the group of men.

'This is *not* what you pay your taxes for.'

Cochran assumed a slightly more satisfied air, his position conceded as it was.

'Given your bank's policy of directing as much of its business as possible through the Cayman Islands, I would suggest it is arguable that you pay your taxes at all.'

A few of the CEOs were slow to stop their guffaws, with even Secretary Peterson smiling to himself. Cochran went to protest but was cut off as the Treasury Secretary – perceiving Mason's strained mood – coughed, and in so doing received everybody's attention.

'Gentlemen, we have to recognize that there is a disconnect between the worlds of Wall Street and Main Street. Wall Street is prospering like never before whilst Main Street is, frankly, on its knees. It might make us feel better about ourselves venting a bit of spleen here and in the press, but it won't make us any friends. More importantly, it won't get us anywhere.'

A sneer had adorned Cochran's face. 'Are you suggesting we kiss up to the terrorists? Is that what you're saying, Richard? This is America; we have a right to make money; the people in this room earn every penny of it. We have nothing – *nothing* – to apologize for. It's Main Street that should be thanking *us*. I mean, who pays their welfare cheques? Who makes it possible for all those Occupy hippies to spend their days protesting instead of working for a living? Huh? Who pays *their* welfare cheques?'

The Treasury Secretary let his gaze fall on the Sovereign Bank CEO. 'Anthony, some people would call the bank bailouts the biggest welfare scheme in history.' Cochran went to protest, but Peterson ploughed on. 'Myself included. We should be ashamed as a group that we let that happen and if we don't feel shame then we haven't learned anything.' Staring around the room now, wanting to be sure everybody was getting this. 'These totally unacceptable attacks might just be a very violent articulation of a very real public mood. We don't exist in a vacuum, gentlemen, we exist in America. We live in a society of real people, many of them without jobs as a result of the economic downturn that many would argue we engineered. And if we don't start remembering that, it is my belief that America will remind us. These attacks are wicked, they are wrong, and the entire law enforcement community is working round the clock to stop them, but I did not ask you here today to use Special Agent Mason as a whipping horse. She's trying to keep you in the loop with a full and honest disclosure. She's been honest enough to admit that they are mostly in the dark at present. Let's show a bit of humility around this table. Let's have a conversation about what we can do to make the bankers of New York safer, shall we?'

Staring at everybody, defying them to contradict his way forward.

The well-dressed Indian-American could not resist pushing his point. 'So, Agent Mason, what practical advice are you giving *us*? What can *we* do?'

'On the record? Be vigilant and cooperate with the NYPD during this troubled time.'

But the room was waiting for the other shoe to drop. The dandy spoke again.

'And off the record?'

Diane Mason hesitated, then felt she owed them absolute candour. 'Take every one of your traders that are net losers off the streets. Send them away until it's all blown over.'

The room was dumbstruck at the logic and the implications. The silence was finally broken by the wire-brush-haired banker.

'That's a lot of people, Ms Mason.'

Special Agent Mason looked slowly around the table, knowing that some of those present would be on that list.

'Gentlemen, to Nemesis they're not people – they're targets.'

24

Webster saw McCarthy before McCarthy saw him. Walking outside the deli, his head turning nervously about, watching to see who had seen him, before ducking out of the cold weather and inside the store. He had sounded cagey on the phone, humming and hawing like there was a lot he wanted to say but felt the phone was the wrong place to say it. Which was right. It had been Webster's suggestion they meet for a coffee in the Village, a suggestion grabbed at by McCarthy.

'Hi, you been here long?' McCarthy extending a hand and giving that extra-pump of friendship in his handshake.

'Literally just sat down.' Webster opening with a lie. Had never been less than an hour early for an unvetted meeting in his life. It took up his time but had saved his life in Beirut and Manila, so he was sticking with it. And this place, dark, with its budget menu and wholesome foods, full of students and tourists, would let him spot anybody untoward before they'd stirred the ethically sourced sugar in their FairTrade latte.

'Coffee?'

'Sure.'

Webster ordered with a hand signal to the deli owner. McCarthy joined Webster at the small, rickety table, losing his jacket and gloves in the warm environment.

'I hope you don't mind me following up like this.'

'No, Doug, no, not at all. And it's Bill.'

'Yeah, sure, I remember.'

Webster looked at McCarthy and knew instantly that the banker wanted him to break the law. He didn't know whether to chuckle or cuss that he hadn't seen this earlier, this way to make money. This way to line his pockets while at the bank. All these years he could have been doubling – trebling – his salary as a trouble-shooter. And he hadn't even seen it 'till now . . . Had he learned nothing from Wall Street?

'So, Doug, you're busy, I'm busy, what can I do for you? And I'm assuming you're not here to tell me somebody's cheating their expense account?'

'No, no.' McCarthy laughing awkwardly at the mood sweetener.

'Good. Because I've been around the block, Doug. If I listed my services, well, I mean, I'd need a business card the size of a billboard.'

More nervous laughter, but Webster happy for him to get the gist of that meaning. When the trader toyed uncomfortably with a sugar pourer he decided a new tack might be in order.

'Doug, can I be frank?'

McCarthy slightly out of his depth. 'Sure.'

'I like to think of myself as like a therapist, a lawyer, you know. Anything you say is between us, doesn't matter what it is.'

'OK, good.'

'And Doug?' Giving a meaningful stare. 'It doesn't matter what it is.'

McCarthy turned the billboard-sized hints over in his mind, still nervous about what he had to say. Christ, it was like taking a hit out on your wife.

'These . . . Nemesis, Bill, I'm not sure if I'm meant to repeat this . . .'

The trader looked at Webster to OK the contents of the meeting.

'Doug, you don't have to say anything, but anything you say will not leave this table, I swear to you. You're not going to ask me to do anything I haven't done before.' *Jesus, do I need to spell it out?*

McCarthy's heart was beating fast now as he wanted to say the words, but once they were out, Christ . . . 'Erm . . . I'm on the list, Bill.'

Webster didn't quite follow, but could see that McCarthy was upset, angry. 'What list, Doug?'

But McCarthy was backing out now, shaking his head, this too much to ask, too much to *think*. 'I can't, I shouldn't.' Because saying it would make it more *real*.

Webster had seen this before. Hell, he'd seen it a hundred times. Civilians sweating tears because they were contemplating things he did before breakfast. McCarthy may have been ex-Air Force, but Wall Street had softened him. This was a world he was meant to have left behind.

The coffee arrived, and Webster poured some sugar into his cup. Quite a lot, a habit he'd picked up during a spell in Kashmir. It was tea back then, but it had given him a sweet tooth for life. The ex-CIA agent took a step back for McCarthy's sake. '52nd, right?'

This reference came out of nowhere to the trader, and

took a few moments to register. 'Oh, yeah, me, right, yeah, 52nd Fighter Wing. How d'you know?'

Webster pulling an amused face. 'I could tell you but I'd have to kill you.'

McCarthy smiled almost sadly at the attempt at humour, the attempt to relax him. McCarthy began to worry again, doubted himself again. What was he doing here?

Then the security chief spoke with a twinkle in his eye. '1st Fighter Wing.'

The banker was surprised. 'Really?'

'Yeah. '89 to '98.'

McCarthy genuinely interested, somehow relieved. A fellow pilot, part of the brotherhood. 'No way. You must have flown in Desert Storm. What were you flying?'

'F-15s – but I was a little late for that, I was part of the no-fly zone afterwards. Good fun, good days.'

'Nice. I was F-16s.' McCarthy grinning at the trump card he'd laid down. 'Over fifty sorties during the Kosovo war. Wow. So you went from 1st Fighter Wing straight into security?'

'No, I went from the 1st into Delta Force. Then after the war I got posted to Nicaragua to help fight the Contras. That's when I started doing . . .' Webster judiciously choosing a euphemism that might ease his colleague's mind. '. . . contract work.'

Webster getting and not getting the hint, but getting enough of it. 'Wow. You've had an exciting life.'

'Hmm.' Webster filled less with false-modesty than the regrets his life had left him with. 'Exciting's one word for it. Anyhow, we were talking about you being on the list.'

'Oh yeah.'

Webster decided to get in there while the trust was at high tide. 'Nemesis? Their list?'

McCarthy paused, thinking about the man opposite – the pilot opposite. Then took the plunge. 'Yeah, the bastards, they're gunning for me, apparently, well, I don't know, it's what I've been told.'

'Who by?' *How the hell did Webster not know this? He was head of bank security – how the hell did he not know this?*

'A guy, Mike Byrne, he's with the Secret Service. Said I should get the hell away, run, go hide someplace.'

Webster noted Byrne's name then assessed McCarthy's mood, making sure he was reading this ex-Air Force pilot right. 'But you don't want to do that, do you? You don't want to run.'

McCarthy allowed the anger to rise up now, the fear-fuelled outrage brimming up inside him. 'Rolling over to terrorists? You shitting me? I don't take it, I dish it out. War is our goddamn profession, right?' Citing the USAF's unofficial motto.

'You want to take the fight to them?' Webster spelling out what McCarthy was afraid to articulate.

'Fucking A. I want to hunt those bastards down and kill them like the dogs they are.' Angry, but also scared, wanting them neutralized before they got to him, wanting to be in *control*.

Webster was as calm as if they were discussing what to choose off the deli menu. 'You want me to fix that?'

McCarthy flinched up at Webster, the very sentiment he was hoping for offered up to him. 'Could you?'

'Probably.'

''Cos that's pretty goddamn . . .'

'Serious? And for the avoidance of doubt, we both know there's only one way to fix a terrorist, right? Complete neutralization.'

'You *are* serious.' McCarthy was quieter now, excited, more nervous than ever. Ordering attacks on positions, he'd done it in Kosovo against the Serbs, enemy people had died, but here, on home soil . . . 'I'm willing to pay.' McCarthy handled his words like nitroglycerine.

'How much?' Webster sipped his coffee, so thick with sugar he could feel the granules sliding down his throat.

'One hundred thousand a scalp.' McCarthy almost ashamed to have said it, then rallying himself, staring with increasing resolve at the ex-CIA operative.

'Dollars?' McCarthy went to earnestly confirm as much, only realizing when Webster smirked that it had been a joke. 'That could add up. Ten terrorists, that's a million dollars. What's that after tax?'

McCarthy waved it away. 'I can get round the tax. That's one hundred K net.'

Webster looking into the remains of his coffee now like he was reading the sugary granules.

'A million dollars? That's a life-changing amount to an old hobo like me. That's a lot of pesos you're prepared to lay out, hombre. What if I get twenty, thirty scalps?'

'There's no limit.' McCarthy felt relieved – euphoric, almost – at being able to *do something* about the death sentence he was under, believing the deal was in the bag. 'Whatever it is it's cheaper than the alternative.'

Webster looked at him, looked outside and about, checking.

'Plus expenses.' Spoken uncertainly by McCarthy. Webster looked back at him. 'Whatever it takes, Bill. I want Nemesis taken out . . . So? Can you fix it for me?'

Webster breathed in slowly through his nose as he drained the last sweet dregs of his drink and placed the cup on the table. There had been a time in his life when he finished his drinks because they were there. These days he tried to remember to enjoy every last drop of them. Too many brushes with death. He thought long and hard then spoke almost regretfully.

'I knew from the first moment I set eyes on you, Doug, that you were the one person at the bank who would want to do something about these Nemesis clowns.'

McCarthy waited, restless at the drawn-out confirmation.

'When I checked your employee record I was *convinced* you wouldn't stand there and take it. That you would take the fight to them.'

McCarthy gave a small nod, agreeing.

'And I knew after that board meeting this morning that you would come to me as your hitman of choice for the job.'

McCarthy could feel a bead of sweat trickling down the back of his neck, realizing now how deep he was into this situation. What if it's a trap, what if it's being recorded, what if it was a mistake?

'And I knew that when you came to me I would have a simple word of advice for you.'

McCarthy nervous and uncertain now.

'What would that be?'

'Don't.'

'Don't?'

'Don't do it, Doug. Don't take the fight to these people.'

The trader was instantly embarrassed and angry at having read this all wrong. 'But I thought . . .'

'You thought what? Thought that you could do what a thousand counter-terrorist police officers in New York couldn't? What the NYPD and FBI and Secret Service haven't got the first idea where to start with?' Not mocking, sympathizing.

'So, what – what now?' The trader felt the heat of having transgressed the law.

'Now nothing.' Answering McCarthy's confused look. 'Doug, there's nothing wrong with what you asked me to do. These people are scum – they're worse than scum. But it's all about waking up alive in your own bed.'

He could sense that McCarthy's paranoia was going to tear away at him and wanted to calm him down, deciding to put himself at risk if necessary.

'Doug, can I tell you something in complete confidence?'

The trader's mind was all over the place. 'Yeah, sure.'

'I'm ex Agency. You know . . .'

Shrugging. Waiting a beat for the initials *CIA* to form in McCarthy's mind, the weight of it not wasted on him.

'I've done things . . .' He shook his head. 'Doug, I need a double dose of pills to sleep at night.'

'What are you saying, Bill?'

Webster put his fingertips on McCarthy's arm. 'What I am saying, Doug is, do you really want to wake up screaming in the middle of the night for the rest of your life? Do you really want the guilt and the memories and the fear of being caught? You've served your country well, Lieutenant. You're a hero. You're a great banker. You're a family man. You've got loved ones, dependants. Let the soldiers fight the wars. Stand down, Doug, stand down. Wake up alive in your own bed, my friend, and live to see yourself reflected in your grandchildren's eyes.'

25

Conrad Kaplan was a serious person's idea of a serious person. His meticulous brown suits, never-creased button-down shirts and mirror-bright brown brogues served only to tighten his already tight persona. His large, black eyebrows and permanent threat of a five o'clock shadow meant his features looked darker than they really were, helped by his permanently furrowed brow and tidy haircut that looked like it was put in place by a mould. He was the type of person who would walk out of a comedy feature telling you that, 'There were seventeen moments of heightened levity in that film.' In the ten years or so that I had known him I had never seen him laugh. I think he smiled once, but the light was bad. He always – *always* – wore the expression of a man considering your last remark as if it contained a clue to the possible destruction of the United States. He left nothing to chance and no possibility unconsidered. He was deadly serious. He was perfect for the NSA and terrific at his job there. And an asshole.

My boss, Diane, Kaplan and I were stood in the car park beneath the Brooklyn Marriott and the New York field office of the Secret Service. We had swapped perfunctory handshakes, both Diane and I keen to get on with our first question, except that he cut in before we had a chance.

'We have nothing to report.'

So that's why he held the meeting between two people carriers instead of our offices upstairs. It was meant to be short. Diane bridled slightly at his offhand manner.

'To us or DC?'

He looked from Diane to me then back again.

'To anybody. Nemesis are completely off the grid.'

I looked at Diane before speaking, checking for any clues as to whether she wanted to escalate this or not. I got none so ploughed on regardless.

'And you're sharing everything here?'

Kaplan twitched his shoulders, accentuating the look of earnestness on his face. 'Look, it's no secret that I'm not happy about everybody getting to sit at the table on this one. We're holding five times as many meetings, and there's a genuine threat of information overload here. But we've all got the same instructions from DC: cooperate. So I'm cooperating. What about your division – anything?'

But Diane wasn't finished yet. 'Mr Kaplan, are you seriously telling us that none of the chatter or intel is even giving us a long list of suspected terrorist organizations?'

He pulled himself up to his full height, which was something under six foot. 'It depends on whether every unhinged blogger is to be included on that list. Every discussion board and website is lit up by these bank killings, and we've got to sift through all of it. If you strip out all the fruit-cakes and practitioners of schadenfreude we haven't got a single, solitary lead. The most solid thing anybody's come up with is your pet theory, Byrne. Bankers who've lost more money than they've made.'

'I'd say Agent Byrne's analysis has given the DoH a good start on pre-empting Nemesis.'

'Agent Byrne's work, whilst commendable, has told us what happened, not what will happen. It hasn't told us how Nemesis had access to this trading data, it hasn't told us why it chose those exact bankers to date over any others, it hasn't told us what motivates them to act on this data and it hasn't told us how the network is structured or how it communicates internally.'

I could see that Diane had to fight the urge to take a step towards Kaplan. 'All very helpful, but in the absence of crystal balls I can't see the trading data shedding much more light on the situation. But if you share what information you have, Special Agent Byrne and his team would have a hell of a better chance of contributing to this investigation. I'm not the President, Mr Kaplan, I don't need your best intelligence, I need your best guess. How do you think they're communicating?'

Kaplan took a moment to sift through his choice of words. He might have been tempted to explode, at which point I would fully have expected Diane to have taken that step forward. Instead, wisdom won out.

'The only way that makes sense is in person.'

It was Diane's turn to furrow her brow. 'But this is an international terrorist organization operating around the globe. They must have channels of communication.'

Kaplan shrugged and looked at the both of us and spoke almost in apology. 'They may have, Ms Mason, but as far as we're concerned they're ghosts. Ghosts in the machine.'

26

'*What's the target's name?*'

'*Douglas McCarthy.*'

'*When do I get to light this guy up?*'

'*Give me a day.*'

'*Oh come on, those people are all over this place. Time is not our friend here.*'

There was a pause in the messages. Then, '*There's always enough time.*'

There was another pause. This time because Alecto was wondering what to type. She typed and hovered her finger over the Enter key. Then hit it.

'*Time enough for us?*'

'*Time enough for everything.*'

'*Tango that. x*'

Alecto looked up at her/Excel's computer screen. In the foreground the figure of a princess – her character – had its back to her. Opposite the princess was a small troll-like creature who gave the princess a small present, a box wrapped with a bow. Then it turned and trotted swiftly away before disappearing in a puff of purple smoke.

The other party had logged off. Alecto twitched a smile and worked to keep it there, watching the purple cloud drift into nothing.

She sat back from the machine. On the screen was *The*

Xia Chronicles, a massively multiplayer online role-playing game, or MMORPG, in the tradition of World of Warcraft. A game based in a mythical ancient China, when it was presumably populated by a myriad of dragons and other beasts. The characters were improbably Tolkien-esque in look and skills, the players were approximately five million people scattered across the globe. The graphics were bad, a world away from today's cinema-quality games, the various missions were ludicrous, and the action took place between an excess of panels and buttons and information boxes and other graphics required to play the under-imagined game. But for some unexpected developments in life, Alecto would never have heard of it, let alone logged on. But even Alecto had to admit that it had one redeeming feature. The online chat between players was untraceable.

The game had started as a project between hackers a decade earlier and morphed and grown via the efforts of the open-source programming community. A global *pro bono* endeavour that had resulted in this substandard game. But it was theirs, it was free and it was run according to the anarchic-cum-libertarian ethos of its players. And because it was all about not being crushed under the heel of *the man*, it was hacker-friendly. Each and every message unmonitored and untraceable. Each and every message existing in a virtual private network between the characters talking at any one time. Each and every message deleted the moment it had been read. No incriminating log-files here. It protected everybody's privacy – as well as saving on server space. It kept their communications private. It kept them off the grid. '*NSA proof*,' he'd told her.

Alecto, in a man's Tommy Hilfiger dressing gown, took a sip from a lemon tea. Then she moved her cursor up to the box in the princess character's hands and double-clicked it. The screen went black. From the bathroom behind her came the sound of the bath running. She looked out of the East Village window as a tiny stream of information was sent to her computer. The view was of the service ducts at the back of the adjacent apartment block. *All this money and he chooses to live here.* The Kansas girl not even beginning to get the logic of Manhattan living.

On the PC's monitor a folder eventually popped into view. Inside it, a large number of photos. Using the mouse, she double-clicked on one. It showed Douglas McCarthy coming out of Sovereign Bank headquarters. Another picture showed him entering the subway. Another showed him jogging beside the reservoir in Central Park. Another, through the window, showed him at his desk. Another showed McCarthy at his desk on the phone, smiling. Another showed McCarthy in extreme close-up, laughing, looking straight into the camera lens unawares. Every office picture taken from a higher-up rooftop opposite.

Then there was a knock at the apartment door.

Alecto's body stiffened.

Somebody from the block? Maybe? Twenty cops with orders to shoot first ask questions later? Maybe that as well.

She quickly logged off from her game and closed the browser to reveal the computer's home-screen – Excel holding a surfboard on a Californian beach, having the time of his life. Then she picked up her compact Desert Eagle semi-automatic.

Already bare-footed, Alecto tiptoed silently across to the door. She stood to one side to listen, her gun at the ready. If there was trouble she was going to use it, of that she was certain. She waited but couldn't hear anything except her pounding heart. After a moment she leaned across and looked through the spy-hole. She rested her forehead against the door, a wave of relief washing through her.

She held the dressing gown closed up to her neck and opened the door – keeping the gun behind her back.

'Man, we thought you were d–'

FiDi stopped mid-sentence on seeing Alecto. Partly because it wasn't a woman he was expecting. Partly because it wasn't a woman with one bare leg sticking out of a dressing gown either.

The young African-American hadn't prepared for this. 'You're not Excel.'

Alecto smiled, slightly more than alluringly. 'Neither are you.'

FiDi's mission was being forgotten in the presence of this charm offensive.

'Sorry, I meant, is Excel there?'

'Yes, he's sleeping.' Alecto made no concessions to opening the door. The message clear.

'Can I see him?'

'Well, you could, but there's a problem.'

FiDi's face asked *What sort of problem?*

'You see, he's got the flu and the doctor said he should avoid any kind of exercise . . .'

'I just want to see him.'

'Well, that's the problem. We just had, you know . . .' Watching the effect of her words on the dead man's colleague with secret amusement. 'He's dead to the world.'

The young man was all but blushing. 'Well, I was told to see him.'

She pulled a face that suggested that she wished that she could help, only . . .

'Has he been getting my calls? I've called, like, every hour this week.'

'Oh, he lost his phone in the bar where we met.'

This was a lot for a young man to deal with, and FiDi instead strained slightly to see round her. A car horn began to sound in the street outside. Once, twice, three times. He reacted to the sound with a sigh.

'I'll be sure to say you called. What did you say your name was?'

'FiDi. Tell him FiDi dropped by.' The horn sounded again and FiDi began to walk away backwards. 'And tell him McCarthy wants him to call, like, yesterday.'

'I'll tell him just as soon as he wakes up.'

Alecto closed the door after the disappearing trader then rested her back against it. She couldn't quite get a handle on her feelings. That had scared her, but it was also thrilling. *Empowering*, that was a word that came to mind. But then her cautious self told her that one more visit like that and she was clearing out.

'Careful.' She spoke the word out loud to herself, reminded herself.

She put down the gun on the table, picked up her drink and wandered into the bathroom. The bath was full and steaming hot, a preposterous amount of bubbles threatening to overflow on to the floor. She turned off the faucet and, pulling some matches out of her dressing gown, lit six scented candles at one end of the bath. The small flames took a moment to fully take hold, but then the candles began to afford a tiny amount of illumination and a gratefully received perfume. She reached back and pulled a cord to turn off the light, plunging the windowless room into darkness before the modest effect of the candles became apparent.

Only now was she ready to take off her dressing gown.

She let it drop to the floor, avoiding the limited reflection the mirror leaning atop the sink might have afforded her. She stepped into the bath, hotter than most people could bear, and quickly hid under the bubbles, the small bath requiring her to bend her knees slightly if she was to lie down. She'd moved quickly and hadn't seen much of herself before the bubbles had closed in on top of her. Hadn't seen much of the burned skin. The thick red threads of scar tissue criss-crossing her body from the neck downwards. Scars that she thought meant that no man would ever want to touch her again. No one, until he came into her life. When he had sat by her bed and looked into her in a way nobody ever had before. Knowing her and accepting her. And, recently, loving her.

Him, the reason she ever got out of that hospital bed.

Alecto looked at the candles flickering, wondering if it was these or the bubble bath giving off the pleasant woody smell – rosewood? Whatever it was, it was pleasant. Relaxing. A world away from her wired existence.

She looked to her right, past the tiny sink, and the tiny

toilet, to the tiny shower cubicle. Where Excel lay crumpled on the floor. His cold skin pale, with a blister forming on his putrefying cheek. Abandoned, like a macabre puppet. Tossed aside, forgotten. Lifeless.

A world away from everything.

27

The drab first-floor office boasted a view of San Diego Bay, if you ignored the naval base that completely obscured said view. On a dull day the eye could also wander over the railway tracks, car parks and towering electricity pylons. Not forgetting the tourist attraction that wasn't East Harbour Drive. An office that even the most shameless realtor would struggle to talk up in an ad. In fact, the realtor had simply written *Basic and cheap, Rent by the month.* And the tenant had thought, *Perfect.* Perfectly undesirable and perfectly overlooked. Perfect for the once-a-week use.

The lawyer with a suit as cheap as the office lay the two cell phones on their sides, facing each other top to tail. Two phones bought with a fake ID, untraceable to him. More importantly, untraceable to his employer. They lay on the chipped, knocked-about desk. The only furniture in the room, not even blinds to cover the window.

The skinny man, tanned but with poor skin reflecting his poor diet, in his charcoal, too-large suit, checked his watch. His knocked-off Louis Vuitton watch used as part-payment for posting bail one time. *10:59:53.* Seven seconds to go. In the early days he had counted them down like an inmate on death row. Now he found himself seeing how late he could leave it to perform his task. His $500-a-week task.

Almost to the second both cell phones began to trill. The lawyer hit the green ACCEPT CALL button on both phones then retreated to a smaller room between the office and the corridor. Here he sat on the only furniture in this room, a solitary plastic chair. Then he took his gun out, a snub-nosed Smith and Wesson Model 60 loaded with a .357 Magnum chamber. He held it in both hands between his legs. If anybody came through that door before 11:10 p.m. he would kill them. His girlfriend, his daughter, his mother. Anybody. Because if he didn't, *they* would kill him.

The two phones side by side made for a poor quality connection. But they made for a great anonymous call. Both parties bouncing their phones through these two. Both parties invisible to law enforcement. Both parties ghosts.

One party was an assured male Mexican. The other hid their voice through a synthesizer that made it sound like a mechanical baddie in a kid's video game. The user didn't care. What he cared about was that his voice was so scrambled that all the audio experts in the world couldn't reverse engineer it to a recognizable owner.

The fifty-five-year old Eduardo Lazcano sat on his couch in his villa outside of Tijuana. He had paused the semi-final of *American Idol* on his PVR, a sixty-inch-wide Lady Ga Ga wannabe frozen in mid sneer. Beside him slumbered his twenty-four-year-old *narco novia*, his drugs bride, a former Miss Venezuela whom he had lured to his high-security lifestyle with a steady train of gifts and the promise of a life of luxury. For the drug lords it was not enough to be feared by their customers and rivals; envy was also required. So they began to add beautiful twenty-first-century courtesans to their money and power, Lazcano's pouting blonde a near-permanent fixture in recent times. But even her undeniable attractions had soon bored him. His wife was alive to his living arrangements away from her, but since her world was infinitely less stressful with her husband elsewhere she chose to overlook it.

Beside Eduardo Lazcano stood his younger brother, Gabriel. He waited with a muted cell phone in his hand, looking to the head of the cartel.

Eduardo spoke gruffly, more from tiredness than ill-temper. 'Does he know that the kidnap of the Secret Service agent was fucked up?'

Gabriel unmuted the phone and spoke with a hand covering the mouthpiece in case anybody was spying on them, lip-reading. 'Are you aware that the American escaped?'

On the table in San Diego a metallic voice from a cell phone replied.

'You sent one man after him. I warned you that was a mistake. Let me deal with it. The usual price.'

Gabriel repeated the message to his brother verbatim. Eduardo's lazy, large-bagged eyes continued to stare at the garish image of the teenager on the large screen. 'Fine. But it's worth twice that if he can bring him to me.'

Gabriel unmuted the phone again. 'That is acceptable. The fee is, however, doubled if you can deliver the package to its new owner.'

On the table in San Diego the metallic voice breathed as it thought about it.

'Trebled.'

'He says he wants three times as much.'

Eduardo looked up. Slowly. Like a well-fed wolf. 'Does he think I do not reward him sufficiently?'

Gabriel knew the implication of the question and took a moment to compose his wording.

On the table in San Diego the mechanical speaker waited.

'We feel the current remuneration is sufficient, as is the latest offer.'

Another pause, the metallic breathing giving no clue as to the reaction of the other.

'OK. Send me eight of your men, and I'll deal with the American.'

Gabriel ended the call and addressed his tired brother. 'Mike Byrne is about to be either dead or our houseguest.'

Eduardo picked up the television remote. 'He better hope he's fucking dead.'

The teenager on the screen reanimated into life, parroting her heroine's words. 'I don't mean to blame you, I'm just trying to tame you. You're an animal, animal. Animal, animal.'

28

Doug McCarthy and his team were wandering along West 59th Street, across from Central Park, having had a couple of drinks at a couple of bars to kick their evening off. The mood in the mid- and uptown districts was noticeably better than near their offices, and Duke, Ace, FiDi, Cartman and DB needed cheering up. And it was true of McCarthy that, no matter what was going on in his personal or professional life, he held his team together. It almost defined him. So tonight was his treat, a bonding meal at New York's newest and most anticipated restaurant from the Roman culinary superstars the Vozzo brothers, Vozzo On Central Park, a name that fulfilled Google's search requirements and left nothing in doubt. Tables in this first week were gold-dust, and it was only as a result of McCarthy shouting very loudly at the concierge service he had signed up to and used exhaustively for the last five years that he managed to finagle a booking.

Even on the approach McCarthy could sense the event. The frisson that accompanies the launch of a new top-end eaterie in Manhattan. A long, sleek Jaguar XJ was parked at the kerbside and a chauffeur was helping a woman with Hollywood A-list good looks and her much older beau out. McCarthy was pleased. A sprinkling of stardust on their evening could be just the fillip his boys needed.

McCarthy and his loudly joshing gang arrived at the door of the restaurant as the Hollywood types were disappearing inside. An impeccably turned-out young African lady stood with a computer tablet in her hand. Her body language told them that they should check in with her before entering the establishment.

She intuitively addressed McCarthy. 'It's reservations only tonight, sir.'

Nobody had expected the undeniably beautiful Italian accent that accompanied her words. Suddenly she went from good-looking to exotic.

'McCarthy. Table for six.'

She glanced down at her tablet, but something about her apprehensiveness told McCarthy at least that something was awry.

'I'm afraid there's been a mistake with the bookings, sir. We can't fit you in tonight. I'm so sorry.'

McCarthy's team were not slow to react.

'You gotta be kidding.'

'Why can't you move somebody else?'

'Man . . .'

But McCarthy had lived in the real world for longer than his young team. In the USAF your word could cost or save lives. In the markets your word was your bond – and calls were recorded just to make sure you understood that. In short, his word was everything, and he knew the value of such integrity, he knew the value that even a superchef restaurant put on its word, on its reputation.

Duke was the most vocally outraged. 'We should ask to see the manager, Louie.'

But McCarthy was way ahead of them.

'We could come back later.' Spoken with incongruous calm.

The African-Italian did not consult her tablet this time. 'No, sir, I'm afraid we don't have anything tonight.'

'What about tomorrow night?'

She stood silently, not wanting to tell him what she realized he already knew.

'Or the next?'

Nothing.

'Or any day in the near future?'

But now she was looking at the sidewalk and McCarthy knew that but for the low light and her ebony skin he would be seeing this lady blush. Eventually she managed to meet his stare.

'Mi scuso, signore.'

McCarthy's team had gone quiet. Each of them had reached the same conclusion: somehow McCarthy's credit must be, or be believed to be, bad and she was trying to save him the embarrassment of saying it. To add to their confusion their boss made to leave before turning back to her.

'Is it me in particular or our . . . profession?'

Her pretty bee-stung lips were twisted in her awkwardness. 'It's the insurance company. They won't cover us if we knowingly accept bankers. We're . . . I'm so very sorry.'

The five young men all but exploded in horror. The drama, the threat to them, the police presence, it was just background noise. It was just something that was happening to other people. But now it had affected them. It had cast them in the role of outsiders. But they were bankers, they were the best of the best. They were furious.

'Oh you gotta be kidding me.' 'We wanna see the manager.' 'Lady, there is no way we are not eating here.' 'Sons of bitches.' 'What the fuck?'

'*Guys.*'

And McCarthy had their full attention. And their begrudging silence.

'Let's go.'

His team were dumbfounded all over again. First being turned away for being bankers then their boss taking it? They didn't have a clue what was happening. They didn't get what McCarthy got: that everything had changed.

29

The Esplanade, Battery Park City. Webster was enjoying a toasted gruyère and pastrami sandwich on a bench overlooking the Hudson River. With a break in the clouds and the sun setting over New Jersey it was quite a pleasant place to while away a few minutes before the meet, cold February day or not. Byrne's tight schedule had not allowed Webster the customary early arrival he would have liked, but he'd still bought enough time on the phone to walk the few blocks around this part of Battery Park City first, just to be sure. But not the whole hour. His routine compromised. *I mustn't allow a repeat of that.* From the corner of his eye he'd nonchalantly watched the Secret Service agent approach. Dark leather blazer jacket, smart jeans, somehow looking taller than the six foot something the file had suggested. Noting that Byrne definitely retained the shape he was in when he carried out the activities he had read about in the past few years – once he'd gotten the non-restricted version of his file from an old friend. It had been hard but he'd gotten it.

As I approached I noted the physique of the fifty-year-old man on the bench. The black wool and cashmere overcoat – *nice* – not completely hiding that here was a man who still had something of his old Delta Force athleticism. The

Sovereign Bank security chief had contacted me out of the blue, and I'd carried out a routine background check: ex-CIA no less. Seen a lot of action down in Central America and Mexico, the CIA keeping itself busy propping up and bringing down governments faster than a scorpion stings, only without the guilty conscience. No doubt he had a capable resumé, the file not mentioning any acrimony at the end of his career. Not that that meant there wasn't any, it just meant it hadn't reached his file. Still, three divorces, one kid in Stockholm, they must have played a part. The rewards of being a covert operative. Maybe he was just burned out – why not. I'd read his file on the way over but was none the wiser as to his motives for the meeting. And then there was that CIA connection . . . The very people who'd vetoed my attempts to pursue Sovereign Bank for their dealings with Lazcano. Was he doing their dirty work? Sovereign's? Both? Or was I joining up random dots to make a picture only I could see? Maybe I was about to find out.

I reached him on the bench. He was sat at the far end, meaning I'd have to sit on his left, his action side. Some habits must be dying hard with this ex-agent.

'Bill Webster?'

'Is it that obvious?'

He smiled self-deprecatingly at me as I sat next to him. 'Mike Byrne.'

We swapped a professional handshake. This was business. He leaned back to get some kind of look at me, an upside-down smile of amusement.

'So, I hear you're the guy who figured out the terrorists' MO?'

Still in touch with some of his old buddies. Still quite pleased with his CIA credentials.

'I didn't know you were in the loop.'

He shrugged in a mock resigned manner. 'Once a spy . . .'

'And why did you stop being a spy?'

The ex-agent gave me a leery sideways glance like *Can I tell this guy here?* 'If you'd asked me five, seven years ago I would have given you the same old same old. Personal shit, the lowlifes they wanted me to cosy up to, this whole new Iran-Contra thing – only this time with drug cartels – across the border. Mexico's going to be our new Afghanistan – you know that, don't you?'

We shared an agreed look on that one.

'Christ, you know the drill, Mike. But that was when I left. If you must know, I guess it came down to money.'

I gave him a *How so?* look.

'Three alimonies, child maintenance, a life of my own, I couldn't afford it. I mean, look at the money being made out there,' casting a hand back towards the Financial District. 'I doubled my salary the moment I walked through the Sovereign Bank door. *And* nobody's shooting at me . . . Well, not yet.'

He grinned, waiting for my amused reaction.

'Fair enough. A person can only take so much.'

'Oh, I took it all right.' Shaking his head again.

'How long you been at Sovereign?'

He leaned his head to one side, recalling. 'Almost five years. Started as a fixer for Human Resources, you know, indiscretions and all that. I felt like a kindergarten cop.' Gesturing like *Haven't people got anything better to do?* 'Then,

as their paranoia went up, I got more and more responsibility until one day the Global Head of Security moved on
and there was nothing stopping me getting the job any
more.'

I gave a small, wry smile. 'Dead men's shoes?'

He returned that upside-down grin of his. 'Figuratively
speaking, naturally.'

I didn't have all day, and he knew how it was. 'What's
this about?'

The good humour fell away from his face and he
looked towards a passing tug boat on the wide Hudson,
its long shadow surrounded by the crimson reflection of
the setting sun. 'I feel pretty bad about meeting you,
Mike. Feel like I'm a stoolie here.' That sentiment was
consistent with his body language. He did seem awkward
about this.

'What's up?'

He sighed a heavy-hearted sigh. 'These bankers, they're
gonna get themselves killed.'

My face told him I wasn't following.

'I don't mean this whole Nemesis business. I mean,
that is what it is. One more divorce and I might have
joined them.' Holding up his hands to let me know he
wasn't being serious, leaning into an imaginary micro-
phone on my raincoat and saying, 'That's a joke, a joke,'
before resuming his place. Awkward body language, awkward socially. Maybe just nervous. Maybe something else.

'It's the Sovereign guys. I'm worried *they're* gonna get
themselves killed.'

OK, now he had my attention. Talking about my number one subject right now, not worrying about whether I

was really recording this, happy to have something like this on the record, in an off-the record kind of way.

He looked away to the tug boat, then looked back at me. 'They're out of their depth with this Lazcano customer.'

'So Lazcano's business wasn't quite legit?'

He smiled cryptically. 'I'm not saying that. Maybe I've got the complete wrong end of the shitty stick.' A little lean towards my lapel. 'For the record.' Smiling knowingly. 'My job is to protect them, you understand. And I can do that because of them or despite them. Am I Mr Selfless of the Year? No. I've got a nice thing going here, Byrne, and if they fuck it up it's still going to be me who carries the can, you know how it is. This is meant to see me through to a retirement, you know, a comfortable retirement. I don't take my luck for granted. I'll never get a deal as sweet as this ever again.' He looked away again. Maybe because he hated the fear of losing his sweet deal. Or maybe he feared the next thing he had to say. 'I met with that Turlington kid before he went down to see his *mysterious* . . .' spoken sceptically, bitterly '. . . prospective Mexican client. I told him not to go. I virtually begged him not to go. But I screwed up. Because I should have locked him in my office until he saw sense. I fucked up, Byrne, I fucked up big.'

He seemed momentarily frail, like a chill wind had blown through him, fighting the anguish.

'It's not your fault, they're chasing profits.' Me trying to probe a little deeper.

Eye to eye now. 'It *is* my fault, Mike. He was just a kid. Just a . . .' He turned his head away. Christ, I think he'd started to well up. He shucked his shoulders, regaining his composure. A sniff to draw a line under it. Turned back to face me. 'If I discover they're planning to hang their asses out there in the Mexican wind I'd like to be able to come to you. I'd like you to be able to help me stop their insanity. Their sense of . . . Jesus, I mean, they think they're untouchable. All that money, they really think this kind of shit couldn't happen to them. It's crazy.'

My nerves were humming with electricity. Webster could be everything I needed to nail the Lazcano case. This was the bit of luck you hoped for. The tip-off. Better than I could possibly have needed, even. If he was telling the truth. The agent in me keeping my guard up. The CIA's nixing of my Lazcano investigation bugged me. Was he still with the Company? Was he not so much working at Sovereign Bank as *embedded* there? OK, unlikely, but once a spy . . .

'Would you be prepared to go on the record? Wear a wire, that kind of thing?'

He hunkered up at that. 'I'd be prepared to save them from themselves. But I need this job, Mike. It's the first time I can remember I've had money in my pocket, and I've got to tell you, I like it. If you're not prepared to work with me, I'm not prepared to work with you. That's how it is.'

I wasn't about to push it to breaking point. For now. 'OK, I get it. And how do you want me to work with you?'

'You came to see Cochran and McCarthy about the threat from Nemesis.'

'That's right.'

'How real is it?'

'I think you could bank on it.'

'Got anything that would help me keep my guys alive a bit longer?'

'Nothing yet.'

'What about the wider investigation?'

'Nothing, that's just it. They haven't left a trail anywhere.'

'No security footage?'

'We think we might have the identity of one of the London suspects soon, but it's a long shot. So far.'

'And no contact from Nemesis themselves?'

'Calls to the *New York Times* claiming responsibility, but no demands, not a thing.'

'Any trace on those calls?'

I looked at him with the scepticism my answer deserved. 'An internet phone somewhere in Islamabad.'

'Pakistan?' He looked at me askew for a moment before grasping the sense of it, almost smiling despite himself. 'Bouncing it around the web? Jees. It's like the internet was designed for terrorists. Give me pay-phones any day.'

He studied the ground at his feet for a moment then sat up, his demeanour telling me he wanted to get away after a couple of last questions.

'The other agencies being helpful?'

I pulled a non-committal face. 'They can't afford not to be on this one.'

'I'll see if I can get any back-channels working. Some of my old buddies might have some scraps of intel of use.'

'All appreciated.'

'Let's keep New York's bankers alive, shall we?'

He stuck out his hand, meeting over. We shook, and I noticed his watch. Omega, at least $4,000 worth. Nice clockwork for a security chief. Nice clockwork for anybody. He was right. He did have a sweet deal.

30

'What a way to spend a Tuesday night, Ash. I'm freezing my butt off here.'

'You can *feel* the cold through that butt?'

'How about you feel my fist through this glove?'

Ashby allowed himself his first smile of the day. The very long, very uneventful day.

They were sat in his Ford Mustang Mach 1 on Barclay Street and West Broadway, just north of the World Trade Centre. Lights out, hungry and cold. Looking around at the buildings – the Sovereign Bank headquarters in particular. Hoping that something would happen, not believing for one moment that it would. Both of them rubbing their gloved hands together, moving their feet for warmth.

'Can't we put the heaters on or something?'

Ashby gave her a look that would have told her he thought she was a philistine if it hadn't been so dark that she couldn't see him. 'This is a 1973 muscle car, Marti. It doesn't have those sorts of features. You have to turn the engine on to make the heater work, and even then you have to wait a half hour for it to warm up.'

'So what are you waiting for? Turn the engine on.'

'Yeah, and I'll honk my horn whilst I'm at it, just in case Nemesis didn't spot us the first time.'

They looked away from each other out of their respective door windows, the banter the only thing keeping them warm. They stared and stared and saw nothing then some more of nothing.

Martinez broke the silence.

'I hate stakeouts.'

'You told me already.' Then he looked at her, hiding the interest in his eyes. 'Byrne stood you up again, lately?'

She looked at the car roof with a grimly amused despair then down into her lap. 'You know I'm here because of him, don't you?'

'*We're* here because of him. And it's the strongest lead we've got. Byrne might be right on this occasion. Anybody wants to get into position for a sniper attack on a Sovereign Bank employee they'll have to do it at night. He may not be the sucker I had him figured as, after all. Hell, we bust this we could be celebrities.' Ashby half-heartedly trying to lift morale.

'Celebrity would be nice, but I'd settle for a warm bed and the company of Mr Nowhere To Be Found.'

'But you want to watch those television cameras, Marti . . .'

'We're finding it hard to make time for each other. I mean, he is. He's snowed right now.'

'They can add ten pounds, you know . . .'

'I managed to book breakfast with him tomorrow. And who says romance is dead?'

'Don't want people saying you look like a fat version of Jennifer Lopez . . .'

'I mean, I knew what I was taking on, so it's OK.'

Ashby looked at her, shaking his head sorry-style. Disbelieving her words and disbelieving she would even try to convince herself everything was all right. 'You haven't listened to a word I've said, have you?'

'Why, what did you say?'

Ashby looked away in defeat but was cut off by what he saw. 'Shhhh.'

'No, I'm serious, what did you say?'

'Marti, *I'm* serious. Shhh.'

Whispered. Knowing each other too long to give a damn about each other's feelings in these moments. She followed his gaze to a dark figure one hundred yards ahead, pausing by the building across the road from Sovereign Bank's headquarters. A dark figure with a sports holdall. The figure looked about, checking who else was about and *watching*. Then the figure disappeared up the stairs of St Peter's Catholic Church.

'Is that place open tonight, Marti?'

'If it is they're a bit late for midnight mass.'

Ashby grabbed the comms device out of its cradle on the dashboard. 'Central, this is Ashby, we've got a 10-10 on the steps of St Peter's. We are preparing to investigate. Over.'

The comms unit hissed back before a female no-nonsense voice came through. 'All units, stand by, possible target. Over.'

Ashby put the comms device inside his pocket then pulled his pistol out from under his jacket, looking to his partner as he did.

'Ready?'

Martinez slammed a magazine into her own Glock with the heel of her hand. 'Just don't screw this up.'

Her partner shook his head as they both got out of the

car as quietly as they could. Both of the detectives pushed their doors closed using their bodyweight, to minimize the noise. Both moved to the nearside building and stayed as close to it as they could as they made their way in the direction of the church. A sudden banging, like a metal door being shoved into place, jolted the night-time air.

Behind Ashby. 'Careful there, buddy.'

Ashby, gun raised ahead of him, already had every intention of being just that. They stepped carefully along the sidewalk until they reached the edge of the church stairs. The gap – the alleyway – between the church and the neighbouring skyscraper was blocked off by a metal industrial door.

Martinez whispered from behind. 'You think that's the sound we heard? Our man climbing over the fence?' Looking through the gap by the gate hinges but seeing nothing, all too dark.

'Could be.'

'I'll go check the church.'

Martinez stepped round her partner, gun held low, moving almost silently up the wide stone steps to the first tall pillar, hiding round it, out of sight of the alleyway, sweeping the entrance to the church at the same time. Nothing. Three big sets of wooden church doors. She stepped towards the first. Pulling, but not shaking, she tried to open it. Nothing. She tried the same with the second and the third. The place asleep, like Lower Manhattan around them. Ashby waited for a sign from his partner. She signalled in the negative.

Ashby pulled out his comms unit – its volume way down – to speak, but a young female voice over the device beat him to it. 'Detective Ashby, this is Officer Truman. A suspect has just entered through the rear fire escape. Over.'

'This is Ashby to all units, do not engage the suspect, repeat, *do not* engage the suspect. Team One and Team Two we will meet you at Assembly Point A. Over.'

'Team One, on our way. Over.'

'Team Two, on our way. Over.'

Martinez had returned to Ashby's position by the alleyway gate. 'What's up?'

'One of the spotters saw the suspect entering the building by the back door, stairwell B.'

Martinez was bothered by something. 'You know, if they're tag-teaming their backup's going to see what's going on before we can even get near the perp.'

'What do you think? Roadblocks?'

'The works.'

'All units, I want the entire block and surrounding area sealed, locked down. Low-key, but nobody comes in or out until I say so. Over.' Ashby had an angry excitement in his eye. 'Time to catch a motherfucking terrorist.'

At the bottom of the skyscraper's stairwell the lone figure stood listening, heart pounding after the need to pull the emergency exit door closed. Not fully shut, as that would possibly re-engage the alarm. But closed enough that an observer would have had to be looking for it to see that it was open.

She was dressed in a black polo-neck, black jeans, black ski jacket and, since entering the alleyway, a black balaclava. All the things required to stay low-key and warm on a night like this. She hoisted her bag up on to her shoulder and looked up at the stairs ahead, which disappeared out of sight, lit as they were by nothing more than dim, fire-regulation wall lights. The task appeared seemingly endless, but the goal was worth every sacrifice. This was what she trained for, this was what she could do. With a moment's psyching-up she took the first of the many hundreds of steps ahead.

The concierge staff of the Barclay Tower were completely relaxed in the presence of the two teams of SWAT officers, helmeted, head-to-toe tactical black, sixteen in all. Four carried bullet-proof ballistics shields. All of them carried MP5 submachine guns. The concierge staff were relaxed because they too were undercover police officers, them-selves part of the stakeout.

On the reception desk was spread a layout plan of the roof of the apartment block, fifty-eight stories up. It showed a large central rectangle, the air-conditioning and other service mechanics of the building. Around it ran a path to each corner of the rooftop. Ashby, Martinez and the two lead SWAT officers were stood behind the desk, going over the plans.

Martinez pointed at the south-west corner of the roof-top. 'That's where the perp's headed.' The view from there directly down on to Sovereign Bank.

And almost as one they looked at the close-circuit television monitor behind the desk showing the black-and-white figure of the suspect mounting the stairs at an effortless pace. Thinking they were unseen. Thinking this wasn't a trap.

*

The woman froze her ascent three dozen floors up. The entrance had become invisible to her thirty floors below, but was that a noise? She looked down, but it was useless. Nothing to see. She stood motionless. Waiting. Listening. Her greatest fear playing out in her mind, the building swarming with police, making her heart and pulse race each other until she got a grip on herself. But she listened more intently. There *was* a noise. A mechanical noise. The elevator. For the briefest of moments she was alarmed by this then reasoned with herself that this was an apartment block. People came and went. *Stay calm. You've come too far. Finish the job.*

Nothing more to hear, she continued on up.

Two elevators. One SWAT team plus Ashby in one, one SWAT team plus Martinez in the other. As the elevators began to rise each SWAT team member felt the thrill of their job. All the training coming down to moments like this. Their minds calm, each one suppressing the excitement of taking down a terrorist on United States soil. But that's what they had been sent to do.

A door. *Please be the top.* She was exhausted, needing to sit down, collapsing, only adrenaline keeping her going. Her jacket open, her balaclava up on her head in the dark, beyond the last security camera. She needed – desperately – to rest, but it would have to wait until she was in position. Once she'd gotten herself set up she'd have all night to rest. She put her hand on the bar to open it, winced at the noise she could only do so much about limiting . . .

*

The elevator doors opened a second apart. Even though they had arrived inside the service block Ashby had asked for no more than the emergency exit signs to be lit. All eighteen officers stepped quietly out into the dim red light. Martinez spotted the north-facing door that would take them out on to the roof and slid the key into it. To her relief it unlocked near-silently and opened just the same. Opening the door no more than they had to, the two detectives slipped silently out and faced in opposite directions, guns at the ready.

Nobody.

Nobody that they could see.

Ashby signalled for the two SWAT teams to follow.

Now the assembled split into two groups. Each group preceded by a pair of police officers carrying heavily armoured ballistics shields.

Now they were going to pounce.

The young woman stopped at the corner of the roof, a low wall running round its outside. She had walked around it and at fifty-eight storeys high had found it to be excellent for her needs. Apart from the route that wound round the flat roof itself, most of the centre was taken up by a grand two-storey high unit with large black iron crosses on it. She was far from being a high-rise architect but she guessed the structure housed the air-conditioning and other such mechanics needed to make the building function. There was bold up-lighting to pronounce the criss-crossed top section of the building, but if she stayed by the edges it shouldn't pick her out.

She settled into one far corner, put down her bag and

looked over the edge. The view over Manhattan was magnificent. Not just the financial district and all of its landmark skyscrapers but beyond, to Liberty, Governors, Ellis and even Staten Islands, all lit up in the still February night. She slipped her iPod earphones on. For her the trip up the stairs was already worth it. But it was the view down towards Sovereign Bank that was the prize. One shot, that was all she needed. One shot and she would disappear.

One team had moved away first, the long way round. Hand signals had coordinated the timing, and the two teams had turned their respective corners to see the figure hunched over its holdall.

Both teams proceeded as noiselessly as they were able to. They crossed over half their respective distances stopping, as agreed, twenty-five feet from the target.

Both SWAT teams were fronted by their ballistics shields. Guns trained above and around these, guns trained on the target. The shields good against gunfire but nothing more.

Everything that could be planned for had been planned for. But so many unknowns. Was any part of the roof booby-trapped? Was the *target* booby-trapped? Each agent knowing that anything other than a head shot could strike explosives that could spell the end of everything for everyone. This was why they trained.

Martinez looked across to Ashby, nodded, letting him know she was about to say . . .

'FREEZE! POLICE! DO NOT MOVE! DO NOT MOVE!'

The target spun round on the spot, screamed, her head-phone wire wrapping around her face, she pointed her equipment at the agents, eighteen officers gripping their weapons, ready to fire if *anything* happened, the woman screaming, dropping everything, hands in the air, desperate not to provoke her attackers, screaming, screaming for dear life, her worst nightmares realized . . .

31

'A photographer?'

'No, a photojournalist.'

'Is there a difference?'

Martinez was resting with her back on Ashby's Ford Mustang, tired after her long night of surveillance. Tired, but still looking great in skin-tight, faded jeans and a cropped burgundy leather jacket. 'Well, only that it was a photojournalist and not a photographer who wet herself in front of us.'

We were stood on a sidewalk in Little Italy. The sun was out, making it feel like the first bright morning of the year. I stood with a small cardboard tray with three coffees in one hand, three bags of deli food in the other. She considered them, unimpressed, but maintained an equitable air of patience.

'I thought you said we were meeting for breakfast?'

I lifted up the food and beverage as I made my point. 'We are meeting for breakfast.'

'This your idea of a date?'

I shook my head. 'It's my idea of a breakfast.' I nodded at the car. 'What's with Eleanor?'

She looked at me pointedly, letting me know my attempt to change the subject wasn't going to work. But she was still confused. She tucked a long, loose strand of her dark hair behind an ear, leaving the ear sticking out. Just a different kind of beautiful. 'Who's Eleanor?'

'The car. It's a 1973 Ford Mustang Mach 1, right?'

Martinez pulled a face. 'Well, let me check my fuck-ometer and see.' She looked at some imaginary piece of equipment in her hand. 'Oh, yeah, so it is. Who's Eleanor?' Wearing an increasingly suspicious scowl.

'It's the name of the Mach 1 that was used in *Gone in 60 Seconds*. The original 1970s version. The same as that one.'

Martinez realized something. 'Ohhh. I see. That's why my geek partner bought it.' She looked down at its yellow body. 'I thought it was that Steve McQueen one with the bumpy streets.'

'Bullitt. No, that was a '68 Mustang GT.'

'Geek.'

'Yeah, I know, but why have you got it?'

She looked round at the glorious car with the same interest she might have shown a mailbox. 'Ashby gets it waxed in sunny Harlem and asked me to drop it in for him.'

'Wow. Letting you drive his beloved car.'

She gave the coffee and deli food another unimpressed stare, noting the three of everything, waiting till I'd seen what she'd seen. 'It's not just us is it?'

I pulled an uncomfortable face that tried to break the news to her that she was right. 'We'll pop in here then we'll go for breakfast, just the two of us.'

Martinez shrugged nonchalantly, leaving me non-plussed as to her mood. Or maybe just surprised about how easy she was making it on me. She stepped up to the narrow, shabby glass-fronted homeopathic storefront, its sun-bleached posters and adverts advertising discontinued products. It was, to all intents and purposes, long shut down. The kind of store you wouldn't give a second thought to. Just how the owner liked it.

Martinez pressed the buzzer. And pressed the buzzer. And pressed the –

A highly irritated Hungarian female came on to the decrepit door-intercom. 'What? What?'

Martinez stopped leaning on the button and looked at me, pure *Get yourself out of that one.*

I rolled my eyes and put my best placatory foot forward. 'Gabriella, it's me.'

'There are nine million *mes* in this city. Narrow it down.'

Martinez smiled at my discomfort.

'Gabby, it's me, Mike.'

Martinez rocked her jaw left and right which I knew was not the precursor to a happy remark. '*Gabby*, is it?' Flashing mock-daggers at me.

A heavy humming sounded and I thumped the door with the heel of my hand. Saved by the bell. Gabriella Hudec was at her traditional place. At the far end, behind the counter-top, playing a video game as if nothing in the narrow, decades-old store mattered. Which it didn't. She was dressed, as ever, like an eternal student. Street clothes that had never seen an iron, but clean nonetheless. Her round glasses reflected the twisted computerized events on her television screen. Gabriella, as ever, utterly unselfconscious of the need for any social graces.

I put the three coffees in their cardboard tray on the counter, then Martinez and I leaned against it and watched the game in question. Gabriella's eerily accurate sci-fi character was creeping through the desolate hull of a grounded spaceship, green smoke drifting across the bottom of the craft, each sound ratcheting up the tension, her female space-fighter halting, crouching, tilting its head to listen before relaxing and standing. Which is when the wall of the spacecraft was torn off and a three-headed figment of some possibly disturbed game designer's imagination grabbed the female character in its jaws and broke her apart with one bite.

Gabriella made a loud complaining noise before tossing her game-pad on to the counter. 'God damn, it impossible to finish this level.'

Martinez turned from the screen to the Hungarian. 'Don't these things give you nightmares?'

Gabriella gave her an emotionless stare as she spoke in her thick native accent. 'I not sleep in sixteen years.' Then she picked up a coffee, turned, slipped off her stool and disappeared behind a curtain at the back of the store.

Martinez looked at me and spoke *sotto voce* out of the side of her mouth. 'Yeah . . . with anyone.'

We were in the basement stairwell. We had already passed through the bomb-proof nine-bolt door at the bottom of the stairs. Then we had descended another bare set of stone steps to find ourselves stood before a steel door, with a warped-mirror effect. Gabriella slotted her hand into a tiny alcove beside it. Inside the recess a red beam scanned her prints. Satisfied, a small, soft thud signalled the basement door beginning to move, sliding left and out of sight, revealing the bright, white workshop beyond. You could keep Fifth Avenue, this was where I shopped.

And she was completely unofficial: off the radar, off the record and off the scale. My go-to girl for all things espionage, surveillance, counter-surveillance and then some.

Martinez surveyed the double-garage-sized room with her usual underwhelmedness. Its white shelves packed with boxes of equipment people in my line of work, legal or otherwise, might want. Only all of it modified by the Aspergers genius plodding across the room away from us.

Martinez considered the same white walls, same white ceiling, same white work bench in the middle and the same white workstation in the corner she had seen before. 'Oh, Gabriella, I love what you haven't done with the place.'

Gabriella either didn't hear or didn't care, but the detective got less than no reaction. The Hungarian put her coffee down at the sprawling workstation in the corner, hit a button on her computer and the half-dozen large screens in front of her dropped their bouncing Möbius-strip screensaver. The screens were large, flat and so seamlessly positioned that you could have watched a movie on them as if they were one massive screen. But for now there were a series of grainy, partial images of a man in a motorbike helmet. She even had Martinez's attention now. Each screen had a different image, which Gabriella talked us through.

'I taken footage of Wyatt restaurant bombing in London.' Her Hungarian accent becoming more pronounced as she became absorbed with her subject. She pointed at the top-left screen, where a quarter of a man's face could be seen as a motorcycle helmet was about to be pulled down on to his head. 'Here's best single shot of motorcyclist we've been given from security cameras in Chelsea area. I then track motorcyclist along route through West London, where, as you know, they lose him around Ealing.' On a second screen a map of the British capital showed the red line of the motorbike's route west. 'At no point along route do we get full facial of rider. However, his visor appears to be bothering him, probably moisture from breathing. As result, on four different occasions he lifts visor to clean inside.' The four remaining screens showed the motorcyclist at different points around London, mostly traffic lights, his hand wiping underneath his visor.

Despite the rather brilliant work on display Gabriella spoke about it unemotionally. Partly because of her condition, partly because – by her standards – it wasn't that brilliant.

Unconsciously, Martinez put a hand on my arm in excitement. 'Have we got a shot of the rider's face?'

Gabriella, still speaking evenly, shook her head in the negative. 'No. But we have partial reflections.'

I was already glued to the screens but out of the corner of my eye I could see Martinez almost mesmerized as Gabriella hit a couple of buttons on her keyboard and the last four screens – each of which showed a different London street scene of the suspect – began zooming in closer, homing in on an individual detail within each. The first towards a shop window, the second a car mirror, the third a driver's car window, the fourth the plastic covering a billboard advert by a bus-stop. Partial reflections.

Each image was hellishly pixelated such that all initial hope began to fade, Martinez's face betraying her sense that this might be a wasted exercise. But then two things happened. Each picture of the street detail began to judder into more accurate focus, as if downloading a big file. Yet still these pictures were painfully partial, a detail here or there, a sliver of the face, but nothing that you could get your mind round, work with. In addition, every picture was warped by the surfaces it was reflected in.

Then Gabriella hit another button and the second thing happened.

The original, and best, quarter shot moved towards the centre of all the screens where it was soon followed by the four partial images. Together they joined together like an overlapping jigsaw, each piece of a differing quality and grade but half a man's face now clearly visible, the man's right side missing completely but rendered as a wire frame.

I gently tapped Gabriella's shoulder. 'Can you enhance that?'

'Of course.'

Another button and another moment of computer wizardry. An invisible paint brush seemed to work down the picture until all the hues and complexions merged to a unified and consistent whole. Then the computer mapped the existing face across the absent wire-mesh side. A real person looking out at us. A real Arab male, late twenties, thirty maybe. Skinny faced, narrow, curiously gentle eyes, a soft mouth.

Gabriella waved an apologetic hand at the screen. 'Remember, nobody's face perfectly symmetrical. Basically, we don't know what right side of his face looks like. But should look like this.'

I was more than impressed. 'Well done, Gabriella. Can

you send it to Park, my AV guy at the Service, he'll circulate it for me.'

I glanced at Martinez. She was speechless, transfixed by the Hungarian's work as if it held the secrets of the universe.

'You said there was something else.'

Gabriella spun round in her chair. 'Oh, yes. Now good part.'

The Hungarian led us through a door at the rear. From here we travelled down a corridor that rounded a corner then doubled back on itself to where a slightly convex metal door with a central wheel for a handle – not unlike a ship's water-tight door – confronted us. She spun the wheel to the left then, judging it loosened enough, pushed it open into a long, wide, arched space. The gun-range.

It was the size of a large, century-old sewer for the very good reason that it was a large, century-old sewer. When Gabriella had bought the place she had been more interested in what was beneath the ground than what was above it. She had given the abandoned sewer walls her signature whitewash and then used the hundred-yard-long tunnel section as her own private shooting alley.

At the near end was a table with various pieces of shooting-range equipment. Targets, used and unused, boxes of bullets, a laptop and a Sig Sauer 229 semi-automatic hand-gun, the same as my own service gun. She handed out ear defenders, which we all put on, then gave me the pistol.

From its weight and balance I held what felt like a modified pistol in my hand. Gabriella nodded towards the target one hundred feet down the range. The outline of a human, rings over key areas of the body, eyes, heart, fore-head.

'Go ahead, try.'

I turned, took a solid stance, raised the gun, sighted down the barrel and pulled the trigger. Or, at least . . . I tried to pull the trigger.

Martinez fought and lost a battle with a grin and coughed pointedly. 'Safety catch, Mr Byrne?'

I didn't look at the gun. 'No. What is it, Gabriella?'

She was wearing as big a smile as I had ever seen her wear, which wasn't saying much. 'Fingerprint recognition.'

I pulled an impressed face. 'Nice.'

She took a lead running from the laptop next to her and plugged the other end into the base of the pistol in my hands.

'Hold it tight.' Talking like a doctor asking me to breathe in for a medical.

We all looked at the laptop, where a computer-rendered picture of the same pistol was now glowing with finger-prints where my hands held it. A message read *Identity Locked.*

She pointed her finger down the range. 'Now try it.'

I turned and fired the gun. Four times. Moving around the target. Heart, both eyes, forehead. All a few milli-metres above dead centre.

Martinez was unguarded for a moment. 'Shit, Byrne, that's some shooting.'

Gabriella eyed the gun, then me. 'How does it feel?'

I balanced it in my hand. 'Were they regular .357s?'

'Yes.'

I was impressed. 'Good. Slightly heavy in the grip. The extra hardware?'

The Hungarian bothered by her imperfection. 'Yeah.'

She took the gun barrel-first from me and presented it to the detective.

'Oh, no, I enjoyed the demonstration but we're actually on a date.' Martinez making sure I didn't miss one drip of her sarcasm.

Gabriella didn't budge but stood, gun proffered handle first. 'I want you to shoot him.'

That was perplexing even for me. I thought Martinez was going to floor her.

'Are you out of your mind?'

'Trust me. He'll be perfectly safe.'

Martinez was trying to understand the situation, her face betraying the range of scenarios she was imagining. It was a bizarre request, but I trusted Gabriella. Enough. Just about enough. Clearly it wouldn't recognize Martinez's hand and would fail to work.

'It's OK, Martinez.'

Martinez looked at me with surprise. Then she took the gun, almost snatched it, from the Hungarian.

'Why him? . . . Why don't I shoot you?' Smiling with more than a hint of malice at turning the tables on the inventor.

Gabriella was completely relaxed about the idea. 'Him, me – you choose.'

Martinez was disturbed by the idea, then the funny side of the situation must have hit her and a wicked smile grew out of her mouth and she pointed the gun at Gabriella. 'Nothing personal, Gabby.'

Gabriella's eyes snapped open.

The scream surprised even me.

I knew somebody being stunned by an electric shock when I saw it, but the actual noise Martinez made was almost like a whinnying horse. The high-pitched scream seemed to elongate with her body, sound and body arching back together.

Then she hit the deck.

Gabriella beamed at me. 'Built in Taser. I call it my Tesla Gun. It's patented and everything.'

I looked at Martinez lying on her side on the floor, incapacitated, just wanting oxygen, her muscles to uncontract and the memory of the pain to go away. She'd live. I looked back at Gabriella.

'What's the trade-off?'

'The battery takes it from nine down to four bullets.'

She picked the pistol up from Martinez's disabled body on the floor. She popped the cartridge and showed it to me. Sure enough, as well as chambering bullets, the top of the cartridge looked like the teeth of a Taser gun.

'You can actually use it as a hand-held stun device, but it's so close up that it's hard not to get shocked yourself, so . . .' Her face suggesting I not try that too often.

The sunlight hit Martinez like a migraine. She shielded her eyes and came to a stop outside Gabriella's store.

When she finally spoke it was unemotionally and with complete sincerity. 'When I get my shit together I'm going to come back here and put a bullet between her fucking eyes.'

'Well, not with the same gun, obviously.'

If looks could kill the stare she gave me would be facing a twenty-five-year stretch.

'So, fancy breakfast?'

The trouper Martinez somehow finding the strength to set aside her physical aches and pains. 'Sure, where were you thinking?'

My cell phone rang with a personalized ring tone. I reached inside my jacket, knowing who it would be.

'Diane.'

'Michael, McCarthy and his team have been locked out of the Sovereign building since yesterday. We can't use him as bait any more.'

I looked heavenward. Bad news. Very bad. 'Do we know where he is?'

'Randall Airfield, Orange County.'

'Why? Is he going somewhere?'

'That's all I know. Michael, I think you'd better . . .'

'Get over there.'

'Right away.'

I snapped the cell shut. 'Martinez, I need to borrow your car.'

The image of Martinez standing on the sidewalk in the rear-view mirror of Ashby's Mustang as I sped away through Little Italy suggested a rather tired figure. And I didn't think it was the result of the tasering.

32

I hadn't stayed below the speed limit since leaving the city and got to the airfield in double-quick time. Randall Airport was a single-strip operation an hour north-west of the city. As I sped along the perimeter road next to the runway I had a sinking feeling that things were too quiet. Maybe McCarthy's plane would be parked here, maybe he'd flown the coop. But it looked worryingly quiet to my eyes. Then I had that thing I always like a little of – luck.

I saw McCarthy's own Mustang coming in to land, his Cavalier Mustang, landing alongside my arriving car. And in the beauty stakes I would have to give it to him, hands down. The polished metal bird was magnificent. A shining aluminium bird of prey that would steal the show down in Reno. I'd visited a race meeting down there a few years back, World War II planes and the like pulling circles at speeds that looked set to tear the old planes apart. Utterly insane and utterly gripping. Every classic plane imaginable being flown to the limit in the blistering Nevada heat. And none prettier, in my opinion, than the P-51 Mustang, the one McCarthy had bought a converted version of. A nose that goes on for ever, a bullet with wings. Beautiful. I was starting to think he might have some taste, after all.

By the time McCarthy had fully touched down I had found my borrowed car overtaking it just as I needed to slow to enter the airport's security gate. A quick flash of my Secret Service badge and I was inside and making my way to a taxi point off the end of the runway. I parked my car nearby and could see the aircraft being greeted by a small group of men fixing a ladder to its side. I recognized them as members of McCarthy's team. So the whole gang was here.

I closed the car door as the pilot began descending from the aircraft. Time to check in.

Through the circular view afforded by the telescopic lens, McCarthy could be seen dropping off the last step of the ladder to the ground where he was met by his young team. They talked energetically as McCarthy took off his helmet, before his attention was caught by something off to one side. The viewer scanned the lens left to see a person walking away from a yellow 70s muscle car. A tall man in a dark leather jacket and jeans. Standing in the view-finder's cross-hairs.

The gun in question was an M-24 bolt action rifle resting on bi-pod legs for stability. A sniper's weapon. An assassin's weapon. Alecto lifted her eye from the rifle and wondered what this new development meant. She pursed her lips, watching the new man join the others with her naked eye, the group five hundred yards away from her position in the longish grass of a hill outside the airport. This was unexpected. Alecto took a wire running from the side of the high-tech telescopic lens and plugged it into the bottom of her smartphone. After a couple of seconds the view as seen through the lens appeared as a film on the smartphone's 4.7 inch screen. She returned her eye to the viewfinder and tracked it over the new man's profiled face. He was talking good-naturedly, if formally, with the group. He turned to point at something down the runway and revealed his face in full. She had to admit to herself that he was a pretty good-looking guy. Tall, very well built, with short, dark hair above a friendly if tough face. Bluish eyes, if she wasn't mistaken. She looked down at her smartphone. Mike Byrne filled the screen. She took a photo. And then another when he turned slightly more towards her.

She pursed her lips. *What to do?*

This would require a conversation.

She swiped her phone's screen and it switched to another app – one running *The Xia Chronicles*, the online fantasy game she used for communicating with other members of Nemesis. The screen showed her princess character waiting by a crudely drawn waterfall. In front of her princess was the troll, sleeping in a standing position, little *zzz*s drifting from its tusked mouth. She tapped on the troll's head and it woke with a start. Then she tapped on a dialogue box and chose *Add file*. She selected the photos of Mike Byrne and sent them as the message.

Alecto knew the online game was always slow when uploading files, more so from a smartphone, so returned her gaze to the gun's lens. She refocused on the target. Byrne wasn't on the move and tracking the sight up his body to his head was an easy – and not unpleasurable –

exercise. Then she heard a ping on her smartphone. She looked down to see a message within the game.

'*His name is Mike Byrne.*'

Her eyes widened. She tapped in a reply. '*The USSS guy?*' '*The same.*'

'*Want me to finish?*'

Her heart started to speed up as she waited for the reply. Then, instinctively – in case the order suddenly came and knowing that opportunities could be fleeting – she slipped her finger over the trigger and resighted the rifle over Byrne's head. A *ping*.

'*No.*'

She scanned the rifle to the right, to the pilot. Once she had him in her sights she looked down and messaged one-handed.

'*OK. What about DM?*'

There was another pause before she got her reply, then, '*No. Abort.*'

'*Why?*'

'*Too suspicious. Confirm abort.*'

Alecto looked unhappily at the phone. She swallowed her impatience, relaxed her stance at the rifle and sighed before typing. '*OK.*'

She was not pleased. She reached forward and flipped the front-lens cover down on the sight then rolled on to her side, frustrated. All the pumped-up adrenaline of a kill having nowhere to go.

I looked at the young men in their camouflaged jumpsuits. Possibly dressed for flying, possibly dressed for who knew what. War games?

'So what gives? You look like you're all in training for something.'

The five young men shared a collective self-consciousness. Only McCarthy shrugged it off.

'No, a bit of desk bonding. Been taking them up in the air for a ride.'

'What else we gonna do now we're suspended?' The young African-American guy.

McCarthy slapped him down with a look but kept it cool as he spoke. 'We're not suspended, FiDi. We've been asked not to frequent our place of work.'

The young Polish man spoke next. 'I say we go to Aspen early. Get in some skiing.'

All the young men nodded, liking that. McCarthy all but rolled his eyes.

'You seem very relaxed about the Nemesis threat. I mean, that's why they've locked you out of your building, right?'

McCarthy bridled slightly at my last remark. He was meant to.

'What would you like us to do, whine about the nasty people with guns? Act like victims? I don't think so, Mr Byrne.' Something about his tone suggested he might be going down a route of his own.

A pumped-up member of his team spoke up, sounding like a jock. 'They want a fight, we'll give them a fight. Bring it on. Boo yah.'

His little speech egged on the younger men, who swapped little high-fives.

Then McCarthy either wanted to speak to me alone or didn't want me hearing more of his team's bravado. If it was just bravado.

'Guys, why don't you go back to the hangar? I'll meet you there.'

They got the message and replied with a few *sures* and left us to it.

My file told me there were six traders on McCarthy's desk – seven before Turlington's ill-fated trip to Mexico. I nodded after the group by way of a question.

'Where's the sixth member of your team?'

McCarthy looked uncomfortable at my question, momentarily unsure of himself when he spoke. 'Excel? He's at home sick. His girlfriend's looking after him.'

Excel. I remembered him from his file, the nickname for Stephen Lewis. Good-looking blond kid from the West Coast, a touch of the young Robert Redfords about him. If they were satisfied he was OK I wasn't going to dwell on it.

I looked after the group as they disappeared into the hangar. 'You know, McCarthy, the whole point about terrorists is that they're not looking for a fair fight. This isn't the WBO, we can't put up a purse and hope that the best vigilantes win.'

'Why not, Mr Byrne? Because as far as I can see your current plan to deal with this Nemesis, or whatever the hell they're called, is to hope they don't kill us before you luck into catching some of them.'

'You have to trust that the government is doing everything it can.'

McCarthy shook his head dismissively and smiled bitterly.

'The government isn't the solution, Mr Byrne, it's the

problem. With all your billions of Homeland Security spending every year you didn't stop 9/11, you didn't stop the shoe-bomber – hell, it was the passengers on flight A118 that overcame the terrorists. People are shooting at us bankers and you're telling us – *ordering us* – to sit on our hands. Just sit there and take it like sitting ducks. Well, I'm here to tell you that we're not going to take it any more. And don't make out the terrorists are a goddamn aberration because we've been treated like piñatas ever since the Credit Crunch. You bleed us dry of taxes every year, and what have you got to show for it? Nothing. Well, let me tell you something, G-man, we've got the money and we've got the resources, so let *we the people* deal with this goddamn problem for once, OK?'

I hoped he felt better for getting that off his chest. I replied in an even manner.

'If I remember it correctly, Mr McCarthy, it was we the people who gave you that money in the first place when we bailed you out. And we the people would have an awful lot more money to secure this homeland of ours if we hadn't had to pump trillions into the quantitative easing required to clean up the consequences of your casino banking. Now, we're trying to protect you and your entire profession but we can't do that if we don't know where you are. Is there any chance that you might want to co-operate with us here?'

His face had reddened during my reply. 'No, Special Agent Byrne, there isn't. No chance at all. If you think we're just a bunch of casino bankers then you're no better than the terrorists.'

I took out my car keys and looked at them for a moment before looking up into McCarthy's exercised face.

'I apologize, Mr McCarthy. There is a huge difference between casinos and banks.'

'Damn right there is.'

I nodded gently. 'In casinos they gamble with their own money, in banks they gamble with ours.'

33

Patterns. They'll save your life.

We're always told to keep an open mind, but, as a wit once observed, if you open your mind too much your brain would fall out. *Patterns*. Life throws them at you. You have no choice but to live by them. Trust in their recurrence. Every time we put our feet on the ground it seems to hold us up. A pattern. A pattern we trust so much we walk down the street without giving a thought to the possibility it might all disappear beneath us. It's how we function. The alternative is madness. *Patterns*. Physics. Patterns so trustworthy we call them laws of nature. We trust these laws implicitly, if we didn't we'd be screaming with terror every time a passenger plane took off. *Patterns*. Even human behaviour has patterns we can live by: people run from danger; lie to me once shame on you, lie to me twice shame on me; Congress is incapable of passing bills that aren't stuffed with irrelevant clauses to do with lobbyist-inspired pork-barrel kickbacks. *Patterns*.

I was thinking about McCarthy's position. What pattern did it fit? Arrogance? Yes. Overconfidence? Definitely. But they weren't the patterns I was worried about. There was another behaviour type there. His mind was elsewhere. He had an investment in something else, somewhere else. A plan? A plan of action? He was a former Air Force pilot. A man of action. Maybe he had a plan and he was going to put it *into* action. I'd seen that pattern of behaviour before. The take-it-into-my-own-hands pattern. Always ended badly. Always. I wondered if Webster could shed any light on it. I wondered . . .

Patterns. They'll save your life.

Like when you're driving along a freeway, thinking about the meeting you've had or are about to have. And the traffic doesn't behave the way it should. When you see four vehicles of the same class – SUVs – all travelling in a long column a few cars behind you. A possible pattern, an unusual pattern. Then the four SUVs, snaking through the traffic together. *Together.* The cars new models. A red Ford Escape, a white Chevrolet Tahoe, a grey Chevrolet Equinox, and then, bringing up the rear, a big black Chevrolet Suburban. Four new cars, all clean, all popular rental choices. Out-of-town killers don't use their own cars when they can avoid it. *Patterns.* Each car carrying two passengers. The pattern of hitmen the world over. The driver and the shooter. The faces Mexican-looking. *Patterns.* Normally I tried not to racially profile anybody, but since Mexicans were making a habit out of targeting me recently I decided to err on the side of caution. I had company driving like crazy behind me. Mexican company. That or Dominoes was late with some pizzas.

Patterns. They'll save your life.

I began to pick up a little speed, pulling away from the traffic about me, an eighteen-wheeler way up ahead. The freeway two lanes in both directions. I was not surprised that the four SUVs slithered their way through the remaining cars until they too were free of the nearest traffic. Then they changed formation. No longer a line of cars, but two rows of two. Somehow feeling like an attack formation. I pulled my service issue Sig Sauer P229 out of my shoulder holster as I did so. I was going to need it.

I slammed my foot down on the accelerator as a gunman leaned out of each lead car behind me.

As I pulled away I heard the sound of automatic gunfire behind me, submachine guns, bullets tearing up the road on both sides of my car, bullets that would soon be tearing me up. Weapons that would prove a dangerous nuisance from a distance, deadly close up.

Ninety miles an hour climbed over one hundred as my borrowed yellow Mustang raced past the eighteen-wheeler and its load of timber. Accelerating, the one thing this V8 muscle car was truly good at, nought to sixty in under six seconds if she was set up right. But that was in the 1970s. On paper, today, my car didn't have much of an edge. Even though I could out-accelerate them their top speed was probably above mine. Reality didn't seem to disagree. Whilst I extended my lead momentarily these straight-off-the-production-line cars were soon gaining on me.

I could see the four SUVs approach the rear of the eighteen-wheeler timber truck. Two stayed in the outside lane. The two on the inside veered right on to the shoulder. All four cars screaming past the truck together.

My biggest problem was the two cars on the left. The shooters in the cars on the right had to lean across their driver, a minuscule respite for me. The shooters in the left-hand cars had clear shots of me. Which is why as soon as I got past the timber truck I jumped into his lane and slowed aggressively, keeping my car three feet from his looming vehicle. That earned me an angry bellow from the trucker's air-horn. But it also bought me the two seconds I needed as the Mexicans dashed past me on both sides before immediately slowing on realizing where I had hidden myself. But all four overshot me for a brief moment, a brief moment I used to ram the rear side of the backmost SUV on my left, the red Ford Escape turning one hundred eighty degrees, the driver trying to right the car, but the gunman with a clear shot of me as he leaned out of his window that was spinning away with the turning car, emptying his gun at me, bullets tearing through my passenger-side windscreen, my hood, the front-right lights, the gunman unsettled as his car turned fully back to front into the inside lane, in front of the truck, me accelerating up the left side, getting parallel with the backwards-facing Ford, its driver on my right for an instant. The instant I put a bullet in his head.

I pulled round the Ford Escape, into the inside lane and floored the Mustang, shooting through the three decelerating SUVs, seeing in my rear-view mirror the eighteen-wheeler pushing the driverless Ford ahead of itself like a snow-plough before the SUV flipped over, the truck unable to do anything but ride rough-shod over it before its own cabin began to lean sideways, the car under its trailer, the eighteen-wheeler rolling on to its left, its load of tree-length logs breaking free behind it as the truck skidded sideways along the freeway to a slow halt, the decimated Ford and its passengers beneath it.

In the confusion my Mustang gained the briefest of ground on the SUVs before all three Chevvies began to chase me down again. My classic American muscle car versus their twenty-first-century technology. It wasn't whether I was going to die, it was at what speed.

For half a mile there was a scattering of commuter traffic which forced my pursuers to break formation and chicane through behind me, but we soon had an empty stretch ahead of us. A wide-open stretch.

The SUVs spread out, taking up both lanes and the shoulder. The wall of cars charged towards my Mustang. Out of each car the shooter leaned. Bullets were ripping the back of my car to pieces. I ducked lower as I heard – or was it *felt?* – the rear lights taken out, as well as the rear windscreen, not to mention the dozens of bullets bursting into the trunk. I only had so much time and so many tyres before my luck ran out. They were no more than fifty feet behind me, only the impediment of the speed keeping the gunmen from wiping me out. But that wouldn't last. All of our cars thundered under a bridge, all of us now bearing down fast on a convoy of maybe six trucks on the inside lane. I approached them from directly behind before going round to their left at the last moment, doing anything to throw the Chevvies – and more especially the gunmen – off balance.

I glanced up at the rear-view mirror. Two cars had stayed with me, presumably the other one had gone up the shoulder on the right. The shooter in the car behind me had crawled out and sat up on his door's window edge, giving himself the clearest possible view of me.

I tore past the convoy of eighteen-wheelers and imme- diately pulled right, in front of the lead truck. But the Mexicans were not going to be fooled twice. Out of nowhere my car was slammed heavily into the traffic bar- rier on the left.

Slammed again.

Slammed again, and the Chevrolet Tahoe stayed there, forcing me up against the barrier, sparks flying out of the side of my vehicle as the protective barrier ground away at its panels. The Mexican looking across at me, angry, furious even, like he wanted to squeeze the life out of me. If he kept this up I was guessing he would.

I hit the brakes, freeing myself from the Mexican's grip, before immediately hitting the accelerator and coming round his right side and ramming *his* car to the left with mine. Only, the math wasn't looking too great. Within seconds another Chevvie – the Equinox – hit me from my right, and suddenly I was being pinioned between the two of them, both leaning into my car so aggressively that I wasn't sure if I was driving forward or being carried. On each side the gunmen levelled their submachine guns at me, ready for the turkey shoot, the Mexican on my left having to lean *away* from me to get a clear line of fire.

Sons of a bitch. I could have sworn the one on my right smiled as he pulled the trigger.

I mashed the brake pedal into the carpet, tearing myself free and backwards from the cars as their respective shooters emptied their guns into the space between them. Into each other.

Both Chevvies suddenly veered out of control, both quickly sliding side on before they both flipped again and again and again, giving me no choice but to negotiate a tight zigzag path between their spinning frames as I continued my escape.

But now the remaining SUV – the mammoth, black Chevvie Suburban – and its occupants had me in its sights, and its shooter was emptying his gun into the rear of my car. As my rear fender disintegrated and flew off I knew I didn't stand a chance like this.

As hard as I figured the car would be able to – and some more for good measure – I wrenched the Mustang to the right up an exit ramp I'd seen out of the corner of my eye. A ramp that stopped almost as soon as it had started. *What the . . .?*

The Mustang flew through the air before slamming heavily into the ground and bouncing back up on its heavy springs and shocks as I found myself on an unfinished road, a dirt track. My entire body had been shaken like a sack of bones and in my surprise controlling the car was an achievement in itself. I didn't have a clue where I was. It was – what? – a site cleared for a possible construction of some kind. What did it matter? The Suburban had followed relentlessly, leaping off the end of the asphalt ramp and on to the dirt road beyond, bouncing ruthlessly in line, ruthlessly pursuing me like a panther chasing a savaged deer.

I wondered how much more Ashby's car could take of this. How badly had it been hit? How badly had it been damaged? Then the gas gauge light began to blink like a badly timed joke.

'Just what do you think you are doing?'

The younger man looked at the older man, slightly nonplussed. 'Getting back to work.'

The foreman, sat on a rock as he was, almost laughed in the negative. 'I don't mean that. I mean *that.*'

And he pointed at the freshly crushed Coke can lying

where it had been thrown on the dirt floor of the chasm they stood in.

The unshaven younger man in workman's overalls gestured around the colossal, freshly excavated gorge, its floor a full one hundred feet below surface level. 'Sam, this place is gonna be a landfill in a week. What does it matter?'

The old African-American man shook his head, disappointed. 'We'll let the good people of Orange County decide what's going in their landfill, shall we, not some litter bug like you. Pick it up.'

The young man tutted under his breath and did as he was told.

'And that one while you're at it.'

The young man looked at another nearby soda can, almost offended.

'But I didn't drop that one.'

The old man took off his protective helmet, wiped the bald top of his head with a blue dotted handkerchief and replaced his hat. 'Pick it up anyways, it'll be character-building.'

The young man had to bite down on a curse, clenching his teeth as he snatched the other can off the floor of the gigantic hole.

The black Suburban was coming up on my previously yellow car's left – the gunman's side. The gunman using the window edge to rest his assault rifle on. Peppering my car with bullets, my only defence the bumpiness of the road, throwing off enough shots to buy me some time, but not enough to save the car, which was seeing every window, square foot of metal and rubber fired at.

I was running out of gas, out of ideas and now, I saw, road. We were all driving at ninety miles an hour towards the lip of something. A slope? A riverbed? Something worse? Then I felt my front left tyre being taken out.

At that exact moment I saw the far edge of whatever hell hole we were approaching. It was some kind of quarry.

Both cars were around two hundred and fifty feet from the edge of the chasm. The braking distance of this car, at this speed was about two hundred and fifty feet.

On a regular road – with working tyres.

Not a dirt track.

I hit the brakes as hard as I could. The other driver clearly had the same realization at the same instant.

A cloud of dust billowed out around us as both cars strained to hold the road, hold on to anything.

I grabbed the door handle.

A rock and a hard place.

I went to pull the door open.

Only it was jammed.

Jammed shut by the pounding the car had taken.

The road running out before me.

Me shoving at the door.

Suddenly no more road to be seen.

Slamming myself against the goddamn door . . .

Both the workmen saw them together, both gasping as one as the two cars roared out into midair, across from right to left, arcing across the sky, their passengers pushing themselves away from their dashboards in helpless terror as both vehicles landed in the centre of the massive man-made hole, the Suburban exploding on contact, its instant fireball taking the Mustang with it, the cars bouncing and colliding together until they crashed into the far wall of the canyon, where they came to a rest.

I rolled what seemed like for ever, desperately trying to slow myself, pushing my arms out to break my speed, slowing, bounding over and over until eventually I stopped. Two feet from the edge. Coughing as much from the cloud of dust about me as the pummelling my lungs had taken.

I heard the explosion as I came to a halt, turned my head to one side to see the *woof* of flames from the gas tanks erupting, a trail of black smoke spewing up after them.

I lay my head back on the ground, wishing to God sleep would take me.

In the soon-to-be-landfill the young workman looked from the wrecked cars to his foreman, once more to the cars then back again.

'I suppose you want me to pick that up as well?'

34

The ancient Mayan city of Calakmul is situated in the south-east of Mexico in the state of Campeche twenty miles from the Guatemalan border. It was known by its people as the Snake Kingdom and was one of the most powerful in all of Mayan civilization. Today it is in ruins, hidden in remote tropical rainforest. At the heart of Calakmul is one of the tallest known Mayan pyramids, guarded by no more than vegetation, insects, howler monkeys and the occasional jaguar. To climb it is to risk personal safety, beset as it is by threats both natural and unnatural. To climb it is to experience one of the wonders of the world. It is from this civilization and this temple that the striking Calakmul Building in the Santa Fe district of Mexico City took its name.

Santa Fe was once a mining town and then a garbage dump. Then, in recent times, it combined the spirit of both enterprises to become a financial centre. After the earthquakes and bulging population crisis in the 1980s, Mexico City's Santa Fe district was developed at breakneck speed. Building activity was frenetic as skyscrapers and aesthetically bold low-rise constructions mushroomed throughout the area. One such building was the Calakmul Building. It is a nine-storey cube of mirrored windows with, on each side, a nine-storey concrete façade, a square with a large circular hole in the centre. It is bold, it is visionary and it looks like a mammoth laundry machine. The locals were quick to dub it La Lavadora. Its tenants were various, but the seventh floor was given over to Banco Orro and the offices of its Private Clients division. Its clients included Eduardo and Gabriel Lozcano.

When the Lazcano brothers were able to stay on the move or visit one of their own residences they used anonymous vehicles with multiple decoys. When a visit was to premises they did not control no such ruses were employed. Instead a fierce show of security worthy of a presidential detail was rolled out. Today was such a day. Today the Calakmul Building and the surrounding streets were in total lockdown.

The exits from the Vasco de Quiroga, Antonio Dovali Jaime and Sta Fe freeways were all blocked by two squad cars each from the Mexico City police department. Though it was not on state business and though it contravened a slate of local and federal laws, such was the relationship — mostly financial — with the Lazcanos that this service was willingly provided. Drivers wishing to enter the cordon were told to not wait but to move on or, at best, be arrested. But this was just the start. The real security was inside the automobile blockade.

On each side of the building stood two Lazcano security guards in their all-black SWAT-like outfits, complete with body armour, dark glasses and ear-pieces. Across the chest of each was held an FN Herstel PS90, a futuristic-looking, compact semi-automatic gun that lay somewhere between a submachine gun and an assault rifle. In use in Afghanistan, Iraq, the United States Secret Service and drug cartels across Mexico. The Mexico City police present simply looked away from this flagrant transgression of national law. See no evil . . .

The entrance to La Lavadora was through a downward pedestrian escalator on one side, a basement car park on the other. The building's usual dark-suited security on the pedestrian entrance was today joined by four of Lazcano's men with guns and body armour. They insisted on seeing the ID and the contents of any bags of all those entering. They offended everybody, and nobody protested. The entrance and exit ramps to the car park were unapologetically blocked by four jeeps and SUVs surrounded by six more Lazcano men. Even if people got past the police road block *nobody* was moving in or out of the car park for the duration of the visit.

Inside, the building's reception floor was patrolled by four more armed bodyguards, as was the elevator entrance on floor seven. Finally, stationed outside the office of the president of Banco Orro's Private Clients division itself were two more Lazcano bodyguards. They, unlike their associates, wore no (visible) body armour, nor did they carry FN Herstel PS90 submachine guns. They wore black suits and carried FN Herstel Five-seveN semi-automatic pistols. They had to show a little tact around the president of the bank, after all.

Not so the Lazcanos.

'How many times will you need one more week?'

Gabriel was dressed pin-sharp in a light-coloured suit with a bright powder-blue open-neck shirt, a handsome man fit for the cover of *Vanity Fair*. Beside him sat his older, gruffer, scruffier brother, Eduardo, in a dull-coloured Hawaiian shirt over khaki pants. A man fit for a makeover. The Beauty and the Beast.

Gabriel Lazcano had asked the question from across a large desk made from Granadillo wood, tan-coloured and streaked with brown. A good wood, a Mexican wood. A Mexican bank proud of its Mexican heritage. The man on the other side of the desk was Señor Huerta, president of Banco Orro's Private Clients division. He was small, fifty-ish, slightly overweight, with pudgy features that on a good day could look homely, stern or comical. But not today. Today his face actually ached from the battle to not let a mask of fear descend over it.

The bank president's office was unostentatious, simple, functional, like the man on the other side of the table. The only concession to ornament was a family photograph on his desk: himself, his wife, his five children, one daughter in graduation robes.

Most corporations award the corner office to their top executives. With the corners of La Lavadora covered by concrete façades, the prize position was in the centre of the floor where the light came in. Beyond the windows was an uninspiring view. The Sheraton Hotel and a freeway and offices after that. The mirrored windows allowed no one to see in during daylight hours without great effort. The Lazcanos had liked that.

The bank president twisted a gaudy gold ring on his little finger. A gift from the Lazcano brothers. In better times. He felt sick, he felt dizzy.

'I thought it was understood that the very act of getting your money through the *casas de cambio* was achievement enough. I don't understand how you can hang Sovereign Bank's losses round my neck.' Not spoken defiantly, implored.

Gabriel, the diplomat, looked from his sleepy-eyed brother to the terrified bank manager. The younger Lazcano's body language was conciliatory, almost apologetic, as only the powerful can afford to be when they hold the fate of somebody in their hands.

'Señor Huerta, my brother and I do not understand the intricacies of the banking world. Otherwise it would be us sitting on that side of the desk, would it not?'

If anybody had watched Gabriel with the sound turned off they would have believed he was talking to a dear friend, so generous was the attractive man's smile. But all the bank manager felt was a searing pain in his lower back, his stress seeping through his body like a rampant cancer. Eduardo staying silent as he had since a grunted *¡Hola* at the beginning of the meeting.

'My brother and I, we are from peasant stock. We have a peasant's understanding of the world. We put money with our bank and all we ask is that it is there when we come to take it out.'

The bank manager limited himself to nodding, because the words were not forthcoming.

'For a decade we enjoyed a very good relationship with this bank, a very good relationship with you. Is not Eduardo here the godfather to your youngest?' Pointing a palm towards the family portrait on the desk.

The bank manager assented weakly, remembering how he and his wife had argued, her disgust at the suggestion, his logic that they would be *safer* if their daughter was a Lazcano godchild, the less likely for the brothers to turn their violence on them.

'And yet now, every time we ask for our money,' gesturing to Eduardo then back to the president, like the Lazcanos were just two simple men, 'you talk of "tradable funds" like we are bankers by profession. All I know is that we entrusted the money to Sovereign Bank in Paris, then our money disappeared.'

The president twisted his pinkie ring then moved his hands under the table to hide his nervousness. But Eduardo's face revealed a hint of a snarl. Hands out of sight might be hands reaching for things hidden. The president remembered himself and quickly put his hands back up, abandoning the ring-fidgeting.

'But I have told you, I have begged you to understand, the only way Sovereign Bank would take the money was into a tradable fund. They made bets – safe bets normally. I told you the risks, I promise you.'

Somehow Eduardo's large frame became more sullen in his chair, more threatening, and yet he gave no word of his feelings. Gabriel shrugged, his persona almost perversely sunny.

'But why didn't the money stay in Paris?'

The president winced. 'Banks move money about all the time. It was the Credit Crunch – their head office needed money in a hurry. I told you they were moving it to New York.'

'Yes, but you told us not to worry, that their star trader had never had a losing year.'

'Yes, yes, Douglas McCarthy ran that fund. *He's* the

man who lost your money. I told you this as well.' The bank president seizing on this new target the way a rock-climber tries to grab at a rope as he falls off a mountain.

But Gabriel was already dashing his hopes on the rocks by dismissing this last remark with a bored hand. 'We know this, we know of Señor McCarthy, we know about Sovereign Bank in New York. But we didn't put the money with these people, we put it with Banco Orro. It is Banco Orro who owes us our $250 million, not these Yankees.'

The Lazcanos had originally only deposited $150 million with the bank, but Gabriel had added $100 million interest for good measure at this end of the problem as well. If the Lazcanos could get either Sovereign Bank or Banco Orro to pay them back – with interest, naturally – they were in very good shape. If they could get them *both* to pay the money back they were in clover. $500 million dollars, a $350 million profit on a $150 million investment. An OK return by drug cartel standards.

The bank president spoke, but only an unintelligible hoarse whisper emerged.

Eduardo sat unblinkingly. Watching the broken man across from him. Gabriel leaned forward pleasantly.

'Sorry?'

'I said,' a cough to clear his throat – to get a grip, 'I said, I need another week.' The nauseous bank president near fainting. 'Please.'

Gabriel sighed, somehow his cheerful demeanour more terrifying than outright anger, hiding unknown, unrevealed feelings.

'Another week . . .' Shaking his head. Disappointed. 'Eduardo?'

A silence fell on the room like a shroud, covering everything. The bank manager almost didn't dare breathe for fear that that essential sound might be heard across the table and cause offence. He was taking small, shallow breaths from just the top of his chest, causing him to breathe more and faster. His rising panic was becoming self-fulfilling as his body sent signals to his brain that it was panicking along with his mind.

When Eduardo eventually spoke it was as if the words came from deep within the bowels of the earth, so low and distant did they seem. '*Puta madre.*' Motherfucker.

Gabriel grimaced to the president like, *I tried* . . .

The president reached out across the table towards Eduardo, pleading hands, begging.

'Señor Lazcano, you know I would give anything – *anything* – to right this situation, but please believe me when I say it is so much to ask.' In his mind the bank president raced through a hundred different laws and internal practices he would have to breach to make it happen. 'One week . . . As the father of your godchild, I am begging you, *begging* you. Please.'

No sobbing, no weeping, but tears pouring freely down his face now, a waterfall of despair. A man for whom the only thing between life and death was the mercy of the man sitting opposite.

Eduardo stood, Gabriel followed. The head of the drug cartel looked at the family photo on the desk. He looked down at the wretched bank president, almost through him, so little did his presence register.

'One week or the doghouse.'

Señor Huerta thanked Eduardo, clasped his hands and

thanked him, not hearing his own voice, or aware that his tears had mingled with the saliva dripping from his thick lips. Only alive to the fact that he had not died at this moment, pathetically grateful to the man who held sway over him. Blocking from his mind the doghouse. Blocking from his mind that which was meant to be nothing but a black rumour. Blocking from his mind a place so terrible that it was only talked of in whispers.

Gabriel smiled like a magnanimous priest. 'Señor Huerta. Do not worry. We know you want to make this right. Please believe us when we say we want nothing more than a long and happy relationship with you and this bank.'

35

Cochran looked like hell. Like he hadn't shaved for two days. Like he hadn't slept in a week. And it wasn't all the result of the outsized tumbler of whisky he was nursing in his hand.

He looked both ways down the plush hallway outside his Park Avenue apartment before closing the door after his guest. He then proceeded to lock two security bolts on the door.

'Mr Cochran, nobody's coming through that door to get you.'

The Sovereign Bank CEO whirled on his security chief. 'You don't know that, Bill. You don't *know* that.'

Webster looked at his boss with a mixture of sympathy and concern. 'May I see it, sir?'

Cochran looked slightly foggy-minded, half elsewhere, half overwhelmed. 'Which bit?'

Webster made a small conciliatory gesture. 'Either. Well, both.'

Cochran mouthed something that didn't come out. Whatever had happened had aged him from fifty-six to a hundred years in as many seconds. He looked down at the amber liquid in his glass and his face began to contort miserably. Then he switched to *think about anything else* mode, trying to put something out of his mind. But first he decided to put some whisky in his stomach.

'There. On the table.' Not looking at it, the bank CEO off somewhere else.

Webster looked around the enormous Park Avenue penthouse apartment. The rooms were majestic, oak and marble finishes with black carpets you could lose a small dog in. He'd heard there wasn't a picture hanging in the Sovereign Bank CEO's pad worth less than most people earned in a lifetime. Looking at them – despite his ignorance of the art market – he suspected it wasn't hyperbole after all. A Parisian café scene with a woman being turned on some ad hoc dance-floor. A chair and a bed, brightly coloured, in almost child-like thick oil strokes. A beautiful young bare-breasted girl from some exotic Pacific island looking nonchalantly out at him. Pictures he thought he'd seen on television in his lifetime, or in books maybe. And those were just the ones he could see in the capacious living room. Plus the pool of vomit. Down the front of a door and beside it. Leading into a corridor to the toilet, no doubt.

Cochran was taking it badly.

Webster's eyes fell on the padded envelope on a 1920s Art Deco table. He didn't have to pick it up to see what it said, but he did anyway, just in case something had been missed.

'Have I got your attention?'

The same message written as before in large letters on the new envelope. Webster clinically spread the messily opened end apart to see if there was anything inside it. Nothing.

He looked up at his traumatized boss. 'And the . . . rest?'

Cochran wagged an impatient, irritated hand at the

table Webster was stood by. 'There, next to the envelope. But . . .'

Webster waited for the bank CEO to finish before he reached for the remote control.

Cochran almost retching on the words. ' . . . mute it.' Covering his hand with a fist, averting his eyes.

Webster pointed the control at a massive wall-mounted television then hit PLAY and MUTE on the controller in quick succession. And from the first frame of the new film he knew he was witnessing a new wickedness that even he in all his black ops days had never seen. He realized that his mouth had fallen slightly open and had to rest a hand against the top of a wing-backed chair for support.

Simon Turlington. The young banker. Drugged. Tied to a chair, his arms behind his back. His face red. Not through cuts or wounds but because the skin had been peeled off. A knife had cut around the edges and it was hanging off his chin. The victim mumbling, still alive through all of it. Lidless eyes, skeletal teeth, a jaw worked by exposed muscles, a vision of depraved horror.

Webster thought he too might throw up. His mind a mixture of outrage and revulsion.

Screw this. Webster fast-forwarded through the film, somehow the abject sadism of the captors' treatment accelerating with the frames per second. Towards the end the camera closed in on Turlington's face, the bloodshot eyes peering out of the red skull. And the young banker said something over and over. The security chief only keeping the sound off at Cochran's insistence.

The film ended and the ex-CIA agent killed the television with it. He stood speechless, appalled. What horse-shit he had spoken in bars and bedrooms when he had told a confidant that he had *seen it all*. He hadn't seen anything and he now knew he didn't want to see anything else. The lack of humanity, the barbarism . . . He had never, ever seen anything to match it.

He said nothing. He said nothing for the longest time. Then, finally, he said the only thing he could think to say.

'I'm so sorry, sir.'

Cochran dared to flick a glance at the television, needing to *know* that it was off. Satisfied he turned to look at his employee.

'I've got an island.'

Webster waited, unsure of the point being made by the wraith of a man opposite.

'I've got an island. In the Caribbean. It's very beautiful and very isolated. You have to catch a small plane and then a boat to get there. It's where I go when I want to get away from it all because when I'm there I really am away from it all. All of this.'

Indicating with his hand Webster knew not what. The apartment? The bank? New York? Then his boss looked at him, his eyes filled with the hope of the desperate.

'I could go there. I bought it through a chain of off-shore companies, for tax reasons originally, but now, of course, nobody would find me.'

The *There must be a way out of this* speech. Webster began to understand the distance between what had to be done and what his boss fantasized could be done.

'Sir . . .'

Cochran looked up at him like he'd only just realized he was there.

'Pay the money.'

'But going to my island . . .?'

'Wouldn't make the problem go away. The problem would just be waiting for you when you got back.'

Cochran looked at him in utter denial.

'Sir, it's like any debt. It just builds and builds. You have to pay Lazcano off. Get rid of him. Put this whole thing behind . . .'

'*I fucking know that, Bill.*' The CEO shouting now. 'Don't you think I fucking know that? I'm just fucking *saying* that's all. Don't be so fucking . . .' Spittle spraying from his drunken, angry, terrified lips. 'STUPID FUCKING SECURITY PRICK.'

Webster looked down at the floor. Proverbial sticks and metaphorical stones had yet to hurt him.

Cochran muttered something, either to himself or the room, Webster couldn't make out.

'Sorry, sir?'

'I can't authorize this . . .' The bank CEO waved at something imaginary in the middle of the room. '. . . sort of thing. I mean, how will I get this through the books? How?' The little boy lost now.

Webster looked him square in the eyes because Cochran had to hear the next thing he said. 'You can't, sir. But your Inner Circle can.'

And for the first time that afternoon the mist cleared from Cochran's eyes.

36

The Brooklyn FedEx office had been filled with people needing to get their parcels in the post *tonight*. The result was that what was meant to be a quick visit by Alecto had turned into a twenty-minute wait. Twenty minutes of keeping her face out of direct sight of any security cameras. Twenty minutes of feeling as awkward as a teenager with volcanic acne you didn't want the world to see.

Sitting for hours, for *days*, in the hills of some foreign land she would only ever dream of visiting in order to kill some locals was a breeze. Waiting behind some old girl who couldn't remember if her niece's Christian name had one or two *n*s was her definition of hell.

Eventually Alecto reached the counter, where she placed the shoe-box-sized package.

The college drop-out on the other side turned the box to face him.

'Overnight?'

'Yes please.'

A middle-aged Iranian woman came up to her colleague.

'Hey, Carl, you seen my purse?'

Carl gave her an exasperated look. 'Can't you see I'm with somebody?'

. The already-annoyed colleague looked him up and

down. 'Yeah, shitty'll get you ahead in life.' Walking off shaking her head.

The young man gave Alecto a *Sorry about my co-worker* look, which Alecto feigned an understanding of.

'How would you like to pay?'

Alecto looked down at the package with the dead banker's trainers in it, being posted back to her own borrowed apartment. 'Cash please.'

37

Diane stood a good foot shorter than me and whilst she didn't exactly dress like a bored wife on 5th Avenue she was as classy as a government employee gets. Today it was a knee-length, double-breasted, felt, crimson winter coat. She once told me she spent all her money on clothes and wine. I couldn't speak for the drink but I certainly could for the threads. But tonight fashion was taking a back seat to practicalities.

Diane and I were stood by the Southport helipad on the southern tip of Manhattan island. We were already feeling the cold of the February evening, and the wind coming in off the Hudson made us instinctively pull our overcoats tighter, both of us rubbing our hands together for warmth.

'Permission to go after Sovereign Bank and Lazcano when this Nemesis business is over, Diane?'

She gave me an arched-eyebrow look for my troubles. 'How do you know it was Lazcano who sent those cars after you? Did you question any of your assailants after the fact today?'

I understood the implied criticism, her looking steadfastly out across the water merely underlining the point.

'You know, Michael, you might want to try leaving

somebody alive one of these days. You might be quite surprised by what you might learn. Key witness statements, incriminating evidence, tip-offs . . . I mean, if it doesn't work out you could just go back to killing everybody.'

Sarcasm was never a good omen with Diane, so I chose not to pursue it. Thankfully our attention was taken with a bright light hovering into view across the water.

'So what's this about?'

I shook my head as we watched the helicopter sweep towards us, raising my voice as it did. 'He didn't say. Just said he thought he might be able to help in an off-the-record kind of way.'

Diane nodded at this information with the same enthusiasm a mother might hear your reason for not tidying your bedroom.

We both hugged ourselves against the gusts and water spray generated by the incoming helicopter in Sovereign Bank livery, conversation pointless now until it had landed. Webster was out of the executive helicopter and shaking our hands almost before it had fully touched down.

I made the introductions. 'Special Agent Mason, Bill Webster.'

He shook her hand respectfully, almost appreciatively. 'A real pleasure, Miss Mason.'

This earned him a trademark raised eyebrow. 'What's this about, Mr Webster?'

Webster glanced back at his ride as if to make sure nobody had followed him over. They hadn't. We had to talk over the sound of the chopper, he evidently wasn't staying long.

'I've been contacted by an employee over in Paris. They want to talk to me about a certain client and the deposits he made three years ago through the Paris office.'

I spoke first. 'Which client?'

He paused the way people do when they have something big to say. Once he'd spoken I found myself forgiving him. 'Gabriel Lazcano.'

I felt my stomach tighten. *This was it.*

Diane spoke, steady in her scepticism. 'And why are you telling us this?'

Webster shrugged affably. 'I can't leave to see my Paris colleague until after the weekend. I have to check out security for our Aspen conference, it's the bank's big annual get-together.'

Diane and I were still not keeping up, so he explained.

'Byrne, I'll let you speak to the Parisian employee first. You can even bring her in, if you want.'

Diane was still unconvinced. 'And what do you want from us, Mr Webster?'

He smiled at her cutting to the chase, respected it. 'I want to know anything you can tell me about Nemesis as it happens.'

Diane went to protest, but he cut her off.

'Nothing untoward, nothing above my pay grade. Just help me do my job of protecting Sovereign Bank, because it's the last job I ever want. I've been following Nemesis, ma'am, and I sense a whole lot of trouble heading our way – and I mean Sovereign's way specifically. Just an above-the-board heads-up, that's all I ask. Have we got a deal?'

Even Diane couldn't object to that. 'OK, Mr Webster, I don't see why that wouldn't work.'

His grin cut through the night. 'I'll text you the details, Byrne. Gotta go.'

And after a quick shake of our hands he did.

38

The detective screamed for the second time that day. At least that I knew of. An excited, schoolgirl, *OMG* squeal. Totally at odds with the news she had just received.

'Martinez, I said *I've* got to go to Paris.'

But she didn't bat an eyelid. 'Yeah, I heard you the first time. And *I'm* coming with you.' Her smile pure mischief, waiting for me to fully grasp her meaning.

We were stood outside the entrance to her stationhouse in Lower Manhattan, her colleagues slipping by occasionally. I looked around us. Cold, dark and I needed to get going.

'How did Ashby take the news about his car?'

Martinez bit her lip guiltily. 'Eleanor? Not well. Like a death in the family, actually.'

'Tell him it was suicide.'

Martinez smiled. 'So, we going now? 'Cos I can run in and get my passport from my desk.'

'Martinez . . .'

'What?' Wide-eyed, innocent, and butter safe from any melting experiences in her lovely, wide, smiling mouth.

'It's business.'

'I know, and I'll keep out of your way. But at least I'd see you on the flight. Ten hours each way, that would be a record for us recently.'

'But . . .'

'And it'll wipe the slate clean for standing me up at dinner *and* breakfast.'

'But . . .' My male brain scrambled and failed to give a good reason not to do as she said.

'Have I been patient of late, Mr Byrne?' A smiling look that dared me to contradict her.

I let out a heavy sigh. 'Yes you have but . . .'

'But what?' Her face nonplussed, *what could you possibly have to say?*

I ran a hand through my hair, looking for the right words. Wondering what words to use, realizing I didn't know my position here.

'You'd be stuck waiting for me at an airport.'

She pulled her head back in something close to amazement. 'I'm not waiting in no plane – Jenni Martinez is going shopping in Paris.' Wiggling her head to let me know how big an event to her that was.

Ah, I got it. I looked heavenward, my turn to smile as I let her know what I thought of that.

Then Martinez pulled a crooked mouth face at me. 'Please. *Please* . . .' Doing that Shrek cat thing that I was powerless against.

'But you . . .'

Her face asking *What – and this had better be good?*

I closed my eyes, dreading the implication of my next words.

'You haven't got a change of clothes.'

And Manhattan lit up as a hundred-megawatt smile beamed out of her face. She leaped at me, forcing me to catch her in my arms. 'I'll do my first bit of shopping at the airport.'

'Really? Where?'

Her face took on a sultry look that made almost forty years of learning fall out of my head. 'Have I ever told you about Victoria's Secret?'

I looked down at her, defeated. 'Who is this Victoria woman? Try water-boarding her – that usually makes them fess up.'

She kissed me and then cocked her head back to look at me.

'I've so wanted to see you, you know that. I've got so much to tell you . . . What shall we talk about in the car?' She rested her head on my chest, savouring having me to herself.

I knew I had stretched her patience in recent weeks, that I hadn't been very present in whatever our relationship was, so I spoke very carefully. 'Well, I have got one phone call to make on the way.'

She shrugged nonchalantly. 'I can live with one. But then you're mine, Mr Byrne – all the way to Paris.'

It hadn't started out as a scowl, but by the time we got to JFK there was no other word for it. Martinez scowled at me with, even I had to admit, good reason. What I had omitted to tell her was that the call was a conference call to the office concerning my itinerary in the French capital. A call that lasted precisely the duration of the journey.

By the time the limousine pulled up beside the Gulf-stream 200 idling in the private government hangar at JFK, I thought the world-class storm brewing meant she wasn't going to speak to me till we got to Paris – or maybe even back again.

I was wrong.

As we reached the bottom of the steps to the private jet Martinez – giving no thought to the politely waiting air stewardess – let rip.

'You know it's not safe to use phones on planes, *Mike*, so you just might have to stay off that thing now.'

Her Latina temper like a volcano. Seemingly inactive until it erupted, burning-hot lava all over you. I snapped the phone closed and dropped it into my jacket pocket.

'Martinez, if cell phones were really dangerous they'd take them off us at the beginning of flights.'

But I'd underestimated the foulness of the mood I'd provoked with my inattention since leaving Manhattan – and it was my bad. She flung a wild hand at me.

'I have been so patient with you this last month, Mike. I have spent hours getting ready just to have you call off a date as I'm walking out the door, I have sat in restaurants by myself because your plans have changed – you even walked out of the movie theatre halfway during that George Clooney flick because *Diane* wanted you. And I have not complained, not once. So if I'm going to get messed around on this trip just tell me so I can prepare myself right now. Is there anything else you have to do?'

I looked at the tarmac then up at her. She was right, right about all of it. 'There's one thing but that's all.'

'One?' The face serious, *speak now or for ever hold your tongue* serious.

'One.'

She nodded like that was settled then turned her head to face the Gulfstream.

'What is that, a Secret Service jet?'

'No, it's not a government jet.'

She stood hovering like her mood could go ten different ways and to ten different volumes, but instead turned on her heel and walked unhappily up the steps past the tactfully retreating stewardess. I followed on, maintaining a wary silence.

Inside the cabin Martinez's frosty politeness towards the stewardess did not fully cover up how pissed she was. She waved a hand at the four luxury leather seats. 'Can we sit anywhere?'

The stewardess had to fight a desire to attend nervously to her neckerchief. 'Actually, I think you're through there.' Pointing at a door in the centre of the oak-panelled wall halfway along the plane.

'Oh *great*. An overnight flight and we're in cattle class.'

Martinez shook her head, marched towards the rear, pretty much flung the door open, took two steps into the room.

And stopped.

I took one step in behind her. Close behind her.

She kept her back to me as she spoke. Her tone had changed. By approximately one hundred and eighty degrees.

'Sometimes, Byrne, you get it so right.'

She turned away from the made-up double bed, the ice bucket with the gold-plated bottle of Armand de Brignac champagne cooling in it, the high-end music system playing Marvin Gaye, and then almost fell into my arms. I looked down into her face, now a picture of contrition, kitten-like shame at ever doubting me, doe-like eyes and crooked mouth proffered by way of a heart-felt and very happy apology.

'Yes?'

Me asking slowly, drawing it out. Me enjoying the indescribable discomfort her outburst on the runway had now made her feel. Then a naughty spark flickered in her eyes and she reached a leg around me and gently kicked the door shut. At its closing click she pushed her lips into mine, squashing their plump folds against me, rewarding me with a harlot's kiss, a kiss meant to reach down into your chest and pluck out your heart. My own little she-devil.

After the longest, most languorous, range-of-emotions kiss I pulled my head gently away. Speaking now as tender as her mood had become.

'We're here to work, Martinez.'

'So get to work.'

I exhaled, pretending to be displeased. 'I'm not happy about this.'

'You want to try being on the receiving end.'

Her *touché* smile was the last thing I saw before the lights went out.

39

'I don't know a thing about you.'

I looked down at the head I was stroking, the head resting on my chest, its long dark hair flowing down across me and on to the mattress. Me not sure if it was my chest or her face perspiring the most. Me not caring after what we'd just enjoyed together. Us enjoying the serenity that follows a marathon sex session. Exhausted and sated.

I gave it some thought, running through our time together, wondering how open I'd been. 'You know lots about me.'

'I'm not saying . . .' She looked up at me with a quizzical look in her eyes, still slightly out of breath, trying to arrange the thoughts in her own mind. 'I'm not, it's not that . . .' She drummed her beautiful non-NYPD-regulation fingernails on my chest. 'It's not that you put *up* walls . . .'

'Uh huh.'

'It's just that you *are* a wall.'

I put an arm behind my head the better to see her, the soft lighting casting into shadow her milk-chocolate eyes and head-turning eyelashes.

'OK, well, what would you like to know?'

She propped herself up, playfully annoyed, her bronze breasts swinging out from beneath her, just touching my chest. And there she was expecting my attention.

'There you go again. You *seem* open but you're impenetrable.'

'Thankfully you're not.'

She fought a smile, but twitched her lips, sexy and amused at the same time. 'I see what you did there, Mr Byrne.' Then she batted a hand across my chest in reprimand as she lowered herself down again, looking at me, her face resting on the interlaced fingers resting flat on my chest.

'Look, ask me three questions, any three questions, and I promise to tell you the whole truth.'

'Truly?' Her scheming eyes alight with interest.

'Truly.'

'OK.'

She took a long moment to think about it, sifting through possible candidates before settling on one.

'Lee Harvey Oswald: acting alone or . . .'

She started laughing through her nose, causing me to laugh as well. She reset her mood and started again.

'OK, OK.' Mentally selecting the one to go with. 'Marvin Gaye or Jay-Z?'

'Oh, I'm taking the fifth on that.'

She gave me a mouth-on-the-ground look of outrage. 'You can't do that.'

'Yes I can, it's in the Constitution.'

'Screw the Constitution.'

'I'm sure you would if you could.'

She tried to reply, but then the dirty little minx inside her won out and she descended into a laugh so filthy it would make a longshoreman blush. Her smell after sex the best smell in the world. Her smutty laugh the most liberated thing in the world. Jenni Martinez, there would never be another . . .

She controlled herself. 'All right. That one doesn't count.' She set her mind to it again. 'Do you cry at the end of *It's a Wonderful Life*?'

Oh. So that's where she was going. Under-the-skin stuff. Weak points. Well, a deal was a deal. 'The end? *Just* the end?'

She liked that answer. 'OK, OK. Erm . . . A song that breaks your heart.'

I gave it some thought then knew what it had to be. '"Friends of Ours" by Elbow.'

'Who?'

'Elbow. They're a band from Manchester.' She looked like she wasn't following. 'England.'

She smacked my chest with a loud slap.

'Ow-w-w.'

'I know where it is. Why docs it break your heart?' Speaking softly. Wanting to know.

'Well, I think it's the sentiment.' Her face saying, *Go on*. I looked up at the cabin ceiling. 'It's a song about a friend of the band's who died. I'm not sure how. Anyway . . . the songwriter couldn't remember what the last thing they ever talked about was – the friend's death was out of the blue. But he knew his friend always signed off conversations with the phrase "Love you, mate." So, whilst he couldn't recall what they had last talked about, he knew what the last thing his friend must ever have said to him was . . . "Love you, mate."'

I continued staring at the ceiling as I thought about the song then looked back down at Martinez only to see her smiling sadly.

'What's up?'

She felt stupid and apologetic and shook away the mood. 'Nothing.'

'What?'

'Nothing. I just think that's a lovely story, that's all.' Brave smile. 'Love you, mate.'

We looked at each other. For a long time. The words *I love you* never having passed between us. Or maybe they just had. She smiled a smile that was meant to say *I'm all right now*. Neither of us believing her. She turned her head and lay it on my chest, doodling with her fingers up and down my left side. The dull roar of the Gulfstream's engines making the moment strangely more intimate, coddling us, making it all the more a million-miles away from everything.

After a while she lifted her head up, a question teed up in her mind. 'Do you trust Webster?'

I wasn't ready for that. '*That's* your third question?'

She chuckled at her misstep. 'No. But you still have to tell the truth. Do you think he's on the level, sending you out like this?'

'He could be.'

'Is that a yes?'

'It's a "not completely". He says he's trying to do his job of protecting the staff at Sovereign Bank, but there's nothing to prove he's playing us, if that's what you mean. He's provided us with a whistle-blower in Paris, and she does want to spill the beans on the Lazcanos. Do I think he's holding some stuff back? Yeah, everybody does. But he's also possibly broken the Lazcano case wide open, so . . .' Me pulling a face of *what's not to like?*

She considered me sceptically. 'He works for a bank.'

I smiled. 'Oh well, case closed.'

She dug a finger into my ribs. 'They're overpaid.'

'Are they?'

'Bankers? Hell yeah. I'd do their job like a bullet.'

I adopted my best *angelic choirboy* look. 'What about the long hours they put in?'

'Hey, I'm a cop. I could do with the break.'

'But they make so much money for their employers.'

'Er, number one, the bank bailouts suggest otherwise and, secondly, *that's their job.* Why would you pay somebody an astronomical bonus for *doing their job*? Teachers don't get mega-bonuses. Steel workers don't. Soldiers don't. *I* don't.'

'Come on, Martinez, bankers need incentivizing.'

'Yeah, you're right. Maybe I'll go see Captain Novak when I get back and tell him I'm not sure I can be motivated to catch any more crooks without a five-million-dollar bonus this year.'

'But bankers are *really* intelligent.'

'How clever do you have to be to almost wipe out the US economy, Byrne?'

'Yeah, but you have to admit that blowing up their own banks then getting the taxpayer to foot the bill *was* pretty clever.'

A smile spread sarcastically across Martinez's face. 'Shit, maybe they *do* deserve their money. Idiot. What do you think the solution to this banking bullshit is?'

'Apart from Nemesis?' I shook my head, resigned to the solution never coming to pass. 'Regulation. Bankers' real genius is for manipulation. Gaming the regulators, gaming the politicians, gaming public opinion, gaming the shareholders, gaming their own risk managers. Bankers game the entire system, which is why it's the system that has to change. Break up the banks that are too big to fail, make the profits go to the people who actually own the bank – the shareholders, not the people gambling with their balance sheets – and pay all bonuses in very, *very* long-term share options. It's all there in front of us. And if a CEO can't explain all the products the bank is selling, fire his sorry ass. Regulate the bejesus out of them.'

'Seriously? But the regulators were asleep at the wheel. They should take some of the blame for the bank bail-outs.'

'The underfunded, overstretched SEC did indeed drop the ball. But the regulator-asleep-at-the-wheel argument only really works if banks are essentially saying, *Hey, we're corrupt and our risk-management is out of control – what did you expect to happen if you didn't regulate us?*'

She pulled a *yet to be convinced* face. 'But regulation hasn't worked so far. Maybe we should deregulate them altogether, and if they go bust they go bust.'

I pulled my best insincere face. 'That *is* interesting.' Like I might want to mull that one over later in the bath.

'Screw you, Byrne.' Said with an amused smile.

'Look . . .' I stretched over the side of the bed to the champagne bucket to grab a piece of ice. Martinez snuggled face down into the warm patch I'd just surrendered, lying naked on the tangled sheets, head side on, facing me. That perfect tanned body content as a sun-kissed feline. I lay on my side next to her. 'The thing with banking is that it isn't a regular business. Banks are a utility, like nuclear power stations. And just like nuclear power stations they need regulating. A lot.'

'Go on.'

'Well, if a mom-and-pop operation running, say, a gas station, ignored safety in the pursuit of profit and there's an explosion, well, the fall-out is . . .' I briefly touched one of her shoulder blades with the ice, causing her to wriggle in discomfort. '. . . limited. However, when a nuclear power station is run by greedy SOBs who just want fat bonuses and don't give a damn about safety, the results are of a more catastrophic . . .' I ran the ice cube all over her back in criss-crosses, eliciting gasps and an arching against the unwelcome cold. '. . . nature.'

I stopped, and she fell back on to her front, where she blew her hair out of her face to look at me. 'Just like banks.'

'Just like banks. The Credit Crunch was banking's Chernobyl. We were hours away from the economy almost being wiped out by the bank's toxic debts, the toxic debts they created in the pursuit of their ever bigger bonuses. And, just like Chernoyl, we'll be feeling the consequences for years to come. Bankers won't, I'm talking about everybody else, the people whose payroll taxes get deducted straight from their payslips, not pushed through offshore scams and tax-avoidance schemes to nickel-and-dime society.'

'But how do banks get themselves into this position?'

'Don't you mean, how do banks *keep* getting themselves into this position? Four times in the last century we-the-taxpayers have had to step in to rescue the banking system because of its excesses.'

'But why would Congress allow that?'

'Why would the people who need millions of dollars in political donations do that? Beats me.'

'OK, OK, politicians are on the make, cowardly, sleaze-bags. But I still don't get why banks would do this. I mean, they don't want to go out of business, do they?'

'Don't they? What's a banker's upside if he takes huge gambles with his bank's cash?'

'A massive bonus.'

'And the downside?'

Martinez gave it a moment's thought before the light-bulb snapped into life inside her head. 'No bonus.'

'Exactly. Or worst-case scenario, they lose their job. Employment risk. They take huge wagers day in day out with other people's money, sharing in the upside and leaving the bank to pay off the downside.'

Martinez whistled, impressed. 'What a perfect deal. It's like a free lottery ticket. Every year.' Then the whole picture formed in front of her eyes like a camera coming into focus. 'Shit, and if they lose so much that even their bank can't pay off their losses, *we* pay off the downside.' Looking at me to reach this same inevitable conclusion. 'That's . . . that's kind of shameless, Byrne. I thought these guys believed in the free market, not government handouts.'

'It's the great irony of banking, Martinez: they're capitalist about profits, socialist about losses.'

'Well, then we shouldn't have bailed them out.'

'What, and let the nuclear reactor completely melt down? It would be *we* the taxpayers taking it up the . . .'

Emphasizing my point by slipping the remains of my

melting ice-cube in between her buttocks. Martinez screamed and spun away from me, gripping my wrist with impressive alacrity.

'Byrne!'

'I'm just trying to make a point.'

'That's not the point I want made up there.' Displaying her usual gift for filth.

'An innuendo, Martinez?'

'I don't want anything in my endo.' Lying on her front again then smiling mischievously. 'Not for now.' Then she returned her mind to the matter at hand, and her mood descended as she tried not to believe the unfathomable. 'Al Capone never had a racket this good. And after wrecking their own banks, wrecking *our* economy, making us cut back on schools, healthcare, policing, *everything*, they used the bailout money to pay themselves *bonuses*.' She shook her head in disbelief. 'You're right, Byrne, they are just gaming the system, gaming everybody. Everybody's worried about the robbers coming in the front of the bank, I'm starting to worry about the people coming in the back.' Martinez pointed a sharp finger at me. 'Don't even *think* about it.' But her anger wiping the smile off her face.

'Hey, easy, Martinez – like Goldman Sachs' CEO said – they're doing God's work.'

She looked like she might spit. 'Which god?' Shaking her head as much depressed as outraged. 'Shit, Byrne, and your job is to protect these mothers.'

'Well, they've been so gracious to we-the-taxpayers for bailing them out I just couldn't say no.'

'If you think about it, somebody like Occupy Wall Street was going to stand up to the bankers at some stage.

Maybe that's just what Nemesis are. The dark underbelly of that protest.'

'People who are mad as hell and not going to take it any more?'

'Maybe.' Martinez was pensive now. She was troubled by something, something she'd maybe meant to bring up all along. She took a long time to say anything and when she did she almost looked through me as she spoke. 'You know, Byrne, one of the things that always impressed me about the Secret Service was the training. When the shooting starts almost every other law enforcement agency is taught to take cover, protect yourself because you're no good to anybody dead. But you guys stand up. When the bullets start flying you throw yourselves between the bad guys and the people you're protecting.'

I lay listening to her dressing up her anxieties as praise.

'Byrne, if Nemesis started firing at bankers while you were around, would you take a bullet for them?'

I exhaled a long, lengthy breath. 'It's my job.'

We lay in the semi-darkness, a world away from the mood we shared when we first entered the cabin. It was Martinez who broke the silence. Speaking so softly that I had to move closer to hear.

'I haven't asked my third question.'

'Oh.'

'Do you want to hear it?'

I looked at her and could see that her heart wasn't in it now. 'Go on. Why not.'

'Who are you thinking about when you hear the line "Love you, mate"?'

Her eyes searched mine for any signs of a confession,

a confession of feelings for anybody else but her, even if those feelings had been in the past. I'd promised to tell the truth and so went to speak –

But there was a knock at the door followed by a courteous female voice. 'Twenty minutes to landing, sir.'

The silence was so heavy between us that it took an effort on my part to break it. 'OK. Thank you.'

I looked at Martinez, feeling reluctance, sensing she could feel my reluctance, but resolving to answer her question anyway.

'Well . . .'

But it was too late, the mood gone from playful to uncomfortable.

She blew out of the side of her mouth to clear some hair from her face, then smiled philosophically and squeezed my hand with her own. 'On second thoughts, I don't want to know.'

40

The whistle-blower looked younger than I'd expected, nothing like her twenty-seven years. A plain girl with a freckled brown complexion and a flat nose, like a boxer's. Half Moroccan, Webster's notes had said. She was small and tidy with the closed air of an academic introvert. Her clothes were stylish and yet too smart, like she'd read up on how to dress rather than possessed any real feel for it. I hoped to God she let herself go occasionally. She looked like she might snap if she were wound any tighter. Still, maybe after work on a Friday night it was her dancing on the bar in the Latin Quarter, pouring absinthe down her colleagues' throats. Who's to say? But right now the shiniest thing about her was the crucifix hanging around her neck.

'Vous voulez un café?'

My question made her smile for the first time since she'd sat at the street café on Boulevard du Montparnasse. Round tables with white metal table tops, waistcoated *garçons* with long white cloths draped over their arms, patrons smoking *vous vissez* style as they read their copies of *Le Monde*. A surprising choice for a Parisian, something so clichéd, so rammed with tourists and bristling with locals. But maybe that was the point. Somewhere public, somewhere she felt safe.

'It is OK, I speak English.'

I returned her smile. 'Is my French that bad?'

She smiled again and blushed. 'Je m'excuse. On peut parler français si vous préférez?'

'No, no, trust me. Let's stick to English, it's better all round.'

I had been bothered by something all the way from the airport and it was only now I had realized what it was. I was missing my gun. I'd had to leave it on the plane, the French authorities not too wild about an armed American agent running round Paris. And I didn't like it. Didn't like it one bit.

I had my back to the café and scanned the cobbled street to see if anything didn't fit. It was cafés and bistros along this side, glass-fronted stores opposite. The buildings above us were a mixture of grand, baroque apartments, older than anything I'd ever seen back home, and ugly retail outlets hastily thrown up in the last couple of decades. To the far right, across the street, was our hire car. Maybe a half dozen other cars also parked on that side only. The customers on this sunny if chilly morning were a mixture of couples, the odd single Parisian, possibly an off-duty soldier by himself. A waiter appeared with the characteristic *Hurry up* fashion I had come to know and love in the French capital. A manner that was half *I haven't got all day*, half *Jesus, I need the John.*

Martinez was sat behind the wheel of their hire car, its engine still idling. The car was a little Citroën C3. As beautiful as it was tiny. Diagonally ahead, on the left, she could see the café. Byrne was sat outside, facing the street, the young bank employee opposite him. She was somewhat disappointed that Byrne hadn't managed to hold the meeting somewhere more appropriate like the Champs-Elysées, or any other major shopping destination. But it *was* Paris, and this was the most romantic city she had ever seen, and she was determined to make the most of their time together, however work-dominated their schedule was. She dipped into her handbag. Plain black leather. That would have to change by the end of the day. As would the lip-gloss she was looking to apply. She smiled at the whole morning of shopping ahead of her. It was nice to take time off from being a police detective. It was nice just being a woman. For all his crap availability Byrne certainly made her feel like one.

And there it was again, that overwhelming feeling of wanting him. That undeniable sense that he handled her just right, the way she wanted to be handled. Treating her as an equal but not slow to take control when she needed a break from responsibility, when she wanted to fall into his arms and be carried by him. It was unlike anything she had ever known. He was unlike anybody she had ever known. And she'd told a half a dozen guys in her life that she loved them and meant it at the time. But this feeling was in a different league. It was every colour of the rainbow, a ticker-tape parade of joy when her hand was in his. And yet . . . she constantly fretted that something bad would happen if she ever came out and said it. Something about their situation, something about him that meant her luck would change. Maybe his constant unavailability was the catch, maybe that was all. Or maybe it was worse. Or maybe she was just writing it off to protect herself from a rejection she feared she couldn't handle. She smiled sadly at her confusion and had to admit one thing to herself. As far as she was concerned, he was the one.

'Where do we start?' She spoke nervously, unconsciously wringing her napkin on the table in front of her.

'Well, first of all, I'd like to thank you for doing this.' I needed to calm her, sensing she was a mouse that might just die of fright.

'I understand. But I must tell you, I am very scared about this. Will I have to testify against this man? The money that came from Mexico, none of the proper anti-money-laundering checks were done. I was amazed by what I found. But also I was scared. This currency house – Banco Orro – was sending money, one hundred and fifty million dollars, from Lazcano.' She shook her head. A fear rising in her. 'The more I read about Monsieur Lazcano the more I . . .' She looked at me directly for the first time since we had sat. 'I am so very scared, monsieur.'

Tijuana, Mexico. I turned towards the American who had watched on as hopefully as a man in his condition could. He made an effort to look up at me in his enfeebled state. He spoke in a mumbled whisper. 'Are you here to take me home?'

I pushed the memory from my mind, but took the lesson from it.

'I'm going to keep your identity out of this, mademoiselle. I promise you that.'

She gave me the first hopeful look all meeting. 'Really?'

*

Martinez, lip-gloss at the ready, turned the rear-view mirror to face herself. She touched the small stick to her lip. Then paused.

Something was wrong.

Something her cop brain didn't like.

She adjusted the mirror to see the vehicle twenty feet behind her.

Two men sat in the front. Serious men. The driver in profile, talking to his passenger.

The left side of the driver's face was completely burned.

She sighed with relief. That was all. Something different. And then, feeling slightly ghoulish for doing it, she found herself looking at the scars running down his face. Severe burns, burns that would change your life. Poor SOB. She thought about the people she'd met with disfigurements like that. Some were stoical, others bitter. Some never forgave those they blamed for the injury, others moved on. Poor SOBs.

Martinez shook her head, almost shuddering at the thought, and went to readjust the mirror.

Only she didn't like what happened next.

Not just the men pulling balaclavas on to the top of their heads.

But the full view of the driver's face as he looked out of his windscreen, directly towards her mirror.

She knew the face.

The same Arab face she had been shown on Gabriella's computer in Little Italy.

The face of the London bomber.

Martinez looked up at Byrne across the street. But she couldn't see him. A waiter was blocking her view. Not enough time to open the window and shout to him. Needing to stop this. *Now*. Putting the car into reverse.

We thanked the waiter as he stepped away.

The young Parisian raised the minute espresso cup to her lips, grateful for something to hold on to, something to steady her hands.

My cell phone rang. *William Webster.*

I was in two minds, then, 'Do you mind?'

She shook her head pleasantly and I put the phone to my ear.

'Hello?'

'Byrne – *he knows.*'

I snapped my eyes up at the young girl. All my instincts telling me the terrible truth. Telling me the terrible events that were about to follow. Suddenly the world in slow motion as it played out around me.

The sniper's bullet ripping through the left side of the young banker's skull. The cloud of blood exploding out of the other side of her head as quickly as the life that left her. The espresso cup flung, leaving her hand.

The screech of tyres. Knowing it was the white delivery van parked behind our car to my right.

Turning.

Seeing the van barely starting to lurch into the street before Martinez rammed the Citroën backwards into it, opening her door as she did.

The off-duty soldier at the table on my left reaching inside his jacket.

Me continuing to turn. Grabbing the silver tray from the already-startled waiter. Turning towards the soldier pulling his hand out. The hand around a gun. Another sniper bullet, tearing through the waiter's hand. The edge of the metal tray in my hand thrust into the soldier's windpipe. My left hand chasing down his arm, grabbing the gun from his weakened grip, ripping it from him, turning, looking right, across the street, seeing the tall balaclavaed driver trying to get out of his van, seeing Martinez slamming her body into his door with all her might, smashing his head between it and the vehicle's frame, seeing a red Fiat Uno speeding from my left, tearing towards me, the passenger leaning his gun out of the window, me emptying three bullets into the Fiat, three holes into the windscreen, the Fiat veering to its left, towards the shop window opposite, me diving to my right, away from the café front, away from the customers, wanting to take them out of the equation, coming up, a long-range rifle bullet puncturing the café window behind me, looking across the street, seeing the van's passenger running round the front of it, submachine gun in hand, blocked by the shunted Citroën, spraying Martinez with bullets, Martinez pulling the balaclavaed driver in front of her, the driver taking the attack, buying herself two seconds of extra life, buying me a shot at her assailant, me firing a bullet into the right side of his head, flinging him on to the hood of the van, firing another bullet into his forehead, to my left, the Fiat crashing through the glass front of the shop.

Then . . .

Time speeding up.

Normal now.

The situation. One sniper a long way to my right plus

two possible survivors, the café soldier and the Fiat passenger. Needing to secure them.

Martinez running towards me as I turned to face the café customer I'd assaulted, a man in his late twenties, small but well built, crew cut, choking from the blow to his windpipe. He was staggering to his feet, looking at me in alarm, escape the only thing on his mind now. I wanted him away from here, I wanted to know what he knew. I was taking the first step towards him when the bullet entered the left side of his face, smashing his eye socket, his left eye falling out on to his cheek as he collapsed on to the sidewalk like a dropped overcoat. The sniper making a deliberate decision to kill him, not me.

But . . .

Then understanding . . .

No witnesses.

That was their plan now.

But the red Fiat Uno inside the store window opposite, beyond the view of the sniper. The car's passenger still a possible suspect – if he was alive.

I dashed across the road, all traffic at a standstill now, Martinez meeting me at the destroyed storefront, by the Fiat's passenger door.

The driver was slumped across the steering wheel, facing us, three holes in his face. The gunman passenger was clearly injured, badly, my mind leaping from securing him to keeping him alive.

Martinez looking at me upset and, for a stupid moment, I thought it was because she had been attacked. Then just as quickly I realized she was horrified at the attacks on me.

But for now a look of *we're still here* between us would have to do.

The Fiat gunman was lying against the door, blood splattered down his window. As I opened it he slumped out, held up only by his seat-belt. His body smashed up. His arm flopped out beside him and I heard it hit the ground before I saw it.

Martinez screaming. '*Mike.*'

Me moving before I even looked, charging at Martinez, not breaking my stride but grabbing her in my hands and lifting her off her feet, running her backwards as I tried to accelerate away from the car, away from the grenade, away from the blast knocking me off my feet, moving my left hand up behind her head as we were flung to the road.

The telescopic lens panned across from the café to the edge of the building to the right.

No line of sight.

At the bottom, on the road, a single female foot could be seen, then it moved, removed from view.

Alecto took her eye away from the rifle's scope. The air now beginning to fill with the urgent cry of police cars around the city. As much as she could do done.

Unhappy, confused, the ex-Army Ranger began to efficiently dismantle the gun.

41

'Stop it.'

'Please, Mr Cochran . . . Please . . .' Turlington half wheezing, half whimpering.

'No, David, I want you to see this.'

'Pay back the two . . .' The effort more than the young banker could bear, the breathing heavy for a moment. '. . . the two hundred and fifty million doll . . .' The last mumbled.

'*Stop it!*'

'David's right, Tony, we've seen enough. *Enough.*'

Cochran stabbed a finger at the remote, stopping the DVD, the first one he had received from the Lazcanos. No less upset by the horrors inflicted on his young former employee but aggrieved by having had to witness it initially by himself, needing others to experience the horror of what he had been living with, share the punishment, the burden, the guilt.

Present along with the bank's CEO in the Sovereign Bank conference room were the COO, its president and its chief legal counsel. Cochran's inner circle. But, much more crucially, Cochran's fellow fire-fighters when the wildfires threatened to sweep through Wall Street during the Credit Crunch. A band of brothers who each knew where the bodies were buried. Each knew what had had to be done to get the bank and themselves through that torrid time.

They were sat in half light at one end of the conference table, next to a wall with a gargantuan flat-screen television on it. The choice of venue and viewing experience most deliberate on Cochran's part. Not here to discuss. Here to close a deal. David Welch, the septuagenarian president, stood from his seat, shaken, and crossed to the long sideboard where a bottle of water and four glasses stood. He needed a drink, and this was the strongest one around.

'How long have you had this?' Falcinelli, the normally slick-looking legal counsel, pulled at his tie and collar for air.

Cochran waved an it's not important hand at the situation. 'Three, four days.' On Webster's advice he had not shown them the second, more horrific film. It was felt that that – showing Turlington's face skinned alive – might scare the Inner Circle into the arms of the authorities. This was about getting the result Cochran and Webster wanted.

The legal counsel nodded vigorously, focusing on the problem, blocking out the film. 'And who else knows?'

Cochran was hit by the exhaustion of suddenly opening up. 'Erm, Webster, that's it.'

Falcinelli still battled his own frightened thoughts. 'OK, OK. And did we take receipt of it at this bank? Did Connie open it? Did she see it?'

Cochran tried to understand his point before flaring up. 'Oh for God's sake, Jack . . .'

'It makes a difference.'

'It does *not* . . . Oh, Jesus, *I* opened it. Nobody else knows about it.'

'You're sure?'

Cochran answered with a threatening look, his stress levels needing an outlet.

The COO, small, taut, took his hand from his eyes, where he had been trying to process the barbarity and implications of the almost-snuff movie they had just witnessed. 'Jack, what did the SEC say about a settlement on this Lazcano business?'

Falcinelli was slightly embarrassed at where he had negotiated to. 'Five hundred million.'

All three others expostulated as one. 'Five hundred?' 'How much?' '*What?*'

Falcinelli opened his hands helplessly. 'Give or take.'

Cochran slapped the table. 'Give or take? Take a dive, more like. It's not like we're Goldman Sachs misleading its customers here.'

But Falcinelli was not in the mood to be their punch bag. 'No, Tony, it isn't. But it *is* like we're Barclays engaging in financial transactions with Cuba, Iran, Libya et al. They got fined $300 million for that, and the SEC is having to be seen to get tougher by the day. You know the mood out there. Lazcano runs a goddamn drug cartel. If the DA gets wind of this before we settle we could all be facing a stretch here, *capiche?*'

Cochran twisted his mouth angrily, went to speak then turned away.

The COO was all business. 'That $500 million figure final, Jack?'

The legal counsel threw up his hands. 'Christ, guys, I'm shadow boxing here. It's not like I've been able to come out and say to the SEC that we turned a blind eye to the money-laundering checks on Lazcano. It was bullshit then and it's bullshit now. I'm couching it all in hypotheticals at this stage. My contact's an old friend, but I can only string him along so long before I have to put out.'

'So it could be much lower?' The COO unable to resist squeezing his colleague the way he squeezed everybody and everything around the bank.

Falcinelli was defensive now. 'Yeah, Martin, and it could be much higher.'

The thin-haired president groaned by the sideboard. 'I told you never to take money through the Banco Orro. We knew their reputation.'

Cochran was ready to brawl now. 'So speaks the Monday-morning quarter-back. Where were you with the bright ideas when we needed the capital in 2007?'

The seventy-three-year-old Wall Street veteran shook his head regretfully. 'If we had just waited for the government rescue . . .'

Cochran began to moan in the build up to a verbal assault on his president. 'David, they let Lehman's go pop, we had to assume the worst . . .'

The COO wanted a grip on the situation. 'Guys, we are where we are. We go to the authorities about this and it's a possible $500 million fine, not to mention the publicity, investigations *and* probable personal liability. Or we make it go away by paying Lazcano his $250 million. Any mathematicians in the room?'

They were silent while they contemplated the dilemma.

The president already needed more water and a quieter life. 'Where do we get that kind of money from?'

There was more silence until the legal counsel spoke. 'The bonus pool?'

The silence instantly froze over. He was met with looks of universal contempt, which made him all but disappear into his suit.

The COO took the reins now. 'No, this has to be buried. We'll have to put it down as a write-off but bounce it through some SPVs, SIVs or whatever the hell makes it disappear from the books.' To Falcinelli: 'Where did we put the sub-prime losses?'

The legal counsel needed a moment to retrieve it from his memory. 'Some special purpose vehicles in the Caymans, but I'd have to check.'

The COO thinking about it. 'OK.'

Cochran felt now was the moment. 'So is that agreed?'

They shared looks that said it all. The COO speaking for them.

'Right. Here's my thinking. We put the money in place, ready to transfer at a moment's notice in case Lazcano decides to pull any more DVD stunts, or worse. But first, Jack and I go back to his SEC friend tomorrow morning and get a final number.'

The CEO didn't like the open-ended feel to this, a meeting that was meant to put this nightmare behind him. 'Guys, don't we just want this to go away? I mean, what will he do next?'

The COO spoke uncompromisingly, too experienced to roll over on anything. 'Tony, the SEC is cleaner. Don't you realize how big the fine would be if they found out we laundered money *and* paid him back as well? A few asshole judges have started throwing out the deals the SEC's been letting us cut. Even if the SEC gave us the usual slap on the wrist somebody on the bench might start

grandstanding and decide to make an example of us all –
and Christ knows they've got the ammunition. Let's not
ride our luck here. We owe it to the bank – and ourselves
– to make sure we didn't walk away from a better alternative here. We all OK with that?'

The COO looked around the room for responses, met
by three nods of various levels of enthusiasm.

Cochran's heart sank that the Lazcanos hadn't been
paid off there and then, that they hadn't been made to
disappear. But he doubted his own thinking. Maybe they
were right, cut a deal and receive the protection of the
authorities. Turlington had been kidnapped on Mexican
soil. Lazcano wouldn't dare to pull a stunt like that in the
United States itself. Wouldn't dare . . .

42

The Gulfstream taking off from Charles De Gaulle airport did nothing to lift our spirits. Neither did the bourbons sitting before us. We had sat in silence since taking our seats opposite each other across a table. My phone and computer tablet were next to my drink, a fact which had already earned more than one unhappy look from my travelling companion. The atmosphere had been fragile since the episode in Paris. The hours since spent disentangling ourselves from the Gendarmerie and Interior Ministry officials with the help of Diane and the State Department.

Martinez looked out of her window, watching the airport fall away beneath us. Maybe pondering the absence of any shopping, maybe pondering the least romantic trip in the history of visits to the French capital. Maybe just pissed that I hadn't spoken to her properly since Boulevard du Montparnasse. After a while, after all the detail of the landscape below was lost in the failing light of the afternoon, she slowly turned her head to me.

'Are you angry at me?'

I was surprised as much by her question as how I must have been coming across. 'No. No, not at all.'

'Then why haven't you said a word to me all day?'

I tried a lie. 'Thinking about the case.'

'Bullshit.'

I failed.

She went to continue but knew me too well. If I was preoccupied with the case I'd need to focus on that before I could get back to us. That was the deal she'd learned to accept. When she spoke it was almost accusatory.

'So do you still trust Webster?'

'He tried to warn us.'

She looked at me, worried. Worried for me. 'We got shot to shit, he didn't do a very good job.'

'He tried to warn us. I . . . I don't know.' Saying it because I didn't.

Martinez looked down at the table. I followed her eyes. She was looking at the gauze on the knuckles of my left hand. Remembering the events of the day. Both of us remembering.

'I'm going to keep your identity out of this, mademoiselle. I promise you that.'

She gave me the first hopeful look all meeting. 'Really?'

Martinez's brow creased as a thought bubbled up in her mind. 'The bit I don't get is why they didn't kill you when they had the chance. You said so yourself, when that off-duty soldier got shot the sniper must have had a clear shot of you.'

Both of us pondered that imponderable. Until I began to understand . . . And felt sickened by it.

'Martinez, they brought a van. They wanted to kill the whistle-blower and . . . grab me.'

'Why?'

Then I suddenly got it. I wasn't a banker with a bad trading year, I was investigating drug money. 'To take me back to Lazcano.'

'But the guy in the van, Byrne? It was the guy from the London bombing.'

'I know.'

That bewildering fact breaking apart my hold on the situation.

'The chances of him being known to Lazcano, Byrne, I mean, as a gun for hire . . . Do you buy that? It only makes sense if . . .'

Then the logic hit us together, us speaking together. 'Nemesis and Lazcano.'

We sat there struck by the undeniable truth of it but utterly perplexed.

'Nemesis were kidnapping you to order? They're Lazcano's people? They can't be, Byrne, they're killing bankers all over the globe. What is this, the biggest smokescreen in history?'

'What if it is?'

'What if what is?'

'What if it is like you say, the biggest smokescreen in history?'

She waggled that head of hers. 'That's impossible.'

'No it isn't. It's improbable, but it's not impossible.'

'But why would Lazcano get mercenaries to go tearing up the world's bankers before coming after you? It doesn't make sense.'

I wrestled with my own confusion over this. 'It doesn't make sense, but it doesn't mean it isn't true. Today's play was all about Lazcano: stop the whistle-blower, grab me.'

Unseen by Martinez, I patted my trouser pocket. Patted the girl's crucifix that I had taken in Paris. Needing to remember her, needing to remember the dead. So angry that I let her . . .

'You're upset about her, aren't you.'

I looked up at Martinez's face and its expression of concern, its look of *don't blame yourself*, and tried to be indifferent, not in the right frame of mind for that conversation. Not in the right frame of mind to think about what I put Martinez through either.

'Come off it, Byrne. I can read you like a book – and not a very good one.'

An old joke between us, spoken softly. We scrutinized each other. Read each other. Her wanting to say everything and nothing.

'Why have you been so quiet today, Mike?'

My mouth started to form the words, some words, but she shook her head. 'The truth. Whatever the truth is, just tell it to me.'

I could see her fatigue, worse than physical, when every emotional step is a Himalayan trek. I took a deep breath and let it out. 'I don't want you to die on my watch, Jenni.'

Her face tightened at my reply. 'You can't do it, can you Mike. You can't just say you care.'

I felt wrong-footed, not comprehending just how wrong my choice of words was.

'You have to dress it up like some goddamn procedural issue, like I'm some prisoner you're transporting from one jail to another. This isn't a goddamn mission from Diane, Mike. This is us. This is everything I . . . You . . .'

Tears began to build in her eyes. She drained her drink. Argued with herself inside her head then made a decision and stood. At that very moment my computer tablet pinged on the table. An email that I quickly scanned. The email I'd been waiting for. Martinez loomed over me now.

'I'm going to bed. You coming?'

'I've got to do this.'

She looked at my bandaged hand. Looked at me.

'You know, Byrne, when I met you . . . I thought . . .' I could see she wasn't sure if she should say the next thing and when she did it was almost blurted out. 'I thought I could stop looking.' Her face creasing up. 'I guess I was wrong.'

She took herself and her broken heart off to our cabin. I bit down on the discomfort these moments brought. I was pissed that she expressed herself so goddamn passionately all the time. Jesus . . . But who was I kidding? What a shitty hand I kept dealing her.

Back to the grindstone.

The communication. It was from Diane. I picked the tablet up off the table ahead of me as the plane experienced a brief moment of turbulence before settling again. I reread the email.

The list of the dead gunmen from Paris. A Bosnian, two Brits, a Georgian and an American. Odd combination. They had to be . . . Yes, there it was as I scanned through their limited early details. All former soldiers. Soldiers. Mercenaries? Former soldiers. Soldiers . . . But why soldiers? What bound soldiers to the Lazcanos? Money? Really? Yet that bothered me. Soldiers don't enter their profession for the money, it's not what motivates them. Could it really be money? I couldn't make sense of that.

Then Martinez's words came back to me . . .

I thought I could stop looking.

Her words washing up against my mind like waves on a beach.

I thought I could stop . . . looking.

Her words . . .

Stop looking.

Byrne . . .

Stop . . .

Byrne, you idiot.

. . . looking.

Why is everything in the last place you look? Because why would you keep looking after you find it? It would be madness to keep looking. It would be madness unless the thing you were looking for wasn't a thing but an answer. A conclusion. A conclusion that could be right for all the wrong reasons or wrong for all the right reasons. The wrong conclusion . . .

Nemesis. I was asking what they were doing, not who was doing it. They were killing bankers, traders who had lost more money than they had ever earned. But it was more than that. It was . . .

I grabbed my cell phone.

Special Agent Mason was sipping a green tea against her better judgement but at her doctor's suggestion when the desk phone rang.

'Mason.'

'Diane, it's me, Byrne.'

'You got my email?'

I was leaning excitedly on the table. 'Got it. Diane, can you run those names you sent me through the database with the following queries.'

'Sure. What are we looking for?'

'Three things . . .'

Mason was already pulling up the file of the London bomber, his half-burned face on her screen along with the top page of his British army record.

'Where they've travelled recently.'

Mason noted the word *travelled?* on a post-it note. Mason intrigued, understanding his inference immediately. The first Nemesis killings. These people part of the attacks on banks.

'What else?'

I rubbed a hand over my face, feeling the day catching up with me. I looked out of the window. The plane was somewhere over the Atlantic, flying through a thin blue sky above a sea of white clouds. It looked like a heavenly bedspread. God, I was tired.

'They're all soldiers, Diane. I want to know where they met and who they knew.'

'You thinking Iraq, Michael?'

'Yeah, but more than that. These are pretty radical people but they're also a disparate group. They did something in Iraq. Something happened to bring them together. Something – I don't know..'

Mason noted the word *met?*

'OK, Michael, and the third?'

'How they're connected to Lazcano.'

Mason's head started up at that link. Her hand hovered before she noted the name.

'Lazcano? You think he's involved with Nemesis?'

'No Diane. I don't think he's involved with Nemesis . . .' I took my eyes off the horizon and looked down at the table. Focusing. 'I think Lazcano is Nemesis.'

43

On the battered table in the cheap office in the cheap district of San Diego two cell phones lay on their sides, head to toe. They rang together. Moving slightly with each vibration. The cheap lawyer in his cheap suit accepted both calls at the same time. As always, the cell phones connected, the gofer lawyer retreated to his antechamber, gun in hand. Out of earshot. Out of trouble.

The phones spoke to each other.

'We screwed up.' The voice at the end of the line was metallic.

'*We?*' The voice in Mexico was unforgiving.

'I . . . I screwed up.' Even the metallic voice failing to disguise the fear.

A silence followed that wasn't broken until from the Mexican end, 'Are you the right man for the job?'

'Sure. Sure I am.'

'We're not so sure.'

'Now, listen, I've worked my goddamn ass off doing this . . .'

Gabriel was stood at the back patio window of his brother's house in Mexico City. The triple-glazed patio glass was bullet-proof, sound-proof. Beyond the glass, always closed for business calls, was a long, narrow swimming pool in a natural stone setting, bright pink dahlia piñatas, tight balls of petals forming a bushy flower, lining the sides. But the younger Lazcano thought only of the possible surveillance cameras, the government agents reading his lips, collecting evidence against the cartel. His hand was held across his mouth as he spoke into the cell phone.

'You were not hired to work hard, you were hired to get results. You promised results. Are you breaking your promise?'

Even the metallic nature of the voice was unable to hide the tightening in the speaker's throat. 'I am not breaking any promises. If I can't grab him I'll kill him as soon as I can, I give you my word.'

Gabriel muted the phone and turned to his brother, who was sitting on a long, curvy white leather couch. Sat beside him was his young Venezuelan mistress in jean shorts and a cropped white T-shirt. She was as interested in the drug lord's affairs as he was in her attempt at sexuality, and thus she had instead settled down to watch a rerun of *Ugly Betty*.

'He's promising to kill him.'

Eduardo's reaction was one of outrage, and he stood up from the couch as he gesticulated through his response. 'Kill him? After all this? He thinks that would be a fucking solution? I want Byrne *here*.'

His girlfriend was having to lean round the drug lord to see the TV on the wall. Pulling a face that said she wasn't happy about it.

'We want the package delivered here.' Gabriel calm.

The owner of the metallic voice calculated how that could be achieved. 'Sure. Sure, that's still possible.'

Gabriel muted the phone. 'He says that's still possible.'

Eduardo stared bug-eyed at his brother.

'Possible? *Possible?*' Repeating the word like it was blasphemous to him, hurtful, insulting. 'POSSIBLE?' The blood rushing to Eduardo's face turned the thickset man a threatening shade of beetroot.

Beside him his girlfriend tutted and waved a hand to indicate he was in the way.

'Eddi, I can't see the television.'

A mistake.

A woman who had only ever seen one side of him.

She had made a mistake.

He had showered her with gifts when he was wooing her, when he wanted her sex, when he wanted the conquest. Treated her like a Madonna when he was getting it. At first. But lately almost seemed to forget she was there, tired of the novelty she presented, bored by her immature interests. And she had never seen the reality, the reason why he headed the Lazcano cartel and why the Lazcano cartel ran the north-west of Mexico.

So she made a mistake.

Eduardo looked down at her. A grotesque smile of pure hate working his mouth. A drop of spittle forming on his fat lower lip.

'You can't see the television?'

The former beauty queen gesturing, *Like, derrr.* 'Of course not, you're in the fucking –'

The last word not out of her mouth before – possessed – the head of the cartel lifted her by the hair at the back of her head, took three big steps towards the plasma television and slammed her face into it. Pulling her head back and looking at the broken levy of blood beginning to pour down her broken Miss Venezuela nose.

Eduardo's voice wired, maniacal, terrifying. 'Can you see it now?'

Then *slam, slam, SLAM*. Gabriel twitched spasmodically with every pounding of the girl's head. He unmuted the phone. Making his contractor hear this. Knowing that on no account should he intervene.

Eduardo was holding the young beauty queen's entire weight up with one fury-filled hand. The massive television had shattered in the middle, a dark cloud at its centre, blackened by mashed-up plasma technology, the young woman's face slashed by the broken screen, her eyes closed and puffing up, darkening, blood running in rivulets from the cuts across her face.

'You always wanted to be on TV. Happy now? HAPPY?' Roared in her pitiful ear.

The ex-model, the never-to-be-again-model, mumbled for mercy, trying to find some strength, any strength to get the word *sorry* to her lacerated lips. Eduardo hated her now. Hated her ugliness. Hated that *she* had made *him* do this.

'*Hija de puta.*' Daughter of a whore.

The last words she heard before losing consciousness. Brought about by Eduardo crashing her head into the screen one last time, with such force that the television broke free of one of its wall-mounts and slid down forty-five degrees until it cracked to a stop on a shelf below. The girl was left with an obtuse triangle of plastic sticking out of her blinded right eye. He dropped her to the ground as good as dead. Finished with.

He surveyed what he had wrought.

He was tired now.

Tired but better for it.

He indicated his ex-girlfriend on the marble floor with an uncertain hand. 'Gabi . . .'

Gabriel's heart ever-so-slowly descended from his mouth. 'I'll see she's taken care of.'

The drug lord slowly looked up at his brother by the window. Spoke calmly now, as if he did not wish to disturb a person sleeping beside them. 'Has Sovereign Bank paid?'

The cell phones lay head to toe in the bare San Diego office.

'The other matter. Have we received payment yet?'

The counterparty was stricken by the unhinged act of violence, the woman's screams, that he had witnessed down the phone.

'No. They are still in talks.'

The phone had gone silent. Muted at the other end. The unbearable part. Then –

'We are concerned that the message is not getting through. Deliver another one. The one we discussed.'

When the synthesized voice spoke next it was with uncertainty. 'But . . .'

'You know what to do. Just do it.'

'Yes, but it might push them into the arms of the authorities.'

Metallic breathing came down the cell phone. Waiting for a response.

But nothing happened. The caller unable to see that the

other cell phone had a message on its screen reading *Call Ended*.

Then the speaker realized that Gabriel had gone. And the speaker realized a few more deaths wouldn't make any difference.

Realized that maybe the Lazcanos were right – it *was* time to send a message.

Time to turn the screw.

44

Alecto looked at the computer screen in Excel's apartment and watched the little troll disappear in a puff of purple smoke. She felt the nervousness that her new instructions instilled in her. She'd been in towns and cities in Iraq when this kind of thing had gone down. Life stopped. Everything stopped. This kind of thing – it changed everything. And there was no denying it, she felt nervous. Battle nerves, but battle ready.

Alecto logged off the machine and padded across the small East Village apartment to the kitchenette area, a heavy object dragging down a pocket of her bathrobe, making it look as sulky as her frame of mind. She checked her watch. 15.46. She turned the faucet on, getting herself another glass of water. Her fourth since the flight. Goddamn flights messed her up. Her sleep, her digestion, her hydration, her mood. *Fucking stewardess telling me not to listen to music. Such shit. Fucking nobody minded on no military flight. No panties-pissing-failed-French-models on those flights jibber-jabbering at you to not play your iPod. It's about fucking control. It's about herding us around like sheep, sticking us in our fucking pens. Teaching us to fear authority. Well fuck authority. Fuck it all.*

In her anger the young woman had overfilled her glass and she instantly felt the pang of guilt that growing up on a farm in Kansas still made her feel about wasting water to this day. The Iraqi desert rather ramming home the point. She turned off the faucet and began to gulp down the water. She was upset, guilty, tormented by her decision to take down her colleague. *But I had to do it, right? We'd agreed the plan. No fuck-ups.* He hadn't argued afterwards. Hell, he'd been nice about it. But, Jesus . . . Taking out one of the team . . . But the plan was the plan. *The plan was the plan, right? Fucking Byrne wasn't meant to . . . I mean, who the fuck is this guy anyway? Fucking kill him, man. What's with all this kidnapping shit? Byrne lives and one of ours dies? Explain that fucking battle plan, man.*

She was confused. Walking up and down now. Working herself up. Nodding to herself. Agreeing with herself as she argued with herself. *If it wasn't for everything that was coming I'd be fucking saying a thing or two about this. He better come through, that's all I'm saying. Man . . . I need to kill me some fucking bankers. And I mean, up close and fucking personal. Sitting in their cosy fucking offices . . . Let's see how they take some heavy metal. Let's see how they deal with a combat fucking situa –*

The intercom rang. A harsh buzzing. Cutting through her internal dialogue.

She checked her watch. 15.56. Not late, but not exactly early either.

Alecto walked over to the door and thumbed the intercom button.

'Yep?'

'Delivery.'

'Third floor.' Alecto hit the downstairs door-release button for five seconds. She looked around. All in order.

She reached into the right-hand pocket of the bathrobe and pulled out the compact, three-and-a-half-inch barrel Jericho 941 Desert Eagle pistol. She held it behind her back, opened the door and looked down the communal corridor while she waited. Two minutes later a young African-American FedEx lady carrying a shoebox-sized package appeared out of the elevator and made her way towards the apartment.

'Miss Daniels?'

Alecto nodded. 'That's right. Could you put it on that table while I get a pen.'

The FedEx lady smiled helpfully as she retrieved a hand-held tracking device from her belt and took a couple of steps into the apartment.

'We don't need a pen, Miss, we use – *oh sweet Lord!*'

The door slammed closed at the exact moment Alecto brought up the gun. 'Give me your fucking wallet.'

'What?'

'Give. Me. Your. Fucking. Wallet.'

The delivery lady didn't know whether to place the box on the table, but – fearing the worst – kept it and yanked out a small brown leather fold and offered it to Alecto.

Alecto snatched it and opened it up. Flipped past the FedEx ID to her driver's licence.

'This your address?'

'Yes. Camden, New Jersey.'

'That place is a shithole.'

'It's got its problems.' The delivery girl worked hard to keep her breathing under control. Worked hard not to surrender to her desire to scream and collapse.

Alecto eyed a photograph in the wallet. 'This your boy?'

'Elijah, yes.'

''Cos now I know where you and Elijah live.'

The delivery woman hadn't even begun to get a handle on what the hell the country hick with the gun wanted, her brain only able to send the message *this is bad, this is bad, this is bad.*

'So if you identify me to the police I know where to come and kill you both.'

The delivery woman barely contained a cry as Alecto scrutinized the ID in her hand.

'I'd know the exact address of the people I had to come and gun down like mangy dogs.'

The delivery woman's face rained huge droplets of tears now. She shook her head. Her world suddenly in that crazy woman's hands. 'I won't tell. I won't tell a soul. I swear on the baby Jesus.'

Alecto almost laughed as she slipped the wallet into her robe pocket. 'Oh, I don't need you to swear on anything because if you tell the authorities *anything* Elijah will die. In front of you. Slowly. Just before you do.'

The FedEx woman shook and shook her head. 'I won't tell. I wouldn't do that. Please don't do that.'

Alecto cocked her head sideways like she hadn't heard what she needed to hear yet. The delivery woman's cheeks were soaked with tears, tears that were still coming thick and fast, her mouth straining to form words that weren't pushed aside by desperate cries of helplessness.

'I haven't seen you.'

Alecto nodded, like *now you're getting it.*

'It all happened so quick.'

Alecto was pleased, like *was that so hard?*

'Don't hurt my little baby boy.'

Alecto laughed. 'I don't need to, you didn't see me.'

The FedEx lady shook her head with big turns, emphatic turns. 'I didn't see you. I'm not seeing you. This isn't happening. This isn't happening . . .' And the articulation of that wish made the last of her defences give out, and she began to sob at the thought of everything she held dear being hurt by this woman in front of her.

Alecto stepped towards her, removed the package from her hands, put it on the table and gently hugged the delivery driver who was all but collapsing in her arms.

'There, there. It's all gonna be OK.'

The delivery lady repeated it in the vain hope that it would make it so.

'It's going to be OK.'

'It's gonna be all right.'

'Thank you. Thank you.' The delivery lady now reduced to the most wretched state.

'Exactly. It's all gonna work out.'

'Thank you.'

Ten minutes later, Alecto, in tight-bobbed corn-coloured wig and FedEx uniform, turned the ignition key in her newly acquired delivery truck. The engine wafted almost silently into life, the dashboard lighting up the only sign of activity. She nodded, impressed.

'Electric. Cool.'

In Excel's apartment nothing moved.

The living room and kitchenette were quiet.

The bedroom was quiet.

The bathroom was quiet.

The person with her mouth gagged sitting next to the bath was quiet.

The person with her mouth gagged, stripped to her underwear and handcuffed to the radiator was very, very quiet.

But not because of her fear of breaking her promise to stay silent. That was the easy part. After everything she had done to bring Elijah into the world, after everything she had done to *keep* him in the world, that was the very easy part.

It was the terror of what she had walked into.

A customer with a gun.

A bathroom for a prison.

A prison with a corpse in the shower. The smell forcing its way into her nose, the stench making her gag. A young white man in a suit. Crouched down on the floor in an unnatural position nobody could possibly maintain unless they were dead. His head lolling against the tiles. His skin a colour she had never seen and never knew a human's could get. A purplish red. A sickly colour off any living spectrum. A bluebottle fly buzzed on to the corpse's face. It skittered across its cheek, down on to its upper lip, before turning towards a nostril, where it disappeared inside.

The person with her mouth gagged silently screamed as she remembered the woman's words before she left.

Take a good look, you hear? That'll be your son if you saw me.

45

The email contained the personnel files of hundreds of allied soldiers. God knows people must have been working closely together to get this over to me this quickly. Stuck on the plane with just a computer tablet, I did not relish the task ahead. To sift through and map their movements and associations for the past decade.

There was no way I had enough information here to be certain of drawing any conclusions, but the events of Paris had told me Nemesis's reach was global and swift. And somehow tied to Lazcano.

Would the files show any mention of Mexico? Any mention of Lazcano? That would simplify the investigation, which is how I knew not to expect it.

There was no algorithm I could crawl across this data with. This was to be the old-fashioned manual approach. This was sifting the haystack a straw at a time.

I looked out of the Gulfstream's window, the sky gently darkening to match the whisper of shade on the horizon. I reached for my coffee and pulled up the file of the London bomber. As good a place as any to start. Where had he travelled? Who did he know? Could he lead me to the Paris sniper? And how the hell had Lazcano found him?

46

'I'm going to have to see your ID.'

Alecto dropped the truck's sun-visor and caught the ID almost without looking as it fell into her hand, like she did this day in, day out. She handed it breezily to the NYPD patrolman manning the temporary road-barrier into both Broadway and Vesey Street. She was smiling and almost winking at him all at the same time, all flirtatious *ooh, a man in uniform.* Her face animated in a way it was never otherwise. Alecto chewing gum and moving it constantly in the hope that, if her face was already out there, nobody would link this version of her to any other. She nodded at the Financial District ahead.

'So road-blocks now?'

The patrolman studied the FedEx ID card, looked up, matching it to her face, her corn-coloured hair. The convincing card made weeks ago, gambling that any cops wouldn't know a real FedEx ID if they saw one. 'Yeah, these terrorists making us all a bit cautious.'

'You can never be too careful, officer.'

He handed the card back. 'You never can.'

Alecto accepted it and deftly slotted it between the sun-visor and the cabin roof. The patrolman signalled to a colleague to lift the manual barrier across the street.

'Thanks, officer.'

Alecto pulled away as the patrolman gave his attention

to the car behind, already forgetting about her. A line of at least thirty vehicles building up down the block.

Alecto pulled the electric FedEx truck up outside the headquarters of Sovereign Bank on Vesey Street. She pulled on skin-coloured surgical gloves and looked at the large glass frontage. Completely covered up with paper. All the banks following suit, thinking they were foiling any sniper attacks. She smiled with scornful pleasure at their mindset. The banks feeling the fear. Delighted they were to make her job a hundred times easier. *If your windows weren't covered up I wouldn't be able to do what I'm about to do. Smiling at the irony.*

Alecto entered the bank's lobby and felt something different, something unusual. The unusual nature of the experience. Not because it was a bank. She could orientate herself around that. It had an expansive front counter, fancy frosted glass panels on every wall space, its name in large, three-dimensional, gold lettering, the words *Sovereign Bank* hanging seemingly impossibly from the air, an airport-style security set-up beyond the automatic barriers for those proceeding further into the building. It had all these things, yet these were not the unusual factor for her.

It was the closeness.

Everybody so close.

Alecto was meant to be five hundred yards away, one *thousand* yards away when she shot someone. Invisible. Removed. An anonymous angel of death dictating who did and did not live. When she shot insurgents in Iraq they were a dot falling over in the distance. No cries, no screams of pain, no blood. Just a dot falling over. But to be this close . . . Hell, she could reach out and touch these people. They were flesh and blood. It changed everything. She'd hear them fall. She'd hear them react. She'd hear them die. Blood would be everywhere. She'd see their faces as the bullets cut into their bodies, into their spines, brains and nervous systems. She'd see them dying, going into shock, reacting. She was surprised that she hadn't been better prepared for that. This was so . . . real. But he would be so proud of her.

She slipped her surgically-gloved hand into the back of her modified courier package. Taller than it was wide, longer than it was tall. Like it might contain a very large hardback book. All wrapped in brown paper, close to her FedEx-uniformed chest, but a slit at the rear where her hand slipped in. Around the Uzi submachine gun.

The Uzi which fired at a rate of six hundred rounds per minute.

Fifty bullets in the clip.

Five seconds of slaughter.

Alecto repulsed by the scatter-gun approach to killing the Uzi produced. The waste. The casualness. Her life where every bullet counted. This clumsy tool for this job doing everything she had been trained not to do.

The urge to just blast away . . . But five seconds. It would be over before it started. Before anybody knew what had happened.

Five seconds of absolute carnage.

Longer if she tapped her trigger finger repeatedly.

But not much longer needed. Or sensible.

Alecto looked around. As she stood by the reception

desk. Three women behind there. Two pretty, one who used to be. Some chairs to her right, people waiting. A group of four businessmen. Selling to the bank or being sold to? Security. Six. Two by the door. Two by the airport metal detectors. Two by the elevators. Very spread out.

She wouldn't be able to kill them all, but gunshot victims didn't do much. And victims was all she'd come for.

Alecto nodded to herself. *Time to make my delivery.*

At first the bullets sounded strangely like fire-crackers in rapid succession, echoing off the hard surfaces, until the ear tuned in to what it was. The sound of death.

The three receptionists momentarily performed a macabre disco dance as they each took one or two bullets in their chests.

Alecto flipped left, trilling bullets at the door guards, dropping them both as the screams of the wounded began to grow. Terror and pain combined. Alecto a show-stopper, cutting the strings of all the marionettes about her.

Turning slightly right, beyond the reception desk, the startled guards, one reaching for his gun, one dodging behind the metal detector. The braver or more foolhardy of the two punctured by bullets, his face contorting along with his body as he fell backwards against a hand-luggage scanner.

Alecto sidling left, quick trigger tap, the hidden guard taking three in the arm and back. Dropping.

The elevator guards with their guns coming out of their holsters. One bringing it up to aim, the other panicking, dropping it as he pulled it out. The more capable drilled with a blast of bullets, the second trying to catch his gun in mid-air, catching instead the ruthlessness of the Uzi.

Alecto aiming right, spraying the businessmen who had yet to properly react, to look over, events too fast, events on Uzi Time now. The damage done to them by her bullets ahead of their ability to comprehend it, knocking the men along their seats.

Alecto pausing to take in the room. Everybody injured or dying . . .

She waved the submachine gun left and right at the wounded, finishing off the clip, every bullet that found a victim again a bonus now.

Until the gun went quiet.

Emptied. Into the people unlucky enough to be in the Sovereign Bank lobby at that time.

Eleven seconds from beginning to end.

She dropped the fake courier's package at her feet.

Turned, pulling off her gloves as she did, shoving them in her pocket.

Accelerating . . .

Flying out the door.

Pointing back into the lobby.

Screaming in the street at the startled pedestrians, at the NYPD officers racing towards her, unholstering their guns.

Alecto running backwards, away from the scene of devastation.

'He's killing everybody! He's killing them!'

Running away as the officers ran towards the door, taking siege positions, calling for backup, shepherding the innocent bystanders away.

As Alecto ran. Not towards her truck but *away*.
Into the crowd.
Round the corner.
Stripping off her FedEx jacket.
As officers raced towards the bank.
Tossing the jacket and wig in a doorway.
Walking towards the Metro. Melting into the city.
Message sent.
Screw turned.

47

'Can he hear us?'

Webster nodded towards the chauffeur behind the driver's screen.

The Sovereign Bank CEO was too in shock to comprehend at first. 'What? Oh, no. No. Bill, what just happened?'

They were both sat on the wide rear bench of a limousine as it travelled towards the Upper East Side for one of Cochran's meetings, Webster jumping in as the only opportunity for face time with his boss right now.

Webster, hotter having escaped the bracing February air outside, pulled open his black wool and cashmere overcoat. Then he gave a helpless, open-handed gesture. 'Nemesis killed three people and injured ten – badly – in the lobby of our HQ approximatcly forty-five minutes ago.'

Cochran wanted to spew rage at his security chief, but the confines of the car inhibited him. He looked out at the midtown traffic, managing his mood down to helpless anger. 'I know that, Bill. The whole fucking world knows that. I'm asking you what happened? What is going on, Bill? Turlington tortured to death. One of our accountants killed in Paris. This – in New York, Bill. What's happening?'

But instead of answering Webster sat there, in two minds about what he was about to say. Wrestling with something that he knew or had to say. His reticence infuriating his terrified boss.

'Bill, what? What?'

'Sir, what I'm about to tell you . . .' Looking him intently in the eyes like *you don't know how fucking serious this is*. 'It stays between you and me until we agree how to deal with it.'

The CEO was bewildered by the challenge to their relationship. '*We?* You work for *me*, Bill.'

'Fine, but I've been your back channel to Lazcano, right?'

Cochran's chest tightened as one of the hundreds of nightmares was possibly playing out in front of him, paranoia suddenly taking hold.

'Are you wired?'

'What?'

'Are you wearing a wire?'

Webster was dumbstruck, momentarily wondering if his boss had lost his mind, then running a hand through his salt-and pepper hair, unable to hide his mood of *I haven't got time for this shit*.

'What the –? Do you think this is a shakedown, sir? You accusing me of a shakedown, Mr Cochran?'

The CEO leaned back into his side of the car now, his frayed nerves betraying him.

'Who knows how people are dealing with all of this, Bill? I mean, we're all on the hook here. Somebody gets cold feet they could sink us all.'

Webster began to unbutton his shirt. 'Come on, check me.'

The CEO waved at him to stop. 'No, no, I'm sorry.

Just, all this, Bill. Look, I'm sorry, please, just tell me what it is. You are the back channel, fine. What did you want to say?'

Webster dropped his pantomime of undressing and sat back, sanity restored.

'I'm saying I think it's worse than you could possibly imagine.'

'Exactly what are you saying?'

There came a long sigh from Webster. Clearly dreading what he was about to impart. Which rattled Cochran even further.

'Lazcano . . . Nemesis . . .' Webster shrugging.

Cochran not comprehending. 'What?'

'It's all Lazcano.'

The CEO was like a dog listening to a child's ramblings. Oblivious to their meaning. Oblivious to their implications. Oblivious until his mind ran through the events of the last week and loose threads suddenly entwined to form a string he could follow blindly along its length. All the way from Lazcano to Sovereign Bank. All the way to him.

Then, uncontrollably, the CEO leaned forward and vomited between his legs. A gutful of half-digested food was dumped on the car floor. He retched loudly, unashamedly, channelling his fear and rage into the loud, twisted moans escaping his mouth. The coffee, whisky and biscuits diet of the last few days splattering his thousand-dollar shoes and five-thousand-dollar pants. And for the first time in his corporate life Cochran did not care a damn. He wanted it to hurt. Wanted to block it all out.

Webster moved his shoes out of the way too late to

avoid some sick splashing back on to them. He grimaced at his boss's behaviour and its effect on him specifically. Then, finally, the CEO sat back in his seat, mopping at his mouth with a handkerchief. His face white, his body spent. Then, with unusual calmness, 'Explain.'

'Sir, Lazcano ordered the hit on the Parisian employee. He must have.'

'No. It was Nemesis, Bill. Even the police are saying so.'

Webster was tight-lipped, shaking his head. 'The police don't know shit, you ought to know that. She died because I told Lazcano she was about to turn state's evidence.'

'You did *what*?' A whole new danger opening up before Cochran – that they could be sunk by somebody *outside* the loop.

'I told him she was about to become a whistle-blower, blow the whole lid off him *and us*. She'd been doing some routine money-laundering checks, realized we had some loopholes in the system and took it upon herself to go back and check all of the large overseas payments for the last five years. Found a truckload of cash coming from the currency houses in Mexico, one of which she traced back to the Lazcanos.'

Cochran was stupefied. 'So the authorities know?'

Webster gave a big, slow shake of the head. 'I intercepted it, got her to progress it with me first. That's when I told Lazcano. Just to let him know there might be a problem. I didn't want him to think we were deliberately spilling the beans on him, you know.' Omitting any mention of Byrne on purpose, seeing no benefit in putting the fall-out from that episode into the mind of the struggling bank chief. Wanting no distractions, wanting nothing except his boss to settle with Lazcano, to lay the whole episode to rest, doing whatever it took. Conversations with Byrne would come later, away from Cochran.

'But Nemesis . . . ?'

'Sir, wake up. Lazcano finds out, Nemesis attack. Do I have to draw you a diagram? Lazcano hasn't told me as much, but, come on, look at the facts.'

Cochran shook his head, the plates spinning out of control, overwhelmed by the angles of attack. 'Oh no, no, no, no. This is too big, Bill. We've *got* to go to the authorities. We've got to lay it all down in front of them. We've got to stop this. Now, *now.*'

'Sir, with the greatest of respect you'll win the battle but you'll lose the war.'

'What . . . What is that supposed to mean?'

Webster expecting this. 'If I may make two points. Telling the authorities will *not* stop this. Lazcano will make the crimes to date look like the entertainment at a children's party. He will make it his mission to murder and maim his way through Sovereign Bank's interests and personnel until you go clinically insane, till you blow out your own brains to make it stop. Believe me, sir, when I say I know these people. I was stationed there for five years, remember.'

Cochran couldn't work his mouth, but his sickened face asked for point number two.

'Also, you have no idea how balls-deep you are in all this, sir. How balls-deep we all are. Trading with an illicit counterparty, money-laundering, obstruction of justice, and that's before the main attraction. That's before Lazcano tells the Treasury that you knowingly sent Turlington and the Parisian girl to their deaths.'

Cochran felt almost deranged by this blow. Holding on to the car door to steady himself. 'But that's just not true, Bill . . .'

'Says the man who lied about his business dealings with Lazcano.' Looking respectfully at his boss like, *See what I mean?* 'Think about how it all looks, sir. Then Lazcano tells everybody how he warned you about Nemesis, how you knew about Nemesis, how you failed to warn anybody else on Wall Street about Nemesis . . . I mean, we're into the Patriot Act here, sir. You *have* to pay Lazcano.'

'No, no . . .'

'And do you think your inner circle will hold together when they're all facing public disgrace? Seizure of assets? Life behind bars? Sir, your inner circle will look like a rat's ass after it's been fucked by a water buffalo.'

Cochran pictured everything he was being told. The events, the inevitable events, as undeniable as they were predictable. Webster was right. One hundred per cent right.

'But Carl and Jack are talking with the SEC to see if they can beat them down on the possible fine. They want to see if we can go straight on this. I just can't engineer it by myself, Bill. We have to make a collective decision here.'

'Hmm.' Webster thoughtful now. 'OK, but one more thing, Mr Cochran.'

'What's that?'

'If you decide not to pay Lazcano I'll have to tender my resignation.'

Cochran considered that event and his subordinate with concern. 'And exactly why would that be?'

Webster's chiselled looks set into stone, trying to convey the magnitude of the threat. 'Because I won't be able to do my job, sir. I won't be able to protect you from what's coming.'

Cochran's body sagged into his leather seat. 'OK, Bill. I get it. I get it.'

'Do you, sir?'

Webster stared long and hard at his boss, his boss somewhere between concession and outrage at the implied insubordination.

'Yes, I get it.'

The CEO looked out at the sidewalk, the shoppers, the life of Madison Avenue continuing apace as his world teetered on the brink.

'Bill, do we want to call off the Aspen conference?'

'Why?'

Cochran looking at his security chief *isn't it obvious* style. 'Lazcano, Nemesis.'

Webster weighed the suggestion but shook his head. 'It's tomorrow, sir, our executives are already flying in from all over the world.'

Cochran nervous about his own shadow right now. 'But security . . .'

'What? You feel safe in New York? Sir, I promise you this: the hotel in Colorado is like Fort Knox. Our own runway, one road in . . . Nobody gets in or out but I know about it. The Bilderburg Group wishes it had our kind of security. Armed guards, the works. Right now I'd say it's the safest place you could be. And if we pay off Lazcano immediately it means that when we get back from the conference all our troubles will be behind us.'

Cochran needed to hear this more than he would ever dare admit.

'Do we know the security firm in Aspen? I mean, can we trust them?'

Webster gave a grim-set version of a reassuring smile and nodded gently.

'You're looking at the security firm, sir. I hand-picked each and every person myself.'

48

Martinez's hand slipped over my shoulder and gave me a squeeze. A squeeze that said *All forgotten*. She slid into the wide leather seat opposite, across the table, and proceeded to do up her seat-belt for landing. She was wearing her work clothes. Collared shirt and jeans. But somehow it seemed all wrong. Not because she didn't look beautiful. She did. It was just that it should have been the new clothes from a Parisian shopping spree.

She gave me a warm smile that told me to go on with my work then looked out over across the water towards a New York bathed in a fiery dusk. I tapped away at my computer tablet screen for a while before she broke the silence.

'Well?'

'Well what?'

'Well, what have you achieved that was worth not coming to bed for?' Smiling at me to let me know she was (mostly) teasing.

I added a sentence to the email I'd been compiling on and off for the last few hours. An email made up of my conclusions drawn from the army records of our Parisian assailants.

'There's been an attack at the Sovereign Bank headquarters.'

Her smile fell away. 'Nemesis?'

'Nemesis, Lazcano . . .' indicating with raised eyebrows

that there probably wasn't much difference. 'A woman dressed as a FedEx employee tore the place up with an Uzi. Three dead, ten injured.'

Martinez looked around herself like *This just gets worse and worse.* 'Did they apprehend her?'

'No. She disappeared.'

'Jesus, Byrne.' Shaking her head. 'Back to square one? No leads?'

'Not quite. They're all injured.'

'Who are?'

'Nemesis. They're all either burns or trauma victims, or military personnel who have required amputations or serious plastic surgery.'

'All of them?'

'All the ones we stopped in Paris.'

Martinez pieced it together in an instant. 'The London Bomber was there; he had facial burns.'

'And the conscript-type at the café? Prosthetic leg.'

'Wow. All of the Parisian attackers? Injured?'

I nodded slowly, still thinking on it. 'And I'd wager a banker's bonus the same will be true of the rest of Nemesis. Casualties of the Iraq war. Damaged people.'

'But soldiers, Byrne, they're your ultimate patriot. They're people who go out and put their lives on the line for their country.'

I thought out loud, as ever, appreciating her take on a problem. 'Iraq Vets have been turning up at the Occupy Wall Street protests around the country. Is it such a big stretch for some of them to want to take it further? Maybe some came back and said, "Look at what we've given our country, look at what the bankers took."'

However, Martinez had a problem with it – the same problem I had. 'But they're working for Lazcano, Byrne. They aren't fighting for a cause.'

'That we know of.' But she wouldn't let go of the inquiring look. She was right. Damned right.

'You said they were all injured, damaged. Could they have been taken advantage of?'

I sighed in frustration at the lack of answers. 'By Lazcano? Maybe, but . . . It seems unlikely. We're, we're missing something.'

'Yeah, like, how does Lazcano even know them? I mean, the Parisian gang was Bosnian, Georgian, British, American . . . They were drawn from all over the world. What the hell is a Mexican drug lord doing assembling a group like that? Where would you find them?'

'Landstuhl.'

She squinted at me. 'Land who?'

'Landstuhl. It's a US military hospital in Germany they evacuate the injured to out of Iraq. Mostly American, but they do what they can for others. This crew all passed through it back in 2007. That's where Lazcano must have met them.'

Martinez sat upright, energized by this new information. 'Can we prove that's where he met them?'

I stretched my arms and rolled my shoulders. It had been a long night. 'Not yet. Maybe never. But that's where he met them. And that's where he recruited them. Somehow.'

'How did he manage to do that?'

'That, Jenni Martinez, is the sixty four trillion dollar question.'

I hit SEND on my email app.

'Have you told Diane yet?'

'Just did.' I finished a long-since-cold cup of coffee. I looked up at her, half thinking out loud, half needing help ordering my thinking. '*Nemesis*. They chose that name for a reason.'

'Yeah, she's the Greek goddess who punishes those that get undeserved riches. Nemesis. I don't like these guys, but I do like their name.'

'But there's a lot of other Greek heroic figures you could draw on. There's Erebus, darkness, Typhon, the storms, Thantos, death, Momus, blame, Moros, doom. Then there's the Moiries, the Fates, and the Furies.'

'The Furies?' Looking at me like I was speaking Greek. With good reason, I guess.

'Yeah, avenging angels. I think they were Tisephone, she punished murderers, Megaera, who punished adulterers . . .'

'She got that right.' Managing even in this conversation to give me the warning and ever-jealous evil-eye.

'Then there was . . .' Struggling to recall it. 'Alecto . . . Alecto. She of unceasing anger.'

Martinez looked at me like she didn't recognize me. 'How do you know all this shit?'

'I went on holiday to Greece once.' Giving her a dead-pan look.

I was rewarded with a suspicious, leery expression. 'So what's your point about all these Greek floozies?'

'Well, maybe I'm just whistling Dixie here, but you'd expect one or more of those names to come up on internet chatter, that's all. I've asked them to look into it.'

'Unless the whole thing is an elaborate smokescreen?' Looking at me like I ought to give that some thought.

My tablet *pinged* as my inbox received an email. Martinez went to speak but was beaten to it by the Secret Service gold star flashing on my cell phone as it began to vibrate. She looked at the image pulsating, indicating, as it did, a call from Diane and decided that whatever she was thinking could clearly wait.

'Hey, what image do you use when I call?'

I gave her an ambivalent smile. 'It's not an image, it's a word.' I hit ACCEPT on my cell. 'Diane?'

'Michael, we've had a breakthrough on the attack at Sovereign Bank today.'

'A breakthrough. What?'

As we spoke I'd opened the new email on my tablet. It was from Diane herself. I popped open the attached file to see a grainy picture from Sovereign Bank's security cameras. It showed a young woman with a corn-coloured bob firing a submachine gun hidden inside a box. I covered her hair with my hand so as not to muddle my mind.

'Michael, we've run the images from the security cameras through the system and she's home-grown. Her name is . . .'

'Alice Armitage, from Chanute, Kansas.'

Mason was in her office, looking at the same picture as Byrne, surprised by Byrne's constant ability to surprise.

'Now how in the hell would you know that?'

She clicked through her various computer windows to his newly arrived email as he spoke.

'She was a sniper with the Army Rangers, Diane. She

was caught in friendly fire in An Najaf in 2006, suffered severe burns and was honourably discharged from the army in 2007 after an extended stay in the hospital at Landstuhl, Germany.'

Mason scanned Byrne's email to that same place and data now.

'Landstuhl's the connection?'

'The connection . . .' I had the ex-Army Ranger's personnel file on my tablet in front of me. 'But not the explanation. What's happening about Alice Armitage?'

'We've put out an all-points bulletin here, and the Kansas police are going to talk to her parents in Chanute: background stuff.'

I all but groaned. 'We really need to speak to her parents. We need to know the why behind all this.'

'Do you want to go, Michael?'

'I can't, Diane, I've got someplace else I have to be, but I want someone good there, someone who isn't going to make them clam up.'

Martinez looked at me as if she could read me like a book and not a very good one at that. She mouthed 'I'll go' and gave me a slightly despairing look.

I genuinely hadn't been trying to angle for that but was relieved by her offer. I mouthed 'I owe you', which earned me an eye-rolled 'I know' mimed back.

Mason was staring up at the office ceiling, trying to untense the muscles in a neck that had been craned over reports all day. She lowered her head and caught sight of a new email on her PC.

'Just a moment, Michael . . .'

Mason read the notice from the US Customs and Borders Protection Agency.

'Alice Armitage just got in today on a flight from Paris, having flown out from JFK twelve hours before. That places her at the attack in Boulevard du Montparnasse. She's the woman who didn't kill you today, Michael.'

As the jet's wheels touched down at JFK I looked at the young ex-Army Ranger's face on my tablet. What the hell was going through her mind? What did she want? What motivated her to kill and not kill?

Questions, too many questions. I needed to find some answers and fast.

'Diane, Sovereign Bank staff have been attacked in Paris and New York today. I think Webster knows more than he's letting on.'

'What do you mean?'

'I think he reached out to us because he knows of specific threats against the bank. I think he knows they're the target. I think he knew that when he talked to us. I think it's time I met with him again.'

'But he's attending the Sovereign Bank conference in Aspen.'

'Then so am I.'

'OK, Michael. And I'll find out the identity of every patient that was at Landstuhl military hospital the same time as Alice Armitage then find out where in the world they all are.'

Mason noted the word Landstuhl on a post-it note.

'Anything else, Michael?'

'The fake FedEx woman had a stolen van. Where's its designated driver?'

Mason paused her writing. 'The police are presuming the worst. She didn't finish her route.'

As the plane taxied towards a hangar I was undoing my seat-belt but paused with a rush of excitement.

'Have they checked . . . ?'

'The NYPD have already visited every house where there was a delivery. Everybody checks out, they think the delivery woman was probably car-jacked after the last delivery that was signed for.'

My spirits sank a little as I stood up from my seat. 'Well, could you send me the FedEx route and everything we know about the people on it anyway? I'll look at it before I fly on to Colorado.'

'OK, I'll get these done, Michael. But Michael . . . ?'

I knew that tone. There was an official sanction coming. 'Yes, Diane?'

'If you get down to Colorado and you don't like anything about it – and I mean *anything* – I want that conference closed down immediately.'

Martinez heard all this and considered me seriously, the three of us thinking the same thing. Thinking that that was a lot of Sovereign Bank staff all in one place. Thinking that, if we were Nemesis, that's where we'd head next.

49

Miami International Airport.

Thirty million passengers each year. Over eighty-two thousand every day. Eighty-two thousand people passing through, departing, arriving, connecting. Eighty-two thousand people anxiously on the go, eighty-two thousand people agitated that they were not at the front of the queue, eighty-two thousand people stopping and staring at airport signs. Every face a face in the very large crowd.

Each person another person.

Like the three dozen injured former military personnel arriving from around the world, their luggage no more than holdalls, rucksacks, sports bags. Thirty-six people out of the eighty-two thousand passing through the airport that day. Faces in a sea of faces. Clean records. No prior reason for the border police to see their names red-flagged. No reason to think anything suspicious about all thirty-six of them as they stood before the departures board over the course of the day, searching out their flights.

Finding their flight.

Heading towards their departure lounge.

Heading towards Denver International, Colorado.

50

Detective Ashby was driving the unmarked Dodge Charger north along FDR Drive not so much like he borrowed it from the police car pool as stole it. Grille lights flashing, siren screaming, tearing through the east Manhattan traffic like a NASCAR racer. I held a roof-strap with my right hand, Ashby's driving making that a necessity if I wanted to stay in my seat.

'We're heading for East 5th Street between Avenue A and B. Got it?'

Ashby looked determinedly out through the windscreen like his stare alone might clear the traffic for us.

'Got it. But you sure *you* got it?'

I nodded. I was certain. 'It's the delivery the FedEx woman didn't make, to a guy called Stephen Lewis. He's a member of Douglas McCarthy's team over at Sovereign Bank. Nemesis have been to his apartment. They might even be camped out there for all we know.'

Ashby pulled the car across three lanes in what felt like one car's length as he joined the exit ramp down towards the south-east edge of the island, forcing me to pull myself in towards my roof-strap or risk ending up in his lap.

Alecto turned on every hob on the gas stove in Excel's East Village kitchenette and left them unlit. They were not the point, they were the distraction. The point was the equipment on the counter.

One digital timer.

One detonator.

One wrap of plastic explosives.

She hit a button on the timer to set the countdown.

She looked up at the bathroom door. One more thing to do. She strode towards it.

The African-American FedEx delivery lady was crouched on the floor, free of her handcuffs now, dressed back in her FedEx uniform, except for the discarded jacket, and no longer gagged by a wrap of cloth. Gagged instead by the compact Desert Eagle Jericho 941 pistol stuck in her mouth.

Alecto spoke with a quiet calmness that belied the sickness that the smell of Excel's rotting corpse in the shower cubicle made her feel.

'Listen, lady. You're not the enemy, you understand? You're not the reason I've been deployed here, you follow? Your death would be what they call "collateral damage".'

The FedEx delivery lady was beyond tears at this stage, feeling hopeless, exhausted to the point of a nervous breakdown, all her strength needed just to keep it together. A bullet in the brain would be some kind of release right now, only her son keeping her going. She searched Alecto's eyes for where the hell this was going.

'Just like we were collateral damage from what the bankers did to us. I'm supposed to kill you. We don't want any witnesses. But you're not a witness are you?'

The delivery driver shook her head as much as she could with three and a half inches of gun barrel in her mouth. Alecto slowly withdrew the pistol from between the lady's teeth as she continued.

'Good. I don't like collateral damage. In fact, I fucking hate it.' Sensing her scared body under her black roll-neck sweater. 'So this is how it's going to be. You're going to hear me leave the apartment. *Then* – thirty seconds later – you're going to fly out of here and run to the bottom of the stairwell like your life depended on it and wait. *Don't* take the elevator.'

The African-American FedEx lady's eyes watched Alecto's face, unable to grasp what she was hearing, only knowing it *might* mean an end. 'How long do I wait in . . . in the stairwell?'

The ex-Army Ranger stood. 'Trust me, you'll know.'

Alecto left the cowering FedEx lady by the bath tub, where she was crouching, craning her neck away from the dead young man, unable to look, unable to generate the tears she needed to wash away the diabolical things she had borne witness to.

Ashby hurled the car right, around a corner into the southern end of Avenue B, forcing a taxi ahead to skid to a halt, stopping sideways, as we drove out wide across its path before getting back in lane.

'Byrne?'

'Yeah?'

'I appreciate you placing the call to me about this.'

'No problem.'

'But whichever way this turns out, whichever way this goes, I want you to know one thing.'

'Sure. What?'

Ashby pulled the Dodge Charger round a slow-moving bus into the path of another, faster, oncoming bus, pulling in front of the overtaken one just in time to miss careering into the other. Still finding time to take his eyes off the road and place them firmly on me.

'I am still majorly jacked about you killing my car.'

Punching his eyes into me. Getting an innocent, sympathetic smile in return.

'Hey, Ashby, they shoot horses, don't they?'

The FedEx woman looked at her watch. Thirty seconds since her captor had left. But she was frozen, unable to move. Doubting everything she was told. Trying to tell her muscles to *get up, get out* but doing no more than rocking backwards and forwards. Then seeing Excel's body. His purple, bloated corpse. Wondering who would stop her boy ending up like that one day. Finding herself rising, getting to her feet . . .

'What else do I need to know, Byrne?'

Ashby drifted the car left into East 4th Street, slapping the siren controls, killing the sound as we approached, the little late-night traffic that there was screeching to a halt as our car rocketed through the traffic.

'They'll be armed. But they might be the end of our trail right now, so we need them alive.'

Ashby stretched his neck like I might have put the nose at the top of it out of joint.

'I'll be sure to remember that when the terrorists start shooting at us.'

The FedEx lady was stood stock still in the small bathroom. She had given it a full minute before daring to stick her head around the bathroom door. She was resigned to a sick trick, a gleeful look on Alecto's lunatic face before blowing a hole in her head so that she could join the boy in the shower. But instead it was quiet. Quiet in the way a place is when it is empty. Really empty. She dared to take a step into the main living area, looked furtively about her, then eked ajar the nearby front door. Nobody through the opening. Nobody through the growing gap. Maybe no one there. Then the only thought that had sustained her filling her mind. *Elijah. My baby.* And suddenly the fear of guns and traps and death evaporated as she dashed for the staircase along the corridor.

We pushed the car doors to and both reached for our guns. Ashby had parked across the street from the apartment, speed more important than creeping up on our target. We started to cross over to the sidewalk outside the brownstone building, holding our guns low towards the ground.

At that moment a woman burst out of the front entrance directly in front of us, dashing headlong down the stairs towards us. A small African-American woman in a jacketless courier's outfit. Ashby tapping my arm, talking quietly.

'The attacker at the Sovereign Bank HQ wore a FedEx uniform.'

However, the woman's panicked demeanour, her looking left and right, her hands everywhere were telling us both that if she was a terrorist it was her first day on the job. But then all of a sudden she was a liability. Seeing us with our guns, not knowing what to make of us, she pointed faintly back into the building behind her, telling us with her gesture that she had just escaped something, some kind of terrifying experience, confirming that what we were looking for was in there, then she was shrinking as we approached, hands to her face, tears erupting over her fingers, realizing – praying – we were cops, hoping to God that whatever she had just gone through was over, safe now and yet still dread-filled, that whatever scared her must have been something –

The windows of the third-floor apartment above exploded out in a twenty-foot fireball, showering the street below with glass and bricks, a physical boom rocking the neighbourhood. Ashby and I instantly both tried to throw some cover over the petrified lady as we took cover ourselves, a sickly ticker-tape parade of debris falling down about us, the flame followed by a cloud of smoke that bloomed out and down on to all below like a volcanic ash cloud. The need to breathe overtaking the need to know if we had been injured or not. The lady's hysteria obscured by the dozen car alarms that had just been jarred into life.

Parked along the street, Alecto had watched the explosion in her car's rear-view mirror. Satisfied with the outcome, she pulled out into East 5th Street. Alecto filled with grim satisfaction at the destruction she had engineered, satisfaction that her erstwhile prisoner had made it to the street.

Ashby, covered in dust, held the weeping FedEx lady in his arms as he surveyed the destruction floating about us. He looked at the police Dodge Charger, which had taken the brunt of the apartment's eruption, windows smashed, roof dented, a layer of bricks and dust over it. He looked all around then looked at me.

'What's happened to your trail now, Byrne?'

I considered the apartment block and its missing wall, paper and scraps floating out of it. Scraps all I had left of Nemesis's plans. I looked down the street at a car braking before turning left with a slight urgency that produced a small screech of rubber. I kept looking after it even though it was out of sight.

'It just headed west.'

51

McCarthy paced the living room of his three thousand square foot Gramercy District apartment, all three thousand of those square feet seemingly in the living room itself, so large was it.

'No. No. NO.'

On a massive horseshoe of a black couch were what was left of his team, Duke, Ace, DB, FiDi and Cartman. They were in shock. They were scared of their boss's fury but more than that they were shocked, shaken. McCarthy marched over to a floating bookshelf of CDs and swept them violently to the right, scattering them over the bowls and vases his interior designer had carefully chosen and positioned, everybody flinching at his anger, but everybody flinching less for the news they had just received.

'*NO.*' Leaning his head on the now-empty shelf, fighting the tears, fighting the – what? What was it? . . . *That was it* – the impotence.

'When did it happen?'

Webster was standing by a Sovereign-Bank-supplied limousine, a black Lincoln Town Car. It was parked outside the departures building at Newark airport. An aged driver was hefting the security chief's bag out of the trunk.

'Half an hour ago. I'm being told the explosion tore the place apart . . . Look, there were no survivors, Doug.'

Even down the cell phone Webster could hear that McCarthy's mind wasn't keeping up, keeping up at all.

'I mean, what's happening here, Bill? What is it, open season on bankers?'

'Nobody knows for sure, but I'm certain of one thing: I think – I *know* - this is personal against Sovereign, they are gunning for us.'

McCarthy looked out of one of his penthouse apartment's vast windows, down on to the park below, keeping his back to his stunned team, embarrassed by the emotions he was fighting. *Turlington, now Excel? What the hell . . .?*

'Personal? How, Bill? Why?'

'I don't know, but they've singled us out. Think about it: Paris, the lobby of our bank and now Stephen Lewis's apartment . . .'

His cell phone felt heavier than a bowling ball to McCarthy. His voice nothing more than a croak as he spoke to Webster.

'So what now? Are you just calling to tell me again that you won't help me to fix this?'

Webster was pulling his large flight bag on wheels behind him as he headed into the departures building.

'Doug, you want to spend the next twenty minutes receiving an apology off me or do you want to hear what I think we can do about this?'

'It's not what we can do, Bill, it's what we are *prepared* to do. I thought we'd already had that conversation?'

'Doug, that was then, that was before it became

apparent that Sovereign had been singled out. We can't bring your team members back, but there is something we can do. You really want to put an end to this?'

McCarthy slapped a picture on the wall in frustration. A picture of a village in Kosovo that he had helped to liberate. People who he had subsequently met and who had answered any doubts about his role in the war.

'You *know* I want to put an end to this. I want to put an end to the sons of bitches who did this to Excel.'

The five team members on the couch behind him nodded miserably, lost in their distress.

'What, Bill, what is it you're saying we can do?'

Webster stopped short of the Continental Airlines first-class desk, out of earshot. 'Look, let's not talk about this on the phone. When you get to the hotel in Aspen come and see me right away.'

Webster killed his phone and let out a deep breath. He knew the bank and its staff were at risk, knew what it would take to save them — wondering who, if anybody, would do it.

McCarthy eyed his crew, the remains of his team. They looked up at him expectantly, hanging on his news.

'Boys, it's time to take the war to Nemesis.'

The words were barely out of his mouth before the quintet of young men leaped out of their seats and roared their anger-fuelled approval.

52

Get the information then get the plane back to New York. Those were Byrne's instructions before he got the FedEx delivery details and suddenly decided to take the first helicopter flight from JFK to Manhattan. Martinez knew he was trying to do the right thing, but why the hell couldn't she join him in Aspen? Didn't he know anything about women? Didn't he know that she was in this dustbowl because it was another way to be near him? Martinez was torturing herself. She was having the debate she had every day: how is this any different from being a mistress? Byrne was married to the Secret Service and even when she did see him there was the constant risk – often realized – that he would drop everything to go back to his real wife. *Diane asks way too much of him. What is he, the only agent on the force? And why does he have to have a knock-out black woman for a boss? Did they have a thing for each other? Was it always work that he had to go see her for?* Then Martinez got annoyed at her own pettiness, knowing it was a proxy for her frustrations and pain. She asked herself the question she asked herself every time they were apart: was a small part of Mike Byrne better than all of another man? And reached the same conclusion every time.

'We're here, sweetheart.'

Martinez came to, alarmed that she had not noticed her whereabouts during her reverie.

The detective stepped out of the brand-new taxi – a Chevrolet people carrier – and could feel the eyes on her, and not just because of the hour, almost 11 p.m. MST. Maybe because this was the nicest car in the whole of the trailer park. A trailer park where the people were sat on the stoops of their shabby parked-up homes watching her suspiciously like all she could be bringing was bad news for one or all of them. Who else got a taxi this far out? Who else was that pretty and well turned out around here? People that good looking were celebrities or hookers or both. And deciding she was neither they decided she was the thing lower than the both of them, a debt collector. Plus the Latina was the only non-white person within twenty-five miles, which made her even more of a curiosity. It carned her suspicious looks and contempt and scorn. More than one man in a scruffy undershirt took one or two steps down their front steps to let her know she was on their turf and that this visit had better not cause them any grief.

The New York cop looked around, lost and disheartened. Saddened that anybody had to live like this. Not recognizing this as the country she had grown up in for the simple reason that it *was* another country. Rural Kansas country and poor at that. Like something out of that Steinbeck novel she had read at high school. *Dirt poor.* That was the term that hit her. Then remembering that maybe this was just their version of a neglected Bronx project. And that made her a little bit ashamed that she hadn't given the reality of the projects much thought for longer than she should have, such was her life at the sharp end, her life of picking up and cleaning up the human garbage that fell into the trash can of life. And feeling momentarily hopeless. Feeling like she needed to get this over with.

'I'm looking for Thomas and Louise Armitage?'

As she expected, nothing from the growing crowd.

'I'm not here to . . .' She shook her head, really not needing to fly this far for this much of this. 'Look, I need to talk to them about their daughter. Could somebody tell me where they live?'

But she was met with nothing but dead-eyed, rock-hard stares until a little girl in hand-me-down Hannah Montana nightclothes pointed a stick at a trailer opposite. Possibly the only one without its lights on.

Jesus, Martinez thought. But then she steeled herself and crossed the dirt of the road to the small trailer home on bricks and knocked on the door. The New York detective looked around casually, like she was taking in the neighbourhood, looking around to see which joker was about to try something, knowing her heart was beating faster as the crowd closed in slightly towards her. Wishing to God the owners would –

'Yes?'

She was confronted by a large, balding man roused from his sleep, wrapping an old dressing gown around himself, keeping one hand out of sight, the hand that would swing the baseball bat up should his immediate fears be realized.

'Mr Armitage?'

Louise Armitage was in what passed for the kitchen, embarrassed by her lifestyle and living quarters. She was, like her husband, in her fifties and, like her husband, had not yet adjusted to their new home.

'Will you take sugar with that?'

Martinez, notepad on lap, almost demurred then realized with a pang of guilt that the coffee might not be the quality she was used to. 'Just the one, thank you, Mrs Armitage.'

Thomas Armitage sat on the couch opposite Martinez's chair, uncomfortable that the young lady before him was being so polite, so respectful. Heck, he hadn't felt that in a while. Didn't know whether to like her or hate her for it. Like a vagrant getting shelter for a single night after years on the road, almost wishing they hadn't been reminded of just how life should be.

'We haven't seen her for almost a year, officer.'

'Eleven months and two days,' his wife said by way of correction.

'I just said that, Lou,' dipping his head like she had made a muddle out of the conversation, like he had it all under control without her help thank you very much.

Martinez received the coffee with a smile, noting that it was in a mug with a near washed-away US Army logo on its side.

'And did you get any indication that she might be, well, angry about anything?'

'Angry?' Mr Armitage snorted as he poured himself a small bourbon.

His wife, the appeaser, explained. 'Well, you know she'd been in hospital?'

The detective nodded and pulled an understanding face. 'Severe burns, I understand.'

'That's not why she was angry, Lou. Tell the lady.'

Mrs Armitage turned on the couch to face her husband. 'Tom, she got shrapnel in her womb. She's never gonna have a baby. You don't think that would make a woman angry?'

Mr Armitage shook his head, the issue as disagreed upon as it was sore to them. 'Lady, I don't know what happened to her out in Iraq, but she went out a patriot and she came back a communist.'

The wife looked like her husband had tossed his drink in her face with those words. 'Tom, how *dare* you. She risked her life for her country, she fought a war to make us safe, how dare you, how *dare* you say that about Alice.'

The husband talked into his glass now. 'Coming back, ranting about the banks.'

Martinez's antennas twitched into life with that last word. 'The banks?'

Mrs Armitage was dismissive. 'Well, it was that subprime time, we were all seeing red.'

'Lou, she wasn't *seeing* red – she *was* red.'

'Now, Tommy . . .' Scared and annoyed at where the husband was taking this.

Mr Armitage placed his shot glass firmly on the table to underline his next point. 'Lady, when she got back from that hospital and saw that we had been foreclosed on our home she talked a streak like she was Cuban or something.'

Mrs Armitage ached to change at least the tenor of the conversation. 'It was a lovely clapboard house in the centre of Chanute, Detective, right by the town square. She'd growed up there, she was bound to be upset.'

Martinez wanted this back on track. 'So, was she angry before the foreclosure or afterwards, after you moved . . . here?' Briefly embarrassed that she didn't want to call it a trailer park but not knowing a better euphemism for it.

The wife was at a loss. 'Well, she's only been here once.'

The husband rolled his shoulders, working up a temper. 'Took one look and wouldn't step inside. Ashamed of her own family. Even changed her name, ashamed of the name we gave her. It's like she shook the dust off her feet when she left here.'

'She was not ashamed, Tommy, she's been upset since she learned she couldn't give birth, you gotta understand . . .'

'It's you that don't understand, woman. She wasn't standing outside screaming about her bodily functions, she was cussing the banks for kicking us out of our house.'

'And maybe that's how you shoulda talked to Mr Anderson when he took away our home because of three missed payments after twenty-four years of never missing a one.'

Martinez looked up from her notepad, not about to let this get away from her. 'Who's Mr Anderson?'

Mrs Armitage's face clouded over even more. 'Oh, the . . . good-for-nothing bank manager who demanded the keys to our family home. But you can't talk to him.'

'Has he moved?'

She shook her head and looked down at her bitter-tasting coffee. 'No. He was found dead in his car pretty soon after we moved here. It was a terrible business. Truly terrible.'

'Yep. Bullet hole in the side of his head.' Thomas

Armitage leaned forward and rested his hands on his knees as he considered it a sadness. 'Whole county was out looking for the killer.' Then his face split into a smile. 'We wanted to give him a medal.'

Then he roared with laughter to his wife's great discomfort.

Martinez had one last question.

'You said Alice changed her name, can I ask what name she gave herself?'

That stopped the laughter, Mr Armitage swapping his smiles for snarls in an instant.

'Alecto. I ask you, what the hell kind of name is that?'

Martinez remembered Byrne's description. Of the ancient Greek furies . . . *Alecto*. That was it. *She of unceasing anger.* She had begun to form an idea, a profile of Alice/Alecto. A profile of a furious ex-soldier. A soldier who had served her country, then had come home only to see what she felt was a betrayal by the banks, then had set on a course of punishment towards the undeserving, set herself up as a twenty-first-century fury. A fury with one deadly plan in mind.

53

It was two in the morning. Everybody had been told to throw on whatever clothes were to hand and come in. Everybody had turned up in a suit, this was the Secret Service, after all, even if some did look slightly dishevelled. Not Diane, naturally.

Special Agent Mason and I were stood at the centre of the open-plan space in the New York field office. This was to be our ops centre till the end of the operation, because we all had the sense we were closing in on our targets. There were thirty special agents sitting in an impromptu semi-circle of chairs and desk-edges or standing. They were tired, but dedication and excitement was their caffeine right now.

Diane did the speaking. 'An agent from a fellow law enforcement agency has supplied us with the name and alias of a member of Nemesis. Her real name is Alice Armitage. We have placed her at the scene of the Paris attack. Her alias is Alecto, from the mythical Greek character of the same name. It is all we have, but it's a start. We have passed this along to the DoH, and they will be investigating it. They are far more likely than ourselves to unearth a trail that can be linked to Alecto. But, as you know, the task of tracking down and neutralizing the threat from Nemesis is the DoH's number one priority right now. Therefore I want each and every one of you to go through all the case files on every bank and see if we can match this name to anything – an account, a password, anything – that can help this investigation. Agent Byrne?'

I pushed up off the desk I'd been sitting against and addressed the room. 'I've drawn up a list of key words associated with this area of Greek mythology. They may prove useful, they may prove fruitless, but it's a lead and, frankly, it's all we've got. Remember, when you go through the financial records, that this is code-breaking. Be alive to acronyms, backward spellings, anagrams, anything and everything. The NSA will go deeper than anybody on this but we cannot take the chance that the answer was under our noses and we could have done something to stop another attack. As Special Agent Mason just said, it's a long shot, but do not let that allow you to be any less vigilant. That's all.'

I nodded at the room and they scattered towards their workstations, leaving Diane and me alone in the centre. She waited for everybody to get out of earshot before she spoke.

'Do you think we'll uncover anything?'

I looked out at the hive of activity already buzzing through the room. 'If we do I'm playing the lottery tomorrow. But you never know, somebody gets lazy, cocky, stupid . . .'

I shrugged.

'You still think you need to go to Aspen?'

And I saw that look she sometimes got in her eye. The *you don't have to do this* look that some might describe as maternal.

'Webster knows a lot more than he's letting on. I need to speak to him in person, and that's where he is.'

'But we're closer than ever to tracking down Nemesis.'

I pulled open the drawer to my desk and lifted out my service weapon in its shoulder holster. I watched Diane watching the gun then me.

'That's when people are at their most dangerous.'

54

'Everybody makes mistakes, Señor Huerta. I made a mistake putting my money with your bank. You made a mistake when you promised us it was safe when it was soon to be gambled away by a Yankee bank trader. Everybody makes mistakes.'

Eduardo Lazcano drew on the last of his fat Te Amo Churchill cigar. A silky flavour, softer than the Cuban cigars he had ostentatiously consumed as a younger man. He had since discovered smoother cigars from that Caribbean island, but his nationalism had grown with the years, and he stuck to cigars from the mountains of Veracruz. Their concentration a flavour he never tired of. Unlike the task at hand.

The nasty, threatening growl of a dog grew into repeated barking, warning barks from a dog that wanted at its prey.

Eduardo looked down from where he stood, stripped to the waist. The sweat rolling off the folds of flesh that were his stomach.

The basement was lit by a strip-light along its low ceiling. It was empty but for the elder Lazcano brother and his bank manager. A man who was tied to an orange plastic chair opposite. A man who was not gagged and yet made no protestations at his plight. A man whose bruised and bloodied face, one puffy eye now for ever closed, was resigned to the end coming soon. The tears had stopped since the first time he fell unconscious, an hour earlier. No human can take much in the way of physical punishment, even the toughest have ways into their bodies and minds. But a plump bank manager? The effort was in *not* hurting him.

Today, however – *here* – pain from Eduardo was merely the collection of a down payment on the debt owed. The real terror, that which had occupied Señor Huerta's mind even when Eduardo had sadistically extinguished his first cigar in his left eye, was what faced him beyond the grille.

One end of the bare room, behind Eduardo, was a grille from floor to ceiling. In its centre, at the bottom, was a three-foot-by-three-foot cage door. Behind it was a three-year-old Staffordshire Bull Terrier in a pen. A fighting dog with a very specific skill. It had been trained to like human blood. To seek it out. To devour it. Its insane barking had been the last thing Señor Huerta had heard when he fell unconscious, the first thing he had heard when he awoke. The bank president even speculated that whatever the dog would be used for was the reason the younger Gabriel was not present. He would never know the truth of his guess, yet he was correct.

'You see,' Eduardo considering a bead of his own sweat that had just hissed into the end of the cigar that he toyed with in his hand. 'It's not whether we make mistakes – we all make them. It is how we *deal* with those mistakes. What steps we take to right the situation. Time and patience have been extended to you, señor, and yet not one peso of our money has been returned.'

The podgy man tied to the chair managed to loll his

head upright enough to cast a one-eyed hazy gaze on his torturer. If his death would be the end of it, if his family was safe, that would be a small mercy in this evil place. The idea of provoking his tormentor was banished from his mind. Dying in a way that least antagonised the Lazcanos was his only – and last – goal on this planet.

The dog's barking had briefly abated, though his excited breathing could still be heard. It gave a small self-pitying yowl then patted backwards and forwards in its concrete cell. Eduardo considered the dog like one might consider a small child going about in small circles on a tricycle. He smiled almost sadly to himself and then flicked the still-lit stub of his cigar into the pen. There was a sudden yelp followed by furious barking as the Bull Terrier first circled itself at a frenetic pace before launching itself back at the grille, front legs up, turning its head sideways as it tried to gain a frothy-mouthed purchase on the bars, wanting nothing more than to chew his way through and be free. To be at the bank president.

Eduardo let out a long, tired sigh and looked back at his prisoner. As he considered him he pulled out a folding knife from his back pocket and opened up its four-inch blade. It was a plain instrument but razor sharp, a talisman from his youth. The knife with which he had killed his first policeman as his initiation into a gang. A long-forgotten gang. Then he pulled out a cigar and lighter from the other back pocket. Señor Huerta watched every move and action with a mind collapsing under the weight of possibilities for this situation.

As he cut off the end of his large Te Amo cigar, lit it, and repeatedly puffed on it to establish a light, the drug lord spoke dispassionately. 'Señor, one last time. Can you or can you not get our money back?'

And the man tied to the chair, beyond hope, shook his head with almost comically exaggerated sadness, like a child.

Lazcano stepped towards him. 'You should have told us that when we first asked.'

Leaning down.

Ramming the four-inch blade into the side of the bank president's gut. A scream escaping the man's throat. The blade cutting, half dragged, half sawing its way around the front of the banker's stomach, screams turning to primal howls of pain as the incision grew to twelve inches wide before Lazcano pulled out the blade, pulling Señor Huerta's intestines out with it, intestines that he grabbed with a red hand and yanked, the bloodied tubes flopping on to the banker's fat thighs. His howls mixing pain with horror now. Only the very real agony telling the weakening man that the mutilated sight of bloody and slimy tubes at the bottom of his torso was in fact his insides.

Lazcano stood and turned. He flicked his bloodied hand at the grille, where the dog caught droplets in his mouth. Droplets that sent him into a frenzy of anticipation, that sent him into a blood-lust that his incessant and violent barking demanded an outlet for.

Eduardo left the room, careful to close the door after himself.

He reappeared behind the grille-wall, beside the dog pen, looking into the basement. The animal was howling with excitement now. Yet Señor Huerta was too shocked by the mutilation, by the pain that accompanied it, to consider the Bull Terrier baying for his blood.

'*Silencio!*'

Eduardo's demand cut through the dog's madness, ensuring silence even from that crazed canine. Cut through his victim's delirium, ensuring his attention.

'Señor Huerta. Before you die, know this.'

With every sinew in his body the dying man attempted to be seen to be listening. He had limited the violence to himself, his family were safe, his death and suffering had not been in vain. He would cry his tears in the next life.

'Señor, because you did not tell me the truth, because you disrespected me, I will now disrespect you. I am going to go from this place and I am going to go to the house where your family lives. Once there, I am going to slowly and painfully kill your wife and sons and then I am going to make your three daughters work as *putas* for me.'

The banker attempted to buck in his chair, uselessly fighting the constraints. 'No, no, *NO.*'

Eduardo drew on his large cigar, enjoying its flavour. Enjoying Señor Huerta's suffering.

'And, señor, I will be their first customer.'

'No, I'm begging you.'

'I will break your daughters in.'

And the man in the chair did what he thought he would never do again. He wept. Wept so that his words were indiscernible. Wept unashamedly because he knew what he had been told would come to pass.

Only the sound of a heavy clank broke the spell.

A heavy lever on the outside of his cell being pulled all the way down. A lever that pulled the dog's three-foot grille all the way up. A dog that took one rapid step in the room then leaped the last five feet towards the banker. The last thing the man ever saw, a Staffordshire Bull Terrier sinking its teeth into his intestines, turning from the chair and trying to drag them out of the man, a man whose terror was boundless, a man who left the world in the greatest state of pain that a man can experience. Body, heart and mind.

The older Lazcano looked on impassively at the medieval cruelty he had inflicted. Puffing on his cigar. Wanting to know that the man that misplaced his money was going to hell. In this life and the next.

Thinking he would not feed the dog again until the Yankee was delivered after the Sovereign Bank conference. Wanting Mike Byrne to suffer the same fate as Señor Huerta. Taking satisfaction in that.

55

As a crimson dawn crept over the shoulders of the mountain-range and washed its pink rays down across the slopes, the Hotel Wolverton could have been mistaken for something impossibly cut and pasted from Gstaad in Switzerland. From a distance – the only view most people would ever get – it looked like a cream-coloured castle, crenellated towers at each corner. The home of an Austro-Hungarian baron, perhaps. But on approaching the palatial building, the tell-tale balconies of its seven guest floors revealed themselves as well as the yawning entrance of the grand hotel itself. Piled all about was snow, lending the setting a further shove towards the Alps in visitors' minds. But this was not Gstaad, nor was it Europe. It was less than twenty miles outside Aspen, Colorado. A hotel that had hosted presidential vacations, UN peace conferences and countless Hollywood weddings was about to receive the entire executive workforce of Sovereign Bank, plus personal assistants and mistresses. Though, to their credit, most of these last two doubled up as both.

The entire hotel had been booked out by the bank. Partly because such a gathering required every one of its one hundred and fifty rooms, partly because it boasted the kind of security that gave presidential security staff a good night's sleep. The grounds of the hotel were bordered either by mountain, valley or imposingly high walls.

There was a single four-mile road servicing the complex. In addition there was a private airstrip that could take anything up to a small jumbo jet — so determined had the owners been to secure the business of the President himself. And secure it they had. The fact that it could land and then hangar almost a score of private business jets did it little harm either. The world's one thousand plus billionaires had been provided with another playground. In a world where banks and corporations thought little of spending millions on their annual shindigs they had found another conference centre. Another six-star conference centre.

Security was tight and it was discreet.

The approach on the route into the hotel was along the side of a winding mountain, and only the most observant would have seen the security personnel in white military snow garb standing sentry at a small distance from the road. But no secret was made of security once the complex was reached. Armed guards manned the illustrious peaked gatehouse that began the grandiose driveway up to the hotel itself. Beyond them the hotel's roof was spotted with snipers and its boundaries were patrolled by Uzi-toting guards accompanied by German Shepherds. Every guard clad in white military snow outfits. Nobody could get in or out without getting past these guards.

Webster guided his black Mercedes M-Class SUV up to the gatehouse of the Hotel Wolverton. The gatehouse was ostentatious, overarching the road with an entrance an eighteen-wheel truck could pull a full load through. On either side of the gatehouse sheer walls rose up and along before meeting a mountainous rock face on one side, a valley on the other. If guests looked upon it as a place that would require heavy artillery to infiltrate they had read the situation and intention correctly.

For the entirety of the drive from the airport Webster had been running over and running over the details of the day ahead. The logistics were enough to give him a headache. He was just grateful that the afternoon would see everybody in the main ballroom, rather than having to send his guards to every corner of the hotel to watch over the bankers.

The ex-CIA agent mulled over the risks, the threat to life and limb that had escalated in the last week. *How have I got myself to this point?* He consoled himself with the knowledge that this was his retirement plan, after all. *But the stakes* . . . Even by his standards, his life of black ops, assassinations both ordered and personally carried out, this, this was something else. A Mexican drug cartel on one side, Nemesis on the other . . . As he rode along the mountain road, chased by the rays of the rising sun, he reminded himself that America was in the middle of a modern-day gold rush where everybody was a prospector. But you didn't look for gold at the bottom of a river-bed or a mine – you looked at the bottom of a street. Wall Street, to be precise. *What had the world come to?*

He smiled unhappily at the thought as he slowed the car before a tall security guard. The intimidating man stood in front of Webster's approaching car as if driving through him wasn't an option, which, given the size of him, perhaps wasn't. The guard indicated for the driver to turn off the ignition, which Webster did. Then he walked round to the driver's side and peered in the electronically lowering window. Without recognition or emotion he looked at Webster but didn't ask to see any ID. He stood back from the car and waved his twirling finger in the air towards the guard in the gatehouse itself. The heavy barricade – which only a fool or a tank would attempt to charge through – was lifted by hidden hydraulics, and Webster's large Mercedes 4x4 came back to life and crept forward and underneath the broad archway at the top of the hotel drive, on through snow-covered gardens towards the palace at the far end.

A silver Audi 8 limousine arrived, slowing to a halt outside the gatehouse, and the tall security guard leaned his white-clad frame into the window.

'ID please.' His accent Eastern European.

The obliging chauffeur, a fiftysomething Japanese-American man, proffered some ID and conference passes to the guard. The guard nodded and returned the cards, repeating the finger twirling instruction to his colleague. After the silver Audi had crept into the hotel in executive comfort the guard saw that there was no one else coming up the road ahead and turned back towards the hotel, where he limped towards the guard house.

56

I was in my rooms at the Hotel Jerome in Aspen City, having arrived a few hours earlier. I'd eaten as quickly as I'd showered and felt dissatisfied with both. That on top of a little more than no sleep made for a bad start to what was guaranteed to be a bad day. Diane was already making sure of that.

'Michael, I want this conference called off immediately.'

Great.

I was sitting on the arm of a couch, Diane was staring at me from the wall of my hotel living room. I'd removed a painting and was using a portable projector linked to my computer tablet to hold a video-call with her. My boss projected on the right, my tablet's computer screen projected on the left. It detailed almost forty individuals that fulfilled two criteria: one, they had stayed at the Landstuhl military hospital in Germany around the same time as ex-Army Ranger Alice Armitage and, two, they had arrived in Colorado by air or rail in the last seventy-two hours. I'd asked for the analysis and Diane did not like the conclusions: Nemesis were crawling all over this conference.

'Diane . . .'

'Michael, you heard what the suspect's parents told Detective Martinez. Alice Armitage is gunning for bankers. Whatever the Lazcano connection might or might not be, it's over.'

'What about the intel on the Greek names I drew up? Anything from our guys? Anything from anybody?'

'I'd say that's about to become fairly academic, Michael. Stop this conference from going ahead. Get those bankers out of there.'

'Diane . . .'

'No, Michael, I know that tone.'

'Commander Becker . . .'

'Forget Commander Becker and forget the Counter Assault Team, Michael. I'm not giving you more rope to dangle Sovereign Bank over the edge to see who bites. We don't know what Nemesis's plans for the conference are, and they've had plenty of time to do something about it. The answer is no, no, no.'

'Diane, I've been up there this morning.'

That wrong-footed her and gave her pause for thought, but her resolve quickly trumped it. 'And what intelligence did we gather, Michael?'

'It's not good.'

'Not good intelligence or not looking good?'

'Hmm . . . Both.'

She closed her eyes on my hotel wall, her shit sandwich of a day having just had an unspeakable relish added to it.

I tapped my computer tablet, which replaced the mugshots of the Nemesis suspects on the left side of my hotel wall with an aerial plan of the Hotel Wolverton complex. What we saw was as impressive as it was depressing. The hotel and its grounds – the hotel itself, swimming and spa complex, formal gardens, airstrip, hangars – were nestled in a natural nook in the side of a mountain. This same mountain provided a perfect natural border – and complete protection – on two sides, north and east. The west was a sheer drop of over two hundred feet into a valley below. That left only the south, the gatehouse entrance. This had high walls extending from both sides that met mountain on the east, valley on the west. A solitary road weaved and descended away to the south. Alcatraz wasn't set up this good. Splendid isolation. And the briefest glance told you . . .

'It's impenetrable, Michael.'

She could see on her own computer screen what I could see on mine, and her face told the story. It was a defender's paradise, an attacker's nightmare. I let her take it in.

'Lord, Michael, get this operation closed down now, this instant.'

'It's not that easy.'

She looked confused. 'Has something happened?'

I shook my head. 'No, but all the Sovereign executives arrived last night, and the security detail hired to oversee the weekend's gathering is Erinyes Solutions.'

'Erinyes?' Her bafflement replaced by suspicion. 'That wouldn't be a Greek term, would it?'

'Ancient Greek. Erinyes is what they called the Furies, the avenging angels of the dead. It was their job to hunt down and punish sinners on earth.'

'Erinyes? The Furies? Jesus, Michael . . . What's Webster's hand in all this? He's meant to be heading up security. Are you telling me he's in with Lazcano as well?'

I shook my head, the bit I couldn't make sense of. 'I have no idea. I spoke to him on his way to the hotel and he told me that Anthony Cochran, the bank's chief executive, brought in a whole new security firm at the eleventh hour, totally overruled him. He sounded pretty pissed about it.'

'So Cochran's in on this? Where the hell is this going?'

'I don't know, Diane. Maybe he is, maybe he's being blackmailed, maybe he just panicked and screwed up. Webster invited me to go up and meet him there, but I haven't been able to get hold of him since that call – or Cochran, for that matter.'

On the projection on my hotel wall I could see Diane putting that issue in a box to one side. 'OK, but the name, Erinyes, they're not just showing their hand, they're showing the whole pack. Why?'

The bad news. 'Because they don't care, Diane.'

'What, you think Nemesis *wants* to be caught?'

I paused before breaking it. 'I think they're going to go down fighting.'

Incredulity spread across her face. 'A suicide mission?'

'If they meet resistance, yeah. That or they're planning on getting out by air at the end of it.' I tapped the long airstrip along the north side of the Wolverton complex on my tablet which lit up, highlighted, on the hotel wall projection.

'But I've seen the flight schedules, Michael. The only planes to land there have been Sovereign's private jets –' And she stopped as she realized. 'That's one audacious plan.'

'They're going out with a bang or a Gulfstream.'

'Michael, if we just drive up to the front door and tell them to shut it down, what do you think will happen?'

'I think half of Nemesis will start defending the place

like the Alamo while the other half will hunt down bankers like it's Columbine 2.0.'

Diane's eyes steeled over. Angry that we hadn't gotten to them sooner, angry that we had let them get to this fortress-like setting, but mostly angry that Nemesis had such murderous plans in mind. She took a breath then asked the question I'd been waiting for. 'What are you proposing?'

I pulled the tablet on to my lap and led Diane through the Wolverton site plans as I spoke, each area lighting up as I tapped on it.

'Daylight has robbed us of the element of surprise. They've got sentries along the hotel end of the approach road here, here, here and here.' The locations brightening on our screens as I tapped them. 'They will need to be neutralized. The gatehouse itself is protected by six guards, and since it's the only way any vehicles are getting in, that needs taking out as well. The gatehouse secured, we make our way up the driveway towards the hotel proper.'

'Where are their hotel guards positioned?'

I exhaled, frustrated. 'That's the bit we don't know.'

'How bad?'

'I couldn't get very close, but I sighted snipers on the hotel roof and saw at least one perimeter guard patrolling along the western valley side. Extrapolate that out and you have to assume they have the grounds covered before we even consider the fact they're running all of the security inside the conference itself.'

Diane shook her head wearily. 'What about flying in?'

I pulled a face that said I had to disagree. 'It's clear

weather, at least for the morning. Parachutists will be dead before they hit the ground. As for helicopters or planes? God knows what artillery they've got down there.' I touched the western valley side of the plans. 'Approaching from the valley below would be cute but leave our men too vulnerable. But . . .' Tapping the eastern ridge of the mountain, 'On this side we could get some snipers of our own into position, then dropping down the eastern rock face could become an option with the right covering fire.'

Diane was stony-faced, setting her jaw against the task at hand.

'When do you think they'll make their move, Michael?'

I paused before telling her my hunch, because that's all it was. 'Noon.'

She spoke with a hint of alarm. 'That's less than two hours away. Why noon?'

I pulled apart the aerial diagram of the Wolverton on my tablet, expanding its image. I then flicked the screen to rotate it backwards so that we saw the wire-frame front view of the hotel itself. I two-tapped the entrance, which saw the picture enter the expansive lobby, abstract in its computer graphics representation. I two-tapped the picture, which brought a set of double doors at the far end into closer view. I two-tapped these. We moved through them into a large ballroom.

'Because the CEO is giving his opening speech to the entire gathering of delegates at noon in the Wolverton ballroom. The entire executive team of Sovereign Bank will be present for it. Nemesis are running out of time, and this is the perfect opportunity to pull off whatever it is they have in mind. Nemesis chose their name for a reason, Diane. They want to restore their idea of justice to America by punishing the undeserving, and in their eyes they'll have a room of some of the most undeserving people on earth.'

She briefly let her eyelids sag. She looked angry before filling with remorse. 'Lord, I wished we'd known this six hours ago, I'd have gotten Becker and the Counter Assault Team on a plane right away.'

'Diane, Becker and the CAT team got my full report, blueprints and attack plan four hours ago as they were boarding the plane I'd ordered them on to.'

I think she had to remember that as the head of the Markets Abuse Task Force she had granted me that authority. Any knee-jerk outrage she might have been about to feel was pushed aside by the wave of relief she was feeling and she almost imperceptibly slumped in her chair, momentarily feeling the weight of the world on her shoulders.

'What else do you need?'

'Becker needs live satellite surveillance.'

'And what about you, Michael?'

'I'm going down there now.'

'But how will you break in?'

'I'm not going to break in. I'm going to walk through the front door.'

'Michael, just wait for Becker. We've no idea what Webster's got prepared down there for you.'

'Or what Nemesis has prepared for him, Diane. Anything extra I can learn could save lives, and I don't just mean bankers, I mean members of the CAT team as well.'

'Michael, it's too big a risk, you'll get yourself killed. I'm ordering you to wait for Becker.'

I reached for the power button on my tablet.

'I'm sorry, Diane, I didn't catch that. I think the hotel's internet's playing up . . .'

'Michael, do *not* go . . . !'

And then silence.

I took a moment to process the coal-hauling I would be receiving on my return then put the tablet to one side. I considered the two Sig Sauer pistols lying on the coffee table in front of me. One my old service pistol, the other Gabriella's tricked-up Tesla model. One with a capacity for twelve bullets, one with a capacity for four bullets and surprise.

Which one would serve me best? Then I half smiled to myself. Forty armed extremists against my pistol. It wouldn't take a Taser to overpower them – it would take a miracle.

57

'What's going on here?'

A tall, thin – but no less strong for it – security guard turned amiably to the hotel employee who had spoken to him in the hangar at the north-eastern end of Hotel Wolverton's complex.

'Just going over security for the conference.' The guard's voice Mediterranean.

The hotel employee, a small but fit middle-aged man with hair that was pointedly combed over to hide a bald pate, was looking about uncomfortably. The hangar had about a dozen military types in white combat gear standing by crates of weapons. Crates that contained very large automatic rifles, dangerous-looking submachine guns, even one crate with some kind of rocket launchers. And whilst he couldn't put names to the M4 carbine rifles, the Mini-Uzis or the M79 grenade launchers, the hotel employee knew that it was way more than he had ever seen used by any other security force at his hotel, including presidential protection. Certainly more inappropriate. And, somehow . . . not right. The middle-aged man suddenly felt a chill that had nothing to do with the weather. An animal sensing danger.

'Has all this been approved?'

The guard, who was standing by Webster's Mercedes

M-Class, could not have been more breezy. 'Sure. James, show . . . Sorry?'

The hotel employee got his meaning. 'Mr Taylor.'

The guard didn't miss a beat. 'Show Mr Taylor the paperwork. It's in the Lexus.'

Mr Taylor looked to a large security guard with a scar running down the entire length of the right side of his face to a snow-white Lexus SUV beyond. The security guard waved him over, and the hotel employee uneasily walked towards him and the car. The first guard pulled out a Beretta 92 semi-automatic pistol and began to screw a suppressor on to it.

The hotel employee waited by the Lexus as the second guard opened the passenger door and began to search through the glove compartment. Behind him there was the soft *phutt phutt* of two silenced bullets being fired. The hotel employee never heard the second one.

58

'Well, could you try again?'

The patient but slightly strained Aspen hotel receptionist smiled a smile that was more professional than it was
sympathetic as she replaced the front desk phone. 'That
was me trying again, ma'am.'

Detective Martinez dropped her hands on to the reception desk and let her head loll back in mild despair. She
took a breath and collected herself. The tried and tested
receptionist repeated again what she believed she knew.

'Mr Byrne left about twenty minutes ago and didn't say
when he'd be back. I'm sorry. Would you like to leave a
message?'

Martinez, feeling bad for taking out her frustrations on
the innocent hotel employee, gave a minimal shake of the
head, a tight smile of her own, then turned and made her
way towards the exit.

She hadn't seen the woman watching her along the
reception desk. Listening for the information Martinez
was obtaining, information that was answering questions
of her own. The woman watched the detective leave the
hotel through the revolving door and followed on after
her.

Outside, Martinez zipped up her burgundy leather
jacket against the weather. She was dressed for Paris,
not Aspen, and was feeling it in her bones. She looked

listlessly up and down the main drag to see if Byrne was in sight. Then she resolved to get a taxi – a warm one – and maybe drive up to the Hotel Wolverton. Then she was spoken to from behind.

'Hi, are you looking for Michael Byrne?'

Martinez spun round hopefully – he'd left a message after all, the first thing on her mind.

'Maybe I can take you to him.'

Martinez knew before she glanced downwards that the woman opposite was pointing a snub-nosed pistol at her. Knew before she examined the face that it belonged to Alice Armitage. The detective knew enough to know that what was going to happen was going to happen and fixed a *screw you* smile on her face.

'Alecto. I've never met an Ancient Greek bitch before.'

The sound of a large SUV pulling up behind her told Martinez they were not staying around to shoot the breeze.

59

Ace, Duke, Cartman, FiDi and DB were standing in one of their twin bedrooms on the third floor of the Hotel Wolverton. They were in a subdued mood but relieved to be there all the same. The experience of being turned away from one of New York's finest restaurants was being repeated across the city – people didn't want bankers on their premises. They feared it made them a target, and insurers were refusing to cover any restaurateur or bar owner who didn't make 'reasonable endeavours' to establish the professional class of their clientele. It had caused outrage amongst the banking community. Boycotts – somewhat redundantly – had been threatened, and the Mayor had been leaned on to force the insurers to cover the food and beverage industry. Even though the bankers were going to boycott anybody who had refused them anyway. It was a mess, and McCarthy's team were glad to be away from it for a few days.

Not only away from it but excited to be in one of America's finest hotels. To have it to themselves, to be amongst their own – to be welcomed. And, though they wouldn't admit it to outsiders, it was good to feel safe. They'd seen the security and knew that for one weekend, at least, they could rest easy.

The room was Cartman's and FiDi's, and the predictable sport was for all five of them to go through each other's bags.

Ace pulled up a sky-blue polo shirt from FiDi's suitcase.

'Shit, FiDi, what you gonna do, play snow polo?'

Duke was tickled by an XXXL T-shirt he had lifted out of Cartman's case. It was black with *Eat Me* written in white. 'Nobody's got an appetite that big, Cartman.'

Cartman ate an Oreo from the packet he was holding, smiling, all of it rolling off him as ever. He spied the logo on FiDi's polo shirt. 'Hey, that's a Phat Farm. Now we're both fat, geddit?'

FiDi went to punch back with some banter of his own until all eyes turned on the polite Pole, DB. He was holding up a pair of Cartman's briefs – and they were elephantine in size.

Everybody wanted to say something but instead everybody collapsed into cascades of laughter. Genuine holding-on-to-each-other-for-fear-of-falling-over laughter. Cartman looked from one colleague to the next, his mind not knowing which way he was going to go until he found himself laughing along with them as well. Ace had to wipe away a tear as he reached for the briefs, but Cartman snatched them – he had some limits.

The laughter continued. Duke tried to say something but couldn't form words for giggling, which just made the others laugh harder. Eventually, after the longest time, they all slowed down together until just little pockets of chuckles were popping up, like balloons let slip by children at a fairground.

They smiled at the floor, smiled at each other. More than colleagues, friends.

There was a knock at the door. Cartman spoke.

'Come in.'

The door opened slowly.

What confronted them drained all the joy from the room. The faces of the five young men turned pale. Because somehow, instantaneously and together, they all knew that life as they knew it had changed for ever.

DB felt faint. '*Oh moj boze* . . .' Oh my god.

60

The polished silver Cavalier Mustang touched expertly down on the Hotel Wolverton's private airstrip. The decommissioned fighter plane could have landed using just a quarter of the runway but in the snow McCarthy appreciated every last foot of it. He looked about himself as the plane slowed to taxiing speed. On his right was a thick line of fir trees that went some way to blocking the view from the back of the castle-like hotel. On his left were two low, wide hangars with their doors open, mountains rearing up behind them. Each hangar housed six Sovereign Bank executive jets. McCarthy managed a small *whatever next?* smile. The hangars were clad to look like log cabins, lest their aesthetics offend the eye. He'd used plenty of camouflage in his time in the US Air Force, but never to make himself look pretty. Then, up ahead, he saw his destination. The largest *faux* log-cabin hangar of all. In it one black and one white SUV, with a solitary man standing next to the former. The trader didn't need to get a perfect visual to know it was Webster waiting.

McCarthy jumped off the last step of the ladder that Webster had attached to the side of his aircraft and down on to the hangar floor. The structure was so large he had been able to taxi in a wide circle and have the aircraft facing back out towards the airstrip, an old habit from his Air

Force days when combat readiness was everything. The two men shook hands sombrely.

'*There is something we can do. You really want to put an end to this?*' Those had been Webster's words to him the night before, and they were eating McCarthy up. He was about to find out what the security chief had meant, and he was about to find out if he liked it. Did Webster really mean to take action against Nemesis? Had he reconsidered Mc-Carthy's initial approach? Was he motivated by the money or did he share McCarthy's moral outrage? Did he expect McCarthy himself to take part in any attack? He had no idea what to expect, but all of the possibilities thrilled him and worried him. He *was* angry. He did want revenge. But if he didn't like whatever it was that Webster was about to propose to him, if he didn't like the exit plan – if he didn't like the risk of being caught afterwards, it was off. He could insist the police or FBI or whoever go in and deal with it. All he knew was that something was about to happen. Finally.

Webster considered the beautiful two-seater aircraft cooling in the hangar. 'What's the range on that thing?'

McCarthy's heart began to race. That was his plane, he was the pilot. Webster really was about to invite him on some kind of attack on Nemesis. But where?

'Er, she's good for two thousand miles, you know, on a full tank.' The trader watched the ex-CIA agent mull something over. 'Why do you ask?'

A reassuring smile spread across Webster's face.

'Hey, you plan for the expected, I'll plan for the unexpected. Excellence in all we do, right?' Quoting the old recruitment slogan at his fellow USAF airman. 'Here, let me show you something.'

The security chief reached through the window of his SUV and came back with a gun in his hand, a suppressor on the end of it. Pointed directly at McCarthy's gut.

A smile flickered across McCarthy's face. Double-cross not entering his mind. Was this a joke? Was this Webster supplying him with a gun, having fun with him on the way? Was this a sting because he'd broken the law here? *What?* What was it? McCarthy not seeing the lethal look that had descended like a shutter over the ex-CIA agent's eyes.

'I . . . I don't understand, Bill?'

'To be honest, Doug, I was kind of banking on that.'

Webster pulled the trigger twice.

Phutt.

Phutt.

61

Commander Becker was a hulk of a man. Six foot and then some. As a younger man he had run towards danger with a recklessness that had won him a chestful of medals but a record full of reprimands. His warrior ego had been as much an inspiration to the men around him as it had been a liability to the officers above him. Always going in first, always staying till the last man was out. A man's idea of a hero. But, ultimately, not his own idea of a hero. Death, in all its guises – the killing and the experience of seeing his comrades and foreign civilians killed – had cured him of that. Cured him to the point of questioning the need for killing on occasions, even questioning the orders of his superiors. He had become more judicial in his willingness to execute on his government's behalf. The political motivation behind the Iraq War had not helped. Politicians' games had cost young Americans their lives, and this cavalier approach to warfare, this lack of nobility, left him drifting. And after a while he was in danger of drifting away from military service, a place of which it can be said with some large degree of truth that, were the person not in the armed forces, he or she might well be in prison. It channelled a need and an energy, but his faith had been tested. He loved the game, he hated the players. One final confrontation with his military masters saw him honourably discharged.

Then he did what any self-respecting ex-marine would do, he hit the bars of South-east Asia. And he hit them hard.

It took his former staff sergeant six weeks to find him, face down on a table in a bar on the Thai island of Koh Samui, wearing little more than swimming trunks and a grin. His former comrade was there to sell him something. A job in the United States Secret Service, defending the President, his inner circle and visiting dignitaries. Becker protested that he had voted for the other guy. His friend told him to use it as a stepping stone to where the real action was: Counter Assault. Which, upon reflection and a whole heap of black coffee, didn't seem like such a bad idea. So he sobered up, cleaned up, turned up and got the job. That was six years earlier. And the balance between the periods of quiet along with the periods of action had suited him just fine. Fine enough to look up an old flame from high school. An old flame who had since married and been widowed from a drunk, then left to raise two children, two little boys. Two little boys Becker was now proud to call his own. Between his family and the USSS Becker had his war and he had his peace. He left his job at the door when he entered his home, whereupon this mountain of a man became all things to his demanding, sports-mad sons. And he left his family at the door when he entered the workplace. Because the workplace meant possible danger and possible violence and possible death. And, on a very bad day, it meant Mike Byrne.

The United States Secret Service Counter Assault Team was flying in a military transport carrier. Stripped of seats, it had webbing dangling from its walls for support and a row of a dozen men sat against each side. Like the security guards they were intent on engaging with, the members of the Counter Assault Team were in white military combat outfits. They were not the natural agency choice for such an operation, but they were the most ready when the call came. Mike Byrne's heads-up to Commander Becker making sure of that.

Becker was chewing a long-since lit cigar between his teeth as he spoke. Personally he hated the things but he'd been impressed by his commanding officer in Afghanistan always chomping on one and knew it made great theatre for the troops. But right now he was more intent on chewing something else off.

'Goddamn it, Byrne, why d'ya leave it so late to call in backup?'

I was driving my rented 4x4 Ford Expedition up the steep pass that wound itself slowly round the white mountain that led up to the Hotel Wolverton. I was wearing a black ski jacket that rode up over my mouth. Good for cold days. Good for covering my mouth from prying eyes when I wanted to speak unnoticed.

'Becker, if I'd called any sooner they'd have sent the Fibis and you'd have spent the day losing money to your team at blackjack back in Newark.'

Becker, the only man standing in the noisy cargo aircraft, held the wall's webbing with one hand, the meaty phone/comms device with his other. His face conceded Byrne's last point but his voice didn't.

'Well, what the hell you got?'

The clear early morning sky had surrendered itself to cloud cover, a precursor to some pretty bad weather forecast for the end of the afternoon. It was meant to come in lower with snow, but nothing that should affect the events of the day. On the left of the car was a vertical drop down into the valley below. On the right were the steep sides of the mountain blanketed by snow. Snow which covered the boulders and trees. Snow that gave cover for the armed security guards discreetly watching along its banks.

'The guards seem to be fixed at five-hundred-yard sentry points at the end of the approach road. I still can't see more than four.'

'Hardware?'

I squinted as best and as subtly as I could at the last sentry as I approached the hotel. 'Hard to tell but it looks like M4s. Give me a moment to go through security.'

I slowed as the road rose up towards the Hotel Wolverton's gatehouse.

A tall, stone-faced security guard limped over to my car then looked into it at me. I held up my USSS ID badge. Impassively he signalled to the barrier guard to lift it for me.

'Go right on through, Mr Byrne. Just follow the road round. Mr Webster is expecting you.'

The heavy barrier rose before me, and I slowly drove down the magnificent driveway, a Colorado winter palace, snow-covered formal gardens on either side of me, their design no more than hinted at under the blanket of white.

'OK, Becker. There's at least three perimeter guards with dogs on the west *and* east sides. I see four snipers on the hotel roof and they have their rifles mounted on tripods. These guys are really dug in.'

Commander Becker was standing erect, a look of concern across his face, the large comms device pushed into his ear, his free hand abandoning the webbing to cover up his other ear.

'Byrne? Byrne, I can't hear you. Byrne? Speak up . . . *Byrne?*'

He gave a fierce stare that was more demand than question of the radio operator near the front of the plane. The young man had headphones wrapped round his head but was shaking it firmly.

'Sir, we've lost him. Lost him completely. Maybe he can't get a signal there.'

Becker slammed the phone against his leg, which earned a knowing look from more than one of his team.

'Goddamn it.' Looking down towards the pilot. 'Can't this thing go any faster?'

He looked down, checked his watch, wasn't sure, wasn't sure if they would make it.

My watch said 10.43 a.m. Becker would be landing at Aspen-Pitkin at around 11.15. A half-hour away. When would the attack happen? Noon? Five past? Ten past? *Before* noon? How much could I achieve by then? How much could I help?

As I neared the hotel at the end of the lavish drive, an Uzi-toting guard in white winter combat gear – they were all in white winter combat gear – signalled for me to turn the car left and follow the road round. It took me around the front of the hotel then, after a right, down the left side of the building. At the rear corner of the hotel another armed guard pointed for me to take a service track left, which ran for a good quarter of a mile, almost to the end of the valley end of the complex, before a tight turn right around a line of fir trees saw me at the wrong end of a runway.

'OK, Becker, the perimeter guards have Uzis but you'll have to tell me what the snipers were using.'

I took the Ford at a steady pace towards the far hangar where Webster had said he would be waiting. My mind was running away with itself with what I might encounter up here. Was the CEO, Cochran, in bed with Lazcano? Was he doing his bidding under pain of death? Under the threat of pain to his loved ones? Lazcano was in a different league of criminals from anything we had in the United States. The product of a narco state where the number of drug cartel foot soldiers outnumbered the country's standing army. They could more than likely overthrow the Mexican government overnight if it wasn't for the fact that the gangs hated each other more than they did the authorities. So if a drug cartel was putting the squeeze on a white-collar Hamptons-type on the Street it was going to be a short fight. In the event what I did encounter surprised me as much as it worried me.

McCarthy's Cavalier Mustang. Staring right out at me.

Then something in my gut told me . . . McCarthy had always been the target at the top of my list. His horrendous year in 2008 put him right in the bull's eye. But Nemesis weren't just going after bank traders who had lost a lot of money, *they were going after people who had lost a particular customer's money*. My mind went back to all the trading accounts that I'd been analysing in my apartment in Brooklyn. And I saw them all – saw them all afresh.

You idiot. Oh, you idiot, Byrne. The bankers who had been killed around the world, they didn't just lose money, they must have lost Lazcano's money. He was punishing them, that had to be it. He wanted his money or their blood, or both. That was the connection, that's what all the dots connected. That's what this had all been about: a customer the banks couldn't walk all over, a customer who could bite back.

Waiting by the car was Webster, who waved a casual hand at me and pointed me to one side of the hangar.

'Becker, I need to get a message to Special Agent Mason. Tell her that all the dead bankers were trading Lazcano's money. Repeat, they were trading Lazcano's money. Becker? . . . Becker?'

But I was getting nothing in return. I was entering the hangar as I reached inside my jacket pocket to pull out my cell phone. No bars. But I'd spoken to Webster earlier, and I'd seen a booster aerial on the hotel roof . . . Then it dawned on me. Nemesis – they must have jammed the cell phone signals.

Crap.

I closed the door of my Ford Expedition behind me, shoved my hands in my pockets and waited for Webster to cross the short distance across the hangar between the retired fighter aircraft and myself. Was McCarthy involved in all of this? Was he working for Lazcano? My mind began to bounce off the different players like a pinball, Lazcano, Nemesis, Cochran, McCarthy, Webster . . . The different events, the different connections, the dead bankers, connected by Lazcano's money for sure. Realizing in that moment – realizing too late – that

Sovereign Bank wasn't the connection: Webster was.

The bank security chief was wearing shades, his own hands in his blue ski-jacket pockets, grinning affably. Where did this bluff go now? How long did we dance? If he was going to come at me heavy there was nothing to be gained by being captured. And then I saw the confirmation that the sands of time were down to their last grains. A dark red spot near a parked-up white Lexus SUV.

Somebody's blood had already been spilled.

Whatever it was had started.

This moment was all I had left.

'Going somewhere?' I nodded at the plane, matching his affability with my own.

He half looked back then waved at it dismissively. 'It's McCarthy's. Nothing but a glorified crop-duster if you ask me. Pretty, though. How you doing?'

Pulling his right hand out slowly. Maybe pulling out nothing more than a hand. Maybe pulling out a hand with something in it. Something like a gun. Not wanting to flick my eyes down to let him know that's where my thinking was at. Not wanting to be so stupid as to wait for a gun to be pointed at my chest. Whatever I did next needed to *count*. But Webster two yards from me, the hand still coming out and me without a certainty, his smiling face not breaking, his eyes giving nothing away, hidden away as they were behind reflective shades – reflective shades that revealed shapes moving behind me at the far end of the hangar, black objects in their hands, men with rifles –

I yanked my hand out of my jacket and pointed my Sig Sauer at Webster just as he finished pulling out his hand.

It was empty.

He calmly smiled and gestured with his open hands, like a magician assuring me he had nothing to hide. But his relaxed demeanour told me I'd called it right. I had to get him between me and the approaching men, I needed him as cover. Not taking the gun off him, I grabbed his right arm and pulled him past me as I got behind him with my gun. He staggered one step then stopped. Then turned. And smiled again, waiting to see my reaction to the joke.

He put out his hand for my gun.

I all but dropped my head dejectedly. Ten men. Ten men with Martinez between them, the two nearest guns pointed at her head. Looking at me apologetically, like she'd let me down. When it was the other way round. Always the same Martinez.

I lifted my gun up for all to see and ejected the cartridge into my free hand before tossing my pistol towards the runway, where it clattered to a halt.

I sighed in defeat and slid my hands back into my pockets. Wanting them to know that I knew the end of the road when I saw it. Webster took off his sunglasses and looked at me with sharply amused eyes as a large security guard walked behind me. I didn't know what the guard was planning but knew it wasn't good. Why else would Martinez be about to scream in alarm?

The butt of the rifle on the back of my head sent everything crimson then –

'*No . . .*' The two guards who had been pointing their pistols at Martinez now switched to struggling to stop her from running towards Byrne where he lay crumpled on the floor.

'You bastards, I'll fucking kill you. Do you understand? I will see you all *dead*.'

Webster, fifty yards away, considered her outburst with a small degree of mirth. He gave a small *away* wave, and the two restraining security guards returned her towards the hangar exit, having to drag her as she kicked and screamed at them.

'Mike! Mike! Mike . . . !'

Webster looking away from her to the unconscious man at his feet. He looked up at the guard who had inflicted this on Byrne.

'Put him in the plane.'

62

'What the hell do you mean, you've lost contact?'

The Treasury Secretary had not been displeased that Special Agent Mason had positioned the financial investigations arm of the USSS to be ready to swoop on Nemesis's operations. It suited his goal of retaking the agency back under his department's wing. But the Treasury Secretary was staggered by the scale of Nemesis's planned atrocity.

They were in the New York field office of the United States Secret Service. A field office that had become an operations centre on a war footing. Outside Agent Mason's small glass-walled office a dozen Service personnel were working in front of an enormous array of monitors which showed satellite images of the Hotel Wolverton as well as the logistics and details of all Counter Assault Team agents involved in the anticipated siege.

In her room Diane Mason rose from behind her desk at the unexpected intrusion into her office.

'Mr Secretary . . . Sir, he was always going to maintain radio silence once he was inside the hotel.'

Richard Peterson threw his hands up with unconcealed frustration. '*This* is the first outing by the Markets Abuse Task Force? You couldn't have started with maybe a case of fraud or something? You had to start with a Wall Street Waco?'

Mason took a breath. *This is what I needed. A politician running a Secret Service operation.* 'Sir, Commander Becker is fully up to speed and is heading up the mission in Aspen.'

'For God's sake, Diane, if it's half as bad as reports say it is we should have *everybody* down there. The FBI, the police, the National Guard, *everybody*.'

'Sir, all the agencies are initiating their own measures, we just happen to be the first on the scene. Also, we have to assume that when Nemesis see our response that the shooting will start. This is by any measure a massive hostage situation by a large group of determined and highly trained individuals.'

'And how the hell would you know they're well trained, Diane?'

'Because we trained some of them, sir.'

Peterson took a moment, half to marshal his arguments, half to listen to the part of him that told him he should listen to Mason. He looked out at the operations room then back at Special Agent Mason.

'So . . . where are we?'

'All radio and telephone communication to the hotel has been blocked, we have to assume, by Nemesis. Commander Becker and his Counter Assault Team will be there at approximately noon, when the conference begins. They're cornered, Mr Secretary, one way or another it's the end of the road for Nemesis.'

'One way or another?' Letting her know with his tone that he was not going to accept a massacre of bankers.

The Treasury Secretary shook his head like this was the sorriest state of affairs he had ever had to hear. It was so bad politically that he even felt bad for the people involved.

He truly believed the financial arm of the Secret Service should be working with the SEC and FBI financial crimes division for the sake of unified regulation and prosecution of the financial sector. And this was the upshot of his first tentative steps on that road. It was a pipe dream backing up behind the political career he saw draining away before his eyes. The best-laid plans . . . His face paled as the gravity of the situation overwhelmed his career and administration ambitions.

'Can Commander Becker avoid a bloodbath here, Diane?'

Mason went to give an upbeat assessment but then the bullshit went out of her.

'He's good, Mr Secretary, but I'm not optimistic. We should prepare ourselves for the worst.'

Peterson had to force something like an exclamation of remorse back down his throat. The bankers were his own, the people he had moved amongst his entire career before going to Washington. Real people who didn't deserve this, people with families, families he knew. He was pensive for a moment then refocused on the task at hand.

'Can Byrne stop it?'

Now it was Mason's turn to fight emotion. 'He was our best hope, Mr Secretary.'

The Treasury Secretary looked up at her, surprised. 'Was?'

The Counter Assault Team were running from the military cargo plane towards six black Chevy Suburbans waiting for them on the tarmac. Without breaking his stride, Commander Becker was speaking into a cell phone as he ran.

'What do you mean, there's no satellite pictures?' He listened to his support staff explain the weather conditions, the complete cloud cover, as he jumped into the front passenger seat of the lead Suburban. 'So, what you're telling me is we're going in blind, is that it? Oh, great.'

He punched the cell phone off with his thumb, the closest he could get to slamming the receiver down. He spoke to nobody and everybody.

'If we find Byrne alive I'm going to goddamn kill him.'

63

On the cheap table in the cheap San Diego office the two cell phones sat head to tail.

'What do you mean, $10 million?' Gabriel as much surprised as he was angry.

'Once I deliver the money and Byrne I'm on the run for the rest of my life. I want to be compensated. $10 million, US.' The owner of the metallic voice believing himself in charge now.

Gabriel, stood with his back to the patio window of Eduardo's Mexico City house, muted the phone and faced his brother on the couch.

'He's doubled his price.'

Eduardo looked up lugubriously from *American Idol* as slowly as a sun-baked lizard. He turned the new development over in his mind, added his Yankee contractor to the list of people trying to steal his $250 million from him. Added him to his list of enemies. The cartel leader gave an almost imperceptible nod and returned to the rerun on the television. Making a mental note to kill his contractor once he'd entertained Byrne in the dog house.

The younger brother unmuted the cell phone and looked out over the narrow swimming pool stretching away amongst the bright-pink dahlia piñatas. 'OK. But only once we have the refunded money in our account, Byrne in our possession and Sovereign Bank on its knees.'

Webster stood impassively in a meeting space off the main ballroom of the Hotel Wolverton, where a few tables and chairs were stacked together against a far wall. He held a small metal disc to his larynx, a wire connecting the device to his cell phone.

'Then we have a deal. I'll be there at the agreed time.'

He killed the call and removed the voice-synthesizing unit.

'What did he say?'

Webster grinned broadly at Alecto.

'We're gonna be millionaires, baby.'

Alecto's eyes sparkled as she threw her arms around his neck, needing to hug just to burn up some of her excess energy, his blue ski jacket and her white cold-weather combat outfit impeding their efforts.

'Oh, Bill, I love you, I love you, I love you. We're gonna have a ton of fun.' Sounding like a sweet little Kansas country girl, which in these moments was all she was.

He held her, but held back slightly, conscious of the work ahead, the people who could walk in. 'But do you just love me for my money, honey?'

Alecto's face couldn't lie, the love shining out too great, too sincere. 'No – but it helps.'

Both of them laughed and then kissed. Then Webster cooled their heels with a *time to get serious* look.

'Right, go get everybody. Time to get this show on the road. Does everybody know their escape routes?'

She nodded, watching him still. 'Yep. Then they'll all meet as agreed for their money.' Watching him. Watching for any last-minute hints of uncertainty.

'Good.'

'And you're . . . ?' The only person who filled her with doubt, so keen was her need for him.

'Am I going to wait for you?' A warm smile spread over his face. 'Lady, your carriage awaits. As soon as the money is transferred text me, then wrap things up and get over to me as quick as possible. Don't wait for the others, I don't want a stampede out there.'

One last logistic bothered her. 'How will that Secret Service guy fit in the plane?'

His smile turned to one of reassurance. 'There's a luggage hold behind the rear seat. It's really quite cosy. Why, want to swap places with him?'

Alecto chuckled lightly, relieved that the plan was still the plan, that they would be meeting the terms and conditions of the deal, getting the full $10 million for not dead but alive. But mostly relieved that her ride out of there was still with Webster.

She gave his hand a squeeze, turned and left. Webster checked his watch. 11.50 exactly. It would be good to get it over with, and with his cover blown he was looking forward to not having to hang around any more.

The door to the meeting area was pushed open and Anthony Cochran walked in, peering at his cell phone through half-moon reading glasses.

'Ah, there you are, Bill. I can't get a damned signal on this thing.'

Webster scratched his nose nonchalantly. 'Yeah, I hear the booster on the roof isn't working. The hotel's looking into it.'

Anthony Cochran looked over his glasses at him, concern in his face. 'Very serious-looking, your people.'

'These are serious times, Mr Cochran.'

The CEO gave his BlackBerry one more look then abandoned the exercise. 'Well, I'd better read my notes. I'm kicking off proceedings in ten minutes. Sort the phone signals out, will you.'

He went to walk away, but Webster tentatively tugged at his arm, halting him.

'Just a moment, Mr Cochran.'

The CEO looked down at his security chief's hand on his arm like he'd put a greasy palm on it. Webster withdrew it.

'Sorry, boss, but I was just wondering what the situation with paying back our friend Lazcano was.'

The banker's gaze grew no less withering as he replied. 'Firstly, he's not our friend. And, secondly, we're not.'

'Not what?'

'We're not paying him back.' Cochran shucking his shoulders like the conversation was over and the matter no longer of concern to his employee.

Webster was struck by the force of the words, felt a tremor in his world, his plans in jeopardy.

'I don't understand, sir.'

The CEO exhaled impatiently, making sure Webster knew this would be *quick*.

'Our people met with the regulators and we can make all this go away for a quarter of a billion. We've come clean about it, there's no going back. We've got a month to settle and we're not allowed to go anywhere near Lazcano. Which is fine by me.' He shook his head, shuddering at the legal wriggling they would need to perform, the sensitive issue of security moving forward.

Webster stood rooted to the spot, dumbly failing to believe it. The sheer stupidity of it. 'What?'

'What do you mean, "what"?'

Webster couldn't believe the moronic decision-making he felt he was witnessing. 'But Lazcano only wanted that much.'

Cochran turned like a man with a boiling rage that needed a target and of the opinion that Webster had just painted one on himself.

'The figure was $150 million, Webster. The rest was the fantasy interest he put on top. And you seem to forget that it was Lazcano who lost his money, not us.'

'He doesn't see it that way.'

'Nobody does when they lose money. We advised him on the investment – he was the one who put it into a tradable fund. Him, not us.'

'Oh, come off it, Mr Cochran. If people knew the risks as you really saw them nobody would invest another cent through their bank.'

'What are you saying?'

'I'm saying a $250 million fine to the SEC won't make this go away.'

'Well, thank you for your *advice*, Webster, but the decision has been made.' Cochran making a mental note to review the increasingly uppity Webster's position once this had all blown over. 'We'll settle with the regulators, take our punishment and get the protection we deserve from people like Lazcano.'

'No you won't.'

'Sorry?'

'No you won't. What the hell has the SEC got to do

with Lazcano? He wants his money back. You think you can buy off your sins, Tony?'

'Sins? Tony? Who the hell do you think you're talking to?'

Webster took a step closer to the CEO.

'I'm talking to a dead man.'

Cochran sensed the shift in the mood, sensed that something was very wrong.

'What did you say?'

'I said, the devil never rests, Tony.'

Cochran, crowded now. 'What? What are you talking about?'

'It's an old Mexican saying, Tony. I'm trying to tell you – for the very last time – that Lazcano has to be paid.'

'No, no – no. This conversation stops now –'

'No, Tony, this conversation starts now.'

Emphasizing the word with a punch to his CEO's stomach that saw the man double over his arm before Webster dragged him up by the scruff of his very expensive suit jacket.

'Lazcano wants to be paid. I want him paid. And if you or any of your fellow scumbags have any attachment to your lives here on this earth then you should want him paid.'

Cochran was gasping for air, his eyes watering such that he couldn't see any clearer than his scrambled, shocked brain was thinking. The ex-CIA agent held him at arm's length in his left hand and delivered a blow to his face with the other, a blow that had blood running from his newly broken nose almost instantly. Pitifully the winded bank CEO tried to reach his hands up to his

441

head, but fear of further assaults left him squirming instead.

Webster was calm, all business. 'Is the money still in place, Tony?'

Cochran stood frozen, in pain and in shock. 'What money?'

'The money to pay Lazcano? Is it still in place?'

'Yes. Yes, I think so. Yes.'

'Well, if he doesn't receive the money in the next fifteen minutes I'm going to blow up the hotel with every one of you cocksuckers in it.'

'Wha . . .?'

The word remained unfinished as Webster launched the CEO away towards a stack of chairs, which he bounced off and down on to the floor, the stack threatening to keel over on to Cochran before righting itself again. Then the service doors swung open and in trooped a dozen Nemesis security guards headed by Alecto. She gave the moaning CEO's form barely a look before addressing herself to Webster.

'We're ready.'

An angry Webster nodded at her, looked beyond her. Being held by the security guards was a doped-up McCarthy with a bullet in each leg. Behind him stood his team, FiDi, Ace, DB, Cartman and Duke, each terrified beyond words. Each knowing they were in the hands of Nemesis and reduced to quivering wrecks as a result.

'All OK?'

She nodded back at him and searched his eyes. 'All OK.'

He extended a formal hand to her, which she took with

a small measure of confusion at the formality until he not only shook it but gave it a minute stroke that only she was aware of. The smallest action that meant everything to her.

Webster looked at Cochran trying to get to his knees. 'Get up, Tony – it's show time.'

He looked at the prisoners again. 'Where's Byrne's girl-friend?'

Alecto pointed behind herself. 'We left her in a lock-up.'

Webster thought about Martinez's fate for a moment then came to a decision. 'There's not enough women in banking. Throw her into the mix.'

64

The ballroom of Hotel Wolverton extended out the rear of the main building. It was as grand as it was large. Just as the building had drawn inspiration from the fairy-tale castles of Bavaria so too had the main conference space of the hotel attempted to emulate the gilded wealth of European aristocracy. It was the size of three tennis courts side by side with a ceiling appropriately high. But any down-to-earth qualities ended there. The dominant colours were burgundy, white and gold. Impossibly long burgundy velvet drapes hung from breathtakingly tall windows. Gilt-covered columns bordered and held up the voluminous room. The walls were made up of twenty-foot-high hand-painted panels depicting European nobility hunting the various animals that made their way to their banquet halls and trophies: stags, game birds, wild boars, then British Raj exotics like elephants, big game cats and, incongruously, a dragon. The only relief on the eye was the enormous glass-domed ceiling that arched high into the air. Tinted white by the lightly falling snow.

The room was garish, tasteless and utterly magnificent all at once.

Fourteen rows of fourteen burgundy-cushioned chairs had been laid out in a square before a raised stage that looked like it had always been there but which had been set up only the evening before. Seated were almost one hundred and fifty of Sovereign Bank's most senior executives, almost exclusively male. Their PAs and 'PAs' were off enjoying the delights of the spa and gymnasium for the duration of the opening speeches. The first day was traditionally something of a soirée with a State-of-the-Bank/Nation speech to the faithful before a day of drinking and an evening of entertainment. As a result spirits were typically high. But not today.

Today the subject was one thing and one thing only: the attack on the bank's Lower Manhattan offices. A genuine shared horror at the plight of the victims, their colleagues – and how close the waters were lapping at their feet. This and the fact that their CEO was running ten minutes late meant that, though spirits were subdued the volume of conversation was not, and what had started as muted chat began to bubble into fuller conversations.

The stage had a clear-glass lectern on one side with eight chairs in a row in the centre. At the back was a massive projector-screen, half the size of the rear wall, which displayed a fixed image of the golden Sovereign Bank logo. When proceedings were running an unusual ten minutes late a door by the stage opened and Alecto, now out of her white cold-weather security outfit and in black combat pants and a black polo-neck sweater, walked on with a slight nervousness towards the lectern. As she placed some notes on it she put both hands firmly on the stand's top. Partly for the pose, partly to stop her hands from shaking. Most people claim to fear public speaking more than death itself. Alecto was no exception and, having served in Iraq, she could make the claim with some conviction. The room began to quieten as the audience recognized an announcement was in the offing though were unsure of who this person was. They didn't pay any mind to the doors at both sides of the rear of the ballroom opening.

Alecto's nerves began to abate as she looked out on the faces. There she saw wealthy men and, some, women. But mostly she recognized the people who had foreclosed on her parents' property in Kansas. She knew they were not the exact people, or maybe even people who were in any way directly linked to it. But she knew they were of the same breed, the same type, the same problem. And this certainty in her mind steeled her nerve and gave resolve to her feelings. She would have taken Webster without the money, but she wouldn't have taken today without what was about to follow.

She was ready.

'Ladies and gentlemen . . .' Waiting for them to settle completely. Waiting as they quickly did. '. . . Welcome to Nemesis.'

And as quickly as the gasps could be emitted, members of her association trotted in from the rear of the room, ten on each side, pointing their submachine guns at the assembled crowd. They had shed their now-unnecessary white jackets and were all dressed in white cold-weather pants and black sweaters. Some bankers half rose only to be tugged and pulled back down by frightened colleagues. A tiny part of the bankers' minds hoped to God this was some sort of sick joke, some sort of twisted drill that had better have some kind of brilliant explanation. But even this desperate hope shattered when more Nemesis members – again dressed in white pants and black sweaters

– began to troop on to the stage. Because before them they pushed the sorry figures of Detective Jenni Martinez, Sovereign Bank CEO Anthony Cochran, McCarthy's remaining team members, FiDi Cent, DB, Ace, Cartman, Duke and, finally, needing the support of two Nemesis guards, McCarthy himself, dragged in on two gun-shot legs.

As the stage-hostages stood in front of a chair each, Martinez nearest the lectern on the audience's right, McCarthy at the far left, gasps were replaced by cries of fear and outrage.

'What the hell's going on?'

'You can't do this?'

'Somebody call the police!'

But the bankers quickly read the situation correctly, that they were penned in, at the complete mercy of over twenty submachine-gun-armed Nemesis guards. And the lack of cell phone coverage began to make an awful lot of sense to an awful lot of people.

It was a trap. And they were in it.

Alecto had their full undivided attention. She turned to the hostages on her right.

'Sit down.'

They did so, McCarthy detached from proceedings by the morphine running through his traumatized veins. His young team sick with fear. Cochran nauseous from both the bruising to his bloodied nose and his pained stomach, and haunted by the events that had come to pass. And, finally, Martinez, impassive, alert, angry. Behind them all stood three Nemesis guards with their submachine guns pointed at the backs of their heads.

Alecto turned to her captive audience and gave an unfriendly smile. The moment – the occasion – she had waited so long for and dreamed of for so many months and years. Ever since lying in her hospital bed after Webster's first visit.

'So, as one nemesis to another, first may I welcome you all and thank you for attending.' In her nervousness Alecto's Kansas accent was coming through slightly more strongly.

An African-American banker in his thirties stood up in the audience. 'You are making a big mistake, lady. This is completely unjustified and w-w-we demand you stop this right now.'

Every last one of his fellow employees rooted for him and every last employee gave no indication of that fact, so scared were they of being singled out. Alecto considered his interjection gravely.

'Gee, you make such an interesting point.' She looked at the guard nearest him on the ballroom floor. 'Would you mind?'

The Nemesis guard reached across a seated man and grabbed the African-American employee and wrenched him violently out of his place and out into the aisle. Murmurs and muffled cries of concern rose up about the seated bankers.

'*Get off me.*'

The banker put up a limited struggle until another guard came forward and the two of them frog-marched him from the room.

The bankers had watched him leave and in his

absence their imaginations ran riot. Fearful of what they might do to him. Fearful of what Nemesis might do to them.

Alecto watched them calmly.

Martinez's mind was racing. Sat on the stage facing the assembled bankers, she was anguishing over what she could do to halt this, most of her mind screaming at her that she was powerless, but a small corner telling herself that there must be *something* . . .

Then a burst of automatic gun fire sounded outside the hall.

A few squeaks of alarm broke through the instant shock of it before fear turned to abject horror.

Whimpers and terror-restrained cries escaped from the bankers, the last vestiges of their confidence buckling. People held on to each other as they were stripped of everything that made them wealthy investment bankers, the certainty that money provides, the gilded comfort their lifestyles and careers afforded, all the layers that separated them from everybody else, all gone. They were reduced to humans laid bare.

The two Nemesis guards came back into the room. By themselves.

'Anybody else?' Alecto eyed the audience with an inviting and challenging look.

The silence spoke for itself. Silence broken only by muffled sobbing.

Martinez's mind whirled. *This has to stop.*

Alecto took a breath and slowly let it out. She was ready. She glanced down at her notes, didn't want to be tied to them, but she had worked so hard on this.

'As I was saying, like, before I was so stupidly interrupted, I actually want to say a word by way of explanation about why we have requested your presence here today. You see, whilst we in the military have been out defending this great country of ours recently, it turned out you, the bankers, had spent the whole time selling it from under us. Instead of coming back to a stronger, better US of A we came back to a bankrupt one. Or maybe, a bank-*corrupt* one.' Smiling at the unappreciated pun, her confidence rising with every word. 'I mean, it left us so confused, you see. Like, we was risking life and limb, giving up our lives and our health, to fight America's enemies. We thought we was all in this together. But it turned out *you* were the enemy. When we got back we found you'd been looting the country like Iraqis in Baghdad after the fall of Saddam. Hell, why didn't you pull over the Statue of Liberty while you was at it?'

A middle-aged Chinese-American woman near the front half-raised a hand and, thinking of nothing but seeing her two children again, braved a question.

'Wh-what do you want from us? Please?'

Alecto fixed her with a menacing grin. 'I want you to shut the fuck up for starters. Think you can do that, or want to join your little friend outside?'

The woman sat low in her chair, feeling the swish of the sword that had just come so close to her. Alecto scanned down her notes, irritated that she had been knocked off her stride, but quickly found her place.

'As it happens, that last question – and I mean last

question,' scanning the audience for anybody who didn't get the implication of that last remark, 'touches on the very topic of today's gathering. You see, us soldiers on the front line, well, we thought we was patriots. We really did. We camped in the deserts, we got shot at, we got bombed, we was away from our homes and families for so long, and we did all that because we thought we was doing right by our fellow Americans. We asked not what our country could do for us, we asked what we could do for our country.' Looking up, hoping they got that. 'We thought we were all trying to make a better America after 9/11, you know, all of us doing our bit. Our bit was fighting the bad guys, your bit was making America stronger and richer. But when we got back you'd made it weaker and poorer. We can't afford to fight wars because you gambled all our money away just so that you few could get rich. I mean, Al Qaida wishes it could hurt America the way you have. When you brought America to its knees you behaved in the most unpatriotic way imaginable. And why did you do it? Why did you wreck America?' Almost free of her notes now, looking at the audience like she might want the answer volunteered, nobody about to do it. 'I'll tell you for why: money. Just so you could have a faster car, a bigger house, a longer yacht, a younger, prettier wife you trashed our country. And then you made the rest of us clean up your mess. Like a pack of Rottweilers defecating on our front lawns.' Shaking her head, staggered by the scale of it all. 'I got buddies can't get no job and they been reduced to begging in the street. And you know what happened to them? They got arrested, that's what. Because begging is illegal in this country of ours. But not – it turns

451

out – if you do it in Congress with a bunch of lawyers by your side. The nerve of you people, lecturing us about taxes and spending when you hocked our future so that you could live your swanky lives.' Stepping away from her notes now. Countless hours of practice making a version of the speech leap to her lips. 'Did you know that in the 1970s one per cent of Americans owned twenty-five per cent of the wealth?' Walking up and down, sweeping her eyes across the rows like the attorney for the prosecution. 'And did you know that today one per cent of Americans owns forty per cent of the wealth? The top one per cent takes home twenty-five per cent of our national income? Now, that ain't right. The top one per cent owns half of all stocks, bonds and mutual funds whilst the bottom fifty per cent owns less than 0.5 per cent of these investments. Now, that ain't right. The top four hundred families have as much money as all the families in the bottom fifty per cent put together. Now, that ain't right. The top one per cent are taking home more of our nation's income than at any other time since the 1920s. Now, that ain't right. Hell, at this rate, in half a century you'll have all of it. That ain't right, people, *that ain't right.*'

She licked her lips, the speech tasting better than she ever imagined.

'I read the bailout cost us $17.5 trillion dollars already. That's a lot of schools and hospitals and jobs. I read that's more than the cost of every war we ever fought in the entire history of our nation. Well, I reckon that's gotta be the most unpatriotic thing I ever heard. The Good Lord said you cannot serve two masters: "You cannot serve both money and God." People of Sovereign Bank, you made that money at the expense of your fellow Americans. We in Nemesis think that's undeserved money. We think it's time to rebalance your good fortune with some . . . misfortune. Time we brought you closer to God.'

Her words hit the audience like blows, their minds in pieces at the unspoken trial ahead of them. This is what it had come down to, the public anger finding a voice and a messenger, and a punisher.

'So what we propose is this.'

She turned to the hostages sat beside her, signalling that what followed involved them.

'Up here, we're gonna play a game inspired by the way you guys make your money on Wall Street. You see, we all know what you do. You make these big casino bets with other people's money and if you win you stake a big claim to the prize money, but if you lose you let your bank or shareholders or, more recently, like, the taxpayers, pick up the tab. How the hell you pulled that one off, Lord knows. You live golden lives, don't you? Lives without consequences. Well, we're going to play a little game of Consequences up here today.' She went to smile but couldn't fake it. The hate was taking over. Only death would satisfy her fury. 'Or, as we prefer to call it,' spreading her arms like a daytime game show host, 'the Wall Street Crap Shoot.'

A shiver of dread ran through the room.

65

Commander Becker's men were spread along the ridge of the mountain that bordered the east side of the Hotel Wolverton. Becker and a team of nine others were looking down on the four sentries manning the approach road to the hotel complex. A further ten were keeping guard on the far side of the ridge, away from the hotel, as they made their way as quickly as possible to positions above the main building. All wore their white cold-weather outfits with their hoods up, white against white.

Becker, lying low on the ridge-summit, looked from Nemesis sentry to sentry through a pair of binoculars, all of them facing away from him towards the road, their images scratchy from the lightly falling snow.

'Have you got visuals on your targets?'

Beside him, four of his team were also lying prone on the floor, aiming their SR-25 rifles at the Nemesis guards below. All four answered in the affirmative.

Becker spoke into a mic wrapping round from a comms device in his ear.

'Brogan, are you in position yet?'

Ten Counter Assault Team agents were spread along a thousand-yard stretch of the ridge. Each was looking down his rifle at the hotel, the airstrip and the hangars to their right. Their leader, Agent Brogan, looked down his line of men.

'We're in position, sir, but we haven't yet got visuals.'

'Well get a move on, Brogan.'

'Sir.'

In the New York field office of the Secret Service the entire staff were ensconced around the desk of the wheel-chair-bound Korean, Park, and his audio-visual set-up. On a large screen on the left was shown an aerial depiction of the Hotel Wolverton's complex with a red dot pinpointing the location of every CAT agent present. The equally large right-hand screen was divided into twenty-four smaller views, the head-mounted cameras of every CAT agent, showing exactly what they saw. Also open were their comms units. The New York field agents present would see it and hear it and, in their own way, feel it as it happened.

Special Agent Diane Mason stood, like every other of the dozen or so agents, in silence. Flicking her eyes from CAT camera to CAT camera. Seeing not much more than a haze of white on each. She pinched her lips between a thumb and a finger. Hard. Needing to break the spell of helplessness she felt.

Webster dropped down into the pilot's seat, sliding his legs into the two wells either side of the joystick. He looked down along the strip, where a light layer of snow had settled. He knew it would cause no problem for the aircraft he was about to take up and proceeded to strap his helmet in place. He cast his eyes over the instruments and controls. He had flown a wide variety of older aircraft in his time but never the Mustang itself. He had wondered if he might be in for any nasty surprises, but the panel had fewer indicators than the one the Wright brothers used at Kitty Hawk. Somebody was looking down on him. He glanced up at the sky, the smile still on his lips. *Somebody, but not any satellites with that cloud cover.*

Webster reached up and tugged at the perspex canopy. After a few false starts it reluctantly rolled into place, sealing in the cabin from the elements. He orientated himself about the few levers and dials. Starter . . . mags . . . fuel boost pump . . . electric primer . . . Nothing too untoward – if he could get the timing right, the trick to firing up these old birds. He held the starter with one hand and went through the procedure with something close to delight. Without fuss the four-blade propeller began to rotate clockwise accompanied by the sound of an electric dynamo before coughing into life with a puff of dark aviation fuel and burned oil which burped out of the nose-mounted exhaust pipes, the cloud floating across the plane and back into the hangar. Now the blades were a furious blur, the Rolls Royce engine roaring its desire to be airborne.

The security chief looked around him. All along the right-hand side of the runway were the hangars housing the dozen Sovereign Bank executive jets. He looked at them, their gold livery dimmed by the overcast sky. A Nemesis guard in white snow combats emptied the last of a large can of gasoline on to the nearest of the bank's private jets. Previous cans of gasoline formed an unbroken line of fuel between each gas-doused aircraft. With the last trickle the guard spilled a thin line of fuel away and out of the right-hand hangar bringing him into the hangar where Webster's Mustang idled.

The Nemesis guard put down the can and looked up at Webster. Webster gave him the thumbs up. The guard immediately crouched by the end of the line of gasoline and held a Zippo lighter to it. The small tongue of flame licked at the fuel for a few seconds before a near-invisible flame appeared above the ground. A flame that snaked away towards the hangar along the side of the runway. Like a line of dominoes the low orange fire rolled along the entire length of the long hangar; each time it passed the front nose of an executive jet fire fanned out towards it, up its front wheel and along its underbelly towards its engine, where an extra helping of gas caused a particular ferocity of heat. The flame ran along the full length of the hangar until all twelve executive jets – the bank's entire fleet – were glowing with the lapping of orange and yellow fire, strangely ephemeral behind the veil of falling snow.

Webster watched all this, a delicious sneer across his face as their gold livery played host to the budding flowers of fire. Where was the planes' lustre now?

Behind him, in the rear co-pilot's seat, sat Special Agent Mike Byrne, wearing a flight helmet. He was strapped in by a seat harness, bound at the wrists, unconscious.

Alecto checked her watch. 12.18. Time for the main attraction. She pulled herself up to her full height.

'Before we begin I want you to know that you have a "Get out of Jail Free" card available to you, if you wish to play it.'

Her announcement only unsettled her audience more as they worried over the next development in this version of hell.

'If your CEO, Mr Anthony Cochran, chooses to pay your bank's debts – in full – to our mutual friend I will bring these proceedings to a halt.'

She looked at him, and the audience followed her gaze, looking at their boss on the right of the stage. His face was a rusty red from the nose bleed he had not been allowed to attend to, his expensive clothes dishevelled and blood-splattered. He sat in bewilderment, his employees unable to grasp what understanding he had with their captors. Looking at him and realizing that in his hands he held a BlackBerry. Everybody thinking the same thing: was this some kind of terrorist punishment or blackmail? What the hell was going on?

From the room came protests aimed at the CEO, angry and confused.

'Pay it.' 'What are you waiting for?' 'Cochran, do it.'

But the CEO could not return their stares, instead staring vacantly down at the BlackBerry in his hand, looking at it, shaking his head.

'Commander, we are in position.'

Commander Becker heard the message from Brogan along the ridge and nodded to himself before speaking. 'Paddy, are you ready?'

Down below, on the approach road to the hotel, a black SUV carrying four CAT agents passed by the outlying Nemesis sentries. The front passenger, Paddy, a burly red-headed Irish-American, discreetly spoke into his mic with an accent that was more Irish than it was his native Boston as the sentry watched on impassively.

'You take the two by the barrier and we'll do the rest, sir.'

Commander Becker, lying in the snow, almost smiled at the insouciance of the agent tasked with the most dangerous part of the operation and watched the SUV slowly make its way towards the gatehouse.

'Agents, on my command . . .'

On the stage of the ballroom Alecto strained a pantomime ear towards the stricken CEO. 'I'm sorry?'

Barely able to make himself audible, Cochran shook his head, pulled at his soft, grey Merino wool suit and finally spoke. 'I can't.'

His colleagues were aghast, the room petrified in its confusion and fear. Only Martinez disagreed. Only Martinez thinking *don't. Whatever it is, don't.*

Alecto righted herself and smiled malignly at the audience. 'Well, folks, he says he can't.' She glanced at her watch. 12.19:46. 'So let the games begin.'

Commander Becker watched the SUV pull up by the gatehouse. Then an agent twenty yards to his right looked up from his sniper's rifle, alarmed.

'Sir, I've lost the visual on Barrier Target number one . . .'

The SUV had blocked his view.

Becker was about to issue an instruction when a thunderous explosion boomed out from the far side of the hotel. Its thunderous noise both worried Becker and forced his hand. Three thoughts darted through the CAT commander's mind: the explosion had been at the rear of the hotel grounds; he had no idea what had caused it; whatever it was was bad news.

From his position inside the cockpit of the Cavalier Mustang Webster watched as executive jet after executive jet succumbed either to the burning aviation fuel or the heat of a neighbouring newly exploded aircraft. Gulfstream after Lear after Falcon after Hawker detonating in an out-of-sequence chain reaction of fire. Tens of millions of pampered banker luxury going up in flames.

The ballroom of the Hotel Wolverton was at the back of the building, adjacent to the runway itself. As a consequence the audience felt as well as heard the aircrafts erupting and immediately feared it was violence aimed at them, every last banker ducking uselessly in their seats as if this action might make any difference to the imagined assault as flames flared up outside the ballroom windows. Alecto watched this and the bankers with a sadistic pleasure, knowing this was just the beginning of their pain. Taking satisfaction that they had no idea what delights she had in store. How she truly was their Nemesis, their Fury.

I felt sick.

I opened my eyes, but the light felt like a burning lamp. I had to close them, but a roar filled my ears as I tried to get a handle on what the hell was happening. I opened them again and then I knew. I was in the rear of a cockpit, and it could only be one cockpit – McCarthy's Cavalier

Mustang. I tried to understand my body. I was strapped in, my legs aching, but not as much as my head. And my hands were immobile. I looked at them and saw that they were bound together, tight, by a nylon cord. I had no idea what was going on. The hotel, Jesus, what had happened? For all I knew that was yesterday. Was it all over? Had Nemesis carried out an atrocity? Was Martinez OK? Oh Christ –

A short burst of anger overtook my mind, and I strained at the binds on my hands, not realizing I was roaring while I did so. I fell back in my seat, my head throbbing, useless against the rope.

'Ah, Byrne.' A voice coming over my helmet's comms unit. 'So glad you've woken up. You almost missed the party.'

Webster. I felt sick all over again.

66

Alecto pulled a pistol from a holster on her hip and walked slowly around the back of the line of eight hostages on her stage. Along both sides of the audience the Nemesis guards presented a double threat to the audience. The Uzis of the gunmen they – in their abject terror – understood. These were very real to them and a source of their living nightmare. What cast every mind into a seeming pit of despair was the gunmen themselves. Almost all of them had visible injuries. Burns across their faces or fire-shrivelled hands. More than one with artificial hands, or arms even. A parade of people that none of the bankers could comprehend, somehow casting their fears towards the more macabre, as if like for like physical revenge might be intended. The lunacy of their predicament and their fright doubling up for the bankers like a bad 2008 sub-prime mortgage position.

'So,' Alecto pausing while she waited for the attention of every last banker, 'the game is simple. I'm going to ask some very, very easy questions and our contestants have to answer them. If they get them right they live. If they get them wrong, whatta you know, they die. Let's see you bankers really earn your money for once. Let's see you do something in your lives that really has consequences for you.'

The audience, repulsed by the sickening exercise being played out, felt the awful shame of being grateful that it was others and not them. Pitying their colleagues and cherishing the slim chance that they had been offered of survival. They hated Nemesis. They hated themselves.

'Our first contestant is your friend and mine, Douglas McCarthy.'

Alecto, into her stride now, looked at the audience with mock enthusiasm but got nothing but hunted looks in return. She shrugged it off and stood behind the wounded trader, semi-delirious from his medication.

'And, Doug, where are you from?' Grinning at the audience.

For McCarthy it was a struggle to speak. His breaths came short and fast and then rage at these monsters fuelled him.

'Fffffffff . . .'

Alecto, perversely playing to the crowd, leaned in close.

'No, I'm gonna need a bit more, Doug.'

Then the words bursting forth with surprising strength but also exhausting him.

'*Fuck you.*'

Standing behind him, Alecto gave an exaggerated frown like she was some kind of children's entertainer magnifying all her emotions for the audience.

'Ahhh . . . *Fuck you*'s not a place. And what's more, Doug, it's not nice.'

The gunshot came out of nowhere.

In the same instant they heard the pistol go off the assembled bankers saw the front of McCarthy's head explode over his legs, his brain, or what was left of it, exposed to the stunned crowd.

Every last decibel of sound seemed to be sucked out

of the room. For a second the space became a vacuum where nothing happened and nothing could be heard, so densely quiet that it was impossible to believe that any noise could penetrate the absoluteness of the silence. The breath, the very sound, stolen.

Then it erupted.

The bankers, despite themselves, began to scream with renewed terror, some outraged, some weeping, some frozen with fear, some almost epileptic in their total unreserved horror at their plight.

A small, round man in the middle became hysterical, half standing despite his neighbours' best efforts.

'Stop it. *Stop it*. Mr Cochran, please stop these murderous people, *please* . . .' His words melting into a wail of despair.

Eyes flicked from the reckless, brave, hysterical woman to the CEO rubbing his BlackBerry with a thumb like he was trying to remove a stain from its screen.

Alecto's face twitched with irritation, and she waved her gun at the man and those immediately by him.

'If you don't make him sit down and *shut up* I will shoot every one of you near him.'

The bankers needed no more prompting, and several pulled him back into his seat, the one next to him forcing a hand over his sobbing mouth.

Martinez looked from the hysterical bankers before her to the lunatic on her right. The man in the audience was on the money. Somebody had to stop it. She slipped her hand inside her jacket and found her cell phone. She knew the signals were jammed but a message waiting to be sent was better than no message at all. As surreptitiously as she could she looked for Special Agent Mason's number.

An anonymous voice shouted out. 'Why won't you do it, Tony?'

Cochran was rocking backwards and forwards, his insides and mind twisted up by the rack he was being stretched on. Everything, *every*thing he had ever worked for – money, power, position – everything was balanced on the finest of knife-edges. To say or not to say? And suddenly he bellowed at the crowd.

'Because we're screwed either way, that's why. Because we did a . . . bad . . . thing. We made a mistake. We'll be ruined. Sovereign Bank, all of us . . .'

Another scared anonymous voice rose up. 'But you can stop the killing.'

Cochran stared back at them wild-eyed, paralysed by the consequences of transferring the money. The regulators knew. They'd done a deal, agreed the terms – the SEC had accepted Sovereign Bank's version of events. They knew everything, everything they'd done. And what a deal. A fine whilst accepting no liability or wrongdoing. It was more than they had dared hope for. But this . . . ? They would trace the payment, the number of laws broken – they'd be paying it twice – it would mean the end of everything. If he just sat tight, if he just waited, maybe there'd be a rescue, maybe there'd be a chance to avoid paying Lazcano, a chance to save the bank, his reputation. He could always transfer the money if Alecto got down the line to him, there would be a way out for him. It was for the best. It was for the best of all his staff. They'd understand. They'd understand eventually. It was for the best, the best, the *best* . . .

Alecto drew a noisy breath through her nostrils as she stared down at the audience. Agitated by the interruptions. Agitated that her game was not being played. So long imagined. She spoke now with less good humour.

'Contestant number two. What's your name?'

Her strained tone of voice was warning enough for Cartman.

'Kevin from Seattle, Washington, ma'am.'

'Ma'am? And so polite too. You can have a real easy one.' Her humour was improving with her performance, and she looked wide-eyed at the imagined children in the audience. 'Over thirty-five thousand US service personnel have been injured or killed doing *their job* in Iraq and Afghanistan. Tell me, Kevin, in the same period, how many bankers have been injured or killed doing *their* job? Is it a) thirty-five thousand, b) one thousand, or c) fuck all? And, remember, deaths from substance abuse don't count.' Laughing theatrically – ever so slightly hysterically – at her own joke.

A hush fell over the room. Cartman knew the answer but was so terrified that the woman standing behind him had a sadistic catch in store that the words stuck in his throat. People shook their heads, whispering prayers, willing him to live.

Cartman stiffened himself and spoke. 'C. None, ma'am.'

The hush became deadly quiet. Cartman braced himself for the end, no noise but tears rolling out of his eyes as he watched his last moments.

'None?' Alecto putting a juvenile finger to her mouth quizzically. 'Is . . . the *correct* answer.'

She moved away, stepping up behind Ace. Cartman dropped his face into his hands and began to sob.

'And who's our next lucky contestant?'

From his vantage point above the entrance on the approach road, Commander Becker watched his four CAT agents in the SUV speaking with the gatehouse guards.

'Have we got a visual on the second guard? What's the status on our men?'

A CAT agent thirty yards along the ridge was straining through his rifle scope, scanning for any sight of the now-hidden guard.

'I'm sorry, sir —'

But then suddenly machine-gun fire by the SUV.

Commander Becker. '*Fire*, take out the targets, *now*.'

From along the length of the ridge sniper fire rattled out as every CAT agent on the mountainside shot each of their assigned targets. The four road sentries fell like rag dolls, one barrier guard spun round and dropped, five dog-handler guards in the grounds collapsed to the ground, three of the four hotel-rooftop snipers rolled away from their tripod-mounted guns, but one rolled out of sight.

Commander Becker stood and bounded down the ridge at a sprint.

'*The gatehouse.*'

Immediately his team of nine CAT agents leaping after him towards the entrance.

*

'What the hell are you doing, Webster?'

I wasn't expecting any kind of emotional breakdown or change of heart, but any information I could gather right now was better than nothing. And why the hell was the Mustang sat on the runway? If he was going to run why didn't he run?

'What do you think I'm doing? I'm retiring.'

Of course, he was waiting for something, something to happen inside that hotel. Something that needed to be stopped. I was looking around the tight space in which I'd been placed, looking for anything that might help me stop whatever the hell was happening.

'Sure you wouldn't prefer to be playing golf in Florida like all the others?'

I had to cut the rope on my wrists, but there was nothing. The galling thing of it was that there was more than likely a survival kit somewhere back here in case the pilot had to ditch the plane and sure as anything there would be a serrated knife in there. But how to get to it?

'Well, I say retire, I've got this one little job to do first. A bit of consultancy work.'

I looked to my right to see black smoke and flames licking out from underneath the long hangar. What the hell had I missed? Had Becker arrived yet? Had he even landed? I looked to my left, the row of fir trees blocking my view of Hotel Wolverton, blanketed in snow. What was going on?

'You're not doing a job, Webster, you're doing a number. All this because a few traders lost a client's money?'

'Well, let's be fair, Byrne, he's not your regular client, is he?'

'What the hell happened? Lazcano ask you to set up a private militia for him? Punish everybody who had a bad trading day?'

I struggled in vain to feel anything beneath my seat. In desperation I started to rub the rope against the side of a metal plate next to me.

'You mean Nemesis?' He laughed. 'Poor bastards haven't got a clue. They actually think they can make a difference.'

I looked at the underside of the rope. Nothing. I wasn't going to be able to cut my way out. But if I sat here while they slaughtered people I'd go mad. Then – belatedly – I registered what he'd just said.

'What the hell do you mean, they haven't got a clue?'

Gunfire was still spluttering around the SUV when Commander Becker reached it. All four doors were open as every agent had tried to get out. Every window was shot through by Nemesis gunfire.

Becker rounded the car and saw a lone Nemesis guard standing over Paddy, who was lying on his back on the floor, about to be shot through the head.

The guard was lifted backwards off his feet as Becker emptied a Remington 870 shotgun into his chest.

The CAT commander dropped to his knees over Paddy's body and scanned the vicinity for more hostiles. As he did so his fellow CAT agents poured past him through the barrier and into the hotel grounds. Becker looked at the three CAT agents from the SUV, lying against the car, each of them wounded. Then he looked down at Paddy, blood around his lips.

'They were ready for us, sir.'

'*Begich.*'

A CAT agent turned back from the hotel grounds and appeared by his side.

'Sir?'

'Evacuate these men.'

'Sir.'

Begich not waiting for more instructions before starting to pull the injured into the gunfire-damaged SUV.

Paddy's face grew dark with remorse. 'Sorry, sir.'

Becker's jaw fixed with an angry resolve that he tried to keep from his colleague. 'You can buy me a drink once we're back in New York. But none of that Guinness crap.'

Paddy managed a limited smile. Both of them knowing his chances of survival were slim at best.

Commander Becker patted his shoulder but then bounded to his feet and was off towards more gunfire. He looked east as he ran and saw ten CAT agents performing controlled slides down the sides of the ridge towards the hotel grounds as they came to join the battle.

Alecto stood behind Ace, letting her gun waver in her hand lightly as she addressed him and the audience at the same time.

'And what's your name?'

'Robert – Robert Taylor, ma'am.'

'So, Robert, members of the US military get combat pay – or Imminent Danger Pay as we call it – for putting their *lives on the line* in combat zones around the world. The value of this bonus is two hundred and twenty-five dollars a month or two thousand seven hundred dollars a year. I repeat, for putting our *lives on the line*, to do our patriotic *duty* we get paid a bonus of two thousand seven hundred dollars a year. Robert, for gambling your clients' and shareholders' money day in, day out, what was the average bonus at Sovereign Bank last year? Was it: a) nothing, b) two thousand seven hundred dollars, or c) *four hundred and thirty thousand dollars?*'

She pulled a clownish face of *I wonder what he'll say?*

Ace spoke but the words came out in a hoarse whisper.

'I'm sorry, the boys and girls didn't hear you.'

'C. The answer's c. Four hundred and thirty thousand dollars, ma'am.'

The tall Texan could not stop himself almost hyperventilating, fearful in the same way Cartman had been, that the unhinged person behind him might have a twisted answer in store.

'Is the *correct* answer.'

Ace slapped a hand over his own mouth, wanting to control his emotions, his breathing, not succeeding at either.

Alecto balanced on one foot and peered over the seated hostages at the CEO down the line. 'Mr Cochran, any more thoughts on paying your debts?' Pulling an unappreciated *will he, won't he?* face for her captive audience.

Detective Martinez looked at the CEO next to her, who was paralysed with more than just fear. She almost whispered to him to stick to his position but she knew she would probably be doing it as a *screw you* to Nemesis rather than as the rational thing to do. She knew from her time with Byrne that Lazcano could make that money

471

sprint through ten different banks in the Caribbean and Switzerland and they would be as open with the authorities as the head of a mafia family.

Cochran stared down at his BlackBerry, his shame rising, his confusion thickening, his ability to make the right call beyond him.

Alecto stepped behind DB, the young stocky Pole squirming as much as he dare, a howl wanting to burst forth from his entire being. Her voice dripped with venom as she spoke to the Sovereign Bank CEO.

'If more of your people have to die to make you wire that money, so help me God, I'll kill every last one of them. And everybody here will know it's *your* fault, Cochran. How many more people have to suffer because of your greed? How much of other people's pain and suffering is enough for you?'

She stuck the gun into the top of DB's head and cocked the hammer, the audience screaming despite itself.

Then Alecto looked up at the sound of gunfire in the hotel grounds.

Outside, Commander Becker was pinned down behind a shot-up statue on the front lawn, exchanging fire with a sniper on the hotel roof. All about him the twenty CAT agents had taken positions behind walls and enormous ornamental pots and anything more solid than snow. An equal number of Nemesis guards were positioned along the front of the hotel behind cover of their own.

Becker didn't have time for this. The *hostages* didn't have time for this. He ducked down and pulled out a grenade-projectile from his utility vest. He slotted it into his Heckler and Koch MP5 submachine gun. He leaned out around the statue and launched the grenade towards the hotel lobby.

The room of Secret Service agents in the New York field office watched in stunned silence at the escalation of the fighting on their screens, every CAT agent's point of view in its own video box on their big screen. A CAT camera was dominating the left-hand monitor where the room could see a sniper on the hotel roof firing down with impunity.

Special Agent Diane Mason looked back at the CAT cameras showing a grainy live feed of the agents shooting and being shot at, two groups of trained fighters holding each other down. She ran a hand over her face thinking the same thing she'd been thinking all morning. *How in God's name did it come to this?*

All around us I could hear the gun battle raging. Becker must have arrived, but what the hell was he up against? Webster came over the intercom in my flight helmet.

'You don't sound happy back there, Byrne. Must be very frustrating not being able to fight it out with the bad guys.'

'Well, there's always you.'

'Trying to sweet talk me now, Byrne?'

'You'll be on the run for the rest of your life, Webster, you know that.'

Around the back of his seat I could see him check his watch matter-of-factly. 'Yeah . . . If only I had a background that could help me with such subterfuge.'

'Being ex-CIA only goes so far. You'll be America's most wanted after this.'

In a side mirror by the instrument panel I could see him half turn round, a wry smile on his face. 'Yeah, but without Bin Laden around it won't feel so flattering.'

Gunfire continued unabated. Whatever else was happening Nemesis hadn't put a stop to Becker and his men. More than that I couldn't surmise. The Mustang was ready to go, the CAT team was closing in, but Webster was sat idling on the runway. It didn't make sense.

'So what are we waiting for, the bankers to come out with their money?'

He rested his head on the seat ahead of me. 'You seem to be in an awful hurry for a man who's going to spend the rest of his short life in the hands of the Lazcanos.'

So that was it. He'd been tasked with taking me to the Lazcanos. It all made sense, terrible sense. Webster had been stationed in Mexico; it was his last stint in the CIA. He would have met the Lazcanos there, he would have wanted money, he would have hooked up with them then and there or would have known he could go back to them when the need arose. Like when Sovereign Bank needed some money *desperately* during the Credit Crunch. Only the money the Lazcanos deposited with Sovereign Bank went up in flames at the hands of a trader. And the bank would have tried to wash its hands of it, but Webster as well as anyone would know how to squeeze even a bank, would know the scale of the operation required to make that happen . . . I was staggered by the plan, but I also saw the sense of it. Martinez had said it: the world's biggest smokescreen. It was brilliant

474

and brilliantly wicked. And it meant he was prepared to do anything.

I wanted to ask him about Martinez, I wanted to ask where she was, if she was a part of it all. But I knew that would be giving a hostage to fortune; he'd use that information against me in a heartbeat. I realized I wasn't worried about her dying on my watch, I was worried about anything happening to her ever, whether I was around or not. I was worried I wouldn't be able to take it again.

I *had* to stop this. I had to stop this *now*.

'OK. I'll do it. I'll do it.'

Cochran tried furiously to hold back the tears as his life, career, money, bank, his everything disappeared with this action.

Alecto smiled to herself then turned to the guard nearest to her on the stage. 'Unjam the phones.'

He immediately exited through the stage door as she turned to the audience.

'If one of you so much as calls, texts or tweets I will shoot the lot of you.'

Watching them, watching them to make sure they got her goddamn message. They had. The ballroom guards looked about – daring one of the bankers to commit suicide with their cell phone. The Sovereign Bank CEO started to tap the message into his phone. Just wanting the pain, the nightmare to stop, for him and his staff. Every tap of his device a nail in the coffin of his life's work. In his present state his mind could see no way through with his career or even his reputation intact. He would be casting himself in the role of pariah, amongst bankers, which took some doing.

In seconds the quarter of a billion dollars his inner circle had lined up earlier in the week would be wired to Switzerland. From there the Lazcanos would bounce it off every tax haven in the world where enough unco-operative principalities would happily assist in the wanton money laundering of a Mexican drug cartel, just as they did with criminals across the globe every hour of every day.

Martinez had watched the events in the ballroom, unable to bear the torture of standing by while Nemesis wrought their destruction and achieved their goals.

'OK, while we wait for Mr Cochran to do the right thing, how about we stop the games and ask a really tough question.'

Alecto stepped away from DB, who was withering with fear in his chair, his face screwing up at the soul-destroying terror of what was to befall him. Instead she moved towards FiDi Cent and placed a hand on his shoulder.

'How about you, my man? How about you show these people what you –'

'Choose me.'

Time stopped for everybody as they saw the female Latina detective stand up at the end of the row of chairs. Looking at the Nemesis ringleader defiantly, standing erect, daring her to bring the sick game to her.

Alecto took a moment to process it then thought *What the hell?*

'My, aren't we the brave one.'

FiDi thanking God in his head that He had sent this

woman to protect him. Praying to God that He would shield her the way she had shielded him.

'Choose me.'

'If you say so.'

'I do.'

Martinez's heart racing like a sparrow's.

67

I couldn't take it any longer. I was trying to force my harness away from the seat, trying to get my bound hands round the back of his seat, do something, stop something.

Up front he was laughing at me, possessed by his buccaneering adventure.

'Webster, this is lunacy.'

'No, Byrne, it's fun, OK? It feels good.'

'Killing people?'

'You make it sound so mundane. You see killing, I see money. I see opportunity. Stop thinking like some public worker ass, Byrne. Get with the twenty-first century. Everything is permitted.'

What the hell was he on about?

I started to feel blindly with my bound hands, feeling around the rear of the cockpit for anything I could do to bring this to a halt.

'So, did McCarthy lend you this plane? What, are you in this together?'

'McCarthy?' Webster laughed, only this time it was hollow, cruel. 'He was trading the Sovereign Bank fund that went south for him in 2008. Lost Lazcano a hundred and fifty million dollars personally. I mean, if you're gonna pick a guy's money to lose, well . . .'

'What's . . . what's happened to him?'

Up ahead he shrugged. He genuinely didn't care. 'In

there somewhere. You have to admit, Byrne, that it's a bit funny. Sovereign Bank *knew* the money was drug money, they were just able to convince the regulators and themselves that they'd ticked enough boxes. They didn't realize that it *mattered* when they lost it this time. That it wasn't just some poor sap on Main Street. Lazcano paid with his bank balance, they paid with their lives. You gotta admire the poetry, doncha think? I mean, who needs regulation with penalties like that?'

'So what's your plan for making money, Webster? You Lazcano's hitman now, is that it?'

'Byrne, I'm just a facilitator of what was going to happen anyway. I'm the guy in the middle skimming off every deal, just like our beloved banks. Lazcano lost the bulk of his investments at Sovereign Bank and he'd like the money back. Sovereign needs to be taught a lesson in respect, and you need to be delivered to Mexico. I just happened to find a bunch of like-minded people willing to do some of the grunt work, that's all.'

'You exploited their anger.'

'Exploitation . . . Finally you get it.'

Then whatever it was he'd been waiting for happened. Because suddenly he sat bolt upright as if he'd received an electric shock.

'He did it. The son of a bitch did it.'

I could see him rapt by something he'd read on his cell phone. And somehow I knew that any news he liked wasn't going to be news I'd liked. I was about to ask, but he saved me the bother.

'Cochran's transferred the money. They've *paid*. Oh, Alecto, you beautiful, beautiful girl. Ah, such a pity . . .'

That last remark confused me just as I was coming to terms with Sovereign Bank funding the activities of a foreign drug cartel.

'Byrne, we are oh so clear for take-off.'

The Cavalier Mustang lurched forward as Webster began to pull back on the throttle. The plane accelerated into the falling snow, the flakes seeming to thicken around us with our speed. Power was raised to maximum, and within seconds I was pushed back in my seat, the fighter aircraft speeding along the air strip at eighty miles per hour, ninety, one hundred, one hundred and ten, one hundred and twenty, and then Webster pulled back on the stick . . .

In the hotel grounds the Counter Assault Team had reduced the Nemesis numbers but were pinned down by the rooftop sniper. Commander Becker had scaled the side of the building and was stood on the railings of a seventh-floor balcony. By millimetres he was able to gain a fingertip grip on the roof, which he swiftly pulled himself up to.

There, just over one hundred feet away, lay prone the shooter who had delayed their assault by precious minutes.

Becker swung himself up, his movement catching the eye of the sniper who swivelled his gun round towards the CAT commander. Allowing Becker to put three bullets into the front of his face, instead of the side.

At that exact moment the Cavalier Mustang roared off the end of the runway, Becker spinning round to see trails of white powder bleeding off the tips of the wings as it disappeared into the white haze.

*

Alecto had listened to the gun-battle outside with little concern, but this new development – the plane departing – caused a jolt of anxiety to cross her face. She glanced in the direction of the aircraft and didn't understand. Trying to keep herself under control, she looked at the Sovereign Bank CEO who was staring at the BlackBerry he had let drop to the floor like it was a gun he had murdered somebody with. She looked at the small Latina woman standing taller than anybody on the stage across from her. The defiant one. Had she spotted Alecto's anxiety? She wasn't sure. *Bill must have his reasons. Bill must have been scared off. I can rendezvous with Bill along with the rest of them next week. He must have had his reasons. Bill loves me. Bill wouldn't do this.* And the lying and self-delusion wanted to make her fall to her knees and scream, but she couldn't, not amongst all this, not in the middle of her moment . . .

The thought of Bill's betrayal – *no, it couldn't be* – made her angry, and she resolved that killing the detective would be an outlet for her building rage. Because Webster *had* gone.

Martinez could see that the sound of the Mustang taking off had changed things for Alecto but she hadn't a clue what exactly, or what she was meant to do about it. All she knew was that she was going to go down fighting. As long as it was fighting.

Alecto was smarting. 'You're that Secret Service guy's girlfriend, aren't you.'

'I'm Detective Jenni Martinez.'

Alecto snorted a small laugh to herself. 'You're pretty.'

'And you're damaged.'

The Nemesis ring-leader visibly flinched. But Martinez

was undeterred, figuring, correctly, that it wouldn't make a blind bit of difference.

'I don't know what crazy promises Webster made to you but he can't keep them.'

'What the fuck you know about promises made? What about the promises made to America? What about the pledge of allegiance? What about my parents' house? What about coming home from having given your country *every-thing* –' Roaring the word at Martinez. 'What about coming back to nothing? What about one country under God? Not two. Not one for the rich and one for the poor, what about one nation? What about justice? What about justice for all – justice for all these money-grabbing bastards?'

Waving her gun at the battered, demoralized, fearful crowd of bankers. But Martinez could see the pain, could see it was greater than the anger.

'This isn't about justice, Alice.'

'Shut up. It's Alecto. My name is Alecto.'

'This won't bring you what you want.'

'Shut up. You're our last contestant.'

'What, before you escape? Have you looked out there?'

Alecto ignored the invitation to look out of the window and violently chambered a round in her gun then raised it towards Martinez as she stepped towards her. The gun wavering in front of the detective.

'How about I put a bullet in your pretty little face?'

Martinez wanted to faint. The primal fear of the end of her own finite existence filled her with dread, but not having another moment with Mike Byrne made her feel an overwhelming sadness. To die here, like this, at the hands of this angry woman? *No.*

'How about you ask me that question.'

'You won't get it right. It's not a multiple choice this time.'

'Try me.'

Alecto flicked a glance up at the window through which she might have seen Webster fly off. Then Martinez made the connection, saw what wasn't adding up.

'He was meant to take you with him, wasn't he?'

Alecto re-gripped the gun, seemingly fighting the urge to pull the trigger.

'He knows what he's doing.'

'He's using you.' Speaking firmly but gently to the ex-Ranger.

'Shut up.'

'Think about it, Alice.'

But calling her by her real name again seemed to be a big mistake and for a moment neither of them knew if Alecto was about to shoot her. And then something sad, sad to Alecto's core, made Martinez want to ask what had tormented her.

'OK, Detective, here's my question.'

The two women looking into each other's eyes. The room silent. Even the gunfire outside seeming to cease.

'How do we stop the bankers ever doing it again?'

Martinez was baffled. 'What?'

'It's the last question. How do we stop bankers bringing our country to its knees ever again? How do we stop them doing it? Ever? You've got thirty seconds, bitch.'

And Alecto, four feet from Martinez, tightened her hand around the gun for the final time.

68

Once Webster had taken off he had banked steeply, pushing the aircraft to something like its limits, before describing a wide circle in the air, almost as if being behind the joystick had got his adrenaline pumped. Or maybe it was whatever money he had coming for doing Lazcano's bidding. Either way he had taken it from nothing to four hundred miles an hour in no time flat.

How the hell to stop this . . . ?

I looked around for some kind of ejector mechanism but I remembered my time at the Reno air-shows. A retired World War II pilot had given a talk in one of the sponsor tents about bailing out of one of these things. There were no ejector seats, you popped the canopy and jumped out. But the lever for that was in the front with my designated driver. The lever was out of my reach.

Think, Byrne, think . . .

'You OK back there?' The laughter in Webster's voice impossible to miss as he tore the inverted plane through the sky. Both of us speaking through our flight helmets now.

'I've had better flights.'

'I know what you mean, I flew with Comair once. We just have a quick fly-by of the hotel to do and then we'll be on our way to sunny Mexico, my friend.'

This was a surprising move, an absurd risk given the circumstances. I didn't understand it. 'Looking to admire your handiwork?'

'No, Byrne. Looking to get my detonator switch within range of all those explosives I have under that ballroom.'

I have never thrown up on a flight in my life, but for the briefest of moments my stomach tightened as if readying to do just that. Jenni was down there. Where was she? Would she be near the blast? Becker's men were advancing. Had they reached her? But, no, everybody was at risk. This ruthless son of a bitch was . . . What *was* he doing? Destroying bankers? Destroying the evidence? Punishing Sovereign Bank? Leaving his trail as cold as possible, knowing that every law enforcement agency would be crawling over his actions for a decade to come? Or, most likely, a combination of all those things. It told me that the extent of his criminality was total. And it told me I had to stop him.

The plane began to descend. I looked out of my right window. Down, far below, through the light but constant snow could be seen the grey smudge that was the Hotel Wolverton. Webster's target.

In desperation I bucked again at the ropes that bound me. Webster must have felt my torment because a hearty laugh came over my intercom. But he hadn't felt everything. He hadn't felt the compact metal object in my ski-jacket pocket.

In the New York field office nobody was speaking, each looking on as their CAT colleagues moved into position. The CAT cameras showed the agents moving around the hotel, closing in on the ballroom. Special Agent Diane Mason watched on, ever vigilant that her own anxiety didn't reveal itself to the rest of the room. Given the disaster that had unfolded before their eyes this morning she took some consolation in the fact that there was nobody she would rather have there than Commander Becker and Michael Byrne. She was watching Becker and his men's progress on the screens before her. She had heard nothing from Byrne since their video call at his hotel first thing that morning.

Something, an instinct, made Special Agent Mason check her BlackBerry. She saw she had a text – Michael? She quickly read it. Then immediately caught a cry in her throat. The message read '*MB on plane.*'

She spoke to the room, unconsciously barking her request. 'The plane that took off. Have we got a visual?'

A youngish, sandy-haired special agent leaned into a mic at the central AV desk.

'Does anybody have a visual on the plane that just took off?'

Almost without exception every view from every camera showed that the CAT agent involved was either pinned down by Nemesis gunfire or involved in action against them. Every agent's eyes flitted from screen to screen to see if any had responded to the question. Then one, camera 16, turned from its view of the rear of the hotel, down along the runway. Without being asked the AV agent at the desk selected this live feed to fill up the large monitor on everybody's left. And there, through the drizzle of snow could be seen the wavering form of the Mustang coming back into view – flying straight towards them.

*

Martinez's legs felt like they would give way at any moment. The gun inches from her face. She spoke but she knew the words would not land home. Not here, not this far from sanity.

'I know the sacrifices you made for your country, Alice.'

Alecto's face tightened as she spoke.

'You're running out of time, Detective. Three . . .'

'Webster's gone, Alice. Don't do this.'

'Two.' Alecto's hand beginning to quiver. The edges of her vision beginning to grow dark, her mind descending into the fog that only the utterly betrayed can know.

I looked down at my hands, bound at the wrist, looked at what I had retrieved from my pocket. Gabriella's Tesla gun magazine.

Using this would be suicide.

'I hope you like fireworks, Byrne, because this is going to look like the Fourth of July.'

Using this might save Martinez.

I jammed the taser's teeth into the back of Webster's seat.

A cry broke out from the front of the cockpit.

I saw Webster's body arch away from his seat, thrusting towards the canopy, testing the constraints of his body harness, before the plane began to barrel on to its side into what I knew would be its terminal descent.

The New York field office agents watched in trepidation for the hostages as the grainy image of the Mustang hurtled towards the hotel in some kind of kamikaze trajectory before suddenly rolling on to its side and swooping past their CAT agent's camera and out over the bordering ridge.

An ice-cold hand gripped Special Agent Mason's heart as she watched Byrne disappear from view and, she believed, her life.

In the ballroom, Alecto had been distracted from her countdown by the roar of the passing plane, Webster's reappearance confusing her, the plane's rapid re-departure almost making her feel mocked, somehow reinforcing the betrayal. She had paused, choking on the words. And Martinez had sensed her anguish, the abandonment she was feeling.

'Alice . . .'

But somehow the word was the wrong word, the very word that could rouse the former Ranger from her mounting nightmare. She spoke her last word deliberately, like she knew it was the end of everything.

'Time's up, Detective . . . One.'

A German Nemesis guard at the rear of the stage was more alive to the dangers facing their group than their leader, had heard the gunfire getting nearer then ceasing. 'Alecto, we must go – *now*.'

She flicked a look at him to catch his meaning.

It was all Martinez wanted. In one motion the detective stepped in and to the side of Alecto, grabbed the gun and pointed it at the German Nemesis guard. Alecto's instinct to start pulling the trigger delivered two bullets to his face before Martinez's knee connected with Alecto's stomach. As the Nemesis ring-leader went down Martinez took the weapon from her hand, to stop the remaining Nemesis guard on stage.

But she was too late.

His gun was raised towards her chest before Martinez could grip the gun.

Death was instant.

The sniper's bullet from above went through the guard's head, knocking him backwards.

At the exact same moment fourteen other CAT agents began to neutralize every Nemesis guard in the room as they fired down from the glass-domed roof and from every door entering into the ballroom, glass showering about the petrified bankers below.

Martinez looked around her, gun in hand, ready to shoot any Nemesis guard that moved.

But none did.

She pointed the pistol at Alecto. Only she wasn't Alecto any more. She was Alice Armitage from Chanute, Kansas, lying on the stage, looking back up at the detective with a vacant expression. As the CAT agents stormed the room Martinez and Armitage existed in their own bubble, away from all the other action, its noise and motion in another universe. Alice said something that Martinez heard as if through a tunnel – *I gave everything* – then she pulled her hand out from under her back to reveal a snub-nosed Desert Eagle semi-automatic pistol. Martinez shook her head, pointing the gun down at Alice's chest. Alice was not deterred and – careful not to swing the gun in Martinez's direction – pointed it under her own chin. And Martinez suddenly understood, instantly dropping her own gun, dropping with it, trying to grab the small pistol, trying to stop Alice. Her word – *No* – drowned out by the gunshot that entered Alice's head. The CAT agents corralling the bankers out of the room, getting them away from potential booby-traps, but everything a blur to Martinez as her tears fell like raindrops on to the young woman's face.

I had lost all sense of direction, of up and of down. Once we had passed the hotel Webster had involuntarily sent the plane rolling over and over itself at ever-increasing speeds. Of that I was certain. What I didn't know was whether we were ascending or descending, whether we would be hitting terra firma now or in a minute or so.

Then something surprising happened. The plane came out of its spin. That tough SOB had recovered enough from his tasering to get some kind of a grip on the plane. I looked out of the canopy and I could see the ground rushing up towards us.

Webster's control of the Mustang had come too late, and we ditched on to the side of a mountain that was less horizontal than we now were. I felt the left wing hit the snow-covered slope, Webster slamming the right side down immediately, the plane bouncing dangerously over the surface like an out-of-control sledge – because that was all it was right now.

I braced myself for what was coming, and it came quick. We hit something, something immoveable in the landscape, and the antique plane's nose dug into the ground as the tail flipped into the air. Then –

Nothing, as darkness overtook me.

69

'I've got no feeling in my hands or feet.'

'You've been tied up, that's all, the circulation, you know. It's going to be OK.'

'I'm an American citizen. My name's Simon Turlington.'

'I know.'

'Who . . .' He weakly spat some blood out that trailed from his bottom lip down on to his chest. '. . . are you?'

'I'm Mike Byrne. I'm with the American Secret Service. Look, Simon, we haven't got much time. I need to know who set up the meeting.'

'Mr Byrne?' Barely audible above the generator down the hall.

I took a breath. 'Yeah.' I wanted to weep for him. I wanted to weep for his parents. 'What is it, Simon?'

'I think they cut my face . . .' The words trailing off. He didn't have much time. We didn't have much time . . .

I had to fight the emotion. 'Who set up the meeting, Simon? I need a name.'

'Sec . . .'

'Sec? Your secretary? No, Simon, who arranged it?'

He seemed to shake his head. He turned his eyes slowly in their sockets and stared at me for the first time. I had to give him the dignity of returning the look, knowing it would haunt me for ever . . .

One bullet left in the chamber . . . Suddenly the American

threw his head back . . . I put my last bullet in the back of his head.

Sec . . . He'd been trying to say 'Security'. Security chief. Webster. Sec . . .

Everything was noise. Everything was roar, a roaring, in my ears, buffeting my senses before softening, before moving away. An aircraft, a helicopter. Where? Where was I? Where was *it*? Then my face, under attack, needles flying into it, I turned my head away and then down and got some relief from the snow pounding my face. I was on a mountain, that was it, the plane crash. I was sat in the rear of the cockpit in the snow. The cockpit, the plane, the right way up. But no canopy, it was gone. Smashed? How long had I been unconscious? I squinted out and looked about. White. White everywhere. Just a sea of white. A world of white. Visibility maybe twenty-five feet. How long? I looked down at my legs. Covered in snow but not hidden in the snow. In this weather it couldn't have meant more than five, ten minutes.

I peered round the seat ahead. No Webster. What had happened to him? Had he been flung out in the crash? Had he bailed out? No, there's no ejector seat in these things and he righted the plane enough for the forced landing. So where was he? Out there.

I looked up and about. The swirling wind lifting and lowering the curtain of snow by turns. The glimpses provided telling me that there were ridges along my left, downward slopes on my right. I had no idea how far the Mustang had tumbled out of control before we had crashed. Was I next door to the hotel? Was I ten miles away? Twenty? I had no idea. What I did know was that the afternoon was ending. It would be dark soon. Then the one question I didn't want to ask myself, that I couldn't afford to dwell on. Was Jenni OK? No, not now, I'd never get through this if I thought about it. That was one for the living.

I groped around for the clasps of my harness. My bound hands made it slow going – and the trauma of the landing made every muscle feel like it had been torn sadistically apart. After a lot of fumbling I managed to ease the harness off myself. The effort had exhausted me, and I took a moment to collect my breath before remembering – he was out there.

I took a hold of the top of the seat in front and tentatively pulled myself up, careful to look around to see if Webster was in the immediate vicinity. Nothing that I could see. Just a sea of white, and part of me started to wonder if he'd been thrown out as we crashed, out there somewhere. Maybe he'd ridden his luck as far as he could, and it was me all alone out here. Well, that was wishful thinking, and I knew it. My priority was to establish Webster's whereabouts and then to see whether setting up some sort of camp by this plane was any kind of an option. But step one was getting out of this cockpit.

I raised a painful leg up and over the right side of the plane and out on to the back edge of the right wing. I followed with my left leg, sliding my rear over the rim of the cockpit itself. I took a moment, my balance not quite right after my concussion, somehow lagging behind my body's orientation. It felt like things were getting better, but right now I didn't want to rush anything, especially with my head throbbing the way it was inside my flight helmet. I held on to the side of the plane, taking a breather. After a brief pause I looked into the front of the cockpit to see if there was anything I could use. Something was sticking out from under the front seat. The corner of a canvas bag. It would be a survival kit. It could have rations, a razor blade, cords, heat blankets, my mind was racing at the possibilities, and I greedily leaned down towards it.

The ties around my wrist made me much less mobile than I would have liked and reaching the bag was a stretch. As my fingers crawled down the front of the seat towards it I thought about the last thing I'd seen before I'd bent down into the front cockpit. The canopy. The reason it wasn't in place was because it had been slid all the way back. That was why it was open. It hadn't smashed apart, somebody had opened it. *Webster.* He would have seen me unconscious and taken advantage of it to get the lie of the land, get some kind of bearings. Whatever his reasons, he could be coming back any –

I heard the crack of the gun at the same instant that a hole punctured the cockpit beside me.

I rolled backwards along the wing, down off on to the ground, the survival kit abandoned. Immediately I was on my feet and running. Staying at a crouch, I dived down the slope and away, not hanging around but stumbling through the snow until managing a low, hunkered-down run, getting myself behind a tall, broad pine. No more shots pursued me. That told me one thing: he was preserving his ammo. He would have landed with what he had on him, and I knew it was not more than a pistol. I still didn't like the odds, but they were better than against a fully armed Webster.

I needed to move the target. I ran what I hoped was in a line that kept the tree between me and wherever he was. Immediately another bullet whizzed close by me, making some kind of clipping sound. Had it hit the side of my flight helmet or was that an overhead branch? I zigzagged between the few pine trees peppering the slope until the ground ahead dropped away some twenty feet. There was a seemingly gentle incline down to my left but ahead just that huge drop, a pine tree reaching up from below it. Choices took time, and I sensed I didn't have much of it, so launched myself off the higher ground towards the pine tree ahead. A bullet followed me over the edge, a bullet that missed. I reached out to grab something – anything – with my bound hands and was rewarded with thick, uncooperative pine branches, briefly – almost – holding one, slowing my fall fractionally, but then falling again to the ground below. Hitting thick snow. Hitting it and bouncing up on to my feet before getting behind a further tree as a gunshot cracked out behind me. He could have as many as fifteen bullets, and that was before he changed clips. I had to think . . .

Now I could formulate a plan. If he leaped after me he handed me the initiative on his fall, if he chose the gentler slope I could keep my distance or look for a chance to attack. If he stayed where he was, well, then we could both freeze to death. The fading light was my firmest friend right now. The man with the gun, the cold, these were my enemies. I couldn't do much about one but I sure as hell could do something about the other.

'Byrne?' Shouted from above. 'I know you're down there, Byrne. I just want you to know that I've had a change of heart.' Where the hell was this going? 'I'm not going to deliver you to Lazcano any more Byrne. I'm going to kill you, you son of a bitch.'

Anger.

Good.

I had another friend.

I made a semi-megaphone with my tied hands. 'I tell you what, Webster. Throw down your gun, and I'll put a good word in with the judge.'

'Fuck you, Byrne.'

My mind racing, wondering what the hell I could do that would take on a gun. How the hell was I going to get in close? I had to get close. I had to get going.

'I'll take that as a "no", shall I?'

He didn't reply. I looked about me as I listened out for him. A branch on the tree next to me had snapped slightly from the weight of the snow. It was thin and didn't look too strong but it was a start. I started to pull at the branch, its sinewy hold on the trunk resisting coming off. I shouted backwards over my shoulder as I worked.

'Tell me, Webster, was it worth it?'

A pause, then, 'Which part, Byrne? It's all been such a ride.'

Reassured that his voice – he – was still on the higher ground, I continued to tug at the tree. The branch began to come off.

'Manipulating the anger of wounded soldiers?'

'I didn't manipulate it, Byrne – I focused it. Give me a little credit.'

The branch broke free. It was about the length of a broom handle, though not quite as strong. I started to strip the twigs off it, my cold, bound hands struggling with the task.

'What about the girl in Paris, Webster? You proud of that?'

'Come, come, Byrne. She was collateral damage and you know it. It was her choice to whistle-blow. I was just doing my job.'

'What does that make the young banker, Simon Turlington? Was that your job, too?'

It went silent up on the hill. Was he coming down? Had he guessed where I was? Was he feeling remorse?

Webster looked down on the silent slope below, through the dense falling snow. It wasn't as heavy as before, it seemed to be lifting, but vision was still limited. Where was his quarry? A small crop of pine trees hid Byrne from view. But his voice was becoming more definite in its positioning. He lifted his flight helmet off slightly to allow him to hear better. One more sound to help locate him . . .

'Turlington, yeah, that was a little bit messy, Byrne. But what do you expect when you get into bed with the devil? You want the big bucks, you gotta take the big risks. Look at me, you think this is *easy*?'

Listening intently, trying to pinpoint exactly where . . .

'What about you, Webster . . . ?'

Webster followed his own best guess and fired off a bullet at a tree fifty feet away. The mountain went quiet, the wind dropping to a noiseless whirl. Then, from a different place way over to the right . . .

'Now that wasn't very nice, was it, Webster?'

'Sorry, Byrne. Thought I saw a grizzly.'

'Shouldn't do that, Webster. They're an endangered species.'

Webster pulled his helmet back down, glared at the whited-out landscape and growled to himself. 'Aren't we all.'

I moved away from my tree again, away from the ex-CIA agent, and started to walk cautiously in a wide semi-circle, away at first then bearing left, back towards the bottom of the slope he would have to use. If he was coming down. Yes . . . There he was, pausing by the top of the incline. He was coming this way. Or thinking about it at least. The cold or Webster were going to get me. I'd be damned if I was going to give him the pleasure. I remembered my taser. I put my stripped branch down and quickly padded my hands against my jacket. I couldn't feel any sign of it, but then I couldn't feel my fingers in these freezing temperatures. But an unfeeling hand inside my pockets confirmed the worst. No taser. Back in the cockpit somewhere. Back to square one. Back against the wall. Having no choice but to do *something*. I picked up my primitive spear. A primitive spear for a primitive man.

Webster licked his lips and immediately regretted it when the moisture instantly turned to ice.

'I read your personnel file, Byrne.'

Waiting for the reply but getting none.

'Had to call in a lot of favours to get it. You haven't been idle, have you?'

Webster began to descend the incline, feeling his way

with his feet, not trusting the slope, his Glock 19 pointed out at the trees below. Walking half forwards, half crab-like, he made his way down, the gloom of the early evening casting the trees into a pall of greyness. The glow of the snow even now casting the setting into a strange other-worldliness before the onset of night.

'Quite the Eagle Scout, aren't we? All very *High Noon*. Tell me, Byrne, do you really believe in the cause? All that risk on a government salary – do you really think it's worth putting your life on the line for?'

Webster found himself getting uncomfortable with the silence now. Silence presaging a plan, an attack. Unconsciously squeezing the butt of the gun. Reminding himself it was he who *had* the gun. Still, Byrne rushing him would get it over with. Better than hide and seek. He had reached the bottom when he stopped to take in the scene. Dark mountain rearing up behind and on both sides of the slope. Ahead a small smattering of trees holding between them their own darkness, their own dangers.

'Do you really want to work for a government that set us on a wild goose chase after 9/11? Do you?'

'Why did you change, Webster?'

Byrne's voice came from his right. Close. Webster flipped round and fired a bullet. But instead of a falling body he heard a fast-moving one, running through the trees ahead.

'What about your fiancée, Byrne? She died that day. She died that day and the next day we flew out the Bin Laden family. We colluded with them after one of theirs killed your fiancée, Byrne. Do you *really* believe in the cause?'

Webster reached the nearest tree and looked around it

into the copse. Nothing. Nothing stirring, nothing doing.

'But you don't, do you, Byrne. Because you quit, didn't you. Quit when Bush tried to pin that whole 9/11 thing on Saddam. What made you come back? Was it the health coverage? The food in the canteen? Or was it the little people, the ninety-nine per cent?'

'What made you change, Webster?'

The voice on his left. Another shot fired wildly at the sound. Another movement through the woods.

'I didn't change, Byrne, *they* did. I gave my life, my *life* to this country. We used to fight communism, we used to protect decent Americans so they could sleep safely in their beds at night. Now look at us. Everything's for sale. The bankers bought our politicians then the politicians bought their debt with our money. Everything's for *sale*. Everything's been *bought*. Look around yourself, Byrne, there's been a coup. I know a coup when I see one, Byrne – God knows I've organized enough of them in my time. There's been a coup d'état in America. No blood spilled, just every last cent stolen. I didn't put my life on the line for thirty years to prop up *this*. We're not meant to be some failed African state where the ruling elite have all the money and power. This is America. This is the United States. We used to lead the way, Byrne, but now we've lost our way. For every winner there has to be a loser. Well, I was sick of being the loser. Screw that every day of the week and twice on Sundays. And if that's the American way, Byrne, then you tell me why I did it. Think about it, Byrne, think about it for a second. We're a country where you eat what you kill. Eat what you goddamn well kill. So I started to kill. And guess what, it tastes great.'

Webster was momentarily high from his outpouring. Then angry that Byrne hadn't reacted. But, no, he felt better. He'd never told anybody, not till then. And he felt better for having said it. He stepped carefully one tree deeper into the copse. Nothing but trees. Nothing but . . . there, maybe there. Something, maybe a bush ahead.

With infinite caution he crept to the next tree. *Definitely something there.* Something still. Something alien to this environment.

The next tree, despite the lowering light, was close enough – twenty-five, maybe thirty feet – to be certain that Byrne was waiting. So far so covered by trees, but now Webster had to decide whether to retreat and attempt to sidle up unnoticed until the very last moment or close it down now.

The impending darkness gave him no choice.

He thought about the situation. Byrne was up ahead and didn't have a gun. He couldn't fire back. The whole thing, it was a cinch. There was a premium for bringing Byrne in alive, he'd have to take a hit on the deal – but there would still be a deal.

Webster stepped round the tree, aimed the gun perfectly and shot as he walked.

Solid steps that did not waver. Three bullets in the head.

The helmet flying backwards off the head.

Impossibly.

Webster almost there now.

Knowing instantly.

His incomprehension and anger rising with every step.

A stack of snow where the neck should be. Byrne's helmet on a goddamn snowman. Some aboriginal snowman with a branch sticking out of what might pass for his left hand. The spear mocking Webster in its primitiveness, his Glock 19 doing nothing more than chasing shadows as night fell.

I jumped out from behind a tree and slammed Webster across the shoulder blades with a branch. He staggered a couple of steps, instinctively flinging out his arms in pain. Holding the branch between my bound hands like an unwieldy club I hit him again, but he was turning and managed to deflect the strike along his rising arm. His Glock was my immediate concern and I brought the branch down on his right hand and wrist, but there was no gun, Webster must have dropped it with my first blow. For a moment he looked like he was going to launch himself at me but then turned away to look for where the pistol must have landed.

We saw it at the same time. Sunk in the snow between us.

He dived at it.

I spun the branch round and plunged its thin end towards the pistol, spearing the gun inside the trigger guard. As he reached for the weapon I flicked it up and away down the slope before he could reach it, into the darkness, into the night. I spun the spear round, bringing the handle uselessly down on the back of his helmeted head, but he charged into me, flooring me as the spear bounced off his shoulders.

I tried to grab his neck, but he was already out of my

hands, out of my reach as he scampered away down the slope in the direction of the gun. He wouldn't find it – but I wasn't going to wait to find out. I sprang up and after him, ready to attack him when he paused for the gun – except that he didn't pause, didn't look back: he just ran. His edge gone, he wanted away, he wanted out of all of this. How the hell were either of us going to get out?

As much as the snow would allow, I ran after him, the icy blasts of wind cutting through my body as I did. He was running, like me, almost blind, charging through the darkening snow and trees, receiving blow after blow from the near-invisible branches, their warning swish ahead giving me a chance to occasionally avoid the same fate. Then he was out of the trees and running across a flat piece of ground. Even with my hands tied up I was gaining on him, the light slightly better out here, the immediate landscape visible, Webster running towards a cliff, having no choice but to jump down on to the lower reaches of the mountainside if he were to escape me, only five paces ahead now, the deadly cold whipping me as I sprinted after him, the cliff edge paces away, Webster about to jump off –

Then stopping himself.

Stopping in that balance-out-of-kilter way that sudden drops force us to do. Diving left or right not an option because there was nothing in front of him, nothing as he turned, too much momentum to stop his forward trajectory, over the edge, over the side of the mountain, helpless to stop himself, falling unless –

I caught him.

As he turned to topple backwards I reached with my

bound hands and caught the sleeve of his jacket, hanging off his arm.

He was leaning backwards some twenty degrees plus. Only staying up because of my precarious hold on his sleeve. His weight perfectly counterbalancing mine, his life in my frozen hands. We stood there taking in the new reality, neither fight nor flight an option for him any more.

Everything had changed. He didn't seem upset by his helpless position. Instead he smiled ruefully. The game over. Knew what I was thinking. *One false move.* Anything sudden and I would release the jacket. He didn't have to ask. He knew. He glanced down at the long drop into darkness then back up at me. His alternative to my help was a fall neither of us could see the bottom of. I adjusted my stance. I was close to the edge, closer than I would have chosen, the snow unsure under my feet, wondering how long I could keep him here.

He looked at me as if time was not of the essence, as if we could stay in this position for the longest time.

'What now, Byrne?'

I weighed it up. Failure meant death to him. I had to be careful. People were at their most dangerous when they had nothing to lose. And Webster had nothing to lose. That, and the cold was killing me. So I cut to the chase.

'Why, Webster?'

He hung out over the cliff like he didn't care how this panned out, almost casual now, distant, leaning his head back, away from me, looking up at the sky like he wanted to really feel the sensation of snowflakes landing on his face, like nothing would ever match that moment for him. Then a change. A shroud of bitterness overcame him.

'You want to know something, Byrne? I'd torn through three marriages, I had a kid I wasn't allowed to see, I lived in a single-bed apartment a North Korean wouldn't have envied, and they told me I could get a second job.'

I looked at him, the muted fury taking over him. 'What do you mean?'

'I asked for a raise a way back, some way to improve my pay grade. My boss at the CIA told me I was allowed to moonlight to top up my salary. Moonlight. *Moonlight.*' Almost howling it at our own hidden moon. 'I'd risked my life and sanity for this country for almost thirty years and they said I could pull two shifts to top up my salary. That's it? I have to get another job to make it possible for me to work for Uncle Sam? For the *honour*? The *privilege*? What am I, *a fucking illegal immigrant*?' After a pause his breathing calmed down and he looked at me, the calm after the storm. 'Screw that, Byrne.'

'So, what? You decided to kill bankers?'

'To kill them?' He really did laugh now. Laughed like he didn't know that my frigid arm was getting tired and I hadn't decided whether to pull him back yet. 'I didn't decide to kill them, Byrne, I decided to emulate them. Do whatever it took to make money and damn the consequences to everybody else . . .' He shook his head with genuine, amused laughter, like he was surprised I didn't get it. Then the moment passed, and he looked at me curiously. Took a long moment to zero in on me, and then something left him, something was absent in his gaze. I didn't understand what at first then . . . Then I realized, realized what it was. For the first time since I had met him he was looking at me without any kind of guile in his eyes.

'Look around you, Byrne.' Looking around like the evidence was here for us to see on this cliff-top. 'Everything is permitted.'

'No it isn't.'

'Really? Well, I think somebody forgot to tell your friends on Wall Street.'

'Our job is to stop . . .'

I stopped, struggling to find the right – the true – words.

'The bad guys, Byrne? Everybody's the bad guy now. The system's the bad guy. What are you going to do, Byrne, when you realize that the bankers dug up your country's yellow-brick road and melted it down to make an extra buck? What will you do when you finally wake up to the fact that everybody's a bad guy? What will you do?'

So that's where his head was at. I decided our fireside chat would have to wait until we got to somewhere safer. I decided to pull him back in.

I decided too late.

The ground beneath us gave way –

Suddenly nothing –

Suddenly we were falling.

The precipice I thought we had been standing on wasn't even that. It was snow and ice. And it gave way beneath us, both of us dropping helplessly, me releasing him, large boulders of snow dropping beneath me, Webster peeling away from me, tipping backwards –

Then I was crashing to a halt. Falling into a bank of snow like a child dive-bombing into a swimming pool. Only nothing pushing me back to the surface. Just snow all about me. Snow I landed in heavy but not too heavy.

After the initial surprise and after realizing nothing seemed broken I tried to hold on to the snow around me, to use it to stand, but it gave way, forcing me to dig, punch my way out, finding some give on one side, smashing myself against it, until it gave way, me spilling out, colder than ever, on to the ledge. I was so cold. I stood, coughing from the shock to my system. Then I saw him in the fading light, a black form in the darkness.

Webster was lying very still on the ledge, lying on his back. Lying in a way I knew he would never move from.

I stood up, needing breaths to recover myself. The falling snow had abated like some malicious joke, like it would make a difference. I looked about me, got my bearings. Sheer rock face on three sides, an abyss on the other, night's cold embrace wrapping around us. I knelt down beside Webster, who was staring upwards at the sky, watching the last of the snowflakes. He was trying to say something.

'I don't . . .'

This was the bit where I was meant to say *Don't try to talk*. But what was the point?

'I don't . . . regret it.'

It was a struggle for him to speak; the ruthless cold made it hard to listen. We both waited.

'I had an epiphany, Byrne.'

I rubbed my jacket and the tops of my legs, a futile attempt to rub warmth and life into them, into my searingly cold hands.

'Yeah, what was that, Webster?'

He spoke gently, the way only a man who knows his time has come and is reconciled to it can. 'Bankers, Byrne.

I worked with them. Went to their meetings. Read their emails. All part of the job.' Trying to smile, failing, eking out the remainder of his life now, wanting to use every last drop to talk. 'I realized that the guys on Wall Street and bank robbers look at customers' money exactly the same way.'

'And how's that?'

'They're both trying to walk out of the building with as much of it as possible without getting caught.'

Finding the tiniest part of a smile. Breathing slightly easier now.

'Wall Street, Byrne . . . It's . . . It's an inside job . . . You do know that, don't you? It's a takedown . . .'

And his last breath slipped into the wind.

I waited a while, feeling the passing of a soldier, however wayward he had been.

I didn't need to look. He was dead. The snow came up. Then my face began to scald. He'd beaten me to it. The son of a bitch had died first.

70

The New York field office of the Secret Service in Adams Street, Brooklyn, was noiseless. It had barely risen above that since the catastrophic events outside Aspen of the day before. After a minimal amount of sleep the agents had returned to their desks, carrying out all of the post-operation administration required. The write-ups, the reports, the daily grind that made up most of their work.

Only, today was more than just wrapping up affairs. Today was the aftermath. The events at the Hotel Wolverton had been bloody and battering for the Service, the fallout as yet unquantified. Colleagues – friends – of those in the New York office had been cut down in the line of duty. Somehow this wasn't just business. Somehow this was personal. People were hurting. Hurting and in some cases grieving. A heaviness weighed on the staff, guilt, anger, loss, a tumbling mixture of moods and emotions. Everybody was taking it badly. Some more than most.

The young agent, Jenkins, walked past Park's desk towards Special Agent Mason's office. Park could see his intent and intervened.

'I wouldn't go in there if I was you.'

'Why not?'

Park raised arched eyebrows. 'She doesn't want to hear anything for a while.'

'She'll want to hear this.'

Jenkins walked past and barely waited after his knock to enter. Park heard his opening remark and understood why.

'Ma'am. They've found the wreckage of the plane. There was nobody inside.'

Before Jenkins could say another word Diane Mason was striding out of her door in a manner that people knew meant all hands on deck.

'Get mountain rescue out, get the Air Force out – get everybody out. Byrne's on the side of that mountain.'

Jenkins bravely – foolishly – tried to impart some wisdom. 'Ma'am, there's no intelligence that anybody survived.'

The people present thought she was about to slap him, so fierce was the beginning of the look that leaped into her eyes. Then she became glacial and turned to the room.

'We're going to find one of our agents, we're going to find Michael Byrne. And nobody sleeps until we do.'

Helicopters from the Colorado Air National Guard swept the mountainsides around the crash site that day. As more heavy snow came in civilian search and rescue teams scoured the slopes with dogs, overnight snow making all and any tracks invisible to the human eye. The teams had had to contend with the worsening weather in an area where the danger of avalanche was high, but hardest of all was the unrelenting woman's voice in their ear asking – demanding – to know where Byrne was.

Nobody was coming back until he was found.

Nobody dared.

*

I couldn't escape the feeling I had messed up somewhere along the way.

I must have fallen asleep.

After Webster had died I did the only sensible thing there was to do. I went through his pockets, used a multi-purpose tool I found to untie my hands then took what clothes of his I could wear over mine and left him semi-naked in the snow. Then I turned back to the boulder of snow I had ridden down the mountainside and scooped out something not unlike an igloo. Then I had crawled inside and slept. The snow shelter and Webster's flight helmet had deadened the sound. I slept fitfully, wary of succumbing to the cold, but needing the energy that sleep brought. Cold, I dug my hands into my pockets. Something was there in one of them. I pulled whatever it was out – my cold hands couldn't tell me the exact shape – but in the darkness I felt it eventually. The crucifix from the girl in Paris. Claire Sancery, that was her name. I'd taken this from her, stolen it. What would she make of me holding it right here, right now? Poor thing. I needed rest. I dreamed it was getting lighter. Maybe. But I needed my rest. As I lay on my side in a ball, dipping in and out of sleep, I heard the wind increasing. Soon it was rushing past my makeshift habitat, pounding my last defences against the elements, a storm to wipe me away, the wind so hard now that it beat down, thumped the snow on my ledge like . . .

A helicopter pilot hovered his Kestrel 500 fifty feet from a solitary ledge one thousand-plus feet up the mountain. He was looking at his colleague, whom he had just lowered on to the same shelf of rock.

On the mountainside, the rescue mountaineer looked down at the frozen, near-naked corpse at his feet. That appeared to be all there was here. Hopes raised and dashed.

Then he noticed a gap in the snow at the back of the ledge and made his way inside.

In the hovering helicopter opposite the ledge, the pilot watched as the rescue worker crawled out of the mound of snow. The worker stood and gave a big thumbs-up.

The pilot flicked on his comms unit.

'Special Agent Mason, this is Mountain Bird Three. Over.'

'This is Agent Mason. Over.'

'Ma'am, we got him.'

71

'Happy birthday to you, happy birthday to you, happy birthday dear New York, happy birthday to you.'

Sung softly, sung beautifully. Sung too goddamn early.

'Wakey wakey, grumpy chops.'

I braved an eye against the Brooklyn morning. There she was, smiling down at me. Always smiling.

'Who is this happy at this time of day?'

The lovely young woman kept smiling at me. 'It's your birthday, Michael.'

I gave Nicole a quizzical look. Even on three hours sleep this wasn't making sense.

'Kid, it's not my birthday until the . . .'

'And it's my birthday, and it's everybody in New York's birthday.'

I raised myself up on one elbow, the smell of coffee giving me some reason to connect with the waking world. I spied the digital alarm clock: 7:13.

'Has Giuliani declared a public holiday that I haven't heard about?'

'No, 'tupid.'

She broke from tidying her black bob to tap me on the head with her hairbrush.

'It's the United States' birthday.'

'What?' Then remembering that if anyone would know she would.

She sat on my side of the bed and put a hand on my chest.

'September the eleventh, 1603, Captain Hudson landed at Sandy Hook near Staten Island. It's our birthday. I thought everybody knew that.'

I had to smile. I stroked her hand as I used the other to sip my coffee. 'I suspect it's just you and the other students in your class. Anyhow, it's not your birthday, Nicole, you're a Native.'

She playfully slapped my chest.

'Half Native.'

'All right. You're allowed to half celebrate it and half resent it.'

She stood up, ready for work now. Her movement had caused her perfume to waft around me. What was that perfume? Chanel something? Whatever it was it would be her scent for ever. She attached a couple of small gold earrings to her ears. Modest, like everything about her. Her clothes, so tidy and quiet. Every day wearing one bright thing, her big brave act. Today a bright crimson neckerchief she had found in a flea market by Washington Square when she was dragging me round on one of her American History tours.

'Talking of half-celebrating, would you like to come out with my class after work?'

I dropped my jaw for effect. 'You're not seriously celebrating New York's birthday, are you?'

She looked from the full-length mirror to me. Shy now.

'Is it geeky?'

'It's the geekiest thing I ever heard.'

'Oh, please come out.' Adopting a Cheshire Cat smile, eyes closed, like the ten-year-old she would probably always be, or certainly had been for the first twenty-five years of her life.

'OK. But only if you take the day off.'

It was her turn to drop her jaw, her mouth dropping open like even entertaining the idea was beyond consideration.

'Michael Byrne, how could you?'

'Easy, just take a duvet day.'

'We don't have duvet days. Do you have duvet days in the Secret Service?'

I laughed. 'Every day's a duvet day in the Secret Service.'

She raised an eyebrow that doubted my words as she sat down again. I took her hand in mine.

'You know, Nicole, if you want to quit we can get by on my salary.'

She shook her head resolutely. 'You're very kind.'

I squeezed her fingers. 'I mean it. Just focus on your studies. No more schlepping up to the Financial District every day. Why not?'

It was her turn to squeeze my hand.

'Because.'

'Because what?'

'Because we don't have a song.'

'A what?'

'We don't have a special song. You know, how can we be getting serious if we haven't got a special song?'

'Nicole, we're engaged. How much more serious can we get?'

Me laughing slightly, but unsure of her mood now. For her part, she was annoyed at how she was communicating herself.

'I don't mean serious. I'm being stupid.'

I looked at her, thinking about something, something not sitting right with her. 'What? What is it?'

She felt stupid saying it but needed to say it all the same. 'It's just that it came up at work, you know, the girls were talking about their special song with their guy, you know, silly stuff, but I realized we didn't have a song, which seemed strange.' Then she shook her head. 'Forget it, I'm just being silly.'

*I didn't know if she was messing with me or in earnest. I'd gotten
that wrong on a number of occasions so was not about to throw caution
to the wind.* 'Like what? "You Don't Bring Me Flowers", what?'

She smiled and tapped my hand, a little sadly I thought. 'No, you
know, a song that means something to us because we shared it
together.'

*Then she looked at me for confirmation that I understood, for
validation of the instinct. She had become serious about it.*

'Oh, I see . . . Well, how about "Born To Run"?'

'No.' *Barely amused.*

'"Glory Days"?'

'No. Not Springsteen.'

'"Straight Outta Compton"?'

'Michael.' *Frustrated now.* 'You can't force it. It just happens, the
song chooses you.'

Looking at me like, please take this seriously. *She was worth
taking seriously. It's what I was trying to tell her. But it was in danger
of becoming one of those conversations that I thought was about one
thing when it was clearly becoming about another, and I didn't have a
clue what the hell what.*

'OK, a song can choose us and when it does you have to quit your
job. And I promise not to play any NWA for a month, just in case.'

*She smiled, mostly for my benefit. A riddle wrapped in an enigma
wrapped in a fortune cookie. She tried to rise, but I stayed her by not
releasing her hand.*

'Seriously, Nicole. Call in now. Tell your boss you're quitting.
He's a jerk anyway.'

*She considered me for a moment then leaned forward and kissed
my brow. Then she looked into my eyes, her face close, but playful, the
way shy people are when they attempt intimacy.*

'It's only till Christmas.'

'Nicole . . .'

'N.O. spells Gotta Go.'

She kissed my lips briefly then stood. She looked like a secretary from the sixties. The retro Vogue look. She looked gorgeous. Not just sexy, which her curvaceous body gave little doubt of, but, in my eyes at least, kindness personified. A gentle soul tripping out into the big bad world every day. I'd feel better when she had tenure somewhere. Wall Street's loss would be teaching's gain.

She walked to the door of our bedroom and stopped to look back. She put on an old-fashioned housewife's faux-racy pose.

'How do I look?'

'I've seen better.'

She gasped in mock outrage but couldn't hold out against my smile for long. She blew me a kiss and walked out.

As she unlocked the front door down the hallway I suddenly remembered Agent Mason had talked of a possible meeting at around six. I quickly put down my coffee mug.

'Nicole?'

The front door slammed after her.

'Nicole? Nicole . . . ?'

I'd call her when she got to the office. I looked out of our apartment window over towards the Financial District. A clear blue day. A good day to be alive.

Then everything grew brighter.

Bright white.

Until it hurt to look at it. Hurt deep inside.

Hurt like nothing I'd ever known.

72

The strip lights above my hospital bed were harsher than my eyes could bear, and after groaning out a breath I closed them again. Then after a while I realized that somebody was present. I slowly looked to my left. Martinez was sitting in a chair by my bed flicking through a copy of *Vanity Fair*.

'Are you in it this month?'

I hadn't meant to shock her but I had. She almost dropped the magazine and put a hand to her mouth. Then, after a long second, put a hand on mine.

'Mike . . .'

I had to close my eyes again, still not ready for the lights just yet. I took a moment then looked at her again. She looked awful. She looked beautiful – she couldn't help that – but she looked drawn. She was in jeans and a sweater from a Jay-Z concert we'd been to. Actually, it was mine but she'd stolen it and used it as the one she slept in when I was away. But right now she looked like she hadn't slept in . . .

'How long have I been here?'

'Four days.' Looking at me intently.

That was it – she looked like she hadn't slept in four days. Not properly, at least. And then there was something else.

'What's up?'

She looked innocent, vacant. 'Nothing.'

Innocent, but not surprised. The way she looked when she didn't want to burden me but would hack her own leg off with a rusty knife if I would *let* her unburden herself. I sighed, as much from fugginess of mind as any impatience towards Martinez.

'What's up, Jenni?'

She looked at her hand lying next to me. The hand that wasn't trying hard to squeeze mine. The hand that was sitting there. Then she looked at me directly. She paused a beat, then got it off her chest.

'Who's Nicole?'

I didn't . . . Then I did. I must have said something in my sleep or delirium or whatever it was. Oh hell.

'She's . . . Look, Jenni . . .'

I wanted to tell her she didn't matter, to appease her, for her sake, but I didn't feel like lying. And I didn't feel like talking that way about Nicole. Ever.

'She's dead. That's all you need to know. She's dead.'

She nodded. Try as she might she failed to hide the scintilla of relief that fact elicited. But then her face drew even tighter, and she reached down for her large, black leather handbag, the one she had meant to replace in Paris. She hooked it over her shoulder and stood up.

'Not to you she isn't.'

And she smiled a smile that told me I wouldn't be allowed to see the tears on this occasion. I didn't have it in me to say more. Not right now. I was tired in a way I didn't know I could be, and all I could do was watch her get to the door and begin to push it open before looking back at me.

She smiled another smile. A smile that loved me but couldn't share me. Then she spoke in a whisper that was all heartbreak.

'Love you, mate.'

73

I'd fallen asleep again. When I awoke I lay there remembering the first time I'd been in hospital during my time in the Service. Like any young buck I had wanted to get out, get out and show my boss it was but a scratch. The chief medical surgeon at the hospital heard my request with a smile that I only realized afterwards was amused. 'You can leave when you're strong enough to push my hand away with your forehead.' Lying in bed as I was, I found that I couldn't. I accepted that I was too weak to leave and stopped fighting it. It was only when he discharged me two days later that he told me that nobody in that position can push away a hand with their forehead. It had made me chuckle. The fact that he was spending his time outwitting his patients.

I looked to the visitor's chair. Diane was sitting there.

'How are you feeling, Michael?'

'Rested.'

'Good.'

'Where am I?'

'New York Presbyterian.'

I located it in my head. I felt better for knowing.

'Hypothermia?'

'Yes, Michael. You slept right through the hullabaloo following the siege at Hotel Wolverton.'

I stretched a little, trying to rouse myself. 'Who says "hullabaloo"?'

She smiled, but something was on her mind.

'How did we do?'

She spoke matter-of-factly, but I knew she hurt to say it. 'Two bankers died, seven were wounded in the cross-fi –'

'I meant our people.'

'Oh. Eight wounded. Patrick Finnegan received a bullet to the spine.'

I looked at her as sharply as I could in my condition. 'How bad?'

She shook her head slowly, sadly. 'Paralysed, for life.'

I closed my eyes and lay back on my pillow. Poor Paddy. Bastards. Idiots. I exhaled a long, noisy breath.

'And what happens to Lazcano?'

'Nothing happens to Lazcano.'

I tried – and failed – to sit up. I pushed myself back, propping myself higher against my pillows, my anger getting me there. 'Diane . . .'

'Michael, there's nothing connecting Lazcano to any of Nemesis's activities except a bunch of greedy bankers making greedy decisions and paying a very heavy price for them. There's no *evidence*. The case is *closed*.'

Her slapping me down before I could even get into my stride.

'We're just going to leave it?'

'Yes, not because we want to but because we have to work within the law. Otherwise we're no different from crooked bankers or murderous drug lords. We have to believe in those rules, Michael, and the way we show that is by acting within them. Always.'

Looking at me like if I hadn't seen the subtext in that

she was happy to repeat it. I went to speak but she cut me off.

'I'm putting you on leave, Michael.'

I saw that coming. 'OK. How long?'

She gave me a firm look. 'Until . . .'

We looked at each other, her watching me while I unpacked that last sentence.

'Take a vacation, Michael. Get some R&R. That's an order.'

'Am I allowed . . . ?'

'No, Michael. You're not allowed. You're not allowed to do anything without my say so. Take a break.'

She picked up her briefcase and herself. 'I'll keep in touch and I'll decide when you're ready to come back to work at the Service.'

And with that she left.

And, lying there, downcast, I thought the same thing I always thought.

Nice ass.

74

I paused by the ultra-smart, slim Maître d' in the restaurant at the top of the Time Warner building on Columbia Circle in New York. He smiled congenially at me.

'Yes, sir, how can I help?'

'I'm just here to see one of your diners.'

He sensed this was a transgression and switched to polite-society blocking mode.

'Have you got a reservation?'

'No. But I've got a badge.'

I flashed him my United States Secret Service wallet. His look of urbane problem-resolution melted into one of concern. Not at the possibility of any real-world issues, but more the possibility of a crimp in his diners' evening.

'If you'd like to wait there I'll get the manager.'

I flashed him my best insincere smile. 'I'm not here to see the manager.' And walked inside.

'Sir. If you'd just care to wait . . .'

I saw him sitting at a table in the far corner. Perhaps the corner was all they had. Perhaps he wanted to keep out of the limelight. Perhaps he didn't feel safe. It had been almost a week since the siege and the only story in town – in the world it seemed – was the Nemesis extravaganza in Aspen. Christmas had come early for the PR firms of Wall Street who were having money thrown at them to 'manage' the situation for Cochran and his bank. But all the money in the world wouldn't turn their shitty reputation into shinola for me.

'Anthony.'

The Sovereign Bank CEO looked up from his main course with that open look that people wear when they don't want to seem rude but don't want to seem inviting. When he saw it was me it turned into a scowl.

'Agent Byrne.'

The tables were round with crisp white linen. Next to his table were four goons who were some hard-on's idea of bodyguards. Black suits and ear-pieces. Who did they think they were – the Secret Service? So that was Cochran's new living arrangements, 24/7 security, the price of supping with the devil. This was one of the best restaurants in the city, so those four gorillas were eating pretty well for hired heavies. As I expected, the nearest stood up and confronted me with a flat hand to my chest.

'Mr. Cochran doesn't wish to be disturbed.'

I considered the hand. I could sense his three boyfriends readying themselves to intervene, their testosterone levels pumping for some of the action, a chance to prove what big boys they were. I looked up at the lean, low-fat, high-muscle man attached to the hand on my chest.

'I'd take that off me if I were you.'

'You're not me.'

He was puffing himself up for his moment in the sun when his employer stepped in.

'Chico, it's OK. I'm sure he's going to be brief. Aren't you, Mr Byrne?'

The goon stepped back, looking at me like a marker

had been laid down. I looked at the banker but pointed at his bodyguards.

'Chico? Who have you got guarding you, the Marx Brothers?' I looked at the bodyguards' table. 'Which one of you's Harpo? Come on, speak up.'

I got four evil stares in return.

'Please take a seat, Mr Byrne, you're causing a scene.'

I looked down at Cochran and his wife, a young forty-something WASP who clearly loved him for his wallet, the age difference and the diamonds dripping off her body attesting to that. I shook my head.

'Like you said, Anthony, this will be brief. And I wouldn't want to put you off your Blackmore Ranch steak, although next time try the herb roasted Maine sea scallop. Very nice.'

'Mr Byrne, would you mind . . .'

'I read your filing with the SEC about Lazcano.'

Cochran winced in embarrassment that such a high-profile issue would be raised like this in public, pulling an admonishing face that I was meant to take as a reprimand.

'Mr Byrne, what happens between Sovereign Bank and the regulators . . .'

'Had better get better.'

He looked at me questioningly, uncertain of my role – if any – in any of this. So I continued to let him understand me all the more.

'You were not very forthcoming, Anthony.'

His teeth clamped together in anger. 'How dare . . .'

'. . . I tell you that it was horse-shit?'

His wife visibly recoiled at what she deemed coarse language.

'Oh, I'm sorry, Mrs Cochran. I didn't mean to put you off your blood diamonds by telling you how your husband really earns his money.'

'Mr. Byrne . . .'

'Has he told you about the young banker, Turlington? Has he told you what they did to him?'

Cochran stood behind his table, putting all his guards on red alert.

'If you say one more word to my wife . . .'

'You'll what, Anthony? Set the Marx Brothers on me? You think that will silence me? Do you really want to see what sort of noise I can make about this?'

The Sovereign Bank CEO looked down at his food, wanting this situation quieted. The room full of diners had gone silent. Half disturbed by the commotion and half fascinated – this was Manhattan, after all. The manager appeared at my elbow, all French and fussy.

'Sir, if you do not desist with this we will 'ave to call the police.'

I didn't look at him. 'Go ahead. But call some paramedics too. They need to treat four comedians for broken bones.'

The Marx Brothers half stood at that remark, but Cochran angrily waved them back down with a minimal gesture that was designed to limit the drama rippling out about him.

'Mr Byrne, say your piece. Say your piece and leave.'

'I want a full and frank disclosure to the SEC concerning your bank's and your personal involvement with Lazcano.'

'I have already told them everything . . .'

'You want them to know. Tell them about Turlington.'

'Byrne . . .'

'Tell them how you sent him down to Mexico to broker a deal.'

'I'm warning you . . .'

'Tell them how Lazcano peeled off Turlington's face.'

A wretched look sprang to his face.

'Stop it.'

'Tell them how Lazcano cut off his hands and feet.'

Mrs Cochran burst into tears. I held up the crucifix I'd been carrying since Paris for him to see.

'Tell them how a young Parisian girl died just to buy her silence.'

Cochran looked paler than the white linen table cloth, unable to cope with his crimes.

'One more word . . .'

'Tell them how Eduardo Lazcano is going to get you and your family.'

The Marx Brothers had had enough and stood at their chairs. And something in Cochran snapped. He was a veteran of Wall Street, brawlers to a man. They came out swinging.

'Agent Byrne, you just don't have a clue how it works, do you? You just don't get what money can buy. I am the CEO of an esteemed Wall Street bank. I own my own private island in the Caribbean that neither you nor Lazcano could ever trace to me, let alone find on a map. My wife and I are about to take an extended break there, Mr Byrne, and when we get back – trust me – the matter will be closed.' He leaned across the table and spoke for my ears only. 'Get used to it, Byrne, I'm untouchable.'

He leaned away and motioned to his bodyguards.

'If you'd care to show Mr Byrne out.'

I turned to face them. Chico put his hand on my chest again. I slapped my right hand on to it, twisted it inwards, bent it backwards till the fingers snapped and used my other hand to punch him in the throat. Diners were now communicating their alarm and began to move away. The gorilla on my left reached out to grab me, but I slammed his arms away and delivered a punch to his solar plexus. There was one guard on my left, one on my right. I flicked a chair between me and the one on my right, he had no choice but to fall over it, me instantly hammering the back of his head with a fist that sent his world into darkness. The fourth upped the ante. He had a steak knife in his hand. He swiped the air with it, clearing the space between us. The smile on his face told me he fancied himself with a blade and was hungry to use it. I stepped away into a space between the tables. He swiped again as he took a step forward. Just what I wanted. The swipe completed I stepped in, grabbed the wrist of the knife-hand, keeping that arm across his body while I rammed a fist into his kidneys once, twice, then three times. He keeled over on to Cochran's table, his hands face down beside his head. I took the steak knife from him and struck it down into the back of his hand as hard as I could, nailing the knife to the table, the hand with it. The guard letting out the biggest cry a man suffering kidney failure could.

I looked at the four Marx Brothers downed. I looked at Cochran cowering with his wife. It was my turn to lean in close to the CEO.

'Nobody's untouchable.'

I strode out of the dining room and past the Maître d', who was in a nervous conference with an equally fearful manager. I spoke as I walked past them.

'I got that wrong about the broken bones. One of them needs stitches.'

75

On certain days the sun doesn't shine on the Caribbean, it makes love to it. Today was such a day. The sun had floated into a cloudless sky a shade of blue reserved for only the highest-rate tax-avoiders and the people that served them.

Napa Island was an island off an island off an island in the Grenadines. It was just a mile across in each direction, a circle of palm trees and exotic flowers ringed by a band of white sands. From its shores no other islands could be viewed, even on the clearest day, even on a day like this. The island itself boasted only one abode, a villa. Yet to call this a villa was like calling the Vatican a church. Twenty thousand square feet of single-storey luxury. Gold, marble, redwood, fixtures and fittings flown in from all around the globe. Eight bedrooms, each with a view of the sea. The master bedroom opening on to the sands themselves, its entire sea-facing wall an open space. It was luxury defined, a gilded residence available only to the likes of Warren Buffett, Bill Gates and God. Or, in this case, a Wall Street CEO.

Cochran lay in the silk sheets, letting the soft swell of the sea wash over him. The sound as gentle as the warm breeze circulating through the exposed room. In his time Cochran had tried everything. Golf, polo, yachting, flying, everything. But it was only five years earlier, when he had bought Napa Island for the bragging-rights price of

$30 million – plus $20 million for the development – that he discovered peace. Only here did he feel that he really was away from it all. His younger wife, feeling the lack of consumerism and society events, could only take it in small doses, but Cochran could have spent a year here. His very own self-imposed castaway existence. Even the staff were ferried in as required, allowing complete isolation when desired. As it was now.

Cochran had never expected to need to hide out on his island, but the fact that he could made him cherish it all the more. A happy accident had seen him buy it through a chain of offshore companies ending in Zurich, where he and a number of colleagues had hidden a lot of their money. That tax wheeze – and the anonymity it had afforded – had resulted in a degree of privacy even he had never expected to need. And for $100,000 a year the Grenadine government provided air and sea security, their military radar posts doubling up as round-the-clock protection from unwanted visitors. The best money, Cochran decided this morning, that he had ever spent.

The Sovereign Bank CEO wasn't in a hurry to wake up but when he realized that he had been staring at the ceiling for five minutes he knew his body had had enough rest. He sat up in bed, his wife gently snoring beside him. He looked out of the room. Out over the sands and the sea to the red-burnished sun lifting off from the horizon. He had always wondered which way round he should have built the villa. Woken by the sun or put to sleep by it? Maybe he'd never reconcile himself to that one. He smiled at the triviality of the nagging thought and committed himself to appreciating the sun glinting off the sea. Glinting off –

– the crucifix.

The crucifix hanging from the post at the end of his bed.

He sat bolt upright, moaning fearfully as he did. Then the moan escalated to an unashamed outburst of terror. He was looking down at his hands. Or, more specifically, his wrists. They had thick red lines around them. And after a moment he realized –

– he threw off the sheet as his wife roused in alarm.

'What is it, Tony?'

But he was screaming now. Trying to escape from himself. Kicking his legs in disgust. Screaming at the thick red lines drawn round his ankles.

'Tony, what is it?' Screaming herself when she saw the marks on his legs. 'Tony what is it? Tony? Are you bleeding? Tony? What's the matter? What's happened?'

But he was up and out of the bed, grabbing his satellite-linked cell phone, punching the speed dial, marching towards the deserted sands, towards the sea.

'Jack? We need to tell the SEC everything . . .'

Down the line his bank's legal counsel in New York. 'What do you mean?'

'I mean everything.'

'Have you lost your mind, Tony? We could go to jail . . .'

'Jack – I said we need to tell the SEC EVERY-THING . . .'

Spitting as he yelled into the phone. Looking down at the lines around his wrists and ankles. Knowing that next time they could be made for real. Looking about himself. On a desert island in the middle of nowhere, nobody as far as the eye could see – feeling watched. Feeling ready to throw up, ready to cry. The banker not wanting the same fate as his young employee Turlington. The banker wondering what he had to do to put the past behind him. The banker wondering what the hell Special Agent Mike Byrne would do next.

76

Evening was taking over the sky, and a cool breeze was beginning to blow away the stifling heat of the day. The cell phone on my canvas bag began to vibrate. I looked down at the screen. The Secret Service star flashing at me. I turned to the computer tablet sitting next to it, connected by a lead. On the screen was a wire-frame map of the world. It indicated that the call was coming – as I knew – from New York with circles radiating out from that point on the map. As the cell continued to buzz I put two fingers over the Caribbean and expanded it. Then I did the same to Barbados. Then I tapped a point on its west coast. After a second a dot started to emit circles around that point too. I accepted the call by pressing a wireless device in my ear.

'Diane. What can I do for you?'

'Michael, I thought I ordered you to take some R&R?'

I turned away from the tablet to look out over the city below.

'I did. I am.'

'Immediately after you left hospital?'

'Well, I won't pretend I went straight from the hospital to the airport.'

'I know you didn't, Michael.'

'How?'

Special Agent Mason's computer monitor showed poor-quality film from a security camera.

'Because I'm looking at footage from a restaurant that shows you interrupting a certain bank CEO's dinner two nights ago.'

'Yeah, well, the thing there is, they gave him my table by mistake. I admit I may have overreacted.'

She switched applications on her computer to one that showed a map of the world, square cross-hairs moving down from New York to the Caribbean, on to a zooming-in Barbados then on to a spot called Mullins Beach on its west coast. She took a grain of comfort from that.

Then she grew serious.

'Look, Michael . . .'

I lifted my head from what I was looking at to concentrate on her words. 'Yes, Diane?'

'Remember what I told you. You're no good to me if you take it all personally. We don't take our work home with us – or on vacation, for that matter. Understood?'

Even though she wasn't there to see it I still gave a little nod. 'Understood.'

She made a noise like she wasn't sure what to say next. 'OK. Well, have a good break. What are you planning to do with your time?'

'Just R&R.'

'Good. Good for you, Michael. You've earned it, remember that. Take care.'

'Take care, Diane.'

I looked at the phone. The call was over. And I thought about Diane, about the work, about taking it home. About undeserved fortune, good and bad, earned and unearned.

I turned towards the American who had watched on as hopefully as a man in his condition could. He made an effort to look up at me in his enfeebled state. He spoke in a mumbled whisper.

'*Are you here to take me home?*'

I took in the view from the roof of the four-storey building I was lying on.

The view looking across Sta Fe freeway in Santa Fe, Mexico City. Across the Camino Real Hotel. Across to the Calakmul Building, La Lavadora. The place where the Lazcanos went to get their money cleaned. The skies darkening, the laundry-machine-like building was illuminated spectacularly from behind its concrete façades, a neon pink on the side facing me, orange on the one running away from me down to the right. And inside this the offices themselves were lit.

The building and the streets immediately surrounding it were locked down by police and heavily armoured bodyguards, the police blocking all freeways into the proximity of the nine-storey office block. Two head-to-toe black-body-armoured cartel security details were patrolling each side of La Lavadora. Extra bodies at the main entrance, extra bodies and SUVs at the car-park entrance. Every bodyguard armed with a submachine gun. Inside I suspected there would be almost as many bodyguards again. Either Banco Orro's Private Client division had gotten skittish of late or the Lazcanos were in town. Either way nobody was going to try to get past that security cordon without a death wish. That was the reaction they clearly wanted. Overkill to kill any ideas of an attack dead in the water.

It was good security. It had served its purpose well. It had kept the Lazcanos alive during the bloodiest period of drug cartel warfare in Mexico's history. Much of the violence meted out by them. It was definitely good security. It had been effective. To date.

I looked back into the telescopic lens of my bi-pod-mounted CheyTac M200 rifle. I had a suppressor on to subdue the flash and sound of the gun. I had a seven-round magazine containing 10 cm long .408 cartridges that could penetrate a car at over a kilometre's distance. But they weren't in their car. Eduardo and Gabriel Lazcano were sat in their bank manager's office on the seventh floor of the office block approximately six hundred and fifty feet away. Offices whose reflective glass had been rendered useless by the bright lights within, at this time of day the occupants visible. And so I could see the older brother gesticulating angrily to a nervous man in a suit.

I aimed my sniper's rifle, bringing the head of the Lazcano cartel into my cross-hairs.

I accounted for elevation, I accounted for wind, I breathed slowly out and pulled the trigger.

Eduardo Lazcano stopped dead mid-sentence. His head snapping back in his chair, the top sheared off.

I panned the rifle to the right, saw his uncomprehending brother, Gabriel, in my sights.

I pulled the trigger.

I watched the second brother join the first as a bullet entered the left side of his face, his body rolling off the chair on to the floor.

I watched the bank manager hide beneath his desk, dragging the phone down with him.

I lifted my head from the lens and looked down at the city going about its business, the police and guards protecting the building, oblivious to the events above them. The world keeping on turning. Life going on.

R&R.

Revenge and restitution.

My body and soul feeling the benefits of it already.

'Why did I rob banks? Because I enjoyed it. I was more alive when I was inside a bank, robbing it, than at any other time in my life . . . But to me the money was chips, that's all.'

Willie Sutton, United States Bank Robber
1920s–1950s

Afterthought

When I was working in finance I had two overwhelming reactions to the Credit Crunch. Firstly, I thought it was glaringly obvious that we had been scammed by the banks. Secondly, I thought that when the public realized what had happened to them – that the bankers had had the party, but we would be having the hangover – that they would get really angry.

Boy, was I wrong.

Once the banks had got their bailouts and brushed the scuff-marks off their knees they went into denial overdrive. Armies of PR consultants and lobbyists[1] had oodles of cash dropped on them in an effort to convince Congress and the public that it was all a misunderstanding, and could banks please be left alone to do what they know best. Which is making money . . . My first Mike Byrne novel, *The Set-Up*, was my attempt to explain – in the most entertaining way possible – my belief that the Credit Crunch was one big Ponzi scheme orchestrated by the banks. But what about public reaction to the Credit Crunch?

On this second point, the brave souls involved in the Occupy Wall Street movement have certainly changed the

---

1 'Banks Find Extra Money To Hire Lobbyists', *Charlotte Observer*, 20 November, 2011. The paper reported that spending by banks on lobbying had increased for the sixth year in a row – $47m in 2011 alone.

tenor of the debate. There is a scintilla of shame attached to the size of bank bonuses at present. Bank bonuses that simply would not exist if the banks had not been bailed out – or if the banks had had to pay for the actual cost of bailing them out. It was this second point – the justified anger at bankers – that I took as my starting point for *The Inside Job*.

It's a funny thing, writing. Sometimes you have one grand idea that you want to pursue for an entire work, other times you sew together different ideas that you hope speak to each other. With *The Inside Job* I had been researching various aspects of the Credit Crunch, trying to understand why people weren't angrier. There are various reasons, of course: the complicated nature of the crimes, the inability to put a face to the exact crimes,[2] the failure of governments to stand up to the banks – it's a long list. Creatively, I was very drawn to the possibilities surrounding the public's reaction to being ripped off – but how to represent that? All works of fiction are, by their very nature, flights of fancy (spoiler alert: *The Da Vinci Code* is not a genuine historical document). But I'm very interested in taking real events as my starting point. You have to work pretty hard to out-sensationalize the crimes that go on about us every day.

Then two ideas crashed into each other. One I'd planned; one I hadn't.

I'd been thinking about how the banks had taken our money, lost it, got bailed out, then used that same money

---

2 Banks are, on the whole, faceless. Lloyd Blankfein, CEO of Goldman Sachs is a rare exception and his zinger that 'We are doing God's work' was a rare moment of insight into his bank's hubristic mind-set.

to pay themselves *über* bonuses. I was thinking about the shamelessness of that – and the impotence that we the taxpayers had felt. So then I got thinking about a *What if* . . . ? Writers love *What ifs*. For many of us, they're our favourite jumping-off points. And my *What if* came to me: *What if there was a client you couldn't rip off?*

That's a bigger *What if* than you might first imagine. Goldman Sachs advised the Greek government on how to massage its debt and dress it up such that it stayed within EU budgetary rules. Goldman Sachs aided and abetted Greece in that deception, and got paid handsomely for it.[3] Has the EU and every country within it cut all ties with Goldmans? I am, of course, being rhetorical. Entire companies get ripped off by banks – think of Goldman Sach's own $550 million fine from the US regulators for misleading its big institutional customers.[4] So if huge companies and entire countries can be ripped off who can't be?

That's when another piece of my research percolated back up in my mind. In December 2009 the *Observer* reported that: 'Antonio Maria Costa, head of the UN Office on Drugs and Crime, said he has seen evidence that the proceeds of organized crime were "the only liquid investment capital" available to some banks on the brink of collapse last year.'[5]

OK, let's put aside the jaw-dropping implications of that quote, the sheer criminality that such a claim suggests the

3 $300 million in fees according to some reports (*New York Times*, 13 February 2010, 'Wall St. Helped to Mask Debt Fueling Europe's Crisis'.)
4 See http://www.sec.gov/news/press/2010/2010-123.htm
5 *Observer*, 11 December 2009, 'Drug Money Saved Banks in Global Crisis, Claims UN advisor'.

banks were involved in, and the contempt shown to both the authorities and the public at large by embracing such illicitly gained monies. Let's just park that for a moment. The question that hit me, as it always does, was *Where was the outrage?* Well, that's the impunity which the banks have come to enjoy the world over.

However, creatively I was hooked. Here was a client that the banks couldn't rip off: a Mexican drug lord. Because they are as bad as they get.[6] I had my (really) bad guy. But that still left the impotence and the lack of public reaction.

Honestly, in my naivety, I really thought we would see public demonstrations against the banks. I thought there would be rioting in the streets by the public at having to face such savage cuts to public services and the accompanied downturn in economic well-being as a result of the banks' direct and indirect actions. Journalists such as *Rolling Stone*'s Matt Taibbi were able to write excoriating pieces about Goldmans, comparing them to Vampire Squids and listing their corporate wrong-doings and still nothing.[7] Nothing. With my author's hat on I couldn't figure that one out. That's when the unplanned idea came back to me.

When you consider what people do for their wage packet,

6 Suffice it to say that approximately 50,000 people have died in Mexico from drug-related violence in the past five years. As an author you would have to cross the line into the horror genre to top the actual acts of violence meted out to the victims. If you are interested, the *LA Times* did a very thorough and very hard-hitting investigation on it over the course of 2011. www.latimes.com

7 See www.rollingstone.com/the-great-american-bubble-machine-20100405 and Matt Taibbi's terrific book *Griftopia* for the full unbelievable details.

it's not hard to get dizzy from the disconnect between public value and remuneration. Teachers are entrusted with preparing the next generation for society and the workplace. Their pay? Peanuts. Investment bankers gamble with other people's money. Their pay? Gazillions. We all know the list; we all know how long it is, and how unjust. But the one that I marvel at is the military. These people don't just exchange their labour for a salary; in many cases they trade their life on this earth. These people actually lay down their lives to make it possible for us to sleep in our beds at night. I won't pretend I agree with the recent wars (the Iraq war was clearly cooked up by Bush and Blair), but that doesn't detract one iota from the genuine – and ultimate – sacrifice these people make. And their salaries? Drum roll please ... peanuts. Certainly, compared to bankers.

So, there were the ingredients, rolling around in my head and eventually coming together to form *The Inside Job*. Because I hate bankers, right?

Well, not really. Some of the nicest people I know are bankers. I had more fun working in the City than at any other employed time of my life. I'd wager a large sum that if you were to test the characters of a sample from any profession you'd get the same balance of good and bad people, pleasant and unpleasant.[8] But I am furious at the system. And I don't believe that bankers are going to be the ones to change it (note their record spending on lobbyists). People can roll their eyes at the critics of banks, play the *Time To Move On* card, but even bankers come clean occasionally. Take this from an Op-Ed in the *New*

8 OK, you're right, I'm not including politicians.

York Times, where a departing Goldmans employee gave this damning summary of the bank's strategy:

> a) Execute on the firm's 'axes,' which is Goldman-speak for persuading your clients to invest in the stocks or other products that we are trying to get rid of because they are not seen as having a lot of potential profit. b) 'Hunt Elephants.' In English: get your clients – some of whom are sophisticated, and some of whom aren't – to trade whatever will bring the biggest profit to Goldman. Call me old-fashioned, but I don't like selling my clients a product that is wrong for them. c) Find yourself sitting in a seat where your job is to trade any illiquid, opaque product with a three-letter acronym. [9]

What Goldmans and the other investment banks did in the run-up to the Credit Crunch isn't irrelevant. It isn't ancient history. It both impacted and continues to impact on our lives. Every closed hospital ward, every laid-off teacher, every cut back in public services is a result of the – inevitable – bursting of their bubble. A bubble that made them rich. Riches they got to keep. We lock up bank robbers, but *banker* robbers . . .

In August 2010, Barclays Bank was ordered to pay the US authorities $298 million for breaching United States trade sanctions with Cuba, Iran, Libya, Myanmar and Sudan. It had disguised the origins of these monies to

[9] *New York Times*, 14 March 2012, 'Why I Am Leaving Goldman Sachs'.

make it possible to move them around the world.[10] The fine was a fraction of the profits made. The government's explanation for not getting tougher on the banks was that it couldn't find anybody responsible, as if somehow banks aren't ultimately a collection of employees making decisions for which they are wholly responsible.[11] That riles me. A lot. Because regular people go to jail, they don't get slaps on the wrist. And I could fill a book with such outrageous real-life injustices, only, I'd rather tell stories and hope people take a small piece of my outrage with them.

One last story. I gave a talk at a prison in the south of England recently. It was dominated by talk of ethics, perhaps a subject they dwell on more than we might expect. It was, to me, a surprising subject for them to focus on but the biggest surprise was that the inmates' real ire was reserved for bankers. Genuine, heartfelt, moral disgust. From *criminals*. We batted it around for a bit until one guy said, 'I mean, I'm in here for holding up a bank with a gun, but who's the real criminal – me or them?' Well, dear reader, obviously, I put him straight on that one. 'If you're going to rob a bank,' I said, 'don't wear a stock and carry a gun – wear a suit and carry a briefcase.'

10 www.bloomberg.com, 16 August 2010, 'Barclays Settles U.S. Government Trade Violation Claims for $298 Million'.
11 *New York Times*, 12 September 2010, 'Follow the Dirty Money'.

Acknowledgements

To the readers: Emma, Susannah M. and Barney M.; first rate feedback as ever.

My agent, Jonathan Lloyd at Curtis Brown, for being upstanding and outstanding.

My editor, Alex, for getting out the red pen.

Richard W. – may blowing up always be in my books and not in the markets.

Bankers, without whose consistent ability to outdo their own shamelessness I would not get the starting points for my novels.

Occupy Wall Street, for saying 'Enough'.

He just wanted a decent book to read ...

Not too much to ask, is it? It was in 1935 when Allen Lane, Managing Director of Bodley Head Publishers, stood on a platform at Exeter railway station looking for something good to read on his journey back to London. His choice was limited to popular magazines and poor-quality paperbacks – the same choice faced every day by the vast majority of readers, few of whom could afford hardbacks. Lane's disappointment and subsequent anger at the range of books generally available led him to found a company – and change the world.

'We believed in the existence in this country of a vast reading public for intelligent books at a low price, and staked everything on it'
Sir Allen Lane, 1902–1970, founder of Penguin Books

The quality paperback had arrived – and not just in bookshops. Lane was adamant that his Penguins should appear in chain stores and tobacconists, and should cost no more than a packet of cigarettes.

Reading habits (and cigarette prices) have changed since 1935, but Penguin still believes in publishing the best books for everybody to enjoy. We still believe that good design costs no more than bad design, and we still believe that quality books published passionately and responsibly make the world a better place.

So wherever you see the little bird – whether it's on a piece of prize-winning literary fiction or a celebrity autobiography, political tour de force or historical masterpiece, a serial-killer thriller, reference book, world classic or a piece of pure escapism – you can bet that it represents the very best that the genre has to offer.

Whatever you like to read – trust Penguin.